The Thorne Legacy
Book I

Legacy of Lies

Winter Adaire

Copyright © 2017 Winter Adaire
All rights reserved
First Edition

PAGE PUBLISHING, INC.
New York, NY

First originally published by Page Publishing, Inc. 2017

ISBN 978-1-64027-380-1 (Paperback)
ISBN 978-1-64027-379-5 (Hard Cover)
ISBN 978-1-64027-381-8 (Digital)

Printed in the United States of America

DEDICATION

This book is dedicated to my father, Leslie, June 26, 1918–June 30, 2004, for the endless bedtime stories I demanded of you as a child and for inspiring me to allow my imagination to soar.

To my mother, Helen, November 3, 1920–March 13, 2013, for making me strong and for encouraging me to believe that anything I could dream, I could achieve. I am grateful for your fiery Scottish spirit that taught me to "pull up my bootstraps and persevere" no matter life's obstacles or heartaches.

I love you both and am thankful you were mine. You are sorely missed.

AUTHOR'S NOTE

Clan Thorne and Thorne Manor are completely fictional, as are all the characters in this book. However, I have incorporated elements of Celtic myth, certain names and historical events, and a historically accurate time line into the backdrop of the story wherever possible. The significance of this will become clearer in books 2 and 3.

The mythical Tuatha dé Daanan, children of the goddess Danu, are said to have arrived in great ships from beyond the stars. After making land upon the western coast of Ireland, they burned their ships so that they could never return home. It is also said that they did battle with an enemy known as the Formorians. These ancient stories are obscure and varied. I have reimagined these mythical beings of lore and woven them into the fabric of a new legacy.

Thorne Manor is based loosely on Kinross House, a neoclassical Palladian mansion built in 1686 on the shores of Loch Levan by Sir William Bruce, who received a grant from King Charles II. The island ruins of Loch Levan Castle, built in the 1300s, can indeed still be seen from the property.

Although few records exist from the time, many scholars believe that Áedan mac Gabráin, AD 532–608, was the son of Gabráin mac Domangairt, "the Treacherous," who was believed to be a grandson of King Fergus Mòr Mac Earca, from whom present-day rulers of Scotland claim descent.

Áedan was crowned Great King of Dál Riata in AD 574, and it is possible that he was ordained by the Christian priest Columba, later to be known as Saint Columba. He was succeeded by his son, Eaochaid Buide, and thereafter, the Cenal Gabráin (line of Gabráin) is said to have continued on into the modern-day rulers of the Isles.

I would like to acknowledge Alexandra Bartlett, Scott Bartlett, and Beverly Peterson for their help, moral support, and endless patience during this process. Thank you for reading the early, incomplete, and *very rough* drafts and demanding to know what happened next. Your encouragement meant the world, especially when I was attempting to mesh the historical aspects of this series with a plotline spanning millennia.

Alex, my love, your insight and editing suggestions were invaluable. Words alone cannot express my gratitude for all your help in that final push to release the finished draft even though you were under deadlines of your own. And, Beverly, I loved all those little red sticky notes! Again, a million times, *thank you* for reading everything so carefully! Scott, I am grateful that you insisted on sending the early draft of my manuscript to colleagues even though I was mortified that it was incomplete. It was the incentive I needed to stop messing around and get it right. I owe you so much for the hours you spent downloading *Legacy of Lies* and sending it out. You became the driving force and the glue that held the project together.

Beverly, Scott, and Alex, when I was ready to toss the manuscript into the shredder, you became my cheerleaders and allies. I couldn't have gotten this far without you.

Special thanks must go to Chris Upkes, for setting up my domain rights and for the incredible website, and once again to Alexandra Bartlett, for your fabulous book trailers. I must also thank Ryan Hughes, my Publication Coordinator, for your help, support, advice and professionalism. You have been incredible to work with throughout this entire process. I am so thankful to have all of you *brilliant children of the technology age* on my side. What a great team we make!

CHAPTER I

LADY IN THE MIST

As long as but a hundred of us remain alive, we will never be subject to tyrannical dominion, because it is not for glory or riches or honours that we fight, but for freedom alone which no worthy man loses except with his life.

—Latin passage translated from the
Declaration of Arbroath, 1320

Icy mist rolled off the obsidian waters of the loch, devouring the shoreline like a ravenous serpent freed from the inky depths. The unearthly cloud reared its head, tasting the air like some primordial creature of lore. Stealthily it ascended the embankment, sliding silently over long-neglected gardens, crawling ever closer to the ivy-choked battlements of an imposing manor.

Vaporous fingers caressed gray stone walls, sifting through vining curtains of green, pressing ever harder against ancient leaded windows, demanding access to the high shadowed chamber where a solitary figure watched.

Denied entry, but undaunted by the flimsy barricade of stone and glass, the hunter shifted, expanding its insubstantial form. Widening its great maw into a macabre parody of a smile, ephemeral jaws sank over the dwelling, swallowing the once-grand edifice in a dank veil of white.

Unaware of the intruder hidden within the roiling mass, the young sentinel rested his head against the chilled panes. His breath momentarily frosted the mist-drizzled window, unintentionally obscuring his face from the spectral stalker just beyond the safety of his haven.

Straining bleary eyes against the eerie predawn light, he brushed a hand to clear the fogged glass. His probing gaze sought gaps and openings in the dense mire, sweeping the shrouded landscape, searching for a clearer glimpse beyond the cloaked gardens of the estate to the murky waters far below.

Something about the mist tugged at his memories. The billowing white cloud unsettled him, made him uneasy. There was an unnatural sense of being separate from the real world, of having stepped into another time, another place. *Ridiculous, of course.* And yet there was that uncanny nudge of déjà vu, an insistent ripple of dormant recollection, distant at first, but becoming stronger, of having done this before.

Rubbing a throbbing temple as a sudden jolt of pain burst behind fatigued eyes, the face of a woman hovered briefly in his mind and then was quickly gone. Fingers dug deeper as the ache intensified and the memory surfaced. Yes, he was certain now. He had sat at this very window and gazed out into the fog, looking for something. For *someone.* But that had been a dream, hadn't it?

Leaning against the pane, he felt the stirring of frosty air as it drafted through cracks in the ancient window where the glazing had failed. He breathed in the cold damp of the room, the frigid bite of night, pulling the *scent* of it, the *feel* of it, deep into his lungs. The icy fog, the brittle air, the bone-deep chill of this house, of this room, was all too real. Clearly, he was not dreaming now.

And yet still he felt compelled to search the loch for that elusive secret that pricked his memories … the secret he had kept as a child … the secret that dwelled in the mist.

Exhaustion beat at him. He should return to the warmth of his bed instead of shivering in this window. Why had he given any credence to the fanciful imaginings of his childhood?

Chiding himself over the absurd vigil, he rose. The faintest glimmer of light caught his eye in that split second as he turned away. Could that impossible shimmer near the water's edge be what he had been waiting for? Could those childhood fantasies actually be real?

It could have been the glint of the moon off the loch, or the flicker of fireflies against the night, but he was almost certain … near the shoreline, a nimbus of light bloomed, something moved, shifted, took form.

Was *she* there?

Though night still held sway over the mist-blanketed landscape, he sensed her presence. He knew the ghostly apparition was the same as the one that haunted his dreams. She was as she had always been from his earliest childhood memories, an ethereal creature wrapped in moonlight, mysterious and otherworldly, beside the loch.

The glowing entity glided effortlessly along the shoreline, carried on the eddying cloud. Vine-like tendrils of white entwined her body, caressing her, gently reaching for her. She was quicksilver, a moonbeam shining through the darkness—elegant, graceful, fluid, enveloped in an ensuing ballet. The mists churned and swirled with every sinuous movement of her slim frame, in harmony with the rhythmic waters of the loch itself.

Utterly transfixed, he watched from his high perch as the ghostly spectacle unfolded far below upon the rocky beach. The glowing lady swept her arms wide in graceful arcs as she drifted and swayed, appearing for all the world as though she was communing with the mist itself. He was mesmerized by the exotic creature, captivated by her dance, entirely caught up in her spell.

Eventually, her movements ceased, and a shiver ran down his spine as the entrancing manifestation languidly turned toward the old manor. He experienced an unnerving stab of alarm, as though he had been found out, as though the vision from the loch was actually aware that he was watching. But surely, the waning night kept him hidden from view. There was no way the spectral lady could see him. And surely, she couldn't *sense* his presence, could she? The ghostly apparition had no reason to suspect that from one of the many darkened windows in the ancient manor, an enthralled audience gazed down from the shadows.

But as the first fledgling rays of dawn touched her face, she looked up. The breath caught in his throat as unearthly blue eyes pinned him. He felt a jolt of something akin to fear as that hypnotic blue gaze locked to his. He tried, but it was impossible to look away. He was ensnared as surely as a wild animal caught in a trap. And in that charged moment as they stared at one another, he knew without a doubt that the ghostly creature had not only known of his presence but had deliberately sought him out.

Those burning blue orbs bored into his, and abruptly, he was pulled ... across the gardens, across the vast distance from the old manor, to the water's edge as though physically hurled through spiraling oceans of space and time. Though he fought, he could not escape the ominous intensity of those inhuman blue eyes.

Some still-rational piece of his hazy intellect insisted that this was an illusion, but his adrenaline-laced senses proclaimed otherwise. The sane portion of his brain wanted to refute what his besieged body was asserting with all its might to be true. This predicament was impossible, and yet some latent instinct of self-preservation screeched a warning. He was in danger! He knew it as surely as he knew he was no longer ensconced within the safety of his bedroom.

Without warning, he was falling as if from a great height, plummeting into those spellbinding blue orbs. But the blue depths that embraced his struggling form turned menacing and green.

Frigid waters swept over his head, imprisoning him as he tried to swim upward but could not. He choked as the viscous realm invaded his nose and mouth, remembering too late to hold his breath. He was in the loch! Oh god! He was actually trapped beneath the icy waves of the loch! But how? He needed to get himself to the surface. But which way was up? He kicked hard but was uncertain of his direction. He fought with all his might, but every moment spent in struggle pulled him deeper into the water's shadowy depths.

Slimy water plants tangled around lashing limbs, ensnaring him further. Long slick ropes of drifting waterweed felt like snakes slithering over his flailing form, sliding into his clothing, reaching for his face. Depleted lungs burned. Gasping for air, fighting, thrashing against the insidious foe holding him under, he realized he had mere seconds before succumbing to this inky, liquid grave.

Deprived lungs desperately pleaded for air, but he was still sinking, down, down into even colder regions of the loch. Staring up through murky green water toward the surface, knowing if he gave into his body's panicked demands, if he took the breath he so urgently craved, it would be his last.

Malevolent vines tightened, no longer slithering, but binding, cutting cruelly into abraded skin like ropes of steel relentless in their evil intent. His clawing hands worked unsuccessfully to loosen the lethal chains. Writhing, whipping his flagging body in an attempt to free himself, his fingernails tore as bleeding fingers ripped impotently against viselike tethers. He was going to die here, and no one but his ghostly assailant would ever know.

With one last fatalistic effort, he gathered his strength. Frantically kicking, propelling himself upward with every bit of self-preservation he still possessed, he threw off the malicious bonds. Another violent thrust, and he broke free of the loch's greedy depths. Frenziedly swimming upward, lungs near to bursting, another desperate kick, and at last he cleared the surface!

The deep wingback chair tipped against a bookshelf with a thud, and the massive, heavily laden piece of furniture teetered dangerously. A large teddy bear in a bright-blue sailor suit landed in his arms, followed by a scattering of smaller stuffies. He was sweating profusely but felt ice-cold.

Still gulping air, the disoriented youth mechanically tucked the bear under his arm and picked up a chubby green dragon from the floor, where it had just fallen. Fighting to control the tremor racking his body, he assessed his surroundings.

"*Holy. Freaking. Hell!* What just happened?"

He wasn't in the loch. He was alive, in his old room, with all the things he remembered from his early childhood. Yet the fire in his lungs remained, his chest still tight from the malevolent dream.

Hesitantly, he approached the window. It was dawn. Gray light filtered through the trees, and a blanket of white lay heavy over the gardens and the water beyond. Nothing stirred in the mist. *Nothing!* Even the birds were silent.

Shivering in the dreary half-light of an early Scottish morning, he blew heated breath into icy hands, briskly rubbing them across his arms and face.

It's June, he thought moodily. *It is June, and it's bloody freezing. And I am in Scotland!*

As he raked still-unsteady fingers through raven hair until it stood on end, a sheepish grin tugged the corners of his mouth.

"Every castle has a ghost, right?" the young man muttered, looking into the solemn eyes of the little dragon he had shoved onto the windowsill. "I guess I just met ours." Drawing another deep breath into lungs that implausibly still burned, he exhaled noisily. "Yeah, you're right, bro, she's got the face of an angel, but she's *evil*."

Briefly leaning a sweat-beaded forehead once more against the chilled windowpane, he gazed down at the small green companion from his childhood.

"Oh, shut up," he said, tapping the little dragon under its chin as if it had answered. "I know she's not real. It was just another freaky dream like all the others."

Chuckling self-consciously, he glanced over his shoulder as if to ascertain that no one had witnessed this one-sided conversation with a stuffed toy. Or his near demolition of the priceless, centuries-old bookcase he had tumbled into.

Sixteen-year-old Ian Thorne quietly righted the large, overstuffed chair still listing precariously against the maltreated shelving and resumed his perch near the window. Thoughtfully, he scanned the spacious bedroom that had remained untouched since he was five. The room still appeared as if the small child who slept there had just stepped out for a moment instead of nearly twelve long years ago.

Everything was exactly as he had left it. The cozy bed with little brown bears on the quilt claimed the center of the room. A small table with two child-size chairs sat in an alcove, dwarfed by one of two enormous diamond-paned windows. The beveled panes of the glass glittered like jewels, and both of the stunning windows commanded dramatic and expansive views of the gardens and the loch below.

A large tawny lion with a wild mane and soft amber eyes lounged on one of the chairs, serenely waiting for the room's owner to claim the other.

Between the windows, an ornate but time-yellowed marble fireplace mantel surrounded a blackened brick interior. A cheery fire had always burned in the hearth when he was young, but the ashes were now long cold.

The tall intricately carved ebony bookcase dominated the second alcove, and the overstuffed chair in which he now sat completed the space. The shelves were crowded with children's books and more bears and other stuffed animals.

Knights on horseback, coloring books, crayons, and a rugby ball all sat patiently, waiting for his return. Only, he had not returned. Not for so many years that he had all but forgotten these once-beloved treasures surrounding him. It was, in fact, so long ago that he could barely recall any part of his life here or the people who had been so important to him.

So why now? Ian wondered.

Why, after dumping him in a boarding school in another country for the past twelve years, had *she* chosen to bring him back here? Why, when he was nearly of age to make his own decisions, to set his own course in life, to be free to do as he damn well pleased, had *she* finally taken an interest in his life?

His friends and professors had become the only family he remembered. Why had she interfered now when he no longer even considered Scotland his home? What had changed?

Ian had no idea what was going on, but he was certain something quite significant had occurred, or he would still be cooling his heels halfway across the world.

Exhaling long and slow, he attempted to detach himself from the anger he hadn't even realized he still harbored. *She* wasn't worth it.

Miranda. His father's wife. His ... stepmother? His *evil stepmother?*

Unconsciously, he shrugged. He hardly remembered the woman who had shunned him, sent him away after his father's death, torn him from the only home he had ever known. The woman who had ignored him, left him for others to raise, sent him to strangers when he was most hurt and vulnerable, a small child with no one else but *her* to care for him.

Who was she, really?

Ian shrugged again. He could not even remember her face. Nor could he recall her voice or anything else about the person who had so unconcernedly discarded him.

Except perhaps the thread of a memory from so long ago he didn't even know if it was real. *Long golden hair, a flowing white dress, a gentle smile, vivid blue eyes, so much like his own, and ... perfume? Subtle, earthy, clean, reminiscent of rain and ... mist?*

No! he thought. *That's just another illusion I've built for myself, another dream I can barely recall. That wasn't her. I don't remember Miranda or much of anything else. I was too young.*

The only face Ian remembered was his father's, and only because of an old framed photograph he had always kept by his bed of the two of them, taken when he had been about five years old. Before his whole world had been irrevocably shattered.

He shoved the memory away. Strange that even after so many years, it still had the power to hurt.

Shivering in the brisk morning air, Ian pulled the teddy bear quilt off the bed. Draping it over his shoulders like a long trailing cape, he went in search of his backpack. The small parcel was the only thing he had time to pack yesterday when he was so unexpectedly summoned back to Scotland.

Spying the crumpled bag near the fireplace, where it had been so carelessly dumped the night before, he rummaged through the few belongings that had been hurriedly thrown together. Shivering, he pulled the blanket more tightly around his body to ward off the damp chill, realizing with a sinking feeling that he had *absolutely nothing* suitable to wear here.

It's June, Ian thought grumpily. *It's supposed to be summer! And here I am with shorts and T-shirts in the middle of freaking Siberia!*

Padding across cold wooden floors on bare feet to the door, he stepped into the darkened hallway, turning left on the landing.

Portraits of long-dead ancestors in gilded frames watched from the soaring walls of the lengthy gallery as their young descendant made his way past a large marble statue of a woman with flowing hair and robes.

The beautifully carved sculpture appeared as though she was leaning into a strong wind. The curve of her face, the graceful, medieval clothing, and the fluid form of her body all seemed vaguely familiar, another tug at his memories. However, he didn't stop to inspect the lifelike figure more closely.

Ian walked quickly, attempting to ignore the phantom fingers that prickled the back of his neck. The silent house and dark, cavernous passage were a little unnerving, as though more than paintings watched from the gloom.

He'd heard odd noises during the night, the creak of floorboards, the scrape of branches against a window, but the house was old, and that was to be expected. Wasn't it? He glanced along the shadowy landing once more. He was completely alone. His imagination was simply playing tricks on his mind.

Ian paused as he reached the door leading to his father's suite of rooms. Somehow, with all he had forgotten, he had no trouble finding the way. Part of him was afraid to turn the knob. What if all that he remembered was gone? What if Miranda, or someone else, had disposed of his father's belongings? Twelve years was a long time.

Brushing a cobweb from the ornate hardware, he rubbed the dirty grit that came away between his fingers. From the state of the manor, it appeared as if no one had lived here in a very long time.

Why was this enormous house so empty? Where was the staff? There had always been people, *happy people*, bustling through the halls. The manor had been filled with sunshine and laughter. And though dirt and cobwebs probably wouldn't have registered to an oblivious five-year-old, Ian was certain the estate would have been immaculately clean. His father entertained too often and, frankly, had too much money for his home not to have been.

Unintentionally holding his breath, Ian forced himself to fill his lungs with air. His own room had remained untouched, a time capsule from the past. Perhaps, just maybe, this suite had been left alone as well. He bristled at the thought of Miranda taking it upon herself to change anything or throw out any of his father's possessions. He swallowed to dislodge the hard lump in his throat, even if his father was dead.

He nervously turned the brass handle and let himself into a room even darker than the hallway. Disoriented at first, unsure if he was trespassing where he should not, Ian hesitated. The dim space felt as eerily empty as the rest of the house.

As jet-lagged eyes adjusted to the gloomy light, he realized that the curtains were drawn shut against the cold gray morning outside. The suite was silent, the massive bed empty.

Crossing to the windows, cautious hands pushed aside heavy brocade draperies. The sun was a little higher now, and some of the cloud cover was beginning to burn off. The mist had all but gone from the loch, and the first rays of yellow sunlight sparkled gently off calm green water. Only the small island floating in the distance was still swathed in swirling billows of white.

Ian could barely make out the gray stone edifice of a ruined castle rising up through the cloud-like haze. The misty island with its crumbling castle, surrounded by the moody waters of the deep green loch, appeared almost like something from a dream, mysterious and isolated from the rest of the world.

Since arriving last night, Ian had felt that same deep sense of isolation within himself. Everything about being in his old family home felt as surreal and insubstantial as any dream he had ever experienced.

Standing at the window, hesitating, awash in emotions that he could barely sort through, he did not want to turn around.

What if everything he remembered about this room was gone forever, like his father?

Well, Ian mulled, fingering the thick draperies, *the curtains haven't changed.*

Eyeing the shimmering cascade of fabric flowing like a waterfall from ceiling to floor, he noted that the cloth was beautiful and the very same color as the deep-red wine his father had sometimes liked to drink. He remembered hiding behind them once, long ago, waiting in ambush and giggling at the tickling he received when his dad had discovered his game.

With a sigh, Ian turned and faced the suite of rooms.

It was exactly as he remembered, exactly as it had been on that terrible June morning when he and his father had set out for the loch. A morning not unlike this one, in fact.

Fighting a sudden intense desire to bolt from the grand bedroom with all its ghosts and memories of the past, Ian reminded himself why he was here.

Enough of the melodrama, he scolded himself harshly. He needed to quash these feelings, shove those thoughts back down into that deep abyss where he imprisoned all his hurts and secret fears. It was far past time for the detached, logical portion of his brain to take over.

He was going to need some warm clothing. Maybe something of his father's would do for now, *until someone could bloody well tell him why, after all this time, he abruptly found himself back in Scotland!*

Turning, Ian allowed his gaze to wander over his father's private domain.

To his left, a high bed with thick, scrolled pillars of dark wood was draped with the same beautiful fabric as the casements. Like the windows, the wine-red hangings flowed from the soaring ceiling, creating an elegant canopy that commanded the room. An old photograph of the baby Ian had been was lovingly placed on the night table next to the bed.

A heavily carved mahogany desk sat in the shadowed alcove of the far window, and two large comfortable leather wingback chairs were pulled up near the ornately carved stone fireplace centered between the tastefully draped casements on the outer wall. Between the chairs stood a small table holding a whimsical green-and-white chess set.

The floorboards creaked under Ian's feet as he crossed the room. The hair stood up on the back of his neck, and once again, he had that eerie feeling that he was being watched by unseen eyes. *This was becoming ridiculous!* His imagination was way out of control. Clearly, he was alone.

Giving himself a stern mental shake, he turned his attention to the chess set, noting that the pieces were exquisite, nearly translucent. An inner glow seemed to emanate from them, as though they were somehow lit from within.

The kings wore flowing robes, with strange crowns on their heads, and the queens were even more beautiful, with long flowing gowns and hair that fell almost to the ground. Their crowns were also unusual, vine-like and shimmery, circling low to a delicate point over their foreheads.

The other pieces seemed to swirl on the board, as if in a kind of dance. They were almost fairylike in their appearance.

Two large antlered stags in the bishop's squares within the white court did not join the dance. Instead, they stood motionless beside the king, as if alert for any possible danger. Their deep jeweled eyes appeared almost sentient, as though guardedly observing the young man who had intruded into this sanctuary.

Great horned beasts, eyes equally aware, glared out from the bishop's squares of the dark court, giving him a strangely uneasy feeling.

This set was very old, Ian's father had once told him, and very precious. He had always been enthralled by the two courts with all their captivating pieces and had begged his father to let him learn to play.

His dad had promised he would, when Ian was a little older. It had been a cherished pact between them, a special treat to be bestowed at some point in the near future. Until then, the beautiful chess set was one of the few things in the house that the young Ian was not permitted to touch.

He had eventually learned to play chess, he thought sadly, but his father had not been the one to teach him.

Ian frowned as he examined the set more closely. Everything appeared to be perfectly intact, but why were the pieces out of order? The White Queen stood in the exact center of the board, not on a square at all, but at the dissection of king and queen's squares four and five. Carefully, reverently, he shifted the delicate figurine back to the safety of the first rank beside her king. He had expected the jewellike stone to feel cold, but instead, it exuded a kind of warmth that was hard to describe.

As he released the queen, a faint breeze caressed his cheek, bringing with it that same illusive scent of mist that had engulfed the estate in the early hours. But that dank cloud that had rolled so quickly off the loch ... *and what had followed* ... had all been a *dream*, right?

Again, he felt those phantom fingers trailing up and down his spine, making his pulse quicken and the hair on his arms and the back of his neck stand on end. At times, his dreams were so vivid that it was hard to separate what was real and what was not, especially when he first awakened.

Those incessant, freaky dreams had messed with his head since he was a baby, but he had learned to hide their effects from those around him, mostly. His roommates at school were aware of his nightly ordeals. It had been impossible to keep them a secret. But not even his closest friends knew just how unnerving they actually were or how precariously close he sometimes felt he was to losing his mind entirely.

Ian absently stroked a finger over the flowing figure of the White Queen as he determinedly ousted those dark thoughts.

Once more, he felt that imperceptible caress of damp air upon his cheek. *How curious.* It was the merest breath, the barest stirring of the ether, but he could have sworn it was real.

Wary eyes probed the recesses of the chamber, searching every shadowy corner, every depressed niche, every darkened alcove of the grand space, thoroughly taking stock of his surroundings. There was absolutely nothing there. He was completely and unquestionably alone. Clearly, his imagination was still jacked up from the nightmare. *Enough already! He really needed to get a grip.*

Crossing to an enormous mirrored wardrobe on the opposite wall from the bed, he pulled on the heavy mahogany door. It came open with a faint creak, displaying an array of shirts and slacks, elegant suits, dinner jackets, tuxedos, and dress kilts, all neatly hung and waiting for their master. The faint smell of woodsmoke and spice lingered for a moment in the air and then was gone.

A drawer at the bottom held more casual jackets and rugby shirts as well as some old fishing garb. This would do.

As Ian lifted out an old polo sweater, he again caught the faint scent of the same woodsy spice. As before, it strongly reminded him of his dad. A sense of loss and longing hit him hard.

Gathering a warm jacket, a couple of long-sleeved shirts, a hooded sweatshirt, and fleece sweatpants, he closed the door and fled from the room.

It had been twelve long years. He should be over this by now. But being back here, like this, in his childhood home, memories of his father flooded over him as though it was yesterday.

So much for cool, detached logic. Ian was going to have to chain that treacherous door shut, push harder against the melancholic thoughts crowding his brain.

He was certain that Miranda had some agenda. Every instinct he possessed warned that he could not afford to let his guard down. Ian could not allow old childhood traumas and memories to weaken him. When he finally faced the witch who had just hijacked his life, it must be from a position of strength. He would not allow himself to become the victim here or be naively drawn into whatever game she had arranged.

Nearing the statue of the medieval lady, Ian heard voices, faint at first.

"I canna imagine where the wee bairn has got himself ta, but nor can I blame him if he's up and run away. That Miss *High n' Mighty* dumpin' that poor child into an empty house in the middle of the night, and she not even due here for another two days. If it was up ta me, I'd tell her just what I think ta her face, but then I suppose we'd both be tossed out on our ears!"

Wee bairn? Ian mouthed silently. *I'm at least a foot taller than she is, and I'm nearly seventeen!*

Ian recognized the voice as that of Mrs. MacShane, the caretaker's wife, who had greeted him with a warm hug and an egg salad sandwich upon his arrival the previous night.

She had apologized for the meager fare, declared in an indignant voice that "he must be *worn ta pieces* after all that *disgraceful pandemonium* at the airport," and ushered the exhausted young man up a wide sweeping staircase to his old room. There she had left him with a promise to return in the morning.

Indeed, it had been well after midnight by the time the battered old jeep had finally turned into the long tree-lined drive leading to the imposing old manor house. Mr. MacShane had been made to wait at the airport for Ian to clear immigration for nearly six hours, during which time numerous phone calls were made by the Edinburgh Airport officials.

It seemed, from the little Ian managed to overhear during this lengthy process, that although he carried a UK passport, there was some confusion due to the fact that he had lived out of the country for so many years without ever once returning to British soil.

Finally, a tall middle-aged man with black hair, wearing a well-cut black suit and carrying an elegant black leather briefcase, had arrived. He respectfully greeted Ian as *Lord Thorne*, ruffled his hair, and told him with a wink that he was not to worry.

Ian inwardly flinched at the designation. *Lord Thorne* was his father's title, not his.

While he self-consciously slouched in an uncomfortable orange plastic airport chair, feeling more and more like a criminal as the hours ticked by, the newcomer laid out several documents for the airport officials, made a barrage of phone calls on a sleek black cell phone, and then miraculously informed him that he was free to go.

Ian's sophisticated rescuer then ushered him quickly through customs and deposited him in the care of a slightly stooped, gray-haired man wearing baggy pants and a battered old tan jacket.

He regarded the elderly man dubiously, noting that the knees of his breeches were mud-spattered, and even his worn boots were caked with dirt. But when those faded blue eyes lit with welcome and the wrinkled face broke into a warm, crooked grin, he relaxed a little.

"Come with me, Master Ian," the wizened little man had said, patting him on the back. "We'll soon have ye home. No need ta fret now. God willin', the worst is over."

Ian truly hoped so as he tried to hide his grimace. *Master Ian?* Who were these people? He guessed it was better than *Lord Thorne*.

The time-withered chauffeur guided him to a beat-up old vehicle. On the fourth attempt, the engine finally gave a grudging, sputtering start, and Ian wondered wearily if they would actually make it out of the parking lot, much less back to Thorne Manor, before morning.

Ian made a halfhearted attempt at conversation during the first few minutes of their journey but found Mr. MacShane's Scottish brogue so difficult to understand that he finally gave up and settled back against the seat, completely drained.

He did gather from their stumbling conversation that the MacShanes had lived on his father's estate for decades, but if anything about either Mr. MacShane or his redheaded wife was familiar, Ian had just been too tired to give it much thought.

The only thing that had really made an impression was his first glimpse of the enormous castle-like structure. Had he really lived here as a child? He had forgotten how grand it was.

"Now, Maigrid, I'm sure he's aboot somewhere." The heavy brogue of Mr. MacShane abruptly brought him back to the present. "He canna ha' got himself far the way he was dressed, in nothin' but shorts and a T-shirt. He'd not likely ta be wanderin' far outside the manor. He's bin livin' in a tropical climate. Thin blood, ye know. And then there's the rest of it. He'd freeze ta death, ta be sure, before he got even a stone's throw down the road."

"Well," Mrs. MacShane commented, "I thought sure he'd still be sleepin', late as ye got him here last night. But I was only wantin' ta peek in on him, poor bairn, especially after that mess at the airport. And his stepmum not even there ta meet him!" Her indignant voice had become quite shrill with this last declaration.

"Now, Maigrid, shoosh!" Mr. MacShane admonished his wife. "The bairn'll hear ye, an' we don't want no trouble ta start out. The situation's bad enough as 'tis."

"I'm not sayin', Hamish," Mrs. MacShane continued, undaunted, "but I'm just sayin', if Master Danny was alive today, he'd be turnin' over in his grave!"

Ian repressed an incredulous smile then shook his head at the absurdity of Mrs. MacShane's thought process. Had he just heard her correctly? But then, the true significance of what she had said hit him. *Master Danny? Daniel Thorne? She was referring to his father!* They must have known him when he was young. Had they been here, then, on the estate when his father was a child?

"Och, now, Maigrid, that don't make no sense, and ye canna help the bairn by gettin' yerself worked up. Now, shoosh!"

Mrs. MacShane opened her mouth to say something more but, at that moment, spied Ian standing uneasily on the landing.

"There ye are, dear!" she exclaimed warmly. "We were so worried where ye'd got ta. What's that yer carryin'?" she asked but then, not waiting for an answer, rushed on. "Ye must be starved! There's a tray in yer room, and Hamish has managed ta get the old boiler workin'. Ye should have hot water in no time. I'm sure ye'd be happy for a good meal and a proper bath, travelin' all this way as ye have." And without missing a beat, she added, "Here, let me take that for ye. Hamish? Grab those from our lad, would ye?"

Hamish, with a good-natured twinkle in his blue eyes, reached for the bundle in Ian's arms.

Ian regarded the short, energetic, redheaded tidal wave and quickly decided that it was just going to be easier to go with the flow where Mrs. M was concerned. He hesitated but then handed over the clothing even though Mr. MacShane looked as if a stiff breeze could blow him over.

"Thanks," Ian stammered awkwardly.

"Come along, now, dear," Mrs. MacShane continued. "There's a good lad. Lord knows if we'd only a known ye were comin', we'd had the house better prepared for ye. Why, Hamish here thought he was ta take ye to some hotel in the city. We never dreamed yer … ah … *Lady Thorne*," she stumbled, "would send ye here with no one ta watch out for ye."

That was an interesting bit of information.

Mrs. MacShane opened the door to Ian's room and settled him at the small child's table in the miniscule chair opposite the large stuffed lion. With his chin almost touching his knees, Ian regarded the enormous platter of sunny-side-up eggs, grilled tomatoes, plump sautéed mushrooms, and hot buttered scones. A small crock of dark purple jam, a cup, and a large pot of what Ian guessed to be tea completed the table.

His stomach rumbled.

"Tuck in, now, dear," beamed Mrs. MacShane.

Self-consciously reaching for a napkin, Ian pondered his predicament. He had so many questions he didn't even know where to start.

"My … um … Miranda doesn't live here?" he asked, hungrily taking a bite of the delicious scone. The warm butter oozed from the roll, and he was tempted to lick his fingers. She was right; he was famished.

Mrs. MacShane glanced at Mr. MacShane, who was still standing awkwardly in the doorway with his bundle of clothes. He slowly crossed to the bed and put it down. Mrs. MacShane took a deep breath, and Mr. MacShane guardedly shook his head.

"I thought ye knew," she answered cautiously. "Lady Thorne left the very same night as ye. She has nae set foot here since."

"Well, Maigrid," interceded Mr. MacShane quickly, "we had best be leavin' the lad ta his breakfast." Addressing Ian, he continued, "Me and the missus'll be gettin' about our chores. We got a lot ta do ta get the house open afore Lady Thorne gets here. If ye be needin' us, we stay in the wee cottage just up the drive."

Mr. MacShane touched his hand to the old tweed cap he was wearing, tipping it in what Ian guessed was a sign of respect, and left the room.

As Mrs. MacShane turned to follow, Ian met her nervous gaze.

"Wait, Mrs. MacShane," he said in a quiet voice. "Why doesn't my ... stepmother live here? Where is the staff? What's happened here? I think I deserve to know."

"Ian," she began, looking over her shoulder at the retreating figure of her husband, "it's really not my place."

"Please," he quietly implored. "I've been away since I was five. I've been cut off from everything here since the day I left. I've had no news of my father or Miranda, or this place. Nothing at all." It had been as if this world ceased to exist once he'd left. In some ways, he reflected, it felt as if he had never actually lived here at all.

An uncomfortable silence filled the room. "Please, Mrs. MacShane," he said again.

Squaring her shoulders as if she had just made a momentous but difficult decision, Mrs. MacShane moved the stuffed lion onto the floor and sat down opposite Ian. Looking for all the world like a giant redheaded fairy in her floral apron, perched as she was on the tiny chair, she leaned in close to Ian. Bright green eyes searched his troubled blue ones. Taking a deep breath, she finally spoke.

"Two weeks after yer father's ... accident, Lady Thorne sent ye away ta America. Ye were so young I doubt ye remember much. Some boardin' school in Hawaii, was it? And she never brought ye back. Now, what ye don't know"—Ian watched as her lined face took on a distant look—"is that very same night that she sent ye away, me and Hamish heard a terrible ruckus up here at the manor. Of course, we come runnin' quick as we could, and there was yer stepma, soaked ta the skin, screamin' like a banshee, standin' outside in the middle of the courtyard. She wasn't wearin' nothin' but a nightgown. Kept goin' on about some ghostly lady walkin' the halls of the house. Said she couldna stay there. There was nothin' on this earth as could make her go back in that house ever again. Even made Hamish go in and get her some clothes ta wear. Had him drive her ta Edinburgh that very same night, ta a hotel. She's no' been back since."

Ian listened in wide-eyed astonishment. It was quite the tale, especially the part about the ghost. Was she making this up?

"A few days later, she sent for all her belongin's and had the house shut up. She let the servants go, all but Hamish and me. We stayed on as caretakers of the place, but she ordered us ta stay outta the house. Hamish walks through now and again, just ta make sure nothin's gone wrong with the plumbin' and such, but there's been no money for upkeep. She'd probably toss us both out if she knew we'd even set foot inside the door."

The spirited redhead tsked in a disapproving way, shaking her head, then sighed. "Now, that's all I know," she continued conspiratorially, "except, Hamish did say, when he went in the house that night ta get her things, that the floors were all wet. There was water on the stairs and all through the halls leadin' ta her room. He thought maybe a pipe had broke, but there was nothin' wrong. He couldna tell where the water'd come from."

Ian swallowed a bite of egg and stared at the woman. *Ghosts walking the halls? No money for upkeep?*

"I ... um," he cleared his throat. Should he ask her, *a stranger*, about this? Well, there was no one else *to* ask. "It was my understanding that my father was ... uh ... pretty wealthy. Why has there been no money to take care of this this estate?"

Mrs. MacShane's green eyes flashed. "Oh, don't worry about that, Ian. There's money aplenty. Its bein' held in trust." Those green eyes narrowed, and he noted the tension around her mouth. Obviously, she knew quite a lot, but would she tell him?

"Mrs. MacShane," he prompted, "regardless of the fact that I've been away for so long, this is my family home. I need someone to tell me what's going on here."

"Yer right, Ian. Yer no longer a child. Ye should have some idea of what ye've come back ta." She sighed heavily. "No, yer stepma shut this place up tight for another reason. Thorne Manor's the official seat of yer clan. The Thorne clan. This estate is treasured by yer people, Ian. There was, em ... some talk *Lady Thorne* didna like." She said the name with no small amount of venom. "Some"—she hesitated—"*some* were suspicious of her after the accident. Miranda was an outsider. She didna get along with the staff. She, uh ... accused those workin' here of tryin' ta scare her, of tryin' ta push her out. So she shut the place up tight, dismissed everyone but Hamish and me. Truth is, even with no pay, there were many as woulda pitched in ta care for the manor." Maigrid MacShane's eyes once more flashed green fire. "No, Ian, closin' the estate was a slap in the face ta the clan, a way of gettin' even."

"So you all think Miranda was somehow involved in my father's death?" Ian was incredulous. *Could this be true?*

"I didna say that, Ian," she denied sharply. "It was just talk. But if yer stepma knows I've said any of this, Hamish and me'll be gone. If ye want ta know more, ye'll have ta ask Miranda Thorne."

"I won't jeopardize your position here, Mrs. MacShane," Ian said thoughtfully. "I was the one who made you tell."

She nodded, those green eyes looking so deeply into his that he was uncomfortable.

"That's why," she went on with a lighter tone, "we were so surprised when outta the blue, Hamish was sent ta the airport ta meet ye. And when the solicitor told Hamish ta bring ye here, well …" She shrugged. "He said Lady Thorne'd be joinin' ye the day after tomorrow. Who's ta say what's in her mind?" She patted his hand kindly. "Now, that truly is all I know. Eat yer breakfast, and I'll check on ye after a while."

Ian slathered a large spoonful of the thick jam onto a second scone and reflected. *This story, this abandoned estate, this abrupt summons back to Scotland*, was a lot to take in. As the heir to this tangled state of affairs, or at least *one* of them, Ian actually had no idea what his status was or the terms of his father's will, but he *presumed* he would inherit all this. Honestly, he really didn't know what to think.

Growing up, Ian had literally been kept in the dark about everything except the fact that his father's body had never been recovered. There had been no one to question, no one who admitted knowing anything at all about his personal affairs. As he grew older and questions about his family and heritage became important, he had hit dead ends. All he knew was that he'd been placed in one of the world's most secure boarding schools for his own *safety*. Ian had assumed *safety* was just another word for the fact that no one wanted him around or knew what else to do with him. At least his father's money assured he'd been *safely* imprisoned and well educated, he reflected cynically.

Ian was also uncertain how he felt about Mrs. MacShane and the things she had told him.

This whole situation bites! he thought moodily. *I should be celebrating the end of term with the rest of my class today and having fun tonight with all my friends at the big luau and beach bonfire. But instead, I'm stuck here, by myself, in this creepy old house with these creepy old people! Oh, all right,* he amended after a moment, *the MacShanes really aren't that creepy. In fact, they have been really nice, and Mrs. McShane is a pretty good cook.* Ian stuffed another amazing bite of mushroom into his mouth. *But still, this...* He raked his hand through his disheveled black hair in frustration. *I don't even know what this is! This whole situation is totally messed up!*

Finally, stomach full, Ian pushed himself out of the tiny child's chair and went in search of his backpack once more. Retrieving his cell phone, he realized it was completely dead. He resisted a very strong impulse to throw it as hard as he could across the room and forced himself to instead take a deep breath and look for the charger.

Everything in the bag was a jumbled mess. Not only had he packed in a hurry, but the customs agents had also dumped the entire contents on his arrival in Edinburgh. *Why am I surprised?* he thought irritably. As he untangled the knotted cord from around a wadded pair of shorts, a button flipped into the air with the final tug. *Great! My only other pair of shorts.* A cursory search revealed it was nowhere to be found. *Really? Can this day get any better?*

Toothbrush, cell phone, and charger in hand, Ian made his way into the little bathroom that had once so long ago been his. Staring in dismay at the electrical outlet, he realized too late that he would require an adapter to use the power in this house—in fact, anywhere in this country.

Yep, he thought ruefully, *this day just keeps getting better and better. I can't even call my friends.*

Ian wondered briefly if the phones in the house were even connected after all this time but quickly realized it would do him absolutely no good. His friends' numbers were stored in the memory of his cell phone, *his dead cell phone,* with no way to retrieve them.

"Who even remembers phone numbers anymore?" he muttered, dropping the phone and charger onto a small bench under the window.

I'll have to ask Mrs. M if she can get me an adapter, he realized, attempting to quell the frustration he had felt since being dragged halfway across the world, *if I ever find her again in this creepy castle.*

Breathe, Ian, breathe, he told himself, staring into the bathroom mirror. Brilliant blue eyes framed by thick black lashes stared back at him. Unruly black hair had fallen forward, hiding winged eyebrows, and deep dimples appeared as he quirked his mouth in a rueful smile. He was acting like a petulant child. Wouldn't his friends laugh to see that? They all swore he had ice water in his veins where his temper was concerned. Nothing got to him but those freaky dreams of his. Or so they believed.

Shoving tousled hair out of a flushed face revealed high cheekbones and strong, classically chiseled features, and for a moment, Ian caught a fleeting image of his father. As each year passed, he looked more and more like Daniel Thorne.

He pushed the memory away. Those memories really did do a number on his head, and he'd already been forced to relive enough of them by returning to Scotland. He didn't want to think about it anymore.

Ian wrestled with the old handles on the small white porcelain sink, finally getting them to turn. A low, soulful moan emanated from somewhere deep in the bowels of the house. The haunting moan escalated to a loud, piercing wail that sent shivers down his spine.

Suddenly, the sink began to shake, and dark bloodred liquid first sputtered and then spewed from the faucet. The loud moaning continued, and Ian jumped back, but not before the awful red stuff increased to projectile force, following the curved trough of the sink up and out, blasting his face and upper body.

He found himself engulfed by a wave of horrid, wet, freezing … *blood?*

Someone grabbed his shoulder from behind, and Ian locked his hands around a wrist, using pressure points and leverage as he spun his assailant into an armlock. Heart pounding, attempting to clear his vision as the vile red substance dripped from his face and body, he forced himself to focus on his attacker.

Shocked, he released the stunned young woman as if he'd been burned. As rivulets of the disgusting *whatever* dripped from his body and onto a rapidly growing puddle on the floor, Ian attempted to assimilate his bizarre predicament.

A fresh-faced, rosy-cheeked girl stood before him with her hand over her mouth, trying not to giggle.

"Sorry, Ian, I didna mean to startle ye," said the still-giggling intruder. "Mrs. MacShane sent me to tell ye that ye may need to bleed the pipes."

"Y ... yeah," Ian stammered, completely mortified, wiping the foul liquid from his eyes. "They're bl—ugh!" He grimaced and gagged as the stuff flowed into his mouth. Clearing it on the sleeve of his sodden T-shirt, he finished inanely, "They're, uh, bleeding, all right."

"No, silly," she said with a broad grin as she struggled to regain some semblance of decorum. "Water's not been run in this house in years. There's air in the pipes and, most likely, rust from the boiler, by the looks of it. Ye need to let the water run for a bit to blow out the lines."

Ian slicked more of the disgusting stuff off his face as it finally dawned on him that the *blood* streaming over him was simply rusty water, and this young woman mirthfully stood witness to the new, very uncool axe-murderer look he was now sporting.

"Keep it runnin'," she continued, her eyes dancing, "until the water starts to clear. It might help to run the tub as well. The rust won't hurt ye, though, to be sure. It just looks kinda, well, ye know ... *gruesome*," she finished, looking him up and down with a knowing smirk.

Ian quirked a winged eyebrow as he stood speechlessly, shaking his head under her laughing scrutiny. Realizing he should say *something*, *anything*, and though he desperately searched his mind, he could find absolutely no words to comment on his *utterly humiliating* dilemma.

She tossed him a dry towel.

"Uh ... thanks." The corner of his mouth twitched in a self-deprecating half-smile.

"My name's Moira, by the way," the pretty blonde announced brightly, as though the young man standing in the bathroom covered in ghoulish red slime were the most commonplace of events. "Mrs. MacShane called me to come help out for the next few days. I expect she'll need a lot more help than just me, by the looks of this place, if she expects to get it cleaned before Lady Thorne gets here. Shame to let a house this beautiful get in such a state, but we'll be gettin' it spit n' polished in no time, just ye wait and see. I'll be clearin' yer dishes now, if yer finished."

And with that, she was gone, leaving Ian still standing slightly dazed in his ice-cold *puddle of blood.*

CHAPTER II

A light breeze skimmed gaily over the loch, creating small shimmering ripples in its flight, while the newly verdant leaves of the forest sighed and whispered secrets shared only amongst the creatures of the woodlands. Birds chirped and squabbled in the surrounding foliage, and high in the sky, Ian spied a sea gull as it winged across the water. A lone seal basked lazily in the sun, appearing to keep an eye on him from a little way down the beach. Its sleek body glistened silver in the pure morning light.

Ian gazed out across the water to the tiny distant island where the gray stone ruins of the tower castle could just be spied above the trees. Mary, Queen of Scots, had once been imprisoned there, he seemed to recall.

Although the sun shone deceptively bright through the lazily trailing white clouds overhead, Ian was heavily bundled in his father's old clothes, as if prepared for an expedition into the Arctic. He shivered as the brisk *summer* air brushed his face and tousled his hair. Long legs swung idly over the murky green water of the loch from a not-uncomfortable perch at the edge of the small fishing pier near the forest's edge.

Ian had followed an unkempt trail through the sadly neglected but still beautiful gardens of the estate, tarrying for a time at the edge of a water lily–choked fountain with a mossy mermaid spilling water from the shell she held into its center, before wandering on. Approaching the loch, he spied the dilapidated pier through the trees far to the right of the gardens. Though it was completely hidden from sight of the imposing manor, he had known exactly where to find it.

Once, there had been a small rowboat tethered here. Ian and his father had spent many treasured hours rowing and fishing from that little boat. It was impossible to believe that it had all been taken away in the blink of an eye. Here in this peaceful place, it almost felt as though no time had passed at all. For a moment, he let himself imagine that his father would soon appear at the edge of the trail, loaded down with fishing gear, and they would be off.

Here, in the midst of this unbroken beauty, filled with so many happy memories, he just could not shake off the feeling that there had been some enormous mistake. Ian couldn't remember any of the events from that morning after they had launched that little boat from the pier, only that the sun had been shining and the smooth green waters of the loch had beckoned.

His father must be alive somewhere. After all, they had never found his body. Maybe his dad had only been injured and had lost his memory. Maybe he would wake up one day, alive and well, remembering who he was and the son who waited for him to come home. Maybe …

Just stop! There was no maybe!

If his dad was alive, someone would have found him. He was Lord Daniel Thorne, an important and wealthy man. The loch had been searched, and boats had swept the area for days. Every inch of the shoreline had been combed. His father was gone. There was no other explanation. It was time to accept it and move on.

Think of something else, Ian angrily chided himself, forcing his thoughts to the events of the morning, which in reality did not make him feel much better.

The girl, Moira, was pretty and not too much older than he was. It would be nice to have a friend in this place. He had made an absolute fool of himself, though, just standing there staring at her while that awful red muck dripped down his face. She must think he was a complete idiot. As more people had begun to arrive to help Mrs. M, he had fled. Not wanting to run into Moira again, the eminent heir to Thorne Manor stole furtively down the back stairs and made his getaway into the gardens.

Ian had never realized he could be such a coward, but the thought of facing the girl whose arm he had nearly twisted out of its socket, on top of being discovered plastered in that gruesome sludge, was just more than he could take today.

I just want to go home, he thought gloomily. *Home?* Now that was an interesting thought. Since when had this ceased to be his home?

Ian wasn't sure but knew without a doubt that Hawaii was where he belonged. Hawaii was his true home now, not Scotland, not this cold, remote, lonely country with too many memories and totally screwed-up electrical outlets.

The crunch of gravel on the path followed by the protesting creak of wooden planks on the old stone pier told Ian that he was no longer alone. He turned to find a smiling Moira making her way toward him. Inwardly, he groaned, wishing the murky green water of the loch would just swallow him up and have it done with.

Resisting the sudden urge to dive into the freezing water and break for the distant island, Ian attempted a halfhearted smile, forcing himself to return Moira's ever-cheery greeting.

"Thought I might find ye here," she stated matter-of-factly, seating herself beside him as if it was the most normal thing in the world. "I brought ye a sandwich," she beamed. "Thought ye might be hungry as it's nigh on three o'clock and ye didna come back for lunch."

Ian took in the bright golden curls framing an open, friendly face and the pretty little dimple that appeared when she smiled. Soft brown eyes laughed into his, and suddenly, he was happy for her company.

Moira passed him an egg salad sandwich and a bottle of apple juice then retrieved the same for herself from a brown paper bag.

"Whew! It's been a long day," she sighed, tossing back those long curls.

Flashing a sheepish grin as his stomach rumbled, Ian gratefully accepted the food.

The pair ate in silence for a few minutes, feet swinging above the green loch, like two children without a care in the world.

"They say that Mary Stuart was kept prisoner in the castle on yonder island," Moira said finally by way of conversation.

"I somehow seem to remember that," Ian replied seriously. Why was it that some things from his past were so easily dredged up while others were impossible to recall? He glanced at her through a fringe of impossibly long black eyelashes, which were the only feminine thing about his handsome young face, and asked, "Have you ever been there?"

"No one goes there," she said earnestly. "There's a dangerous current all around the island, like a whirlpool. Boats have a hard time gettin' to it, though I remember hearin' that yer family may have had some secret way in. They say the island's haunted." Moira took a drink of her juice. "Yer family owns that isle, Ian. It's part of the estate. Did yer dad ever take ye there?"

"I don't remember."

Ian examined the distant shoreline. The water did seem rougher near the island. "There's a pier, though," he commented. "It looks really old, but like you said, someone must know how to get onto the island. After all, they built the castle there."

"Yes. Sometime around the eleventh century, I've heard."

Moira squinted out across the loch. "A pier, you say? I canna see it. I didna know such a thing was there. Yer eyesight must be really good."

Oh, he shouldn't have said that. Ian had let down his guard with this good-natured Scottish girl. There were certain things about himself that he'd learned to hide. His best friend Braxton called them *his freaky skills*, but his abilities were definitely out of the ordinary. His eyesight was crazy good, far beyond that of anyone he knew, as well as his hearing and sense of smell.

"Ye were young when ye left, weren't ye? Five or six, as I recall? Is it hard bein' back?"

Ian released a long, slow breath. "Yeah." After a slight hesitation, he continued, "I don't really even know what I'm doing here or why, all of a sudden, Miranda sent for me. One minute I'm in class, and the next thing I know, I'm on a plane. No explanation, no nothing!"

The frustration on his face and in his voice was evident.

Moira put an arm around his shoulder, pulling him into a quick hug, and, just as quickly, let him go. The movement seemed somehow natural, and unlike the girls he went to school with, Ian found her presence comforting.

"Somethin's goin' on for sure." She nodded. "I doona think the MacShanes know just what's happenin' either, though. Still …" She trailed off. "Well, keep yer chin up, Ian. Lady Thorne'll be here in a couple a days, and I'm sure it'll all come right in the end. It's *you* who's the rightful heir to Thorne Manor and all that comes with it. She canna really make ye do anything ye doona want to, can she?"

"I guess not," Ian acknowledged, beginning to relax a little. Moira was right. He wasn't a small, powerless child anymore. Miranda was his father's wife, but he was Daniel Thorne's son and heir. Honestly, what *could* she do to him? Clearly, she didn't suddenly want to welcome him home as her long-lost son. She obviously had no place for him in her new life. So what was her agenda?

"I hear ye've a birthday comin' up in three days. Maybe that's somethin' to do with all this."

Ian eyed her quizzically. "How did you know that?"

"Just somethin' Mrs. MacShane said this mornin', that's all. Ye'll be seventeen?" Moira nodded knowingly. "Yer the same age as my brother, Conner. I'm nineteen, but no reason we can't be friends. I figure ye might need a friend while yer here, and besides"—she winked—"I hear all the gossip in the kitchen and the village. I can be yer spy. It'll be just like in the movies."

Merry brown eyes laughed into his vivid blue ones with reassuring warmth.

"How many brothers do you have?" Ian hoped she didn't catch the wistful edge to his question.

"Just the one, and believe me, he's enough of a handful." Golden curls bobbed as she grinned conspiratorially. "There are five of us in all. I've three older sisters. Da kept tryin' till he got his boy." She sighed in mock horror. "Poor Mum! And poor me! Conner'll be joinin' me at university in the fall."

"You're in college?"

"Yes, at Aberdeen. I'm just home on holiday. Mrs. MacShane needed some help up here, and I was glad to do it. I'm savin' for a car." Moira flashed a radiant smile, and the excitement in her voice told Ian just how much she wanted it. "Da' would help, but with five of us, I hate to take it."

"Sounds like you have a great family." Again, Ian hoped she didn't catch the envy he tried to hide.

"We're close." Moira nodded and gave Ian a look that told him she understood.

"Well," she announced briskly, "I'd best get back to the house. There's still a lot more to do." Tucking an errant curl behind her ear, she scrambled to her feet. "It's goin' to be a long night, but we'll get'r done."

As Moira gathered up the remains of their makeshift picnic and turned to go, Ian realized she was wearing only blue jeans and a long-sleeved T-shirt against the freezing June weather. He felt suddenly self-conscious in his arctic gear. "Hey," he called after her, "aren't you cold?"

"Nae." She called back in her ever-cheerful voice. "Sun's shinin', and it's a glorious day!" Spreading her arms, she spun in a circle with all the exuberance of a child. "So far," she added breathlessly, glancing briefly at the sky. "One thing about Scotland," Moira chuckled, "if ye don't like the weather, just wait half an hour and it'll be different. From the looks of ye, though, I'd wager yer havin' a hard time of it. It's warm in Hawaii, no?"

Ian nodded.

"Well, keep those clothes close. This is about as nice a day as ye'll see here." She winked. "Ne'er cast a cloot till Mey's oot, but in yer case, best make that June."

"What the heck does that mean?" Ian shot her a puzzled grin, uncertain what to make of this ambiguous bit of Scottish wisdom.

"I'll tell ye later." Moira laughed over her shoulder, turned a quick corner, and was gone.

Completely bemused, Ian stared at the empty path where she had just been. He suddenly felt much better, happier. Moira was like *pure* sunshine. Things were definitely looking up.

He swung his feet back over the edge of the pier and gazed out toward the swirling waters surrounding the castle island. The loch was immense and beautiful, with a mix of foliage and broad trees along its shoreline. Deep green water reflected the pale blue sky overhead, and the bits of fluffy white clouds cast shadows over the mirrorlike surface as the sun dipped in and out. The sound of waves gently lapping the supports of the pier lulled him, and for the first time since his arrival, a sense of peace began to take root.

The breeze picked up slightly, lifting the water's surface into small foamy streaks of white, and the tops of the trees began to sway rhythmically, as though unseen hands brushed fingers to and fro through their branches. The mild soughing of wind through the forest and the symphonic rustle of leaves added to the peaceful choir of nature. Ian lay back, closing his eyes, allowing the sun, the gentle breeze, and the soothing sounds of his environment to wash over him.

The snap of a branch followed by the startled shriek of birds as something large crashed through low brush in the nearby forest jolted him from his repose. The continuous birdsong that had barely registered suddenly ceased altogether, and he looked around to see if Moira had returned.

The abrupt hush sounded louder to his ears than the earlier melodies of nature, and the complete absence of the cheery squawks, squabbles, and trills unsettled him.

That noise had come from the opposite side of the forest, far from the path Moira had taken, but he could see no one. Ian waited for another rustle of underbrush or the telltale sign of movement, but the eerie silence droned on.

A prickle of unease brought him warily to his feet as he scanned the forest. Hair stood up on the back of his neck as Ian cautiously and thoroughly took stock of his surroundings.

He was suddenly aware of just how isolated he was from the manor.

A low, dense mist now lay across the loch between the castle island and the shore, and every now and again, the vapor roiled and churned as though something swum just out of sight beneath the thick white shroud.

The Loch Ness monster lives in Loch Ness, not here, he reminded himself with a self-deprecating jab at his wayward imagination. Still, he was not sure if he was more unnerved by the thing in the water or the thing in the forest.

Ian inched his way off the dock and away from the swirling mist but wondered distractedly if predators like wolves or bears roamed the woods. Hawaii had wild pigs, which under certain circumstances could be dangerous, but surely, Moira would have warned him if there was anything to worry about.

It's probably just someone's dog, or maybe a deer, Ian chided as he turned toward the track Moira had taken earlier. Glancing back, though, he couldn't quite shake the feeling of being watched. The movement in the forest had ceased; however, the birds had not resumed their antics.

Ian tugged the sweatshirt's hood up over his head. As Moira had warned, the weather had definitely changed. The breeze off the loch had a decidedly icy bite to it now. How was it possible for it to be so cold here in the middle of summer? Definitely time to return to the manor.

It was then that he thought of his dream from the morning. Without intending to, he veered away from the trail and instead found himself heading for the distant shoreline. He felt silly and a little embarrassed about his suspicions the farther he got from the forest and soon pushed the incident from his mind entirely as he neared the scene of his bizarre brush with the ghostly vision who had decided to drown him in the loch.

Would there be any sign of that mysterious lady who had visited the water's edge at dawn? he wondered. *Would there be footprints?*

Of course not. She had floated on the mists. She had been a dream. *A dream,* Ian mused with irony, *that I have only ever had here at Thorne Manor, and not since I was five.* Or had he dreamed of her in Hawaii? Yes, well, maybe. But those dreams had been different. He had certainly never taken that suffocating plunge into the loch in any of his dreams, that he could recall anyway. And the lady in the mist had never seemed so … *evil,* until today.

Still, he poked along the rocky shoreline just to be sure.

Ian scrambled over the rough pebbles and small rocks, head down, looking for anything out of the ordinary. Stepping over bits of driftwood and other debris thrown up by the waves, he saw nothing one would not expect to find on such an isolated and remote shore.

There was no use looking for footprints on such a rock-strewn beach. A stampede of elephants would have left no imprint on the hard, rocky ground, let alone a solitary, graceful woman.

It was only as he turned to make his way back to the house that he noticed something glinting in the dying rays of the sun.

The object was small, resting upon a nest of dried waterweed within the hollow of a piece of driftwood. It was almost as if the shining item had been deliberately placed there. Had the sun been at a different angle, he would not have seen it. *A priceless jewel upon an altar to a pagan god.*

Now, where had that thought come from?

Bending to retrieve the small figure, Ian gasped as he realized what he held in his hand. This was a beautifully carved figurine of a woman with a long flowing dress and hair that hung almost to her feet. She wore an unusual crown, vine-like, circling low to a delicate point over her forehead. The emerald-green lady seemed to glow with an inner light, and the figure, although carved of hard, cold, jewellike stone, appeared almost to be in motion, swaying in a gentle, rhythmic dance.

The Dark Queen from his father's chessboard!

Who would have dared to remove such a priceless object from the house? he wondered angrily. *And why then would that same person just discard it among the rocks and debris on this beach?*

Shaking with rage, he reverently cradled the exquisite object in his hands.

Ian stormed up the rocky path like a roiling black thunderstorm blown in from the loch, not stopping as he reached the manor.

Still seething with anger as he entered the massive french doors leading into the house from the gardens, he barely registered the smells of lemon oil, floor polish, bleach, and other cleaning products that assailed his nostrils.

He heard the faint buzz of a vacuum cleaner coming from somewhere in the house. Windows had been thrown open, and the pale-blue silk curtains in the downstairs salon flapped in the breeze.

Ian stood at the bottom of the impressively carved staircase leading to the upper gallery and shouted, "MRS. ... MAC ... SHANE! MRS. ... MAC ... SHAAANE! I WANT TO SPEAK TO YOU NOW!"

Two blond heads peeked over the balcony of the upper gallery, and a flustered Mrs. MacShane hurried toward him from the direction of the kitchen. A cobweb was tangled in her hair like a silken headpiece, a dark mark smudged her cheek, and she was quickly wiping her hands on a stained old towel.

"What in heaven's name is goin' on here?" she asked breathlessly. "What's happened to ye? Are ye all right?"

"Mrs. MacShane, I found this on the beach. Do you recognize it?" Ian demanded through clenched teeth.

The disconcerted housekeeper looked at the delicate object Ian was holding so carefully in his palm and visibly paled.

"It's … it's the Dark Queen." Ian did not miss the slight quaver in her voice. "It's the Dark Queen from yer father's chessboard."

"*Yes*, it is." Ian's blazing blue eyes flashed dangerously, barely controlling a temper that seemed to be surfacing more and more. "Someone stole this from the house and threw it away on the beach. I saw it this morning, so it was taken sometime after breakfast."

"Come with me!"

Mrs. MacShane grabbed Ian by his free hand, pulling him with surprising strength at a dead run up the staircase, along the gallery, past two gaping girls, and into his father's room.

The chess set resided serenely on the little table, every piece where it should be, except two. The White Queen once again stood peacefully in the exact center of the board, gazing benevolently upon her subjects.

The Dark Queen was missing.

"Who's been in this house today? One of the people you brought in here is a thief," Ian grated out.

Mrs. MacShane collapsed into one of the leather chairs and clutched her throat, breathing hard.

As Ian impatiently waited for the gasping woman to catch her breath, reverent hands placed the Dark Queen in her rightful square on the board. Carefully retrieving the White Queen, he returned her safely to her court.

"It's … it's not what ye think," she began.

"Then," Ian gritted, "explain it to me."

"No one stole this, Ian," she stammered, pushing up from the chair. "It was …" Again, she hesitated, eyes raking his face then flitting over the room almost frantically as she sought her answer.

"Was what?" he demanded.

Pursing blanched lips, she stared at him for a long moment.

Ian watched the short red-haired woman impatiently. For a second, her green eyes bore deeply into his, making him highly uncomfortable.

Finally, as if coming to a difficult decision, she answered, "It was a warnin'."

"A warning?" Ian repeated in a voice flat with disbelief. "From whom?"

No answer. She met his incensed gaze for a brief moment then looked away.

"What kind of a warning, Mrs. MacShane?"

Nothing.

"Who put it on the beach?" Ian prodded.

Still nothing.

Tense fingers that ached to throttle the woman instead pushed hair back from his furrowed temple in frustration.

"I don't know what kind of games you're playing here, but even though I no longer live here, this is still my house. Stay out of this room from now on." He eyed the keys jangling at her side. "In fact, lock it. And give me the key. Now."

"It wasn't me, Ian. It was—"

"Who?"

She shook her head. Her gaze was filled with such sadness that he almost felt guilty.

"Who, Mrs. McShane?"

Eyes downcast, she refused to look at him.

"Something … *other*," she mumbled.

"What did you say?"

"Nothing."

"Other?" Ian asked again in that same flat tone, refusing to allow any sympathy to enter his voice. "You mean a ghost?"

Her head jerked up again, searching his face for something she obviously didn't find. For a moment, it seemed as if she would answer, but she did not.

In truth, the morning's dream had made an impression. Ian wasn't certain that if she had said yes, he would have disbelieved her.

Silently, she handed him the key. This stoic refusal to answer was more frustrating than the cryptic statements. She knew more than she was saying. Mrs. McShane was obviously lying to protect someone.

Ian drew an exasperated breath and motioned for her to leave.

Not budging from her spot, that somber green gaze rested on his face in obvious distress. Ian knew he wasn't prepared to physically remove the obstinate woman from the room, so how did he make her take him seriously? He had absolutely no experience being in a position of authority over someone so much older than him.

They stared at one another in a kind of stalemate.

Finally, with troubled eyes, she spoke. "Ian, I swear I don't know who took it. I got three good girls a helpin' me here today. I've known 'em since they were bairns, and all three of 'em are as honest as the day is long. I'd stake my life on it. Not one of 'em has left this house since they showed up this mornin', except Moira, ta bring ye some food. I'll talk ta the girls. The doors've all been open today, so it's not impossible that someone else got in here, but it makes no sense that they'd take somethin' so valuable just ta get rid of it in such a way. I'll check the rest of the house too, just ta make sure nothin' else is missin'."

Ian wasn't going to let her off the hook so easily. "You've already said you don't believe it was stolen."

"No. The chess set is priceless. If someone came in here ta steal somethin', I believe they would've taken all the pieces, not just the queen."

That did make sense.

"Why did you say it was a warning, Mrs. MacShane?"

She exhaled slowly. "Things go on here, Ian. Strange things that canna always be explained."

"Like the *ghost* who chased Miranda from the house?" Ian couldn't keep the skepticism from his voice.

"Yes," she mumbled, color tingeing her cheeks.

He nodded. No part of his upbringing had equipped him to deal with something like this. His temple was beginning to pound. Raising a winged eyebrow, he waited for her to elaborate.

"Yes, Ian," she finally answered. "I think it might be a warnin'."

"A warning about what?"

The little redhead sighed deeply then determinedly met his probing blue eyes. "I know what the Dark Queen means ta me, Ian, but ye have to work out what it means ta you."

Enough! Ian had had more than enough of this cryptic conversation. For the first time, he looked fully at the infuriating woman before him. Though seemingly spry, she was fairly old, and she looked tired. He noted the cobweb still clinging to her hair, the dirty smudge on her face, and the grimy apron that spoke volumes about the hard work she had been doing since dawn to bring his family home back to some semblance of its former glory.

This old woman had been working the entire day while he'd been lazing in the sun, and he had just berated her. Ian's gut told him she was harmless, but she was eccentric. He was certain she wasn't telling him the truth, or at least not the entire truth, but this woman had obviously been trusted by his father if she had lived on the estate as long as she said she had.

Calmer now that the Dark Queen had been returned and no damage had been done to the other pieces, Ian's conscience jabbed him. He spoke quietly but in a voice that broached no argument. "I would appreciate it if you would let me know what your girls have to say. I would also like my father's room locked from now on while people are here. And I will keep the key."

Dipping her chin in agreement, she adjusted the keys at her waist.

"And, Mrs. MacShane," Ian added guiltily, "I'm willing to help you get this house in order. I'm stronger than those girls you have helping you, and I'm not afraid to work."

"No, Ian!" she asserted, suddenly very flustered. "That wouldn't be right. It's not yer fault this house is in such a state."

"Nor yours, from what I understand. Let me know what I can do."

"It'll be fine, Ian. Ye should spend some time gettin' reacquainted with your home."

He nodded thoughtfully. "The offer stands."

Instead of leaving, Mrs. MacShane placed both hands on Ian's shoulders. Bright green eyes looked straight into his. "Ian," she said levelly, "I've been with yer family for more years than I can remember. I took care of yer dad when he was a baby, and I was here when he brought ye home after ye were born. I've loved ye both, and it hurt bad when Daniel ... when we lost yer father. It hurt even more when Lady Thorne chose ta send ye away. Ye were so little and afraid after what'd happened. Ye just kept starin' out at the loch with those big, sad eyes. Ye were so stoic it near broke my heart, yet ye never cried. Ye just kept askin' for yer dad."

Tears welled up in her eyes as she continued. "I know ye doona seem ta remember me, bein' so young when ye left, but ye can trust me ta look out for ye. I owe it ta yer father. And, Ian, as long as I draw a breath, I'll do what I can ta protect ye. By Scottish law, though, yer dad's marriage ta Miranda put her in charge of ye, and this house, and for that matter, everything else too, after he went missin'." She paused. "Well, at least for the time bein'," she finished uncomfortably. "If it'd been any other way, I'd never have let ye leave here. Now"—she brushed away a tear—"keep that key. I think yer right about keepin' this room locked."

With that, Mrs. MacShane swept him into a crushing bear hug. "Remember, Ian," she whispered, "I've loved ye since ye were born." Abruptly releasing him, she quickly walked to the door. "I'll bring yer supper up ta yer room in a couple of hours. Kitchen's a mess. I think ye'll be more comfortable eatin' in there, at least for another night."

Ian suddenly felt like a deer in the headlights. Shaking his head numbly, he mumbled something unintelligible. How had she done that? She had just completely and effectively turned the tables on him.

Acknowledging the shame he felt for the way he had treated this perplexing old woman, Ian stopped her before she could leave. Never in his life had he spoken to an adult that way. True, someone had removed a rare and priceless object from his father's room, but it was clear that she had been almost as upset about it as he was. *Unless it was all an act.*

Now, where had that thought come from?

Ian didn't recognize himself and the strong roller coaster of emotions he had been experiencing since his arrival. This house was opening old wounds, and he really needed to get a grip. Normally, he was the calm, logical voice of reason among his friends, but he felt ill at ease here, unsettled, as if something was jarringly wrong. The last thing he needed was to make an enemy of Maigrid MacShane on his first day in Scotland.

"I'm sorry for shouting, Mrs. MacShane," Ian said quietly. "No matter the situation, I should not have been disrespectful."

"Thank ye for that, Ian. There's no harm done." She heaved a sigh. "I know its hard comin' back inta this house with all its reminders of the past, but in time, ye'll make new memories. And eventually, those old demons'll cease ta haunt ye."

Ian's eyes snapped to hers. Once more, she had espoused a cryptic piece of wisdom that on the surface seemed quite innocent. But Ian was not fooled. Just what exactly did she mean by that? Just what exactly did she know that she wasn't telling him?

CHAPTER III

The figurines on the chessboard emanated that gentle, luminescent glow, and Ian realized that today had been the first time he had ever touched any of the chess pieces. It both hurt and shocked him that someone had removed the Dark Queen from the safety of his father's room and then simply dropped her on the beach, where she could have been easily broken or lost to him forever. For some reason, this beautiful chess set, more than anything else, was a symbol of his bond with his father. Ian felt somehow closer to him just by being in its presence.

Late into the night, as he tossed and turned in his little bed, the day's events played out endlessly and would not allow him to rest. *Only Moira left the house today. But she wouldn't. Why would she? Why would she take the Dark Queen, only to discard her on the beach? It didn't make sense. Moira wouldn't—no, she wouldn't ...*

Ian finally murmured and fell into a fitful sleep.

He dreamed that *a redheaded fairy with luminous wings flitted through his open window and came to alight upon his shoulder. Her bright green eyes gazed merrily into his.* "I've loved ye since ye were born, and I'm watchin' over ye," *she whispered in his ear. Then with a wink, she flitted up, hovering for a moment, and flew away.*

Turning on his side, he restlessly stretched, bunched his pillow, and finally slumbered more deeply.

Ian drifted peacefully in the calm blue ocean waters of Hapuna Bay. The sun was warm on his skin, and he and his friends floated lazily on their surfboards, waiting for the stingy ocean gods to send more waves. The ocean was flat today. No matter, it was enough to enjoy the sun and the limited freedom the school allowed them.

Suddenly, she *was there on the shore, the lady who often appeared in the mist. She had been visiting him since he was a child, keeping him* company in his dreams. Was he dreaming now? Must be a dream, 'cause he always forgot when he woke up.

She beckoned to him, silently calling him to come to her. The mists swirled and plumed, and her eyes met his across the distance of the turquoise water. The ocean began to churn, turning to murky green. Her motions became more urgent, almost frenzied. He began frantically to paddle his surfboard into shore. He had to reach her. Somehow, he knew his life depended on it.

Suddenly, he was no longer on his surfboard but in a small rowboat. The boat was rocking, a hole had appeared in the bottom, and water was rushing in. They were too far from shore. His father was beating his oar against something dark in the water. The thing was rocking the boat, trying to capsize the tiny craft. The boat tipped, and he felt a shock as the icy water engulfed him. His life jacket was torn from his small body. Something grabbed his legs, pulling him deep under the frigid waters of the loch. His father was there, grabbing ahold of the dark thing that held him under. He needed air; he was going to die. He breathed the water into his lungs. Strong arms carried him to the surface of the shadowy green water, but he was suffocating, choking!

Ian kicked himself away from the tangled blankets that held him prisoner and, with every last bit of strength he possessed, propelled himself halfway across his bedroom. His heart was pounding in his chest, and he could feel that he was breathing too fast. His body was drenched in sweat. No longer disoriented, he realized he was in his bedroom and he had had another bad dream. No, this time he was calling it a nightmare. The dreams were getting worse and much more realistic.

Forcing himself to calm his breathing, Ian staggered into the little bathroom and flipped the switch. Flinching as the bright, harsh light pierced his eyes, he momentarily shut them against the merciless glare. A moment passed before he was able to force them open and make his way to the sink. He put his mouth to the faucet and gulped at the icy water flowing from the tap. The reflection that greeted him from the mirror was a little frightening. His face was waxy and pale, and his deep-blue eyes looked bruised and haunted. Wild raven hair was soaked and matted, and his T-shirt and pajama bottoms were drenched.

Stripping out of the soggy mess he was wearing, Ian crossed to the tub. He'd give anything for a hot shower right now, but the tub had only the handheld device that always reminded him of an old-fashioned telephone. Turning on the tap, he noticed with relief that the rust had subsided and at least he wouldn't have to bathe in *blood*.

When it was warm enough, he eased his tall frame into the old claw-foot tub and, still shivering, sprayed himself down until he felt a little more human. He could have gone to another room, he supposed, and had a real shower, but in truth, he was more than a little spooked. He had no desire to go wandering through the enormous dark manor in the middle of the night.

Finally dressed and warm, Ian returned the sheets to his bed and burrowed beneath the blankets. Still uneasy, he had left his bathroom light on and cracked the door so he would not have to sleep in the dark. *Just for one night*, he told himself.

As he turned on his side and was about to close his eyes, his drowsy gaze settled on the small figurine on his bedside table. The Dark Queen glowed softly in the dim light of his bedroom. *The same chess piece he'd returned to his father's locked room earlier in the day.* A chill went through his body as he leapt from his bed and bolted his door.

Ian raised his sword, its lethal, bloodied blade glinting silver in the fading light. He stood wearily, watching the advancing horde. Already, they had fought long and hard, and exhaustion was a constant foe.

The stench of smoke and blood assailed his nostrils. Drums pulsed, metal rang against metal, and the sounds of screams and thunder were deafening.

Over the raging battlefield, struggling knots of fighters twisted, blocked, and slashed, trying not to trip over bodies strewn over the ground. The first ranks of shrieking Cruithne, the painted ones, crashed into a line of shields. The shields shivered under the impact and fell back.

Amid the turmoil and chaos, Ian blocked a war hammer and glanced quickly at the lithe blond warrior fighting savagely at his side.

Long battle braids whipped as she blocked a deadly blade and cleanly took the head of her aggressor. She had blood running from her temple and an ugly gash on her left shoulder. Against insurmountable odds, her shining sword sliced through the guard of another and then another. Strategically placing her back to him as she prepared another defense against the onslaught, beating back an enemy that came on ruthlessly, she called to him. *"No one thinks we will stand."*

He knew her. He should know her; she was so familiar.

With the rising howl of the wind and great crashes of thunder, a storm broke over them in sheets of hail and freezing rain. The deadly clash of swords turned to a rhythmic clang as Ian emerged from a shattered slumber, his heart racing.

He wasn't on a battlefield, but it had seemed so real. He could still feel the heavy weapon in his hands. He could still smell the smoke and the blood and the rain.

Someone was pounding quite insistently on his door and calling his name. "Ian! *EEEE ... AN!* Are ye all right in there?"

"Coming," he answered, his heartbeats wild and irregular. "Coming!" Throwing off suffocating blankets, he staggered out of bed. He stumbled as he unbolted his door, and was met by a very agitated Moira.

"Ian," she gasped, concern showing on her pretty face, "are ye all right? I've been knockin' forever!" She bustled past him, setting down the breakfast tray, and turned to scrutinize him more closely. "Ye look terrible! Didna ye hear me beatin' on the door?"

"No," he replied, taking a deep, orientating breath. "Rough night. Bad dreams."

"Oh," she said sympathetically. "Is that the reason ye had yer door locked?" She poked him mischievously in the ribs. "To keep out the monsters?" Soft brown eyes twinkled, and a smile played at the corners of her mouth.

"No!" he denied a little too vehemently. "It's just ..."

"It's all right, silly, we all have bad dreams sometimes." She looked around the room. "If truth be told, I'm not sure how well I'd like stayin' here either, in this big old house, all by myself like ye've been. Actually, I think ye've been pretty brave."

Puffing out his chest a little, he shrugged almost convincingly. "Nah, I'm good."

Moira laughed at him good-naturedly. "All right, tough guy, eat yer breakfast. I'll be back in a bit to get yer tray." As she turned to go, she spied the emerald-green lady on the side table. "Ooh, that's real pretty, Ian, where'd ye get such a thing?" Her eyes widened as it dawned on her. "That's no' the Dark Queen from yer dad's room?"

"Yeah," Ian said uncomfortably.

"Mrs. MacShane told us what happened yesterday. Guess ye brought it in here for safekeepin'? Can't say as I blame ye. Mrs. McShane cleaned yer father's room herself yesterday, so I've no' seen the entire set. Judgin' from this, it must be beautiful. It's real old too, I hear. I'm sorry, Ian, I doona have a clue who woulda taken it. I'm just glad ye happened on it on the beach." Moira's curls bounced as she earnestly nodded. "Seems a real piece of luck, ye findin' it as ye did. I'm happy no harm was done to it."

"So Mrs. MacShane cleaned my dad's room?" Ian asked, trying to keep the suspicion from his voice.

"First thing yesterday mornin'." Moira nodded again, curls bobbing. "Guess she thought ye might want to move in there. Bed's bigger and bathroom has a proper shower. It's a grand room to be sure." Blushing, she confessed, "I peeked through the door just as she was lockin' it up tight last night. She gave ye the key?"

"Yes," Ian acknowledged softly. "I have it."

What time had that been? he wondered. *The room had not been locked when he'd entered with Mrs. MacShane, and* Ian *had been the one to lock the door as they'd left.*

"All right, then," Moira chattered on, oblivious to his suspicions. "I'll leave ye to yer breakfast." Already to the door, she added, "Kitchen's clean as a whistle. Ye'll find sandwiches and such at midday when ye get hungry. Mrs. MacShane stocked the fridge and pantry for ye too. Eat up, now."

"Uh, thanks."

"Oh! I almost forgot. I saw yer phone charger in the bathroom. Thought ye might be needin' this. It's an adapter. Ye canna plug any of yer American electronics straight into our electrical outlets. My aunt has a wee bed-n'-breakfast in the village. Caters to American tourists, so she always keeps a couple about. Here ye are, Ian." The lively blonde cheerfully handed over a small beige two-piece gadget. "Make sure ye plug the big piece into the wall first and then the smaller one into that, or ye'll burn up yer things."

"Thanks, Moira. Yeah, my phone's dead. I was going to ask Mrs. MacShane if she could find me something so I can call my friends. I didn't have time to tell anyone I was leaving." Ian was touched by her thoughtfulness.

She flashed him a sunny smile that warmed him to his toes.

Ian made his way down the grand staircase past an ancient suit of armor to the main reception hall on the ground floor. Passing through tall french doors to his right, he entered the majestically opulent *small salon*.

Whoever had named this room had to have been playing an elaborate joke. The *small salon* was enormous by anyone's standards.

Its high gilded ceilings, shimmery blue silk draperies, and elegantly carved mirrors and furniture made him feel as though he was walking through a palace. Tall leaded windows looked out over the front courtyard and the deep, tree-lined drive to the forest leading up to the property. An elaborately carved gold-gilt french settee centered the room, facing an extravagant white marble fireplace, with two similarly carved chairs on each side completing the seating area. A long lavish french sideboard with scrolled legs and a delicate pale-green alabaster top resided against the wall opposite the seating area and fireplace, and two smaller seating areas with low tables were positioned precisely and symmetrically at each end of the beautifully adorned room.

The salon was almost too perfect, Ian mused. It looked like a set from a movie or a room in a museum where a person might tiptoe through but never dare to sit or touch anything.

He crossed through the salon to a doorway at the far end, entering the beautifully appointed dining room.

Ian took a moment now to really appreciate the high ceilings, with scenes of ancient battles so magnificently portrayed. Three immense chandeliers, spaced evenly over the elongated chamber, glittered with sparkling crystals, washing the room with a dazzling dance of jewel-like light. Every surface was either paneled in intricately carved black mahogany or painted with stunningly depicted events of long past.

Two massive fireplaces with larger-than-life carvings in the same black mahogany centered the walls on either side of a long, stately table, while three majestic diamond-paned windows faced out onto the loch at the end of the far side of the room. The swagged draperies were a deep azure blue with striking gold accents that shimmered in the soft morning light.

Ian remembered that a hidden panel on the side of one of the fireplaces gave access to the kitchen, but he couldn't remember which one. He didn't have to guess for long, though, for at that moment, a golden-haired girl with a striking resemblance to Moira entered the dining room loaded down with so many sheets that she could barely see around them.

"Oh, Ian," she gasped, out of breath. "Ye startled me. I'm Martha. Ye've already met my sister Moira, I think. I'm just headed upstairs to make up the beds. Kitchen's through there, if yer lookin' for it."

"Thanks," replied Ian. "Do you need any help with that?"

"Oh no, thank ye. It wouldn't be proper, but I appreciate it all the same." Flashing the same cheery smile as her sister, the heavily laden girl sidled past and disappeared into the salon.

Ian was amazed at the resemblance. She was almost a twin of Moira, but maybe a year or two older. He almost went after her, though no doubt she would once again refuse any offered help. He was really beginning to feel guilty about doing nothing in particular while everyone around him worked.

Instead, he wandered through the secret door, noticing how thick the walls were between the two rooms.

Mrs. MacShane, humming a happy tune, was just putting four doughy loaves of bread into an oven to bake. There was a dusting of flour on her face and floral apron. The large kitchen smelled of cinnamon and apples and freshly baked scones.

Ian didn't know what he'd expected in an old house like this, but the kitchen was a charming mix of old and new. The appliances were all stainless steel. Their modern, almost-industrial look was offset by stone floors and walls and a fireplace big enough to cook a cow. It probably had been used for that very thing in times past, he mused.

A big farm table in the center of the room was laden with bunches of root vegetables and bowls of apples. It was obviously the heart of the kitchen, where food was prepped and meals eaten.

Various cooking utensils and copper pots hung from a suspended rack within easy reach, and sprigs of dried herbs were neatly hung from another suspended rack beside them.

The room was basically square with a couple of alcoves and a door and windows on the back wall facing out onto the gardens and loch.

"Oh, there ye are, lad," she exclaimed warmly. "I hope ye slept well last night. There's some hot cinnamon rolls just behind ye on the counter, if ye'd like one."

Closing the oven door, she confessed, "I just love bakin'. We'll have some lovely, fresh bread in just a bit for sandwiches. I'm about ta start a nice stew for this evenin' as well. Fresh bread's just the thing ta go with good, hearty stew." Pushing back a couple of strands of loose red hair, she gave Ian a warm smile.

He cleared his throat and said guiltily, "I'm really sorry about yesterday, Mrs. MacShane. I was rude. You've been nothing but kind to me since I arrived, and I had no right to yell at you." Ian had been dreading this encounter, and shamefacedly met her bright, knowing eyes.

"It's behind us now, Ian," she said seriously. "I was as upset as ye ta find the piece'd been taken from the house. Best keep that door locked for the time bein', just ta be safe."

Turning to the wide stove, she adjusted a knob and positioned a large copper pot over a burner. "Oh, and, Ian, I did have a thought that ye might want ta move inta yer dad's suite instead a stayin' in yer old room. I just put ye in the nursery first 'cause I'd cleaned it quick before ye come and I knew it'd be familiar. Ye've grown up a lot, though," she added, taking in Ian's tall, athletic frame.

Ian hadn't even considered moving from the nursery. It made sense, though he wasn't certain about all the memories his father's room seemed to dredge up.

"Bed's nice and big in yer dad's room," she continued, placing a big bunch of carrots on the cutting board. "And bathroom's got a proper shower. 'Course yer welcome to stay wherever ye want. There's lots of other rooms ye could choose too." A large kitchen knife began to make quick work of the orange tubers. "Or maybe yer comfortable where ye are. Lord knows yer dad fell asleep with ye many a night, ye snuggled in his arms, with his long legs dangling off the foot of that tiny bed." She sniffed and pulled a handkerchief from a pocket in her apron.

A quickly rinsed colander of already-cubed potatoes was dumped into the pot after the carrots.

"Lady Thorne'll be here tomorrow," Mrs. MacShane added, talking as she went about her chores. "Said she's bringin' ten or more people with her, so if ye want that room, I'd stake a claim ta it sooner rather than later."

What?

The tone of her voice told Ian that she did not much approve of Lady Thorne's plans. "We'll only have time ta clean the first and ground floors, so she'll like as not be needin' most all the bedrooms up there. Wouldn't put it past her ta install one of her friends in yer dad's suite before ye could stop her."

Ian hadn't imagined that Miranda might be bringing anyone with her. He guessed he hadn't given her arrival much thought at all. He certainly wasn't happy with the idea of some stranger taking over his father's room, *sleeping* in his father's bed.

"Moving to my dad's suite might be a good idea," Ian quickly agreed, as unhappy with the thought of houseguests as the redheaded woman aggressively pounding spices into a pulp with a heavy mallet was. "I'll … uh, shift my things after lunch. Thanks for the heads-up, Mrs. MacShane."

Ian leaned against the counter and bit into a hot, gooey cinnamon roll while Mrs. M bustled about the kitchen. *Amazing!* The rich spices and sweet, creamy frosting burst on his tongue, and he nearly groaned aloud. *Oh man! Could this woman cook!*

Scooping up another, he accepted a steaming cup of amber tea.

"I've been meanin' ta ask ye what yer preference for food is. That is, yer dad wasn't one for meat. Ate eggs, a' course, I saw ta that—needed the protein, ye know—but preferred vegetables and such."

Ahhh, all those egg salad sandwiches. Ian hid the grin. "I seem to recall him eating fish."

"As ta that, he'd catch 'em sometimes but mostly brought 'em back for Hamish. Remember that, do ye? Yes, he loved the loch, loved ta be out there on the water, but I suspect half the time he didn't even bother ta bait a hook."

Ian didn't remember *that*. "No, I don't eat meat either if I can avoid it." Funny, he'd never realized his dad was a vegetarian.

"As I thought. I'll whip ye up a thick vegetable-n'-barley stew for this evenin', then. Was one a Danny's favorites."

Danny. Huh. Ian was glad his dad had people around who knew him so well and cared enough to remember all those special things about him, but he couldn't help being jealous that others had gotten to spend so much time with his father when he had so little.

CHAPTER IV

As Ian strolled the gardens, he checked his message mailbox. He'd only given the phone about an hour on the charger, but it was enough for what he needed.

Eight voice messages, fourteen texts. He speed-dialed his voice mail first.

"You have eight missed calls," the impersonal female voice informed him. *"First unheard message sent Saturday, June 17, at 8:42 a.m., Hawaii-Aleutian standard time."* Good! The phone worked.

"Bro, where are you?" Ian recognized the excited voice of Braxton Markus, his best friend. *"Grab your board. A bunch of us are headed to the beach. Waves are awesome! Headmaster said we could go as long as we take Malcolm and Nader."*

Josh Malcolm and Rand Nader were two former SEALs who had joined the ranks of what amounted to a small private army that protected the highly exclusive *International Academy of the Pacific*. Students were never allowed off campus without bodyguards, though technically, the private beach below the cliffs was on school property. Still, the headmaster took no chances when students were on the beach or in the water. He always sent at least one of the highly proficient ex-military water-rescue guards. Ian had often wondered why any of those men would have given up such exciting careers to guard a bunch of kids.

"Second unheard message," continued the impersonal female voice, *"sent Saturday, June 17, at 8:55 a.m., Hawaii-Aleutian standard time."*

"Bro, where are you? We gotta leave. Sorry, man. We're gonna lose the waves if we wait any longer," Braxton's apologetic voice told him.

"Third unheard message sent Saturday, June 17, at 8:57 a.m., Hawaii-Aleutian standard time."

"Hey, Ian," greeted Kimo, another good friend. "All the school's surfboards are being used, and they're awful, anyway. Can we borrow your board?"

"Fourth unheard message sent Saturday, June 17, at 8:59 a.m., Hawaii-Aleutian standard time."

"You haven't called back," an amused Kimo informed him, "so I'm taking that as a yes. We'll take good care of it. Thanks, bro."

"Yeah, *bro*," Ian said aloud, grinning. "You waited a whole two minutes before you decided to steal my board? You're gonna pay for that, Kimo!"

"Fifth unheard message sent Saturday, June 17, at 4:58 p.m., Hawaii-Aleutian standard time."

"Ian! Where are you, man? The beach was great! Did you finally take my advice and ask out Trish or Beatrice? I want details!"

Braxton was one of those guys girls loved even when they wanted to slap him. He joked around sometimes and might slip out to meet them, but Ian was pretty sure he was all talk. He was too popular and actually too respectful with past, present, and future girlfriends to really be the love-'em-and-leave-'em kind of jerk he sometimes pretended to be.

"Sixth unheard message sent Saturday, June 17, at 6:09 p.m., Hawaii-Aleutian standard time."

"Dude! WHERE ARE YOU? I've sent you like a gazillion texts!" Brax's voice was sounding a little testy. "Not still mad about last night, are you? You know we didn't do anything but hang out for a while on the cliffs. Come on already. Get over it!"

"Seventh unheard message sent Saturday, June 17, at 6:22 p.m., Hawaii-Aleutian standard time."

"Hey, Ian, I just heard you left for Scotland last night. Didn't see you because … well, you know … " Ian could picture him checking over his shoulder to make sure he wasn't overheard by a teacher. "But I didn't know you'd left the country! No probs, though. It's not like I'm your best friend or anything. Call me as soon as you get this." Brax's forthright voice let Ian know he was unhappy.

"Eighth unheard message sent Sunday, June 19, at 9:17 p.m., Hawaii-Aleutian standard time."

"*Dude! We just got back from lacrosse practice and found our room trashed!*" an out-of-breath Brax informed Ian. "*The furniture was thrown all over the place, and there was water all over the floor. Your locker was broken into, and your bed was slashed to pieces. Nothing of ours was taken, but we don't know if anything of yours is missing because we don't know what you took with you. CALL ME!*"

The text messages said roughly the same thing.

Wow! He'd missed a lot in two days. Who would have broken into their room? None of the guys had anything really valuable apart from their cell phones and maybe an iPod, but every kid at school had the same thing. To do so much damage was just crazy.

Ian's shoulders sagged despondently. *Has it really only been two days?* he wondered miserably. That didn't seem right. He counted back. *Wasn't today Monday?* Somewhere he'd lost a day. The time difference?

He'd been pulled from school on Friday afternoon as he practiced self-defense moves in his *Krav Maga* class. The unique style had been developed for the Israeli Defense Forces and combined techniques of judo, jiujitsu, Muay Thai, Wing Chun, savate, boxing, grappling, and wrestling.

An Israeli bodyguard for one of the upperclassmen had been persuaded to take over some of the mandatory martial arts training that all students at their school received. He had introduced the highly efficient methods of defense combined with brutal counterattack measures while stressing that students should first seek to avoid confrontation. If this became impossible, the goal then progressed to finishing the fight as quickly as possible.

Many of his classmates were the sons and daughters of high-profile leaders, diplomats, or others who required safety and anonymity for their children. Security at the school was beyond tight, and the headmaster believed it important for all students to at least have the basic skills to defend themselves.

Some learned enough to get by and chose other activities to fill their physical education requirements. Others, like Ian and Braxton, embraced the training and thrived on the strict discipline of the advanced *Krav Maga* instruction, with its focus on threat neutralization and simultaneous defensive and offensive maneuvers in real-world situations.

The class had progressed as usual from a rigorous warm-up session to a series of *katas*. These were fluid movements designed to meld aggressive and defensive techniques into something resembling a dance. Constant reinforcement and repetition of the movements made them as familiar as walking or running. They became reflexive and could be employed quickly and without thought.

Ian and Braxton had then paired off to practice punching, kicking, and blocking before progressing to "defense against knife attack" techniques.

As usual, the last few minutes of the class were given over to sparring, which was the closest thing they could get to real-life fighting and honed their instinctual skills.

"Brax, Ian, you're up," Ari called in his thickly accented voice. "I want you to neutralize your opponent in five seconds." He clicked a stopwatch. "Go."

Brax charged Ian with a front kick and a flurry of punches as Ian moved in, blocking swiftly and easily. He closed the gap, sweeping his right leg behind Brax's right knee. Planting his foot, Ian pivoted in, following through with his left hand at Brax's nape and right palm over his face, forcing him off-balance and down. Brax would have hit the mat hard, but Ian controlled the fall, smoothly leveraging Brax's arm into a lock and forcing his face into the mat. He subdued him completely, leaning a knee into his back, and applied pressure to the pinned arm.

The class let out combined cheers, whistles, and good-natured calls to Braxton of "Better you than me, bro."

"Three seconds. Good job, Ian," Ari acknowledged.

Ian offered Braxton a hand up.

Brax glared. "Ugh, Ian! You ever hear of pulling your punches? It's like getting hit by a freight train."

"I didn't punch you, and I controlled your fall."

"Yeah, but you're so freaking fast."

"Are you hurt?" Ian knew he wasn't.

"No, but you're making me look bad." Brax glanced over to where several girls stood watching.

"Suck it up, cupcake. You're getting soft."

"No. I think you're developing superhuman strength. If you get the urge to put on tights, though, were gonna have to talk."

"Analysis," Ari interjected.

"Ian's a machine!" someone yelled out. Good-natured laughter erupted.

"Ian's just scary good ... He's unstoppable ..." other voices echoed.

"Brax is scary too. Ian's just ... better ..." someone else contributed.

Brax glowered at his classmates.

"Not relevant to my question," Ari said empirically. "It is important to size up your opponent. Sometimes you don't have the time, but in a class like this, we all are aware of one another's strengths and weaknesses. So what happened?" Ari cocked a brow as he paced in front of his students. "No one?"

A few murmurs resounded, but no one spoke up.

"Right." Ari was all business now. "Braxton went immediately on offense. He had the intimidation factor going for him, but that never works with Ian. Ian always has a strategy. Instead of stepping back, he immediately got inside Braxton's guard. *Think* about what you're doing in these training sessions. You may not have that luxury in a real-life setting. Paying attention now can save your life someday."

Heads nodded in agreement. A few shifted restlessly, shaking out arms and legs in preparation for their own bouts.

"All right, next pair," Ari called. "Ian demonstrated perfect control. I want to see that from everyone."

Ari was always serious and reserved. The instructor's rare praise secretly pleased him.

"So hey," Brax whispered as they moved to the back of the group. "I've got a date tonight. Can you cover for me at bed check?"

"No way, Brax. If you get caught again, you're going to get expelled."

"Nah, probably not even detention. We're just going to the cliffs to watch the meteor shower." He wiggled his eyebrows and smirked wickedly.

"I don't even want to know."

"Hey, man, half the school goes there."

"TMI, Brax. Too much information."

"Yeah, about that, bro. You've got girls lined up out the door, but you don't date 'em. Trish and Beatrice are standing over there right now drooling over you, and they're *seniors*. You've gotta stop comparing every girl you meet to the one you keep dreaming about. Here's a hint, Ian. *She's. Not. Real.*" Brax patted him on the head. "I'm just saying this because I care, bro."

"Get your hands off me."

Brax grinned. "Cover for me. You know you will."

"Ian Thorne, please report to the headmaster's office," came a tinny female voice suddenly over the loud speaker.

"Oh nooo!" Braxton put his hands on his face and shook his head in mock horror. "Don't tell me you've been breaking rules on the sly."

Ian groaned. He elbowed Braxton and hissed as he walked by. "That's going to be *you* in there at midnight when you get caught."

"I almost never get caught."

Ian shook his head in utter disbelief.

"Text me if you need help breaking out of detention, Ian. I've got that down."

Ian and Braxton had been best friends since the age of five, when they had both found themselves dumped at the prestigious International Academy of the Pacific, on the Big Island of Hawaii. The school was remote, fortified like a fortress, and hosted students from all over the world who required heightened security, anonymity, and specialized instruction while still preparing for excellent universities.

Braxton's mother hadn't survived his birth, and his father headed a covert military team that had put him on the radar of international terrorist organizations.

Both of Ian's parents were dead, and though he was heir to a fortune and title, no one, especially his stepmother, seemed to have known what to do with him. It didn't matter. He had long since gotten over it, or so he convinced himself.

Though polar opposites, the two had become fast friends, although Braxton spent an inordinate amount of his time getting into trouble while Ian spent even more attempting to keep him out. Brax was the closest thing he had to a brother, and Ian couldn't imagine life at IAP without him, screwball schemes and all.

As he reached the office, he was met by the intimidating, no-nonsense head of security, Antony Desmond, who ushered him quickly across campus to the dorms.

Ian's initial fear that Brax had finally gotten them both into major trouble over some reckless, harebrained prank evaporated with relief as Desmond hastily explained.

"Your mother, Lady Thorne—"

"*Stepmother*," Ian interrupted.

"Your stepmother," he corrected, "contacted us a few minutes ago. It seems your presence is required at your family estate in Scotland on a matter of some urgency. You've been booked on a flight leaving out of LAX at midnight. We've got to get you on the next plane out of Kona to make that happen. You're still under IAP's protection and jurisdiction until you leave American soil, so you'll be met by a bodyguard as you disembark in Los Angeles and be escorted to the international terminal. There will be an air marshal aboard both flights, and he will make himself known to you. If anything about either flight or any of its passengers makes you uncomfortable in any way, you are to let the air marshal know."

Yeah, Ian knew the drill. He'd just never been the recipient of IAP's special brand of "travel protection," given that he'd never been allowed to travel anywhere by himself before, let alone outside the country.

"You've got ten minutes to pack." Desmond radioed for a car and waited outside while Ian haphazardly threw clothes, comb, toothbrush, cell phone, and charger into a backpack. Grabbing the framed photo of him and his father off the nightstand, he stuffed it too in the pack. He glanced quickly around the room at the two sets of bunk beds, wardrobe lockers, and table under the window that served as a desk.

"Damn it, Brax!" he muttered.

Ian pushed pillows under the blankets on the top bunk of Brax's bed so it looked as though it was occupied. Hastily, he penned a note for his roommates and taped it to the inside of the door. If their dorm mother entered, she would leave the door open so only Dieter or Clive would find it.

The white piece of notebook paper stood out starkly against the brown door.

TALK HIM OUT OF IT!

They would know as soon as they saw the room what he meant.

If Braxton doesn't listen, he thought gloomily, *I'll be on a plane, and Brax will be in detention.* He was really pushing the headmaster. How much more before they actually *did* decide to expel him?

Desmond tossed Ian's backpack into the trunk before he could protest, phone and all. Ian had no time to let his friends know he was leaving. They literally ran for the gate upon their arrival in Kona, and Ian boarded his flight so quickly that he'd had no time to do anything but power down the device.

So here he was in Scotland, wandering aimlessly through the dilapidated grounds of an estate he barely remembered. It actually felt a little strange to not have bodyguards stationed throughout the area. Security had become a way of life that Ian simply took for granted.

Ian missed his friends and felt cheated that he hadn't got to enjoy the celebrations they had planned. He, Brax, Dieter, Clive, Sadek, and Kimo had all been together since kindergarten. Others had come and gone, but these six boys were one another's family.

Their backgrounds and ethnicities were all so diverse, but it didn't matter.

Ian grinned as he wondered if Braxton was indeed "serving time" in the headmaster's special classroom for wayward offenders. He'd probably be forced to write a paper on *Hezbollah* or some other radical organization then watch a movie on US military schools and warned that if he didn't curtail his extracurricular activities, he could most likely expect to see one firsthand in the near future. Hell, Brax could probably recite the entire film verbatim by now. *Really, the headmaster needed to come up with something more original,* Ian mused.

Braxton's father, Devon Markus, was an American Special Forces officer who was deployed all around the world. The idea of military school actually appealed to Brax on several levels.

Devon's life seemed dangerous and exciting, and both Braxton and Ian idolized him. In those rare instances when he was able to break away from his unit, he included Ian in their family outings and other *bonding* adventures, having somehow been granted permission by an executor of the Thorne Estate.

Ian was grateful that Devon had taken the time and interest to look out for him and to make those arrangements with the enigmatic entities controlling his life. Brax's father always took the time to teach, play, and listen to him as he did with his own son. Colonel Devon Markus was, in truth, the closest thing to a father Ian could remember.

As much as Devon played the father figure for Ian, Braxton was, in every way but blood, his brother. They did everything together, and although their personalities were very different, they were inseparable.

Brax was a dark-haired, athletic boy who had a tendency to say just what was on his mind regardless of the consequences and was something of a daredevil. He was outrageously funny and, if not the instigator of every madcap adventure at school, then most likely involved in some way. Ian, being a little less inclined to break *every* school rule, spent much of his time keeping his best friend out of trouble. Life around Brax was never dull.

Ian's other two roommates, Dieter and Clive Jiles, were two sandy-haired twins from South Africa. Their mother was a doctor, and father a diplomat to some obscure foreign embassy. Ian suspected that story was a cover, but at IAP, even among your closest friends, you learned not to ask.

Another member of their close-knit group was Sadek Khalifa. His father was a deposed prince of some Middle Eastern oil kingdom. He wasn't allowed to say which one, and Ian secretly suspected that he didn't know.

Ian was also certain that *Khalifa* wasn't even his surname, but hey, many of his classmates' identities were a secret. Like Ian, he knew almost nothing about his family. A distant cousin was his only contact, and Sadek swore he told him very little *for his own safety*.

However, Sadek sometimes did get to travel with his cousin's family during the holidays throughout Europe and the United Kingdom. Once, he had even gotten to see the pyramids in Egypt. Although Sadek said the family was always surrounded by bodyguards, at least he got to see the world, which was more than most of the inmates at IAP did.

Yeah, those words, *safety, secrecy, security*, and *anonymity*, seemed to be the buzzwords at IAP. Ian understood that many of his classmates were the cherished children and heirs of world leaders, royalty, and billionaires, but jeez, really? Sometimes the drama and intrigue got a little deep.

And then there was Kimo Kalehana, a local boy from Waimea who had attended the elite school with Ian since the beginning. His father had something to do with legal counsel and immigration for the academy. Even though Kimo had not moved to the school dorms until he was twelve, and often went home on the weekends, the six boys had become fast friends.

On a couple of rare occasions, the boys had been allowed to spend their holidays at the Kalehana's ranch in the hills above Waimea, with Kimo's uncle Jake, herding cattle. It was Jake who had taught them to ride horses and provided the big-brother sort of mentorship they all craved.

With the rigid security protocols, Ian was frankly amazed any of them were ever allowed off school property, but he suspected surveillance teams kept track of their whereabouts. He wouldn't be surprised to learn that drones or even satellites were trained on them at all times. Ian had actually spied snipers in the trees up on the Kalehana ranch. He didn't ask or even want to know. Any freedom away from their prisonlike school was an enormous gift.

It wasn't that they were mistreated ever; it was simply that their lives were strictly planned out and controlled by those sworn to keep them safe at all costs. Education was important, but secondary to the mission, even though the school was touted as one of the world's *premier preparatory academies.*

Study time was enforced, but Ian had never really had to study *anything*. It just all came so easy. He'd learned to pretend, though. He didn't want to seem different from his friends, even though he knew he was.

All in all, Ian had a very happy existence at IAP. He felt close to his friends and "adoptive" family, and in truth, Hawaii was the only *home* he remembered. Memories of Scotland had seemed far away, more like a dream he'd once had than anything tangible.

As Ian tried to calculate the time difference between Scotland and Hawaii, he was already pressing his speed dial. He couldn't remember exactly what time it was now on Big Island, so if Brax was asleep, he'd just have to tough it up.

"Hello?" came a sleepy, muffled voice through the receiver, and then a completely alert, "Dude! Finally! Where have you been? Why didn't you call me?"

"Sorry, bro," Ian answered, happier than he cared to admit to hear his friend's voice. "Phone was dead. Couldn't charge it until this morning." Ian could hear a commotion in the background.

"Bro, you've got some enemies!" Kimo's excited voice announced.

"Give me that!" exclaimed Brax. "You can talk to him in a minute. Yeah, anyway," he continued, once again addressing Ian, "we're in Ari's room. The bodyguard dorms are *sweet!* It's like a hotel over here. Headmaster thought it was safer until we find out who broke into our room."

Ian heard a scuffle. "Better put that down, Brax!" came a muffled voice through the phone. "Ari told us to *'touch nussing'!*" Kimo mimicked in Ari's stern accent.

"He wasn't talking about *my phone!*" Brax informed him in exasperation.

"What time is it there?" Ian asked.

"A little after midnight," Brax returned.

"So ... yesterday, someone trashed our room?"

"Not yesterday, man, three ... four hours ago," broke in Kimo again.

"Three hours?" echoed Ian, a little confused. "Oh, we're eleven hours later here. Anyway, they didn't take anything? They just messed up the room?"

"Not messed up. *Destroyed!*" Brax told him. "That picture of you and your dad is missing from your nightstand, some of your clothes are ripped up, and your sheets and mattress are totally shredded. They didn't really touch our stuff. Just threw everything all over the place."

"Maybe they heard someone coming before they could finish," interjected Kimo.

"Yeah, maybe," continued Brax. "So, Ian, anything you left here that someone would want?"

"Nothing!" Ian let out a low whistle. "I have that picture of my dad and me." He had, in fact, slept with it under his pillow last night, he thought self-consciously, and it was still there, but he wasn't about to tell his friends that. "I brought my phone and my iPod. That's all I have that's worth anything, except my surfboard, and that had better be in one piece when I get back," he added accusatorially.

"Sorry, bro," said a completely unremorseful Kimo. "It was Clive and Dieter's last day, and the waves were bitchin'. We waxed it up nice and new, though."

"Thanks," Ian sighed sarcastically. "Sorry I missed it. So how long are you staying in Ari's room? And who all is there?"

"Just me, Kimo, Dieter, and Clive, but those two are asleep. They have to be at the airport by six in the morning. Desmond moved everyone else to another dorm for the night. There's yellow police tape across our door and everything. Pretty cool, actually," Brax added cheerfully.

"They called the police?"

"Nah, not with all the military types they have around here. They're investigating it themselves. The campus is on lockdown right now. Too bad you missed it."

"Yeah, too bad."

"Hey, guys, I'm losing my battery. I'll text you later. Get some sleep. And don't break my surfboard." Ian laughed as the phone went dead.

Oh well, at least I got to talk to them for a couple of minutes. He felt better. He really didn't mind them using his board, either, and they knew it. He had bought it three years ago from a graduating senior and had every intention of sharing it. It wasn't the greatest, but it allowed them to get out in the waves, and that was what counted.

The room situation was another thing, however. *Weird, really weird. Nothing like that has ever happened at school since I've been there, and I missed it. Well, I've missed more than that,* he thought dejectedly, his cheerful mood from moments before evaporating.

The deafening sound of helicopter blades overhead intruded on his brooding thoughts. Ian heard it before he saw it. The sleek black object appeared suddenly above the treetops and circled the manor house. Something about its effortless speed and strength reminded him of a great black shark circling a tank in its deadly pursuit of prey. He watched as the helicopter gracefully dropped from the sky and landed on the vast lawn at the back of the house.

Curious, Ian observed the scene as an elegant brunette lady stepped from the craft, followed by two men in business suits. The lady looked cool and sophisticated in a creamy white jacket and slacks. A heavy gold necklace at her throat glittered in the sunlight, and another large bracelet shone equally bright from her wrist. She said something to the two men, and then all three turned and walked toward the house as the pilot powered down the rotors.

Miranda, he guessed, *but a day early?*

Ian stepped uncertainly into the shadow of a large tree. Why did he feel so uncomfortable? Surreptitiously, he watched the procession as Miranda gracefully led the way, flanked by the two men. *The queen and her court* came an unbidden thought. The queen's stride faltered for a brief moment as she gazed up at the house. Then she noticeably squared her shoulders and purposefully approached the imposing structure.

Interesting, thought Ian, remembering his conversation with Mrs. McShane on the morning of his arrival.

In the bright sunshine of the lush but overgrown gardens, the idea of ghostly women walking the halls of Thorne Manor seemed all too ridiculous. However, Ian knew firsthand from the past two nights spent alone under its roof that Thorne Manor could certainly be unnerving in the darkness and most definitely had its own secrets.

He was beginning to think there was more going on in the house than he had at first believed. Whether a *ghost,* however unlikely, actually walked the halls or someone was playing tricks, Ian hadn't yet decided. He didn't actually believe in ghosts. Or at least he hadn't.

Ian would have to think about that later. Right now, he was about to meet the woman he'd spent his childhood hating—well, maybe *hate* was too strong of a word. *Strongly resenting* would do for now.

The young heir to Thorne Manor squared strong, athletic shoulders, as he had seen Miranda do moments before, and, in a convincing imitation of Miranda's determination, strode purposefully toward the house.

CHAPTER V

"No, no, Maigrid," the cultured, feminine voice soothed, "it is I who must apologize. I was so dreadfully sorry not to have been here when Ian arrived. I was able to conclude my business in London a day earlier than expected and persuaded Dr. Manard and Sir Lawrence to accompany me. It has been so many years, and I was *so* looking forward to seeing Ian. No matter if things are not quite ready. We will make do."

Ian entered the kitchen in time to see a flustered Mrs. MacShane cock a disapproving eyebrow. Miranda and the two men stood with their backs to him, and all four were as yet unaware of his presence.

"I am sure," the redheaded housekeeper replied, barely able to keep the skepticism from her voice, "he will be delighted ta see ye as well, *Lady Thorne*. And as ta the house, the ground and first floors are ready for ye, though we had planned a simple stew for tonight's supper. I believe there is time ta make other arrangements, however, if ye and yer guests would prefer somethin' more formal for the evenin' meal."

Ian noted that Mrs. MacShane's tone was polite but held no warmth.

"No, Maigrid," the velvet voice continued, "I am sure the stew will be delicious. Perhaps you might find some greens for a lovely salad as well, and I know that the cellars will have some excellent bottles of wine to pair with our meal. My chef will be arriving in the morning and will relieve you of the burden of having to organize the meals."

Mrs. MacShane visibly stiffened. "'Tis no burden, Lady Thorne. I was in charge of all the meals for the Thorne family for thirty years. I can cook for a small dinner party or a large reception. If ye have a menu in mind, I'd be happy ta see it prepared." Her demeanor was strained, speech forced. Although the conversation was polite on the surface, uncomfortable undercurrents could be felt strongly in the room.

"No, no, please don't concern yourself," Miranda answered with finality in her deceptively soft voice. "It is all taken care of." Flashing a cool smile that in no way rang sincere, she turned to leave.

Ian stood awkwardly in the doorway, consciously aware of the friction between the two women. Four pairs of eyes simultaneously turned his way, aware for the first time that he had joined them.

Miranda regarded the tall raven-haired boy for a brief instant, cocking her head slightly, before the corners of her perfect mouth turned up into a radiant smile that struck Ian like a blow. She was dazzling!

Long dark hair framed the most exquisite face he had ever seen. Luminous, porcelain skin set off classical high cheekbones, a perfectly chiseled nose, and a full, voluptuous, almost-*pouty* mouth.

But her eyes ... eyes like blue arctic seas, deep and clear, while at the same time icy and pale, imprisoned him. Her eyes were like those of the ice wolves he had seen in pictures, riveting and hauntingly beautiful. Her gaze was almost hypnotic, piercing, delving into the deepest secrets of his soul.

For a moment, it was as if the world itself fell away. Nothing else existed but him and this exquisite creature, locked together in an endless universe where time and substance no longer existed. Those magnificent eyes held him captive. He lost all thought of anything but the desire to stay there forever, ensconced in their icy fire.

A small laugh emanated from one of the men. "Don't worry, she has that effect on all of us." The second man chuckled, and the spell was broken.

Feeling slightly dizzy, Ian struggled to gain some semblance of control over himself. Embarrassed, staring down at his feet, he realized miserably that he still wore his father's oversized, mismatched clothing.

Miranda moved forward, resting both perfectly manicured hands on Ian's shoulders. Her perfume was light but intoxicating, and Ian found himself feeling even more off-balance. One cool hand gently lifted his chin, and he again found himself staring into those mesmerizing ice-blue eyes.

"Oh, Ian, darling! At last! I'd have known you anywhere. You look so much like your father."

Miranda bestowed another of her dazzling smiles on the disconcerted young man, rocking him to his core. "Pay no notice to those two." She nodded conspiratorially over her shoulder. "The color of my eyes is somewhat unusual, so people often stare just a bit when we are first introduced. No matter, you'll quickly become accustomed to me, *again*."

Linking slim arms through Ian's, she gently propelled him forward. She strolled with him to the kitchen door, into the dining room, and through to the salon, chatting soothingly in her melodious voice.

The simple act of walking calmed Ian and gave him a chance to compose himself.

I'm fine, he told himself, *I'm absolutely fine. Yeah right! As long as I don't have to look at her.* What had just happened to him? He felt as though he had been hit by a bus. Ian recognized that Miranda's one-sided monologue was designed to put him at ease, and was grateful for that brief opportunity to pull himself together. Obviously, she was aware of her effect on him and was giving him the time he needed to recover. This situation was all so bizarre.

"So now," Miranda was saying, "tell me what this is you're wearing. Surely, this look is not all the rage in Hawaii?"

"Not a'tol," Mrs. MacShane interjected. Ian hadn't been aware that she had followed them from the kitchen. "The lad came ta us with nothin' but a pair a shorts and some T-shirts. I imagine those things he's wearin' belonged ta his father. There's a trunk in the attic with Lord Daniel's old school things. I had Moira lay some clothes out for Ian in his room. They should fit quite nicely, I should think, and'll be much more … suitable, I'm sure." Her tone was brisk and matter-of-fact as she attempted to regain control of the situation. "Would yer ladyship like me ta show ye and yer guests ta yer rooms now, or would ye wish me ta come back later?"

Miranda turned that icy gaze on Mrs. MacShane. "No, thank you, Maigrid." That velvet voice slid over them all like a silken breeze, low and cool and cultured, but did nothing to conceal her irritation. "I will show them the way. I will, of course, be staying in my old suite, and I will want Dr. Maynard and Sir Lawrence in the adjoining suites close by."

"Master Ian is stayin' in his father's room, unless, of course, ye prefer we move him?" Mrs. MacShane's tone was innocent, but the ensuing tension in the room escalated to an almost-unbearable level.

"That won't be necessary." Miranda smiled coldly, but her voice cut like shards of ice. This time, there was no mistaking her displeasure. "I'll see you in a bit," she spoke to Ian almost affectionately. "I'd like Dr. Maynard to have a look at you as well, darling, just to make sure all's well." She showered Ian with a warm smile and turned away. "Come, gentlemen. Let us get you settled."

Both Ian and Mrs. MacShane stood speechless, watching the retreating figures. The tense redhead let out a long, slow breath and turned to Ian.

"You don't like her," Ian stated. It wasn't a question.

"I doona trust her." Mrs. MacShane cupped Ian's face into warm hands and looked deeply into baffled blue eyes. "I'll be close by." She nodded, as if trying to reassure him. "Now scoot upstairs ta yer new room and try on those clothes we found for ye."

Reaching the top stairs leading to the first floor gallery, Ian heard a commotion from the entry hall. Glancing down over the rail, he spied Mr. MacShane and the helicopter's pilot bringing some luggage through the front doors.

Absentmindedly making his way along the landing toward his father's room, he tried to clear his muddled brain. Ian had been prepared to dislike Miranda, but now, he didn't know what to believe. She confused him. He couldn't even form a mental image of her appearance in his mind. All he could remember were those ice-blue eyes and the sense he'd had of wanting to remain there for eternity, or even longer, ensconced in their frozen fire. At the same time, he'd felt lost or consumed. Ian was dazed, unable to think clearly.

One thing, however, was clear to him. Miranda and Mrs. MacShane had an intense dislike of one another. Why, then, he wondered, had the MacShanes been the only two people Miranda had not fired when she closed the house? Nothing about any of this made sense.

As the mental fog began to subside, it occurred to Ian that Mrs. MacShane had said Moira was laying out clothes for him in his *new room*.

How was that possible if he alone possessed the only key to that room? His eyes traveled the length of the gallery, past the marble statue of the lady, and sure enough, the door was open.

Feeling betrayed and more than a little out of sorts, he passed through the doorway. A crackling fire blazed in the hearth, the lovely chess set resided serenely on its small table between the two wing-backed chairs, and there on the floor, between the fireplace and the table, knelt Moira. She was sopping something out of the rug with a thick white towel.

Ian cleared his throat, and Moira glanced at him over her shoulder. "Oh, Ian, there ye are! Did Mrs. MacShane tell ye we'd found some proper clothes for ye to wear? I've laid 'em out on the bed."

Ian's gaze traveled to the large four-poster bed, and there as she'd said were several pieces of clothing neatly displayed.

"Um, Moira," he said, turning his attention back to the bubbly blonde still diligently working the towel over the rug, "what exactly are you doing?"

"Oh!" She blushed. "I brought yer clothes in and put 'em out for ye, nice and neat, and then thought I'd build ye a cozy fire to warm up the room. There's a storm comin' in." She nodded knowingly. "And I thought it'd be real nice for ye. Anyway, when I knelt down to lay in the wood, I realized this carpet here was soakin' wet. Really strange, huh?"

"Yeah," Ian hesitantly agreed.

"If it'd been rainin', I might a thought the water'd somehow come down the chimney, but ye know as well as anyone it's been dry as a bone the past couple a days. I canna think where all this water's comin' from," she chatted on. "Ye know, yesterday afternoon, just after we'd shined up the floors along the gallery, it looked like someone'd spilled a mop bucket. There was water all along the landin' and down the stairs. We didna check this room, because of course, Mrs. MacShane had already locked it. Did ye notice the carpet bein' wet yesterday when ye and Mrs. MacShane came in here to check the chess set?" Moira now stood, sodden towel in hand, and brushed back a stray curl.

"No." Had the carpet been wet? He wouldn't have noticed. He'd been too upset. "How did you get in here? I made sure this morning that this room was still locked." Ian's tone was accusatory.

Moira seemed not to notice. "Oh, as to that, Mrs. MacShane gave me her key. Ye know there are two to every door, in case one's lost or … somethin' else was to happen. Mrs. MacShane keeps the spare keys. Ye know she was the cook and housekeeper here for more'n fifty years. Now"—she dropped her bundle near the door—"take a look at what we've found for ye!" She flashed Ian an excited smile and bounced over to the bed.

Her enthusiasm was contagious. Ian could never stay cross for long in her presence. He'd try to sort through his jumbled thoughts and suspicions later, when he was alone. For now, he really was happy to see what Moira had found for him.

"One of yer dad's old school trunks had lots of things about yer size. Of course, they're mostly school uniforms, but they're still real nice, all the same."

Ian looked at the assortment of navy blue slacks and blazers. There were V-neck sweaters, white button-down shirts, and a warm woolen coat. The shirts, blazer, and sweaters had a school crest over the left chest.

Ian had never worn a uniform at his school in Hawaii, other than matching T-shirts on field trips or a football or soccer jersey with his school colors. He touched the emblem almost reverently. This had been his father's, when he was about his age.

The crest was navy and gold, with a gold lion raising a paw above a shield. Within the shield were four quadrants. A gold crescent moon resided in the upper left, and a closed circle or full moon resided on the right. Below, in the bottom left, was a boar's head, and on the right was an open book and what resembled a genie lamp with a flame. Below the shield bore the school motto, *A Posse Ad Esse*. Latin, he guessed but had no idea what it meant.

A navy-blue-and-gold-striped shirt was folded and placed to the side, and as Ian lifted it, an old photograph fluttered down to the bed.

"It's an old rugby shirt," Moira told him. "It's got blood all over the front. I didn't realize at first, but then when I found this photo tucked inside, I thought ye'd want to see it." Those pretty dimples deepened as her eyes lit with pleasure. "Look! It's yer dad."

Ian picked up the photo and saw a jubilant young man with a trophy raised high in his right hand. He was being carried on the shoulders of his teammates. It was a chaotic scene of elation and cheers, a triumphant moment in time captured on film. The young man had suffered a bloody nose, and his jersey was covered in a dark crimson stain, but was euphorically oblivious to his injuries. Only the exuberance and sheer joy of victory shone on his face.

"Yer the spittin' image of yer dad. Ye wear yer hair a little longer, though, and there's somethin' different about the eyes," she mused. "That'd be the only way anyone could tell ye apart."

Ian turned slightly away from Moira's excited gaze, not wanting her to see the suspicious moisture welling up in his eyes. Pretending to study the photo from a different angle, he held it up to the gray light filtering in from the window and furtively brushed a sleeve across his face.

"Thanks, Moira," he said quietly, struggling to gain control over his emotions.

Moira ruffled his hair in that lighthearted manner of hers and picked up a shirt and blazer. "If ye want, I could remove the school crests from these. They're just patches, and it'd take me no time a'tol. That would smarten 'em up right n' proper, I should think."

She delicately worked her thumb around the edge of the emblem, testing the thread and gently lifting as she went.

"No!" Ian answered too hastily. "I like the crests. They're perfect just the way they are. Thanks anyway, Moira." He couldn't bear for her to remove the emblems. He loved that these clothes had belonged to his father, and he wanted to keep them just as they were.

"Well, if yer sure, then, I'll leave ye to settle into yer room. Dinner should be around eight in the dinin' room, I should imagine, and Mrs. MacShane was makin' some sandwiches if yer hungry now." She paused, as if to say something more, and then looked as if she'd thought better of it. "There's a storm comin' in, though, Ian. Don't get yerself too far from the house if ye go out. Weather comes on fast here, and ye could find yerself in trouble before ye knew it."

She scooped up the wet towel, tossing Ian a sunny smile as she closed the door behind her.

Ian could indeed see the black storm clouds through his window as they descended on the manor. The sunshine and warmth from earlier in the day had been swallowed up as if it had never existed. He moved closer to the crackling fire, appreciating its comforting warmth. Sinking into the leather armchair, he gazed pensively into the flames.

A light knock on the door brought his attention around just as Miranda poked her head in.

"Ian," she said, smiling. "I hope I'm not intruding. I thought you might join me for some lunch in the salon. I asked Mrs. MacShane to bring us some sandwiches and tea, although you might prefer something different to drink? Don't typical American teenagers prefer fizzy soft drinks?"

Ian noted her emphasis on *American*, not really sure how she had intended it.

"Um, yeah," he stammered, trying to breathe normally. *What is with me?* "That sounds great," he answered more evenly. "And tea is fine. I like tea."

"Perfect!" She sounded delighted. Entering the room fully, she glided to the bed.

Ian heard the soft sigh.

"Daniel's school uniforms." Elegant hands touched them gently. "These should work nicely for you until we can arrange some things of your own. Oh!" She gasped. "And this! I've never seen this picture. The two of you could be twins!"

Ian watched Miranda closely as she studied the old photograph. She seemed genuinely moved. Graceful fingers stroked lightly over his father's young image. She then turned her gaze to the bloody rugby shirt, a slight frown appearing between perfect brows for a brief moment.

"I know you have some questions of me, and we have many things to discuss." Her face held a wistful sadness. Carefully, she laid the picture back on the bed. Abruptly straightening, Miranda flashed Ian that same conspiratorial smile that had so devastated him earlier. "I'll leave you to change and then meet you in the salon in a few minutes?"

Ian nodded.

"Lovely."

Ian hurriedly changed into a pair of slacks, shirt, and pullover sweater. The pants were a little long and large in the waist. His father must have been a bit older when he wore these, or perhaps Ian was simply not as tall and filled out as his dad was at his age. He preferred to believe the former. Either way, he was going to need a belt.

Spying the backpack that Moira had stowed next to the massive armoire, Ian dumped its contents onto the bed. As he rummaged through his belongings, he lifted out the photo of him and his father. It must have been taken just before the accident, he thought sadly. Ian looked to be about five years old in the picture, although he couldn't remember having posed for it.

He retrieved the belt and carried the photo to the nightstand. He then placed it next to the other one his father had always kept there and compared the two. Actually, Daniel Thorne appeared the same in both. Thick black hair framed a ruggedly handsome face. Deep, mischievous blue eyes gazed out at him, and he wore a playful smile, as though concealing some special secret. His dad's smile brought out the same deep dimples that girls Ian knew had always teased him about. They looked masculine on his dad. Maybe they weren't so bad, he decided.

Ian pushed down his sadness. He just couldn't afford the luxury of those emotions when he needed to face Miranda in the next few minutes.

As he compared the two photos side by side, he smiled at the chubby, happy baby he had been. He must have been no more than a year old in the one his father had kept. Ian could see his resemblance, though, even then to his dad. Bright blue eyes stared out of a grinning cherubic face framed with a tumble of black curls. The five-year-old Ian looked much the same, just *older*. The older Ian's boyish features held that same secret mischief as his father's. *Twins*, Miranda had said. Would he grow up to look exactly like Daniel Thorne? He'd like to think so.

"Darling!" Miranda exclaimed with a smile as Ian entered the salon. "Come, sit here." She motioned to a chair next to the settee, where she reigned, coolly beautiful, elegantly at ease, looking every bit as though she belonged in this luxurious setting.

The salon glowed in the soft golden light shed by the dance of lambent flames in the elaborate white marble fireplace. Overhead, a crystal chandelier cast glittering, iridescent stars onto the ceiling, and the pale-blue silk on the antique chairs and settee made Ian feel as though he had entered another century. The brightest jewel in the room, however, was Miranda. Her radiance outshone everything else.

As Ian crossed the gleaming parquet wood floor, she poured two cups of steaming amber liquid from a cobalt-blue teapot etched with lacy gold filigree.

"Dr. Maynard tells me the weather is growing worse and a storm will be upon us in under an hour. The helicopter will need to leave soon, or he won't be able to get out at all." Lifting a porcelain teacup, she took a delicate sip. "As he needs to return to Edinburgh tonight, we have only a few minutes for him to look at you."

Noting Ian's puzzlement, she continued on reassuringly. "Dr. Maynard just wanted to do a short examination … you know, heart rate, blood pressure, listen to your lungs … He was a great friend of your father and just wanted to be sure you're feeling well."

"I'm fine," Ian replied uncertainly. "They give us a physical exam every year at school. I'm never sick. In fact, I've never even had a cold."

"That's marvelous, darling! I'm *so* happy to hear it!" Miranda remarked with another of her radiant smiles. "But," she continued persuasively, "Dr. Maynard just wants to take a quick look to be sure. Oh, Ian, humor us, please, just this once, if you would."

"Well, okay, I guess. But really, there's never been anything wrong with me. Like I said, I've never been sick in my life."

Miranda raised an eyebrow, giving a knowing look to Dr. Maynard, who had just entered the room and now stood behind Ian.

"Just like Daniel," she commented.

Only then did Ian take a good look at the man who had arrived with his stepmother's entourage earlier in the day. He'd been too distracted by Miranda when he'd met her in the kitchen to notice anyone else, or anything else, for that matter.

Dr. Maynard strode forward, extending his right hand to Ian.

Ian stood, and after a formal handshake, the doctor smiled in what he guessed was meant to be a reassuring manner. That smile, though, Ian noticed, did not quite reach those surprisingly cold eyes, and something about the man put him instinctually on alert.

Miranda's Dr. Maynard was fairly tall, just under six feet, with sandy brown hair and a slightly weathered, suntanned face, as though he spent a great deal of time outdoors. He appeared to have an athletic build, although it was a little hard to tell because of the cut of his dark very well-tailored suit.

The stranger didn't seem quite comfortable in that suit, though, Ian observed, although why he thought that, he really couldn't say. The doctor was maybe in his early forties, younger than Ian's father would have been had he still been alive. They couldn't have gone to school together. His father would have been, what, fifty-one by now? Maybe fifty-two? That seemed so old. Especially when compared to Miranda's still stunningly youthful appearance. Had this doctor and his father really been friends?

Steel gray eyes assessed the young son and heir of Lord Daniel Thorne, noting his hesitation. "Come, my boy," Dr. Maynard said in a brisk, no-nonsense way, guiding Ian to the chair he had just vacated. "Let us get this done so you can enjoy your lunch and I can get back to Edinburgh."

The doctor opened a black leather briefcase and pulled out a clipboard with what appeared to be a standard-form medical chart. "Right. Hmmm ... now," he began, "you are sixteen?"

"Seventeen in two days."

"Yes, I see. Do you know your height and weight?"

"Um, six feet or so and about a hundred and ninety pounds."

"Closer to six two, I'd guess," Miranda commented.

"Hmmm, hmmm," Maynard nodded, making an entry on the chart. "That sounds about right. Tall for your age," he mused. "Daniel was six foot five, as I recall, so you probably still have some growing to do. Without x-rays, I can't be sure. It's highly possible you'll be close to that height. All right," he continued. "Never been sick, you said?"

Ian shook his head. "No," he mumbled. There had always been those brief, sharp headaches, but he had been checked out at school, and for some reason, he was loath to let him know.

"No measles, mumps, chicken pox?" Dr. Maynard ticked off as he touched his fingers to Ian's neck and throat, gently palpating the lymph nodes.

"No," Ian said again.

"Open your mouth," he said, placing a wooden stick on Ian's tongue. "Now, say 'Ahhhhh.'" The doctor placed a thermometer in his mouth.

"Normal," he announced. "Now, Ian, I know it's a little chilly in here, but would you mind removing your sweater and shirt? Just for a couple of minutes. Here," he continued, guiding Ian to the hearth. "You can stand by the fireplace so you'll be warmer."

As Ian somewhat embarrassedly complied, Dr. Maynard retrieved a stethoscope and blood pressure cuff from his case.

Ian stood naked from the waist up, with the slightly oversized pants belted low over his narrow hips. Really, he had no idea why he felt so self-conscious. He'd spent his life in shorts and a T-shirt or just plain board shorts and nothing else at the beach. This felt somehow different, though, being the sole focus of both Dr. Maynard and *Miranda*.

Miranda raised her eyebrows, and Dr. Maynard commented, "Good symmetry, good musculature development. You look like an athlete. What sports do you play?"

"Uh, at school I run, swim, play lacrosse, soccer, and football. I also surf whenever I get the chance."

"Good, good. Any injuries from your sports activities or at any other time?"

"No."

Again, Miranda and Dr. Maynard shared a look that Ian didn't quite comprehend. "All right. Now, Ian, I am going to listen to your heart and then check your blood pressure, then we'll be close to being finished here."

As Dr. Maynard pulled the blood pressure cuff from Ian's right arm, he commented, "Everything looks perfect. I'd just like to check one last thing, if you don't mind, just to be thorough, you understand." He then pulled an empty syringe from his case and a rubber tourniquet.

"Oh no!" both Ian and Miranda exclaimed sharply at the same time.

"Really, James, is that necessary?" Miranda gasped.

"Yes, Miranda. Yes, I believe it is. You can tell so much from the blood, and Ian has been living in a tropical climate. So many nasty parasites and bugs," he commented, shaking his head. "There have been recent outbreaks of *Zika* and *dengue fever* throughout the Hawaiian chain, just to name a few. I'd just like to take a look. One syringe. It'll be quick, and then it will be over. I'll feel much better knowing that

I've checked him out as thoroughly as is possible, given that we are not in a clinical setting, where I could actually run other tests."

Again, Miranda and Dr. Maynard exchanged a look that Ian didn't fully fathom, and then Miranda turned to Ian.

"All right, darling. You can do this, yes? It will all be over before you know it."

Ian looked into Miranda's ice-blue eyes and was lost. He barely felt the rubber tourniquet tighten above his elbow, and as Miranda chatted on about a dinner party in his honor, he descended ever deeper into those hypnotic arctic pools.

"All finished," Miranda said brightly. She gently brushed Ian's cheek with cool, soft fingers and gave him another of her devastating smiles.

His knees nearly buckled, not from the loss of blood, but from that inexplicable power she seemed to have over him. *I have really got to get a grip! What is it that she does to me? Why can't I just behave normally around her instead of acting like a tongue-tied eight-year-old? She's my father's wife, for heaven's sake! Breathe,* he told himself. *Just BREATHE!*

A short time later, Ian, again fully dressed, faced Miranda across a tray of tea and sandwiches. "How do you take your tea?" she asked. "Milk and sugar? Mmmm, me too." She smiled wickedly. "The sweeter, the better!" She passed him a cup of the fragrant, steaming brew. "You know, when I was a child, I wasn't allowed to have sugar. I suppose this is my way of making up for it now."

Ian tried to imagine her as a little girl and failed miserably. She reminded him of the goddess Venus, who was born fully grown from the sea in all her glorious immortality.

OMG, Ian! Where did that come from? I mean it. GET A GRIP! Don't look in her eyes. Do not look in her eyes! Ian looked down, pretending to study his teacup, and took a sip. It's sweet, creamy warmth stole through his body, relaxing him a bit.

"So are you British? You don't have a Scottish accent," he ventured at last.

"No. Actually, I was born in Egypt. My father was a kind of archaeologist ... among other things. I lived all over the world when I was young, and as a result, I speak several languages. However, I received my higher degrees from Oxford, and so I suppose the accent stayed with me." Another siren smile had Ian gripping his cup a little too tightly. "As did my penchant for sweet afternoon tea."

"How did you meet my father?"

"We met at a reception at the British Museum, in London. I was working as a liaison between the Cairo and British Museums in an effort to"—she hesitated—"*repatriate* certain artifacts."

"What does that mean?" Ian asked.

"Well," she said thoughtfully, "during the time of Napoleon, and truthfully, even prior to and after his reign, many important Egyptian artifacts were taken from my country. Pyramids, tombs, and temples were plundered, and the wealth and entire history of a great civilization were simply stolen or disappeared. I was, and for that matter still am, involved in a dialogue to return as many of those items as possible to their rightful country of origin. As you can imagine, the politics are … delicate. Because of my early upbringing, especially in Egypt, and my father's connections in the world of ancient antiquities, I am uniquely qualified for such a job. I am also now employed by the British Museum as a consultant and am involved in many of their acquisitions."

Classy, intelligent, and beautiful. No wonder his father had fallen for her. Ian watched as she unconsciously brushed her dark hair away from that lovely oval face, and wondered how old she was. She looked really young, maybe in her early twenties, but Ian knew that to be impossible. She possessed a degree from Oxford, and she had married his father thirteen years ago. She had to at least be in her thirties, but he knew that wasn't the sort of question he was supposed to ask a lady.

As if reading his mind, Miranda smiled. "I was twenty-six when I married your father, Ian. He was thirty-nine, and I know that some people thought I married him for his wealth and title, but that absolutely isn't so. I loved Daniel. Hmmm, truly, everyone loved Daniel. He was a beautiful, strong, intelligent man with a wicked sense of humor that kept me laughing."

She met his gaze straight on as Ian studiously attempted to look away. "I know you have some hard questions for me, and I am prepared to tell you whatever you want to know."

Ian shifted uncomfortably under her forthright gaze. Here it was, whether he was ready for this confrontation or not.

"I am well aware that you think I abandoned you, and I am certain that you have some strong feelings about that." She reached across the small tea table and lifted his chin so that she could look him directly in the eye.

"Let there be no secrets between us. I am going to tell you what happened to your father and why you were sent away. Ask me what you will. You are old enough to know the truth, and it is time you knew the facts behind his disappearance. Only ... Ian," she continued more softly, "you were with him the day he disappeared, and I don't know how much you remember. I don't want to dredge up old pain, so tell me if you don't want to have this conversation."

All the anger, all the hurt, and all the loss Ian had suffered reared its ugly head. He fought hard with himself to remain calm, to push down the loneliness and anguish he had endured. His hands shook, and he buried them in his lap so she wouldn't notice.

Miranda seemed to understand, as she gave him a moment to collect himself. She busied herself pouring more tea and serving Ian some finger sandwiches, as if he could actually swallow anything with the huge lump in his throat.

"Ian?" Her voice was very soft. "Tell me if you want me to stop."

He nodded without looking at her.

"It was your fifth birthday and your father's fortieth. Did you remember that you were born on the same day?"

"No," he replied huskily.

"Maigrid had made you a birthday cake, and we were planning a party for you. Just a few children from the village were coming. Hamish MacShane had brought in some small ponies from the upper pasture, and we had dressed them in paper armor so you could pretend to be knights and ladies. Each child had a costume. We wanted you to be surprised, so after breakfast, Daniel bundled you up and took you out on the loch so we could prepare everything. Your father loved to fish, and you loved to go with him. He kept an old wooden rowboat tied to the pier, and that was always what the two of you used."

Ian nodded mutely. Yes, he remembered that old boat.

"The party was set to start at eleven, and you hadn't returned. No one was really worried, as Daniel was always losing track of time when he was out on the loch. Hamish was headed down to see if he could wave you in when we heard you screaming. The wind was whipping in off the loch toward the house, or we might not have heard the sound. A thick mist had suddenly rolled in, and we had to follow the sound of your cries to find you. You were sopping wet on the shore, still choking from the water in your lungs. You weren't wearing your life jacket, and there was no sign of Daniel or the boat. You couldn't tell us what had happened. *A black thing in the water grabbed you*, you said. You kept calling for your father. No one knew how you got to shore."

Miranda paused and took a deep breath. She cleared her throat and then took a sip of tea with a hand that trembled just a little.

Ian could say nothing; his throat was so tight he could barely breathe.

"The first two days were horrible. We kept hoping that Daniel had swum to shore and was hurt or unconscious. We began dragging the loch and searched the shoreline for miles. We even sent scuba divers into its depths. Finally, on the third day, they located the boat. It had sunk far from shore in very deep water. When they brought it up, there was a large hole in the bottom of it."

Miranda heaved a heavy sigh, swallowing a couple of times before she could go on.

"A day later, they found your small life jacket tangled in some weeds. It was clear that the jacket's straps had been cut from your body with something sharp, probably a knife. The hole in the boat was also suspicious. It was too large and looked as though a sharp object had repeatedly hammered at it from underneath. Where at first it had appeared as some kind of freak accident, it was suddenly ruled to be a deliberate attempt on both your lives."

Miranda closed her eyes for a brief moment as two glittering tears dropped from long thick black eyelashes and rolled slowly down her cheeks. She brusquely brushed them away.

"Well, Ian, I think you know," she hesitated, her voice taking on a slightly bitter note, "or maybe you don't know, that Scotland is a *clan country*. Outsiders are often met with suspicion and are rarely welcome. Daniel's clan suddenly closed ranks. *I* was the outsider, and I, it was decided, had the most to gain from the death of you and your father."

Miranda took another sip of tea. Her chest heaved again in a heavy sigh.

"If you were both dead ..." Her voice broke. "If you were both dead," she repeated more evenly, "then it stood to reason that *I* was the one who would inherit everything. Suddenly, the British authorities were investigating me as the person with the best possible motive. Not only had I just lost my husband but I was also now fighting to prove my innocence in the matter. Neither the authorities nor Daniel's friends or clan wanted you left in my care. The biggest problem, though, for me was that I knew Daniel's killer was still out there, and if he still wanted you too, then I had to find some way to keep you safe."

Miranda briefly placed her cold hand over Ian's and then withdrew, as if she wasn't certain of his reception to her touch.

"Daniel's solicitor came up with the idea of placing you someplace remote and well guarded. When we finally located Daniel's will, the bulk of it was sealed and not to be opened until his death. I will explain this in a minute. The part we could, by law, immediately access, the part regarding *you*, strangely stipulated that if anything happened to him, and for some reason you could not remain at Thorne Manor, you must always live within the proximity of a large body of water."

Miranda shrugged and raised her eyebrows. "Strange, I know. Thus the decision to place you in the school in Hawaii. Although you may not have been aware, there are many children of powerful and high-profile individuals who depend on the anonymity that the school provides, and it is very well guarded."

Oh yes, Ian knew firsthand of the school's reputation and was well aware of its security procedures. He'd been locked away in that prison-like fortress for twelve years.

"We moved you quickly and in secret. I wasn't allowed to leave the country, as I was under investigation, so Alan MacTarran, your father's solicitor, went with you. You were so little and so hurt, but I had to let you go."

Miranda glanced at Ian as if to read his reaction to what she was telling him.

"I wasn't free to travel until almost a year later, and I came to Hawaii to see you. Your counselors told me that you were only just beginning to settle in there and that your constant nightmares had finally subsided. They felt that seeing me would reopen old wounds, and since I was still not able to return home with you, it was best you not know I was there."

Ian listened numbly, trying to digest the information she was giving him.

"We know no more about your father's death now than we did then, and so I never felt it safe to bring you home. I have monitored you throughout the years and was told that your perceived abandonment by me, and your animosity toward me, had become your shield against your pain. You had grown into a happy, healthy young man, and I did not wish to jeopardize that."

"Ian," she said. Miranda's voice, though still low, held some urgency. "I am still not convinced you are safe here, but the terms of your father's will stipulated that it was to be read within the walls of Thorne Manor. Because his body was never found, it has taken nearly twelve years for Daniel to be declared legally dead by Scottish law."

She gently rested her hand over Ian's clenched one. "He went missing on your birthday, Ian. I am so sorry, but we will be needing to take a look at that will in two days' time. It's a rotten birthday present, I know. Life is rarely fair, Ian, and you have had more than your share of heartache. I need you to be strong, and you will get through this."

Ian regarded Miranda in a daze. He was trying to take in all that she had told him, but he just could not wrap his mind around it. Miranda was his enemy, not his friend. She had never been on his side. Or had she? His dad had been *murdered*? Someone had *tried to kill Ian* too?

No matter how screwed up or off-kilter his life had felt up until now, it was nothing compared to what he was feeling at that moment. Ian felt as if his whole world had just tilted on its side and he was in a free fall.

"Ian? Ian?" Miranda was speaking to him. "Are you all right?" She was standing over him with both hands cradling his face. She gently attempted to raise his head so that she could look into his eyes, but Ian steadfastly resisted.

"I need to be excused," he blurted and, without a backward glance, rose and bolted up the stairs to his room.

Ian rummaged in his pocket for his key as he ran. Finally, within the sanctuary of his father's spacious bedroom, with its familiar, rich wine-colored fabrics and heavy dark furniture, he locked his door and then leaned into it for support.

He slammed his fist against the hard wood but it did nothing to blunt his anger or his grief. He punched it again. He wanted to feel the pain in his hand instead of the vicious ache that squeezed his heart.

Somehow, hearing Miranda speak of his father's death had made it all so final. Ian had secretly been holding on to the hope that his father would return to him. All these years, he had refused to truly believe he was permanently gone, and now he knew that that fanciful dream had been dashed forever.

Ian crossed to a window and stared out at the cold gray sky. Dr. Maynard was just stepping into the sleek black helicopter on the outer lawn. Even on the ground, it reminded him somehow of a powerful and deadly shark. He watched as the black predator lifted into the air, ascended over the tree line, and then quickly disappeared from sight.

The room had taken on a distinct chill, and he mechanically crossed to the fireplace to add another log to the smoldering orange-red embers. He stoked the fire and then stepped back quickly as a sudden gust of cold air blew down the chimney, churning up flaming-hot ashes.

Ian shivered as the frigid wind hurled large splats of rain against his window. The rain quickly became torrential, and then suddenly the storm turned to ice, pelting frozen white hail so hard against the ancient windows that he was unsure if they could possibly withstand the force. The onslaught was so furious and frenzied that he covered his ears with the palms of his hands in an attempt to block the pounding assault, backing quickly away from the glass.

Late in the afternoon, as the storm subsided, the world outside Ian's window became engulfed in a dense blanket of swirling white mist. Even the air in the room felt thick and wet. The sensation was almost surreal, as if Ian's physical form no longer existed. His body felt neither heavy nor light. It was a strange feeling of being almost insubstantial, made of nothing. His mind was still active, but his body simply *was*.

Mrs. MacShane tapped at his door. "Ian, may I come in?" she called.

He really didn't feel ready for company but knew it would be rude to send her away.

She entered with a pot of tea and a tray of cookies, placing them on the desk in the alcove. The irony of the tea wasn't lost on Ian. It seemed that both the Brits and the Scots believed that every occasion called for a pot of tea. They couldn't seem to go five minutes without it, he reflected ruefully. Well, fine. He was beginning to get used to the hot, sweet milky beverage. And really, it was thoughtful of her to look after him.

"Ye look good in those clothes, Ian. They seem ta fit just fine," Mrs. MacShane commented. "Moira hung the rest of yer things in the armoire. Do ye think there's enough, or should we try ta find some more?"

"No. Thank you. I'm sure they'll be fine."

"Ye had a talk with Lady Thorne? She told ye about the day yer dad disappeared?"

Ian nodded.

"She talked ta ye, then, about why she sent ye away?"

Ian nodded again. "She said my dad was murdered and she wanted to keep me safe." Ian watched for her reaction to that. "She said the person who killed my dad tried to kill me too."

Mrs. MacShane nodded but had a strange look in her eyes.

"She also told me the authorities and the clan accused *her* of killing my dad and wouldn't let me live with her."

"Aye, that's true." Mrs. MacShane took a deep, ragged breath. "We doona trust her. She *would* tell ye she sent ye away ta keep ye safe." She blew out another deep breath. "Miranda took ye from yer clan, Ian. *We* woulda' kept ye safe. Ye'd a been raised amongst yer own, with all the love our hearts could give."

"She said the person who killed my dad is still out there."

"That's true. We've never found the person who tried to hurt ye, Ian."

"Mrs. MacShane, I know you don't believe her, but it seems like she really cared about my dad. It seems like she tried to do the best she could. If only you hadn't shut her out, maybe I wouldn't have had to go away."

"Yer defendin' her now, are ye? After all she's done?"

"What has she done?" Ian asked earnestly. "She sent me away to keep me safe. She brought me back to hear my father's will. She had Dr. Maynard check on me to make sure I am healthy. He even took some blood to check for parasites."

Mrs. MacShane turned white as a sheet and stood very still.

"They took yer blood?" she whispered. *"Ye let them take your blood?"* Mrs. MacShane cried in disbelief. She grabbed Ian by his upper arms and shook him. *"SHE TOOK YER BLOOD? IAN, WHAT WERE YE THINKIN'?"* she fairly shrieked at him.

Ian attempted to pull from her grasp, but he didn't want to hurt her. This unhinged, screeching woman had completely lost it, and he was beginning to be really afraid of her. She seemed frenzied, almost demented.

"If you'd only talk to her," Ian reiterated anxiously, contemplating how best to restrain her. "She seems very convincing."

"OF COURSE SHE SOUNDS CONVINCIN'! SHE'S HAD TWELVE YEARS TA MEMORIZE HER SCRIPT!" Mrs. MacShane screamed at him.

"Take your hands off him, Maigrid," Miranda commanded from the open doorway.

"What's yer game, Miranda?" Mrs. MacShane confronted her vehemently. "Ye had no right ta touch this child. Ye had no right ta *take his blood*!"

"Enough, Maigrid! Don't force me to have you removed from this house."

"Ye canna, and ye know it," Maigrid spat venomously. "Neither of us may know what's in the sealed portion of Danny's will, but one thing's been spelled out since the beginnin'. Hamish and me'll always have a place here, and there's nothin' on this green earth that ye can do ta change that."

"For now." She had spoken quietly, but Miranda's arctic eyes were blazing. "Keep your hands off Ian," she repeated. "And, Maigrid, I want you to know"—Miranda's voice now took on a dangerous tenor—"Lawrence is staying in the room next to mine, and he is armed. Tell your people that if anyone should attack me the way they did that last night I spent here, Lawrence will shoot to kill. I've arranged for even more protection by tomorrow for Ian and me. Keep your people away from me. Keep your people away from us."

Mrs. MacShane sputtered and then turned to Ian. "I ... I'm sorry Ian," she said tearfully. "I didna mean ta scare ye. I'd n-never hurt ye. S-surely, ye must know that." She turned and left the room.

"I think Mrs. MacShane's gone off the deep end," Ian said softly.

"I think you may be right," Miranda grimly agreed.

She put her arm lightly around Ian's shoulders. "Listen, darling, I've got a lot of people coming in the next two days ... for various reasons, but mostly because your father was a very important man and several of them will need to be present when the will is read. It won't be a very happy birthday for you, I'm afraid, and so I've decided to hold a small banquet in your honor tomorrow night. Unfortunately, there will still only be a lot of stuffy grown-ups, people you don't know. But I truly did want to mark your birthday in some way. Anyway, I know you haven't been here long, but I was wondering if there was anyone in particular you would like to attend? Have you met anyone yet from the village?"

"Um, yeah," Ian stammered. The emotional roller coaster of the past few minutes had given him whiplash, and he was struggling to maintain his equilibrium. "Moira is really nice. I don't know her last name, though. She's been helping get the house ready for you. I'd like her to be there, if it's all right with you?"

"Hmmm," Miranda said thoughtfully. "She would be one of the MacTairn girls, I think." She smiled. "They're all mostly *MacTairns*, *MacTarrans*, or *MacTorns* around here. You know, from your father's surname, *Thorne*. An ancestor of yours many centuries back ruled this area, and though the name was *Anglicized*, the clans have endured. Of course, many other surnames have come and gone too. People marry, people move away, but your name is an old and powerful one in this region. I think Moira would be a lovely addition to our evening. I'll see what I can do."

She tightened her arm around Ian's shoulder in a quick hug and then released him. "Now, Ian," she said seriously, "I am staying in the room next to yours. Look"—she crossed to a concealed panel in the wall and pushed it open—"I am just through the sitting room in here on the other side. If anyone bothers you or you just need to talk, don't hesitate to come to me. I'll lock both doors opening onto the gallery, but this side door between our rooms will remain unlocked if you need me."

"Uh, thanks," Ian mumbled, completely dumbfounded. Why was he even bothering to lock this room? The whole world, it seemed, had access to it. In fact, it was beginning to feel like Grand Central Station. After she had gone, he checked the panel leading into the sitting room. He'd had no idea it was there. How many other people knew about it? he wondered.

Everyone, he decided. *Everyone, that is, except me.* Ian closed the panel, checking for some way to lock it. There wasn't any. Of course there wasn't. And that surprised him because … ? *I wonder how many other secret panels and passageways there are in this house. If I'd grown up here, I probably would have explored until I found them all.* Really, it could have been fun when he was little, but now, when he wasn't feeling exactly confident about the people around him, he'd trade it all for his small dorm room in Hawaii and the friends he had made there.

Maybe he should just move back to the nursery. But then, he'd have to explain why. *I just have to get through the next two days, and then I can go home,* he promised himself. *Two more days, two more days. I don't care what anyone tells me after that. I'm going!*

Feeling a little better about his resolution to leave as soon as possible, Ian poured a steaming cup of tea and collapsed back into the leather armchair by the fire. He really was getting used to the stuff. *Must be my Scottish roots.* And it really was nice of Mrs. MacShane to bring it to him. *Even if she is a deranged, crazy lady.*

"*Mysterious and kooky, they're altogether spooky, the MacShane famileee,*" Ian sang under his breath.

That evening, as Moira served steaming bowls of rich, hearty stew to Ian, Miranda, and Sir Lawrence, she said shyly, "Thanks for askin' me, Ian. I'm honored to come. I won't be seein' ye tomorrow durin' the day, though, or the next, for that matter. I've got to help my aunt Bridgett. The village is fair crawlin' with tourists because of the summer solstice. This time of year, they all flock to the area to visit the stones and cairns."

"Summer solstice? Stones and … corns?" Ian repeated, nonplussed.

"*Cairns*, silly," she laughed. "They're really just piles of rocks, many of 'em put there thousands of years ago. Some were burial chambers, but others"—she shrugged—"who knows? And circle stones are … well, they're circles of tall rocks, some brought from hundreds of miles away. There are sites scattered all over the British Isles, though not many are as large or in as good a shape as Stonehenge."

Moira had forgotten she was supposed to be serving, and Ian grinned as she earnestly waved the ladle.

"Ye've heard of Stonehenge? Ye know, on the Salisbury Plain in England?" she continued, oblivious to the amused glances she was receiving from Ian and Sir Lawrence. Even Miranda seemed so far to be taking their bubbly server's preoccupation in stride.

"Our climate is harsher the farther north ye get, though, so the ancient places tend to get more weathered and beaten down. Some of the cairns and circles date back to around 4000 BC. They're as old or older than the pyramids."

Interesting. Ian hadn't realized that.

"There are those that say they were built by the Druids as magical places of worship or places of power. Others say they're way older than the Druids. Who's to know, really?"

Moira began to serve the soup once more, carefully filling Miranda's bowl before moving on to Ian's, though she continued her history lesson.

"The circle stones were also used as a sort of calendar. The sun lines up *just so* during the summer and winter solstices. Ye know, the longest and shortest days of the year? The summer solstice almost always falls on June 21. In some ancient pagan religions, a person born on the solstice was thought to be blessed by the gods."

She carefully ladled a heaping portion into Sir Lawrence's bowl as she added, "The twenty-first is yer birthday, isn't it, Ian? Ye see"—she winked—"I knew ye were special."

"Right, Moira," Ian replied sarcastically. "If only."

"No, truly." Her eyes lit with mischief, and she flashed him a sassy smile that showed her dimples. "A solstice is a '*no time*,' when our world mingles and unites with the '*otherworld*' and magic abounds." She tried to make her voice sound scary. "On the summer solstice, the veils between the two worlds are at their thinnest, and fairies walk the land. Ach, Ian!" She laughed at his look of blatant disbelief. "Any self-respectin' Scott knows that!"

"Funny girl!" Sir Lawrence laughed outright. "You'll make a welcome addition to that boring dinner party Miranda has planned for tomorrow night to torture Ian with."

"It is not my intention to torture Ian!" Miranda retorted indignantly. "Regardless, the gathering tomorrow evening would have been a formal affair. Because we are also celebrating Ian's birthday, albeit a day early, I have planned a wonderful treat for him. Something to welcome him home and to remind him of his Scottish heritage."

"All right, all right," Sir Lawrence said laughingly, raising his hands in surrender.

Ian liked Sir Lawrence. He was funny, with a self-deprecating sense of humor and a way of immediately putting people at their ease. The smile lines around his thoughtful hazel eyes gave him the approachable air of someone who refused to take the world too seriously. The touch of gray at his temples belied his youthful, boyish face, and his slightly tousled, sun-streaked hair only added to that illusion of youth. Like Dr. Maynard, he had a tall, athletic build, but unlike the doctor, he seemed as comfortable in his well-tailored suit as he would have been in shorts and a T-shirt on a rugby field.

Later that night in his room, Ian reflected on the events of the day. Although in many ways it had been tremendously draining, it had also been cathartic and had given him answers he'd desperately needed. He had begun the morning thinking Miranda was his enemy and ended the day admitting that there was a strong possibility he had misjudged her.

Ian had been shocked by the admission that his father was murdered, but that information also helped him put the pieces together regarding his own predicament and the reason he had been shipped off to Hawaii.

He had hated Miranda for abandoning him, but in retrospect, his life in Hawaii had been filled with close friendships, a great deal of happiness, and unique experiences he wouldn't trade for the world. His life without his father would have been far different had he remained here, but in reality, he could not believe that he would have been any happier growing up in Scotland.

Suddenly in the mood for one of those *fizzy American drinks*, as Miranda called them, and maybe another one of Mrs. M's cinnamon rolls, Ian decided to raid the kitchen. The manor didn't seem so spooky at night with Miranda and Sir Lawrence staying here with him, he observed.

Ian let himself out onto the darkened gallery and made his way toward the stairs. Who knew? Maybe he'd run into the ghost. After all, she was probably a relative or something. And hey, he was up for a ghostly adventure as much as the next teenager staying in a haunted house, especially when he knew that Sir Lawrence and Miranda were just down the hall. Why not? He grinned at the absurdity of his thoughts.

Light still spilled from the majestic salon where Ian had drunk tea and talked with Miranda, casting a swath of soft golden light to guide his way.

Padding silently on bare feet across the shadowy entry hall, Ian slowed his pace as he identified the furtive whisperings of a hissed conversation. Mrs. MacShane was just inside the door of the salon and gesturing animatedly to someone Ian couldn't quite see.

If I cross into the light, Ian thought, *they might think I am spying on them. On the other hand, if I stand here listening, I really will be spying on them.*

His decision was made for him when he heard Mrs. MacShane hiss, *"They took his blood!"*

Ian stood stock-still. "And that's not all," she continued, wringing her hands. "That championship rugby jersey with the bloodstains all over it is missin' too. Moira brought it down from the attic this mornin' by mistake and then left it with Ian when she found the picture. It's gone, Áedan! It's been taken from his room! I've looked everywhere for it, and it's nowhere ta be found!"

Áedan? Ian heard a man's voice answer her but couldn't hear what he said. The pair moved away from the door toward the dining room, and Ian caught a glimpse of a very tall male with long raven-black hair that fell to midback. His face was turned away from him, but he had the impression that the man was young, late teens, early twenties? And strong. A weight lifter?

As they passed into the next room, Ian realized he'd been holding his breath. He slowly exhaled.

Safe back in his room, Ian speed-dialed Brax. "Hey, bro! About time! You don't call, you don't write …" An enthusiastic voice greeted him.

"I just talked to you this morning."

"Oh yeah. Well, it was the middle of the night for me. What's goin' on, dude? How's Scotland?"

"Get me out of this loony bin!" Ian answered with feeling.

"That bad, huh?"

"You have no idea!"

"Your stepmom? The *Wicked Witch of the West* bringing the pain?"

"No. Actually, she's about the only normal one around here. She's really kinda nice."

"Seriously, dude? No way. Not possible."

"Look, there's this *nutjob* cook—housekeeper, whatever—who used to work for my dad, who I just can't figure out. There's a girl named Moira, who seems really nice, and she's really cute—"

"Oooooh," Brax interrupted

"Shut up, Brax. Anyway, but Moira works for Mrs. MacShane, and they seem really close—"

"Mrs. MacShane?"

"The nutjob."

"Oh."

"And I just found out that my dad was murdered—"

"No way!"

"And they tried to kill me too—"

"What? Today?"

"No! When I was five, with my dad."

"Wow! Bad blood, man."

"That's why they sent me to Hawaii."

"Oh!" Silence. "Ian? Hey, man, are you okay?"

"Yeah, Brax. I just need to get outta here. I just want to come home."

"This is home, now?"

"Yeah."

"Whew, Ian. Sounds really bad. What can I do?"

"Nothing, bro. Nothing. Things just don't feel right here. I just needed to tell somebody in case—"

"In case what? You think somebody might actually try to hurt you?"

"I don't know. I'm not sure what's really going on."

"Yeah, man, definitely sounds like you need to get on the next plane outta there. Just keep me in the loop." There was a pause. "But hey, Ian, I'm in your will, right? I mean, if something happens to you, I do get your surfboard and your iPod."

"Sure, Brax. Anything else? My phone, my computer … ?"

"Yeah, that'd be good too."

"Thorne Manor," Ian continued, "my trust fund … ?"

"Nah, sounds too dangerous. If you can't deal with all those crazy people, you think I want to?"

Ian snorted. "No, man, if I die, it's all yours. You gotta take the good with the bad, bro."

"Well, forget it, then." Another short pause. "Listen, Ian, just watch your back."

"Yeah, I'll try."

"Do better than try, bro. We've got plans to ditch this place when we graduate. We're gonna see the world. If I have to dive the Great Barrier Reef without you, I'm gonna be *really pissed*!"

"Well, I wouldn't want to piss you off, Brax. I've seen what happens when you lose your temper."

"Okay, then, we're good."

"Yeah, we're good." Ian tried to sound enthusiastic. "Hey, did you find out anything more about the break-in?"

"Nah, they think it was just some kind of a prank that got outta hand. Nothing else has happened."

"Pretty weird, huh?"

"Compared to what? Sounds like you've got plenty of *weird* happening on your end too."

"Yeah. This whole place is straight out of a soap opera."

"Sounds real fun! Better you than me, bro."

"So anyway, the phone works both ways, Brax. Stay in touch."

"I tried to call you, but I keep getting voice mail."

"Oh. You have to dial a country code first. Zero, one, one, four, four, one, four, one, I think. Uh, I'll text it to you."

"No probs. Keep me posted, bro."

"Yeah."

"Bye, Ian. And I mean it! *Watch your back*. And just remember, you've got *freaky skills* no one knows about. Put 'em to use. And don't forget, excluding *me*, you're better at *Krav Maga* than anyone, maybe even than Ari. I'd like to see the two of you paired up someday." Brax let out a low whistle. "That'd be a match to bet on!"

"Yeah, I'll remember that if I have to use martial arts to take out the housekeeper," Ian joked. He pictured the short elderly Mrs. MacShane. "Talk to you soon, Brax," he said, shaking his head at the ridiculous image he had conjured. "Take care."

"You too, Ian."

Ian touched the red phone icon, disconnecting the call. He did feel better. He'd forgotten to tell Brax about the blood. But really, what difference did it make? He'd think about what he should do tomorrow. He was suddenly just too drained to worry about anything else tonight.

Lying down on his father's bed fully dressed, the young heir to the ancient manor, presently overrun with suspicious characters, byzantine plots, and enough intrigue for a Hitchcock film, was asleep before he could exhale.

CHAPTER VI

Ian was awakened by the sound of a helicopter. He'd slept the deep, dreamless sleep of complete exhaustion and was at first disoriented to his surroundings. He groaned as he realized it was already nine o'clock in the morning.

The dreary gray light and chill in the room told him that the sky was still overcast. As he crossed to the window, the clouds, indeed, threatened rain. Five men were disembarking from the same black helicopter that had brought Miranda to Thorne Manor the previous day. He recognized Dr. Maynard, but the rest of the faces were new. As they traipsed toward the house, Ian saw that they were all men of various ages. Three, including Dr. Maynard, were wearing suits, and two were dressed much more casually. All carried an assortment of garment and overnight bags.

Ian showered and dressed then headed downstairs to find breakfast. The two casually dressed men he had seen from his window were rummaging through pots and pans and inventorying the kitchen. "Deez iz terrible!" one was exclaiming theatrically. "Ow, am I expected to prepare a deezant meal wiz deez awful cookwares?" Ian hurriedly backed out of the melee, not wanting to become the object of their wrath.

"Ian," Mrs. MacShane gestured him into the salon. "There's breakfast set up in here. Lady Thorne's *chef* has arrived," she stated heatedly, "and we're to stay out of his way."

"Thanks," he mumbled, sidestepping Mrs. MacShane. Still feeling uncomfortable in her presence, he busied himself piling sunny-side-up eggs, sautéed mushrooms, and fresh fruit onto a plate so that he didn't have to talk to her.

He noted her distressed sigh as she left the room.

After breakfast, Ian escaped to the garden and then made his way to the rocky beach. Water broke roughly onto the shore, driven by the angry black rain clouds farther out over the loch. The dark mass hovered just above the ruined castle on the distant island. Lightning forked the sky, quickly followed by the rumble of thunder.

Soon, he would have to return or risk being caught out in the deluge.

The air smelled clean and fresh, tinged with the earthy, wet tang of the loch and pungent crispness of the grass and forest. Over it all was that intense evocative scent of rain.

Wind whipped the waves into a frenzied white-capped furor, and the first frigid drops of moisture were carried in on the squall. Ian turned and made a run for the manor.

As its crenelated roof and square turrets came into view, Ian marveled at the imposing structure. Against the angry backdrop of the storm, it looked more like a haunted castle from a Frankenstein movie than a family home. He knew it had been built by one of his ancestors in the sixteenth century as a Renaissance palace. Why it was now called a *manor house* instead of a castle, he couldn't fathom.

Arriving out of breath and soaked to the skin, Ian dropped his sodden coat over a wall hook and removed his muddy tennis shoes in a small alcove just inside the back door of the kitchen that led in from the garden. He skirted the kitchen's perimeter quickly, trying to escape the notice of "*zee chef*" and "*zee chef's helper*" but only partially succeeded. As he reached the secret panel leading into the dining room, the culinary virtuoso exclaimed, "I cannot work like zees! Ow many more people will be needing to run sru zees kitchen today?"

Ian didn't stick around to answer that question, deciding it was time to make himself scarce.

Once again dressed in dry clothes, he wished he'd brought another pair of shoes with him from Hawaii. Moira had said there was a trunk of his father's things in the attic. Maybe there were shoes too. Anyway, he was bored. Ian wished Moira were here today. There was just nothing to do. He couldn't go outside. There was an old TV but no reception. He didn't feel like reading. Maybe he could explore without getting in the way of all the bustling people scurrying about in preparation for this evening.

Navigating the long gallery in stocking feet, he passed along rows of portraits of highbrowed ancestors now long gone from the world.

Strange how the family resemblance had carried through the ages. All the males had that same raven-black hair and identical vivid blue eyes as Ian's. There was no denying his relationship to these people. They were all so similar; only their clothes and the style of their hair were in any way different.

For the first time, Ian noticed the walls contained mostly portraits of males. He supposed, with the chauvinism of past ages, the portraits of his female ancestors were not deemed as important. It was really a shame. He would like to have observed some of his female ancestors too, although maybe he just hadn't come across them yet. This manor was so vast he had barely covered a tenth of it during his time here.

Interspersed between the portraits were various weapons from different centuries. Swords, shields, knives, pikes, and spears were displayed alongside other items of war he didn't fully recognize.

Ian knew from history books that Scotland had a brutal and bloody past marked with uprisings, massacres, and clan wars. British rulers had treated the inhabitants of these Northern Isles harshly, ruthlessly attempting to repress their indomitable spirits by hammering them into submission. Only by sheer grit and determination had any of the Scottish clans or culture survived.

As he came upon a framed parchment, he noted that it looked old, but certainly not as ancient as the date suggested. A copy of some document, Ian guessed, written in both Latin and English.

THE DECLARATION OF ARBROATH
Year of our Lord, 6 April 1320
Submitted to Pope John XXII

At nos non imperium neque divitias petimus, quarum rerum causa bella atque certamina omnia inter mortalis sunt, sed libertatem, quam nemo bonus nisi cum anima simul amittit.

FOR AS LONG AS BUT A HUNDRED OF US REMAIN ALIVE, WE WILL NEVER BE SUBJECT TO TYRANNICAL DOMINION, BECAUSE IT IS NOT FOR GLORY OR RICHES OR HONOURS THAT WE FIGHT, BUT FOR FREEDOM ALONE, WHICH NO WORTHY MAN LOSES EXCEPT WITH HIS LIFE.

Ian's blood surged hotly through his veins, and chills raced up and down his spine. Those words, more than any other piece of history in this vast estate, spoke to his heart, told him where he came from, told him *who he was*.

He looked again at the faces of his ancestors. Though all elegant and strikingly attractive, there was also something powerfully charismatic about them. And even though the varied portraits had obviously been painted at different times and by different hands, an underlying element of danger bled through.

These people had been warriors, all of them, surviving barbaric wars and the capricious rule of fickle monarchies. They had to draw on their prowess with archaic weapons and unimaginable physical strength. They must have had highly developed instincts and superior intellect to navigate the erratic currents of their times. The fact that this manor still stood and had remained within control of his family for over five centuries validated the strength of their tenacity and resolve.

Ian snorted. If anyone could hear his thoughts, they'd certainly call him a snob. But he wasn't counting himself into that equation; he'd done nothing of any merit up to this point with his life and was undeniably soft by their standards. He was referring to *them*.

Not for the first time, he marveled that this magnificent manor was like a museum, or more accurately, like stepping centuries into the past. It was a shame more people hadn't had the opportunity to see and appreciate these treasures. Actually, it was unbelievable that a single family could actually have amassed such a vast and varied collection and that the evidence of his heritage was still intact centuries later.

Ian had already visited the stunning ballroom, a two-story library crammed with priceless leather-bound books, a billiard room, a smoking room, a study, an armory, and numerous other rooms, all obviously used for some illustrious purpose in the past. His head was beginning to swim with the sheer magnitude of this place. He needed to stay on track, though. Now, he needed to find some footwear or risk his safety in the retrieval of his muddy shoes, hopefully still drying in the kitchen alcove. In a pinch, he could wear a pair from his father's room, but they were all about a size and a half too big.

Really, he should have just carried them to his room, but after all the hard work by Mrs. MacShane and Moira and her sisters to get this house so pristinely clean, he hadn't the heart to disrespect their efforts and track dirt over those beautiful floors.

Finally making his way to the far end, Ian somehow remembered there was a small staircase leading to the third floor, probably used mostly by servants in times past, as it was nothing as grand as the wider, more central flights. Actually, this staircase led to the *second* floor, he corrected himself. The *first floor* in this country was the *ground floor*, and the *second floor*, the *first*. Too confusing, he decided. Anyway, maybe the stairs continued on up to the attic.

Yep, he thought. There was the staircase just where he remembered. Good. There were just too many people arriving now. He could hear the muffled murmur of voices drifting up from below, and he definitely wanted to stay out of their way.

The steep passage didn't continue up to the attic as he had hoped, but Ian knew there had to be another flight of stairs somewhere nearby. Mrs. MacShane had said they hadn't cleaned up here, so he had no fear of disturbing anyone. He'd just check the doors along this upper gallery until he found it.

As he walked, Ian noticed that a door was ajar a few paces down the corridor. *That's probably it,* he hoped, heading toward it.

Slowing as he approached, Ian was surprised to hear the raised, indignant voice of Mrs. MacShane as she exclaimed, "Yer lucky ta get that! They've taken over my kitchen! She's got a French chef preparin' *haggis*! I've never heard'a such a thing!"

Ian heard a low, masculine laugh. "Did I say I wasn't grateful? Egg salad is one of my favorites."

Rolling his eyes with a grin, Ian suppressed his own chuckle. *Mrs. M and her egg salad sandwiches.* Somehow, the man's assertion that he liked those sandwiches didn't really sound sincere.

Ian recognized the voice as that of the man from last night. *Áedan?* Here he was again, Ian chided himself, listening to a conversation not intended for him. He started to back away but then hesitated. Why were they being so secretive?

"How's Ian?" asked the man.

Ian plastered himself against the wall. Well, that cinched it! If they were going to talk about him, then he was going to listen, just for a minute.

"How do ye think he is?" Mrs. MacShane retorted fiercely. "He's confused! Miranda's got him tied up in knots. Ye of all people should know how persuasive she can be. Áedan, what were ye thinkin' bringin' that witch into our midst?"

Áedan brought Miranda here? That didn't make any sense. The tall raven-haired man he had glimpsed in the salon last night certainly wasn't the helicopter pilot. Ian had seen the pilot in the hall yesterday with the baggage.

His brain suddenly wasn't tracking properly. That sharp headache that so often came out of nowhere suddenly splintered from behind his eyes to the base of his skull.

Tense fingers massaged a throbbing temple as Ian waited to hear the man's answer.

"I wasn't thinking, Maigrid." The voice sounded angry. Bitter.

"Have ye talked to MacTarran? Has he got the will yet?"

"The will is still locked in a vault at *the Royal Bank of Scotland*. It'll be released tomorrow and then brought here to the estate by armored truck."

The will? Who was this person? Ian was still trying to place the man's accent. A bit of a Scottish brogue, a bit British, and something else that he couldn't quite identify.

"Áedan, ye've got ta get ta that will!" Mrs. MacShane was demanding of him.

"There's nothing I can do until it's delivered to MacTarran tomorrow."

"Ye shoulda come sooner."

"It wouldn't have made a difference. You know I couldn't have just waltzed in here and announced myself. And getting here wasn't that easy, Maigrid. I had to wait until we got closer to the solstice."

"All right. Just stay outta sight, Áedan. I fear what might happen if anyone was ta see ye. We can't afford any questions about ye. And I'll try and get ye some clothes. Yer too conspicuous in that medieval tunic and those leather trews."

"Just say I'm in a rock band, if anyone asks." His voice sounded amused.

"No one'd better be askin'," she retorted testily. "And ye look more like ye wandered in from a Renaissance fair. Stay hidden, Áedan. I mean it."

Ian backed toward the stairs as quickly and silently as he could move. Reaching the dark, narrow passage, he raced down the steps two at a time then bolted to his room.

What in the heck was going on? Mrs. MacShane and that man were trying to get the *will*? Why? *Think, Ian, think!*

What could they do with the will? Hide it? Change it? And this guy, Áedan, was here to help her. And what about this MacTarran person? Wasn't MacTarran his dad's attorney, solicitor, or whatever you called them here? Did he know what Mrs. MacShane was going to do? Was MacTarran plotting with them?

Attempting to sort through his chaotic thoughts, Ian paced back and forth. Mrs. MacShane had told Miranda that she and Mr. MacShane would always have a place at Thorne Manor and there was nothing that Miranda could do about it. His father had obviously trusted them. Were they trying to get more? Were they trying to cut Miranda out of the will? Mrs. MacShane clearly hated her. It had probably been Mr. and Mrs. MacShane who had chased Miranda away from Thorne Manor right after his father died. Could the MacShanes be the ones who had his father murdered?

Ian needed to tell someone. *Miranda?* Could he trust her? She was definitely not in this plot with Mrs. MacShane and Áedan, whoever *he* was. She seemed, in fact, to be as much a victim in this as Ian was. She was also the only one who really seemed to be on his side.

Yes, he decided. He needed to tell Miranda.

Ian crossed his bedroom to the secret panel and pushed through it into the sitting room. It was a comfortable, elegant room with pale gold-and-green upholstered furniture and sumptuous, graceful window hangings to match. A gilded sideboard with a rich green marble top doubled as a bar on one side of the room, and orange-and-yellow flames danced languidly from the depths of a carved limestone fireplace.

A portrait of Miranda hung above the mantel, gazing out over the room with those icy frost-blue eyes of hers. Long dark hair flowed gracefully around that perfect, flawless face, and the corners of her mouth turned up with just a hint of a mysteriously provocative smile. She looked no older now than she had when the portrait was painted.

A tea tray with two cups resided on the green marble-topped coffee table in front of the down-filled sofa. Soft classical music was playing in the background, and the scent of Miranda's exotic perfume filled the air. The door to her room was slightly ajar, and Ian crossed to it, raising his hand to knock.

He hesitated as he heard voices. Perhaps he should come back later. But then, just as with Mrs. McShane earlier on the second-floor gallery, Ian realized that this conversation was important and definitely not something that he was meant to overhear.

"He's the very image of Daniel. There is no disputing the relationship," Dr. Maynard was saying gravely.

"There's no birth certificate, no record of his birth at all! We can locate no one who knows who his birth mother was. There is absolutely no way to prove that he's Daniel's son." Miranda's voice was distraught.

"Do you mean to tell me that you never asked him?"

"Of course I asked. He told me she died giving birth to Ian and it was too painful to talk about."

"Miranda," Dr. Maynard said pacifyingly, as if trying to reason with a child, "the blood is … unusual, but the DNA test is conclusive. The two of them couldn't be more alike if they were clones."

"What do you mean *unusual*?"

"I can't say right now. Just *unusual*. It could be due to some contamination at the lab or variable in the processing. I need to run more tests."

"You've still got the rugby shirt?" she asked tensely.

"Yes."

"Well, keep it hidden!" Miranda ordered fiercely. "They can prove nothing without Daniel's DNA."

For the second time today, Ian backed away from a doorway and fled.

Ian sat huddled in the overstuffed armchair in the nursery and stared moodily out his window over the churning dark water of the loch. Lightning split the sky, and thunder crashed overhead. Rain ran in rivulets down the ancient leaded windowpanes like tears, distorting the view into an impressionistic landscape.

He had to figure out what to do. He had to tell someone, but whom? Ian knew he needed help, but who could he trust? Should he call the police, or bobbies, or whatever they were called in this country? Would they believe him?

Miranda had said this was clan country. Would the clan be on Ian's side or Mrs. MacShane's? And what about Mr. MacTarran, his father's solicitor? Was he involved in Mrs. MacShane's plot to get the will?

And as if that wasn't enough, what were Miranda and Dr. Maynard up to? They had taken his blood so that they could prove what? That he was Daniel Thorne's son? Or that he wasn't? Miranda, *Lady Thorne*, was a very well-connected and powerful woman. Would anyone believe Ian's word over hers?

Ian pressed his speed dial, and after several rings, a sleepy voice greeted, "Whassup, bro?"

"Brax, I need your help."

"Yeah?" Brax said, repressing a yawn. "You know it's two in the morning, Ian? This had better be good."

"Brax, this is important. I think I'm in trouble. Can you get a message to your dad?"

"Yeah, maybe. It might take a couple of days."

"I know he's Black Ops, Special Forces, so ... can you have him do a background check on Lady Miranda Thorne?"

"I thought you liked her, bro. Ian, my dad can't just get involved in civilian issues. He's not allowed to use his position for personal gain."

"Tell him she's a terrorist."

"Is she?"

"No, but listen to me for a minute." Ian gave him a brief rundown of the events he had failed to mention when they'd talked earlier and then told him about the two conversations he had overheard. Brax, now fully awake, blew out a long, slow whistle.

"Lady Miranda Thorne," Ian repeated. "I don't know her maiden name, but she was born in Egypt thirty-nine years ago and works for the British Museum."

"Okay, okay, I'll try, Ian."

"And I don't know if he can find out anything about Maigrid and Hamish MacShane—are you writing this down, Brax?"

"Yeah, Ian. I'm writing, I'm writing ..."

"And an attorney named MacTarran. So anyway, Brax, let me know, okay?" Ian murmured, trying not to sound as shaken as he felt.

"Watch your back, bro," Brax told him. "I mean it, Ian, this sounds serious."

"I know. I'll try." Ian hung up the phone.

The rain let up almost as quickly as it had begun, although the sky remained dark and threatening. Ian would have liked to stay hidden in the nursery for the remainder of his time in Scotland; however, he knew he needed to stop feeling sorry for himself, and *he needed a strategy.* He couldn't avoid Miranda or Mrs. MacShane forever, and so it made sense to spend as much time around each of them as possible in hopes of learning something more.

As he left the relative safety of his old room, voices carried up from the entry hall. "I thought you weren't arriving until tomorrow," Miranda was saying to someone.

Ian looked over the rail to find a tall middle-aged man with black hair wearing a well-cut black suit, carrying an elegant black leather briefcase, standing below.

"I heard there was a party here tonight," the newcomer answered in a deceptively mild voice. "I'm sure the omission of that fact was an oversight when we spoke yesterday, Miranda. I just thought I'd pop in a day early and make myself useful." The man smiled innocently.

"Of course, Alan," Miranda said stiffly. Ian could see the tension around her perfect mouth. "I'll ask Mrs. MacShane to make up a room for you."

Ian descended the staircase, noting that this new arrival was none other than the person who had helped him at the airport. Had they been introduced, then? Ian couldn't remember hearing his name, but he'd been so tired and disoriented anything was possible.

"Oh, Ian," Miranda said as she noticed him. "There you are. I believe you have already met Lord Alan MacTarran, your father's barrister. I am told he met you at the airport upon your arrival."

"Um, yes," Ian answered uncertainly. "It's nice to see you again, sir. Thank you again for your help." So this was the man Mrs. MacShane and Áedan had said would have the will.

"It was my pleasure, Ian. It's good to see you too." *Lord* MacTarran extended his hand warmly. After a vigorous handshake, he asked, "How are you getting on here? Is everyone treating you all right?" The question seemed innocent enough; however, Ian noticed the barely concealed animosity in the look that passed between Miranda and Lord MacTarran.

"Yes, I'm fine. Thank you."

"Good, good!" His gray eyes sparkled, and he gave Ian a wink. "Although, Miranda," he continued, turning to her, "Ian should have been brought back to Scotland at least once a year to keep his visa valid. By not following the rules, you created a hell of a lot of paperwork for me."

"Really, Alan? I think you are perfectly aware of the reason that didn't happen." Miranda's tone was icy.

"And, Miranda," he said, speaking as though he hadn't noticed her enmity, "I hope you won't mind if I make myself at home in the library for an hour or so? Daniel kept some papers that I probably should have a look at before tomorrow."

"What kind of papers?" Miranda asked suspiciously.

"Ancient titles, deeds, and land grants to the Thorne estates. I have copies, of course, but I will need to compare them to the originals and have them notarized before we can sign off on the will tomorrow."

"I would prefer that you wait until tomorrow morning, Alan. My own legal council will be happy to assist you with whatever you need then." The arctic tone removed any doubt as to the blatant hostility she felt toward the man.

"As you wish, Miranda," Lord MacTarran said genially.

Ian had to admit he was smooth. Not once did MacTarran's relaxed, good-natured facade waver.

Mrs. MacShane appeared behind Ian at the top of the stairs. "Alan," she cried warmly. "I'm so glad yer here!" She hurried down to greet him.

"I've only just arrived, Maigrid. It's good to see you too," the urbane Lord MacTarran returned her greeting affectionately.

Definitely on Mrs. MacShane's side, Ian decided.

"Maigrid, would you be so kind as to settle Lord MacTarran into a guest room? I'm certain he'd like to rest before the party this evening," Miranda commanded in a wintry voice.

As Mrs. MacShane led Lord MacTarran up the grand staircase, Ian commented, "You two really don't get along. I thought he helped you after my dad died."

"Yes, he did, Ian. But he didn't do it for me. Anyway," she continued, forcing a warmer tone into her voice, "enough of that. I have something for you." Suddenly, her devastating charm returned. She flashed him one of those smiles that made his knees weak, and linked her arm through his.

"I've laid out a tuxedo and some dress shoes in your room for tonight. They just arrived from Edinburgh. I know they are going to be perfect." Her enthusiasm was contagious, and despite himself, Ian found the corners of his mouth turning up in a slight smile. Even with all his suspicions, he found himself responding to her. The woman's charm was truly lethal, and Ian realized anew that he was definitely out of his league.

"Oh, and, Ian, I'd like to introduce you to Sean and Eric."

Two well-muscled men stepped from the shadows of the opposite doorway and nodded curtly. Ian hadn't even known they were there. They both wore dark suits, but something about their bearing made him think of them as disciplined military types. Both men wore their hair military short. One was a little taller than the other and probably in his midthirties. He had a strong square face and nondescript brown hair. The other was a little younger, a little shorter, and a little darker, but both appeared equally powerful. The two men had an alert, no-nonsense air about them. Ian noticed the bulge under their suit jackets and guessed they carried handguns.

"Sean and Eric will be staying with us for the next few days, Ian, just to make sure that things go ... smoothly. They'll try to stay out of your way, but I wanted you to know that you may find one of them shadowing you if you leave the house. And, Ian, if you should run into any ... problems or feel unsafe, you are to call for them."

"You mean they're my *bodyguards*?" Ian asked in disbelief.

"*Our* bodyguards," Miranda said firmly.

Ian felt the warning bells going off in his brain. *Bodyguards* or *jailers*? he wondered as he made his way up to his room.

The glittering ballroom was full of people Ian didn't know, and he was extremely grateful for Moira's presence. She looked beautiful in a pale evening gown of some shimmering fabric that subtly shifted color from soft gold to bronze as she moved. It perfectly complimented her flawless, creamy skin and brought out the rich, tawny gold in her hair and eyes. Ian knew nothing about women's clothing, but it looked expensive. Had Miranda chosen it for her?

Moira's quick wit and sense of humor did much to calm Ian's frayed nerves.

The majestic ballroom was a larger version of the salon, with similar furnishings and enormous mirrors. Soft music resonated from the keys of a lovely old grand piano and a tall golden harp, where a man and woman entertained Miranda's guests.

Miranda steered Ian around the ballroom, introducing him to elegantly dressed individuals sipping champagne and cocktails, whose names and titles he could never hope to remember. As usual, she was the most exquisite jewel in the room. She literally glowed in a diaphanous white silk sheath that clung softly to her perfect, graceful frame. It wrapped over one shoulder and then flowed out from her body as though carried on a soft, gentle breeze. Her long dark hair had been partially pulled up in the front in loose tendrils and curls and then fell in soft waves to her waist. She reminded Ian of a Greek goddess.

There were about fifty people in attendance, not including those serving drinks and hors d'oeuvres. Most were older, Ian noted, reserved, and distinguished, although Miranda's immediate circle seemed to break that mold. Her friends seemed younger, perhaps in their thirties or forties, and far more *something*. *Athletic? Dangerous?* Ian chided himself. Now he was just being paranoid.

As they approached Lord MacTarran, Ian noticed he seemed to be in a heated discussion with three other men. The conversation broke off abruptly as they drew near.

"Ian!" Lord MacTarran shot him an affable smile. "Lady Thorne." The reserved manner in which he stated her name and the slight mocking bow he bestowed upon Miranda spoke volumes of their strained relationship.

"Lord MacTarran," Miranda returned his greeting. Only the slight elevation of her chin and the cool, icy glint in those pale eyes gave any hint as to her own feelings toward the man. "Gentlemen." She inclined her head toward the other three. "Ian, I would like to introduce you to Lord Macolvy, Lord Emery, and Sir MacCrichton."

"It's very nice to meet you," Ian automatically responded, feeling the tension and noting the sidelong glances shared between the four men.

"And I am very happy to finally meet you, Ian," said Lord Emery, extending his hand to Ian. The other two followed suit. "Daniel and I were at Cambridge together," he continued. "I must say, you are the mirror image of your father. I am so sorry to be meeting you under these circumstances."

Cambridge? Ian had no idea. Everyone, it seemed, knew more about his own father than he did.

"Thank you, Lord Emery," Ian responded again, vaguely wondering if he should say something else. He was blatantly aware of how completely unprepared his upbringing in Hawaii had left him for this type of society. He found himself intensely grateful to Miranda for smoothing over any rough spots in the evening and, if possible, was even more acutely aware of her poise and charm.

How could he ever be expected to take his place at the helm of his father's empire? This was an alien world where Ian knew none of the players and barely understood the social rules of engagement at this highest pinnacle of society. On some level, he felt eerily like he'd done this before, but that illusory sense of déjà vu wasn't enough to give him any comfort or competence.

"If you will excuse us, gentlemen," Miranda intervened, "Ian *must* make the acquaintance of Lady Malbourne before we adjourn for dinner." She guided him quickly away, and Ian was aware of the sharp but barely audible exhale and tightening of her jaw. Glancing over at the goddess-like woman on his arm, he glimpsed the momentary unguarded look of hurt that shone in her eyes.

"Are you all right?" he asked. Even though he wasn't really certain where he stood with her, that fleeting look of distress and vulnerability brought out his protective instincts.

The expression was immediately replaced with one of icy calm. "I'm sorry, Ian. Those men think I killed your father. I can barely abide being in the same room with them."

Her comment jolted him, and for a moment, he scrutinized her flawlessly perfect profile as though he might find the truth there.

She turned to him a little sadly. "I apologize, Ian. I should not have said that in front of you, although you cannot possibly imagine how difficult those men have made the past few years for me." She flashed him a brave smile and changed the subject, guiding him over to Moira.

"And now"—Miranda's eyes suddenly glinted with mischief—"I must have a word with Sir Lawrence. We've prepared a little surprise for you, Ian, and Lawrence has promised to help me."

Ian watched her glide gracefully across the ballroom. She was like a glittering magnet, drawing the gaze of both men and women. She moved easily through the crowd, smiling graciously, stopping to speak briefly with one group or for a polite handshake with another. She was elegant, dignified, and confident. As usual, Miranda left Ian feeling off-balance, confused.

Moira, however, quickly wove her usual magic, and Ian soon found himself relaxed and laughing.

Finally, everyone was ushered from the room, and Miranda returned to Ian, linking her arm through his. With one of her conspiratorial smiles, she led him into the salon, where they were greeted by two men in resplendent Scottish regalia carrying bagpipes under their arms. Ian couldn't remember ever seeing a Scottish piper before and stared at the full ceremonial uniform with great interest.

The men wore dark-green-and-blue plaid kilts, ruffled white shirts under ceremonial jackets with gold embroidery, and matching dark-green-and-blue plaids across their shoulders. The plaids were pinned with large silver brooches that contained gleaming blue stones in their center. A kind of horsehair "purse" hung from their waists, and Miranda whispered archly that it was called a *sporran* and most often used to conceal a flask with a "wee dram of whiskey." White spats covered black shoes, diced hose were secured below the knee, and feather bonnets were perched jauntily on their heads.

As both pipers blew into their bagpipes, a long wailing sound filled the air. One piper moved to the door of the dining room, and Miranda guided Ian to stand about six paces behind the man. Beyond the piper, Ian watched as the already-seated guests rose to their feet.

Oh no! Was he really going to have to enter the dining room this way?

Trying to conceal his rising panic, he glanced at Miranda. *What. The. Hell?* She actually *grinned* at him with such genuine delight that Ian *knew* there was no way of escaping.

The piper led the way slowly into the room, playing a traditional Scottish processional tune, and the other piper fell in behind Miranda and Ian. Ian had no other choice but to go along with their plan.

The small procession proceeded past the standing guests through the magnificently bedecked room. The pipers moved to either side of Ian, and he was guided to the place of honor at the head of the table. Moira was already in place at Ian's left, and Miranda moved into position on Ian's right. As the final, soulful wail of the bagpipes faded away, the guests clapped politely, and everyone took their seats.

Ian's face burned scarlet red. He hated being the center of attention, with all eyes on him. This was supposed to be a birthday treat? He struggled not to tug at the high, tight collar of his tuxedo shirt and shifted uncomfortably in his chair.

Miranda inclined her head graciously, thanking everyone for coming, and the low buzz of conversation gradually resumed. Two tuxedoed waiters made their way around the table, filling wine and champagne glasses.

One asked Moira and Ian if they would like soft drinks instead.

"Coke, if you have it," Ian responded.

"Of course, sir," the waiter said formally.

"None for me," Moira answered with her dimpled smile. "Water'll do me just fine."

Sir Lawrence, who was seated next to Moira, leaned in to Ian and, in a low, amused tone, asked, "So what do you think, Ian? Great fun, yes? Or"—he winked across the table at Miranda—"cruel and unusual punishment?"

"Oh, Lawrence," Miranda gave him an exasperated sigh, and deliberately turned to speak to the man on her right.

"Just wait, Ian. It gets better." Flashing Moira and Ian a cheeky grin, Sir Lawrence lightly tapped a spoon against his water goblet as he rose from the table. The silvery chime brought all eyes to him.

"I've been asked by our lovely hostess, Lady Thorne, to begin our meal with *The Selkirk Grace*. As you are all aware, Lord Ian Thorne, our young guest of honor"—he raised a champagne flute and saluted Ian—"has recently returned to us from America, where he has resided these past twelve years. Sadly, Ian has never had the privilege of experiencing the time-honored ceremony of a Scottish *Burns Supper*. As this esteemed tradition is also a celebration of life, our hostess has deemed it a fitting way of welcoming him home."

Sir Lawrence cleared his throat and arched an eyebrow at Miranda before once more addressing the room in general. "I am certain many of those present are aware that, *most regrettably*, I am not Scottish," he said, sighing dramatically. "However, I will do my best to honor this ceremony with the proper accent it deserves." Raising his champagne glass once more, he recited:

> *Some hae meat and canna eat,*
> *And some wad eat that want it;*
> *But we hae meat, and we can eat,*
> *And sae let the Lord be thankit.*

The grace was met with applause, light laughter, and shouts of "Hear, hear!" Glasses were raised, and the toast was complete. Sir Lawrence took a bow and returned to his seat next to Moira.

Ian raised his eyebrows. *That was it? All that buildup to that silly toast?* Well, fine then. Now at least he could relax.

"Well done, Sir Lawrence," Moira giggled. "Ye've got the accent to a *tee*."

A young woman seated herself at a harp and began softly singing as a rich, creamy soup was served.

"Your chef didn't know how to prepare cock-a-leekie soup, Miranda?" Sir Lawrence's eyes lit with mischief.

"You're evil, Lawrence, and I refuse to be drawn into this dialogue." Miranda laughed indulgently. "Yes, I suppose Jean Claude could have prepared cock-a-leekie soup. However, after I informed him about the haggis and he threatened to throw himself in the loch, I didn't actually have the nerve to ask him."

"Do ye mean, then, to do a *traditional* Burns Supper tonight?" Moira asked with a gurgle of laughter.

"I believe it's customary for special occasions," Miranda smiled. "This is part of Ian's heritage. I had hoped that it would be an interesting experience for him."

"Well, then, Ian," Moira giggled again, those merry brown eyes dancing, "Yer in for a rare treat."

What? The ceremony wasn't over, then? He groaned, wondering what other embarrassing rituals he would be asked to participate in this evening.

After the soup was cleared, everyone was asked to stand, and the bagpipes again led another procession into the room. The two pipers entered, followed by an elegantly tuxedoed man carrying a silver tray with many small glasses of amber liquid. Lastly, strode the puffed-up chef, nose haughtily in the air, carrying a large covered silver tray.

The procession made its way to Ian, and the tray was placed in front of him.

Sir Lawrence moved to stand behind Ian, and as the final notes of the bagpipes sounded, the chef removed the silver cover with a great flourish. Assorted groans, laughter, and whispered comments emanated from the guests.

Ian stared down at what appeared to be a bulky meatloaf shaped into a face of some kind. *A cow?*

"You may all be seated," Sir Lawrence directed. He took a glass of the amber liquid and waited until all the guests were served.

"The things you make me do," he said good-naturedly to Miranda.

Her eyes widened innocently. "Darling," she winked, and a roguish smile played at the corners of her mouth, "I have no idea what you could possibly mean by that."

Shaking his head in mock despair, he lifted his whiskey glass. "*Address to a Haggis,*" Sir Lawrence recited with all the good-humored, theatrical pomp he could muster.

> *Fair fa' your honest, sonsie face,*
> *Great chieftain o' the pudding-race!*
> *Aboon them a'ye tak your place,*
> *Painch, tripe, or thairm:*
> *Weel are ye wordy o'a grace*
> *As lang's my arm."*
>
> *The groaning trencher there ye fill,*
> *Your hurdies like a distant hill,*
> *Your pin wad help to mend a mill*
> *In time o' need ...*

He's got to be kidding! Have I just entered a parallel universe? Ian wondered incredulously.

> *His knife see rustic Labour dight ...*

Sir Lawrence drew a knife and began sharpening it.

> *An' cut you up wi' ready sleight ...*

He plunged the knife into the haggis, to the accompanied laughs, gasps, and groans.

> *Trenching your gushing entrails bright ...*

He cut it end to end, to more laughing and groaning.

Like any ditch;
And then, O what a glorious sight ...

With the knife, he gouged at the haggis, making long, lethal cuts. Some were now finding this uproariously funny, while others were clearly appalled.

Warm-reekin, rich!

Oh, gross! Ian looked at Moira as though Sir Lawrence had lost his mind, while she tried to stifle her amusement with her napkin.

"It's part of the presentation, Ian," Moira chortled. "Have ye ever tried haggis?" she whispered mirthfully.

"I don't think so. Is it good?" he whispered back uncertainly.

"It's ... well ... it's an acquired taste."

"Do you like it?"

"I like it just fine, but I'm used to it."

"What's in the glasses?"

"It's whiskey, to toast the haggis."

"You're kidding, right?"

"Don't be disrespectin' the haggis, Ian," Moira said, laughing.

Ye Pow'rs wha mak mankind your care ...

Sir Lawrence was still reciting.

And dish them out their bill o'fare,
Auld Scotland wants nae shrinking ware
That jaups in luggies;
But, if ye wish her gratefu' prayer,
Gie her a haggis!

Sir Lawrence lifted his glass, as did the rest of the table.

"Gie her a haggis!" They all laughingly hailed in unison and drank their whiskey.

Ian was absolutely speechless. He watched in dismay as a good-size portion was carved and put onto a serving plate.

"And now," Sir Lawrence announced, holding the platter aloft, "the first serving goes to the guest of honor. Happy birthday, Ian." The laden plate of *whatever was in that mush* was ceremoniously placed in front of Ian.

No! No! No! He didn't just give that to me to eat!

"Ah, go on, Ian," Moira urged, laughing still. "It won't hurt ye."

"You're joking, right?"

"Just try it, Ian." She jabbed him good-naturedly with an elbow. "Everybody's watchin'."

"Darling, just take a small taste. You don't have to eat it if you don't like it, but you never know unless you try," Miranda whispered.

Ian's face was crimson. He speared a piece with his fork and placed it in his mouth. He chewed. It was *mushy, gamey, horribly disgusting*—possibly the worst thing he'd ever tasted. As he started to bring his napkin to his mouth, Moira stayed his hand.

"Ian," Moira whispered earnestly, "ye can't spit it out in front of all these people. Just swallow it."

"I can't," Ian whispered miserably, trying not to move his lips. "What should I do?"

"Ian," Moira whispered more sharply. "They're all watchin'. Swallow it if it kills ye!"

Ian swallowed as his stomach lurched. *It probably will kill me,* he thought darkly. He gulped his soft drink to wash the taste from his mouth. He drank more. There was a funny aftertaste in his mouth that wouldn't go away. The cola seemed very sweet, almost too sweet. He reached for his water.

"Brave boy," Miranda teased. "I'm proud of you. They'll serve a bit of haggis to everyone at the table now, Ian, but I doubt very many will eat it. It's not a favorite of anyone but the Scots. We've got a lovely prime rib and mashed potatoes coming next. I'm sure you'll enjoy that."

Ian's stomach felt as though he'd swallowed a rock. The haggis was now trying to come up, and he could barely pay attention to what Miranda was saying. *Prime rib? More meat? No!* He couldn't swallow another thing. Just thinking about it made him want to retch.

Ian was suddenly hot. His face felt flushed, and he was beginning to perspire. His body felt shaky. His head began to throb, and the room seemed to shift and roll as though he were sitting on the deck of a boat.

"This haggis isn't bad," Moira was saying. "Do ye like haggis, Lady Thorne?"

"I've never cared for it, I'm afraid. The young people here all seem to enjoy the ceremony of the haggis, though, and so I thought Ian might find it entertaining."

Ian could barely focus on what was being said. He had to excuse himself. He knew he was going to be sick. As he tried to rise, Moira exclaimed in alarm, "Ian, are ye all right? Yer white as a sheet."

"I'll be fine," he mumbled. "I ... I just need some fresh air."

"Oh dear," Miranda remarked. "The haggis isn't sitting well with you?"

"No, I'm f-fine. J-just, uh—excuse me for a moment."

Ian swayed as he made his way out of the dining room. Somehow, he got himself up the stairs and to his room. He fell across his bed as chills and waves of nausea racked his body. His head pounded, and his stomach was on fire. His body shuddered as a blistering inferno scorched his insides. He floated deliriously on a sea of pain for he knew not how long.

"Ian?" Mrs. MacShane stood over him. "Ian?" Her voice was far away. "*Ian, are ye all right?*"

She was there as if in a dream. He couldn't answer. He felt cool hands on his forehead. He felt his body repositioned on the bed. His jacket was stripped away, and he heard another voice in the room. "Ian!" She was shaking him. He just wanted to close his eyes and sleep. "Ian! Ye've got ta sit up! Listen ta me." He drifted. "Ian!" She was shaking him again. "Ye've been *poisoned*. We've got ta get ye outta here."

He heard the voices of the two bodyguards challenging someone. There was a scuffle, a strangled curse, and then a thump as a body hit the floor. A second thump followed, and he heard a man from a long way off saying he needed to tie someone up in the bathroom.

"The solstice is no' till tomorrow." Mrs. MacShane's announcement bordered on hysteria. "Ye'll be needin' *her* ta help ye get across tonight."

"I've placed the queen in the center of the board, but it's not like making a phone call, Maigrid," said the hard, clipped male voice. "It could be hours ... or days."

He was repositioned once more. "Áedan! He's not goin' ta last! He needs the *Talis of Tara!* Now! Hurry, Áedan! Is it still hidden in the frame?"

Ian heard the sound of shattered glass as the picture frame by the bed was smashed. "I've got it, Maigrid. It's here."

A chain or necklace of some kind was slipped over his head, and a silvery medallion glinted in the light. Almost immediately, his pain lessened and a soothing sense of calm stole through his body.

"Áedan," Mrs. MacShane cried frantically, "we've got ta get him away from here now!"

Strong arms lifted him, and Ian hazily registered that they were in a dark, narrow passage of some sort. He groaned, nearly vomiting as they traversed seemingly endless sets of stairs.

Ian dreamed of cool air and rain on his face. He was being half-carried, half-dragged by someone, and they were running. He smelled the wet grass and the earthy, verdant scent of the forest. He registered the faint scent of woodsmoke and spice. Through a haze of pain, he perceived brilliant blue eyes blazing out of a strong, determined face framed with wild black hair. The man carrying him was breathing hard, but his stride didn't falter.

He heard Mrs. MacShane cry out, and then icy waves broke over his head. He was suddenly submerged in frigid liquid. He registered shock as his lungs flooded with water. He was drowning! Arms like steel imprisoned him against a broad chest. He struggled against the unyielding bands trapping him beneath the waves.

He kicked and flailed. His head barely cleared the surface before he was again pulled under. Choking, sputtering, his deprived lungs desperately pleaded for air. He was in the loch! *Oh, god! No! His nightmare had come to life!* Even as he fought his captor, a part of his mind accepted the inevitable. This was how it ended. He was going to die here in this wretchedly cold, watery grave, *just like his father.*

CHAPTER VII
THE VEILED ISLE

Ian drifted. He heard soft music, almost like a woman's voice, carried on the wind. She called to him from far away, whispered for him to come to her. She sang to him in a pure, clear, lilting voice that echoed in his mind. *Come to me, Ian, come to me.*

Ian tried but couldn't reach her. He searched for her but couldn't find her. Her ethereal melody was at first a silken thread, fragile and impossible to grab ahold of, her unbroken clarion chant unremitting. *Ian, I'm here,* she called. *Reach for me. Come to me, Ian, come to me.* Her music wrapped him in golden warmth. Her voice became a lifeline, and then an anchor, a siren's song that both sheltered and beckoned. Ian struggled to reach her. He fought against the shadowy depths that consumed him.

Other voices found him. Another shimmering light reached out to him. This one seemed so familiar, like the other, but not. His soul moved joyfully toward it, brushing softly against its essence. Its feel was bittersweet and reminded him of sadness and loss. He reluctantly drifted away, but it wrapped him in silvery threads and rewove those that had been broken. It anchored him more securely and brought him carefully and more fully into the keeping of the music of the *golden angel*. Whispers and murmurs invaded his dream, but his golden angel continued to sing to him, continued to beckon and entreat.

Finally, she appeared in a bright golden light, peaceful and calming to his battered spirit. Silvery blond hair that trailed to the floor flowed out from a radiant, compassionate face. Brilliant blue eyes, bluer than any Ian had ever seen, looked into his soul. Her visage was one of gentle serenity. She truly was an angel, but without the wings. A long flowing white dress wafted and fanned from her slender body, carried on a breeze he couldn't feel. *Be at ease, Ian,* he heard in his mind.

Am I dead? he wondered.

You are safe, Ian. You are home, he again heard in his mind.

Home? She hadn't really answered his question. *Am I ... in heaven?*

She delicately stroked his face. Her touch was as soft as a butterfly's wing, but Ian felt healing strength and warmth infuse his body.

Rest, child. All will be well, she told him, and he did.

A gentle, perfumed breeze caressed his fevered skin. Arms cradled him, lifting his head so that he could swallow a sweet, refreshing drink. "A little at a time," a soothing, dulcet voice crooned. "This will help you. Take what you can. Soon your strength will return."

Ian swallowed slowly as his raw, parched throat was bathed in a light, honeyed liquid. He tried to open his eyes but failed. He was simply too tired. He drifted dreamlessly in a gentle sea of pale, luminous colors. Time fell away as he glided over endless azure oceans. Sometimes his angel's incandescent blue eyes harbored him from the burning and pain in his body as he struggled toward consciousness. Always, she guided him back to a place of safety.

Ian felt as though he swam laboriously up through deep, dense water. His limbs seemed heavy and sluggish. He persisted until his movements were easier, freer. Finally, he pulled away from the impenetrable depths that swallowed him. Slowly, he became aware of the cheerful sounds of birds as they frolicked in nearby branches. In the distance, the sound of waves crashed over a shore—or was it a waterfall? The water's mellifluous music was steady and unremitting, adding a fresh, moist aura to the air.

Luxuriant, billowy wafts shepherded the fragrant scents of jasmine and honeysuckle and deep-green woodlands to his awakening senses. His closed eyelids registered the golden dappled light coursing over him in a gentle ebb and flow. His fingers moved lightly over the silken fabric that covered him. His body felt airy and insubstantial, but not uncomfortable.

Ian's eyelids fluttered open. Gentle rays of sunlight shafted through a green canopy of leaves, creating intricate shadows over the creamy, carved arches and domed ceiling of the room where he lay. The tall gothic arches boasted no glass, leaving the room open to the gossamer breezes that sighed through the green curtained leaves outside and gave him the impression of being in a tree house.

Light scattered itself in silver and gold glints over the rich celadon silk that covered him. He wore a strange garment made of the same pale green, with gold embroidery at the high rounded neckline and cuffs of the long sleeves. As he pushed back the coverlet, he saw that the tunic reached to nearly midthigh, and he was also wearing loose breeches in a similar but sturdier fabric.

Ian felt no alarm at finding himself in this strange and beautiful room, only peace. He had no desire to attempt to sit up or move from this place of immense comfort in which he found himself. The vibrant sounds of nature were soothing to his battered body and spirit. He shifted to his side and saw that the low bed on which he lay was beautifully carved, like the rest of the room. Its pale stone resembled intricately twined tree branches that met and burst into fronds and leaves and flowers above his head.

Eight elegant gothic arches rose from the floor like the points of a crown, and the circular dome of the ceiling balanced delicately on top. The arches more closely resembled doorways than windows, and the room actually reminded Ian of a small temple.

Beyond the arches, Ian saw terraces and gently sloping paths and stairways that led to other templelike structures at varying elevations. The effect was of a giant carved tree of ivory stone with many graceful domed structures perched amid its strong and massive branches.

Willows and climbing, flowering vines of honeysuckle, jasmine, and roses tumbled over the arched domed edifices, balustrades, and terraced walls, providing privacy and perfuming the air.

The soft rustle and swish of fabric alerted Ian to the entrance of an inordinately lovely tall blond girl carrying a silver pitcher and a golden goblet. Condensation glistened over the curved surface of the pitcher, as if its contents were very cold.

"You return to us at last, Ian," she smiled, pouring some of the liquid into the goblet before placing them both on a small vine-like table next to the bed.

She had an alluring heart-shaped face with wide sky blue eyes, a small pert nose, and soft, full mouth. Long, filmy layers of flowing coral-and-red silk clung to her body, flowing out from slender hips to trail behind her on the floor as she walked. The neckline and long narrow sleeves of the coral underdress were richly embroidered in gold, and the sleeveless crimson oversheath fell in an inverted V from her knees so that it was shorter in the front than in the back. She wore a wide gold jeweled belt low around her hips, and a golden jeweled circlet over her forehead held back long shining hair. She reminded Ian of a princess from the time of King Arthur.

"He wakes," the girl called to someone beyond Ian's line of sight.

"I felt him," answered a lovely, melodic voice, and then the angel from his dreams glided to the side of his bed. A soft, luminous light emanated from her, filling the room with a radiant warmth as the shadows retreated. Cool fingers touched his cheek, and the brilliant, incandescent blue eyes he remembered from his delirium met his own bemused blue gaze with tender affection.

Just as she had appeared in his dreams, a long white flowing dress sheathed her slender body. She, like the other young woman, also wore a wide golden belt low on her hips, and a golden circlet held back floor-length platinum-blond hair. In the center of the circlet was a single shimmering white stone in the shape of a teardrop.

She was exquisite, dazzling, even more spellbinding than Miranda. Pale eyebrows arched slightly over those stunning blue eyes. Her alabaster skin was soft and luminous, like smooth, shimmery satin. High cheekbones in a regal oval face sloped to a full, voluptuous mouth. A straight nose and strong but utterly feminine jaw and chin made up the most perfect, classically beautiful features Ian had ever seen.

He thought it was impossible for any woman to be more magnificent than the one standing before him. She exuded strength, wisdom, and a kind of raw power that was almost paralyzing. Only the compassion and kindness in her astonishing blue eyes prevented Ian from shrinking before the overwhelming force of her presence.

And there was something about her that spoke to his soul. Some long-forgotten memories tugged at his consciousness, but he could not retrieve them. They remained disconcertingly out of reach, just beneath the surface.

"You thirst." It was a statement, as if she already knew the answer. "Come." She lifted the goblet and then sat next to him on the bed. "Partake of this. It will do much to restore you to health."

The other young woman helped him sit, while the angel held the goblet to his mouth. Ian cupped his hands around the heavy chalice and drank deeply of the cool minted, honeyed beverage.

"Where am I?" he asked in a voice gravelly with misuse as he handed back the empty cup. Already, he was infused with a curative vitality. The residual ache in his body began to fall away, and the weakness in his limbs was replaced with the promise of renewed vigor. The heavy fog of exhaustion withdrew as his mind cleared.

"You are safe," she said simply in her serene, lyrical voice.

Both women spoke with a soft, lilting accent that he couldn't place.

"That wasn't really an answer," Ian mildly reproved as he evaluated the strange beauty all around him. He tried again. "How long have I been here?"

"Not long." Once again, her answer was cryptic, though her voice and manner maintained that unruffled serenity.

"Okaaay." Little warning bells were beginning to sound in his mind as the haze lifted from his brain and some semblance of strength returned to his body. He noted the cloaked, sidelong looks the other woman was giving him.

Ian pushed himself up so that he could sit higher in his bed. Even that small effort drained any energy the sweet mint drink had supplied. His forehead beaded with tiny drops of sweat. Still, he needed to understand what he was doing in this place with these unusual women. He needed to know what had happened to him. Though he searched his brain, he couldn't seem to remember how he might have come to be in such an exotic environment.

"Maybe we should begin again," Ian said as calmly as he could. After the events of the past few days, his skills of diplomacy were wearing thin. "I would very much appreciate it if you could tell me where I am." His voice was polite but now had a distinct edge to it.

"It is not that I am disinclined to answer you, Ian. It is simply that the information you seek is perhaps more complicated than you might believe." Again, that serene, unperturbed composure as she dismissed his question. It was beginning to alarm him.

"Try me." He looked unflinchingly into her neon-blue eyes.

"You presently reside within the *Mountain Court of the Veiled Isle*. As to how long you have been here, time means little in this place," she continued vaguely. "We do not reckon the passage of time as in the mortal realm."

"*Mortal realm?*" Clearly, he was still dreaming, or one of *them* was delusional. Ian was inclined to believe that he was the one hallucinating, given the current state of his health. He glanced around at the carved temple in which he now resided, the sweeping, graceful landscape beyond the tall, stately arches of his room, and the two dazzling women who now shared his company.

"This is not a dream, Ian. Soon, much will become clear."

Can you read my mind? Ian wondered, looking intently into her eyes.

"Yes, Ian, I know your thoughts."

That snapped his mind to attention. "Well, that's just ... uncomfortable," he muttered as he fell more deeply into her blue gaze. "Who are you?" The last was barely above a whisper.

You know me. You have always known me, Ian heard her voice in his head. *I have always watched over you. We were together often when you were a child. When you were taken across the vast oceans, far from your home, I came to you in your dreams. Search your memories, Ian. You will find me there.*

"I am called Niamh," she said aloud. She rose. "Soon we will open your memories, and then you will understand."

What the hell? Ian wondered before he could stop himself, highly disconcerted with the effect she had on him and the idea of Niamh knowing what he was thinking.

"Open my ... memories?" he asked aloud. "What does that mean, anyway? What do I need to *understand* that you can't tell me now?"

"Rest, Ian," she said gently. "All will become clear."

He could actually *feel* her subtly willing him to relax. He wanted to obey her, to close his eyes and slide back into that still, tranquil safety of his dream state before he had awakened, but he fought it, pushing back.

"Why are you afraid to tell me the truth about what is happening here?" He was becoming agitated. If he had felt stronger, he might have risen from the bed and tried to find a way out of this place.

Niamh's golden light grew brighter, engulfing him like a warm, safe blanket. Part of his mind registered the sedative-like effect it was having on him, but the other injured, exhausted part of him was beyond caring. He laid his head back against the soft cushions of his bed.

"I am Caitria," the other woman said, lightly touching his arm. "I will not be far, should you require anything or should you wish to rise. I will return with broth to break your fast."

"Can you read my mind too?" he asked resignedly. He knew he should be concerned by this bizarre situation, but his mind, like his body, felt slow, anaesthetized, drugged maybe.

"A little. Not like Niamh."

Ian wearily closed his eyes. Perhaps when he awoke, he would be back in his bed at school, or even in the nursery at Thorne Manor. Clearly, despite the assurances of the mysterious blond angel, who, if he was entirely truthful, seemed very familiar to him, he was having one heck of a crazy dream. Or maybe someone had slipped him a hallucinogenic drug. That seemed about as likely as anything else.

"Áedan arrives." Niamh smiled gently at Ian as his feathery black lashes fluttered open. "He will wish to see you."

Both women greeted the tall, imposing raven-haired man who had apparently saved Ian's life and then withdrew from the room. The lacy shadows again encroached, and the chamber felt almost bereft as Niamh's golden glow retreated with her.

Ian gaped at the stranger. A jolt of adrenaline raced through his veins, jump-starting his heart and giving him a renewed spike of energy. This was the first time he had actually seen the face of the man who had rescued him.

It was like looking in a mirror!

Startling blue eyes blazed out of a strong, handsome face. The man was a few years older, maybe twenty, taller and more muscular, but beyond that, he could have been Ian's twin.

Ian no longer had to wonder what he would look like when he was fully grown. His twenty-year-old self was standing in front of him.

The man wore a long-sleeved, high-necked tunic and fitted trousers, similar to Ian's unusual garb, but in unrelieved black. The pants were tucked into high black boots, and a heavy belt cinched his trim waist, emphasizing narrow hips and broad, muscular shoulders. An ornate jeweled dirk was sheathed at his side. His long hair was tied back, and although his appearance was almost *courtly*, there was a sense of something wild and even dangerous about him.

"So, Ian, you've met *Niamh the Radiant*. What did you think?" he asked with a disarming grin. His menacing countenance changed completely with that smile. Deep dimples gave him a boyish appearance, and mischief lit his eyes.

As Ian continued to stare, completely at a loss for words, he spoke again. "We haven't been formally introduced, Ian. I am Áedan." He looked gravely into Ian's eyes and continued. "I am your brother."

Ian felt as though the wind had been knocked from his body. For a moment, he couldn't catch his breath. "I … I don't understand," he finally stammered. "How is that possible?"

Could this *Áedan* really be telling the truth? Ian searched desperately for some fragment of information from his past that would make sense of all this. Nothing in his memories from his early life had even remotely prepared him for this situation. His father had another son? He had an older brother? Why hadn't anyone told him? He wouldn't have been alone after his father's death. He wouldn't have felt so *abandoned*.

Áedan casually leaned his tall frame against a twining stone column and levelly assessed Ian. "I know this situation seems difficult to comprehend, Ian, and it is, in truth, a little … complicated. However, I will try to answer some of your questions."

Ian attempted to force his mind to function properly but, in the end, could only continue to stare at the raven-haired stranger with the face of a dark angel.

"Why didn't I know about you?" he finally managed to say. Outwardly, Ian appeared calm; however, the mistrustful tenor of his voice and the underlying tension in his body were unmistakable.

"Ahh," Áedan thoughtfully regarded the distraught young man in the bed. Ian had dark shadows beneath his eyes and had lost some weight from his ordeal. The trauma of fighting off the poison, along with the uncertainty of his present situation, was very apparent in the strain that showed on his youthful face. "Did Niamh say anything to you about opening your memories?"

"Yes. What does that mean?" Ian asked warily.

Áedan appeared to be evaluating Ian and considering what or how much he should say about the subject.

"You are not quite who you think you are, Ian."

Obviously. If it was true that he had a brother, what else hadn't he known about himself and his family?

"Your memories were bound when you were a baby so that you would have no knowledge of this world or its people until you were old enough to understand the significance of your heritage."

"Why?" he challenged. "Why wouldn't *our people* want me to know who I am? And actually, *Áedan*, I don't understand how something like that is even possible—*binding* my memories, I mean."

Ian scrutinized his doppelganger closely, waiting for him to continue.

"You and I are not exactly ... *mortal*," Áedan said carefully, watching Ian closely for his reaction. "We are members of an ancient race known throughout history as the *Tuatha dé Dannan*."

"Uh-huh." Ian didn't even attempt to disguise his skepticism.

"Our people are the guardians of this realm, which is not part of the human world," Áedan continued as though Ian had made no comment.

Ian nodded as though in agreement, all the while searching the immediate area for an escape route just in case. Did this guy really believe what he was saying, or was this some kind of an elaborate joke?

"Two separate bridges between our worlds exist, both hidden and protected within the boundaries of lands owned by our family. The lands and holdings of the Thorne Estate have guarded the gateways to this *otherworld* for centuries."

The mention of the *Thorne Estate* caught Ian's attention. Was this something to do with his father's will? he mulled suspiciously.

"*Seriously, Áedan,* you expect me to believe this?"

Áedan pinned Ian with those startling blue eyes. "Yes, Ian, I do. You are presently in the Mountain Court of the Tuatha, which is far beyond the boundaries of the mortal realm, and all who dwell here are powerful immortal beings."

Ian let out a long, slow breath and assessed Áedan with a quiet dignity and self-possession far beyond his years. Normally, he was reserved and thoughtful, using his intellect to his advantage, quietly assessing his situation instead of blurting out his thoughts. But it seemed the filters between his mouth and brain had ceased to function. And Ian was so tired of being lied to, of being moved around like a chess piece on a board.

"You know, earlier I was thinking I might be crazy," he said bluntly, "but you all are kind of ... well ... certifiable."

Áedan lifted one winged black eyebrow and, with somber blue eyes, announced simply, "I know it sounds that way. Look, Ian," he said seriously. I realize this is all but impossible to believe. And yes, it sounds completely crazy, but *look* around you. You can see the truth of what I'm saying. You can *feel the Magic* of this world."

Ian did actually have to admit that this place *felt different*. There was a tingle of something in the air, a crackle of power that imbued everything with a kind of vibrant energy. There was a nearly tangible undercurrent of something primitive and intense, almost like lightning before a thunderstorm, though subtler.

The air *smelled* different here too. And somehow, deep inside, Ian felt the truth of Áedan's words. This world called to him like an old friend, but denial sprang forth immediately. This was so far beyond anything a *sane* person could believe, *should* believe.

"So you said we're not exactly ... mortal," Ian said guardedly. "Are you really telling me that *we, both you and I,* are *immortal?*" Again, Ian's probing, steady gaze examined Áedan's inscrutable face.

Áedan gave an imperceptible nod.

"You expect me to believe that I am *immortal?*" Ian asked in disbelief. "I'm just like everyone else I know. I'm still growing, I get bruises, I bleed, my body is still constantly changing, and I don't have any special abilities."

"You have just turned seventeen. Of course you're still growing, and in the outer world, you are far more susceptible to injury. But you have more innate Power than you know. And had you not been sent away from Scotland, we would have already helped you become acquainted with who you are."

Áedan forged ahead before Ian could voice his protest.

"Your memories were bound when you were an infant for your own protection and should have been reopened long before now. I suspect you've had strange dreams all your life, and as you've gotten older, they have become progressively more persistent and realistic."

Ian went very still as the reality of Áedan's words came crashing down upon him. The reference to his dreams hit home.

"Yeah," Ian acknowledged grudgingly, expelling another long, slow breath. "My dreams have been pretty interesting lately." *That's putting it mildly,* he thought without humor.

"So you're telling me I'm not *Ian Thorne* but some kind of … of … *alien* … or something from this other realm?" Ian seared Áedan with his intense blue gaze, as if to pull the truth from his very soul.

There was a subtle but noticeable hesitation before Áedan responded. "Of course you're Ian Thorne."

Ian's eyes narrowed. Something in the way he answered didn't ring true. "But there's more to this, right? Who were my parents? How could my dad be immortal? He's *dead*, Áedan. Haven't you heard?"

"Your father was a great man, but he was mortal."

"So my mother …"

"You are the son of an immortal goddess," Áedan replied calmly.

Ian sat in a dazed silence for a moment. "My father was married to a … *goddess?*" He nearly laughed aloud. This was becoming more far-fetched by the moment.

Áedan merely watched him with that inscrutable expression that made all of Ian's defensive instincts flare.

Ian struggled to wrap his mind around this information. *Impossible,* he decided in a kind of incredulous disbelief, his intellect riding him hard. If any of this was true—*big emphasis on the if*—his father had really been keeping a lot of secrets. *And,* Ian mused his way through this hypothetical story, *he must have really been an astonishing man.* How did a person, a *mortal*, go about meeting a goddess, let alone having a child, *children*, with one? Surely, he would have remembered something from his childhood to indicate his life was a little *unusual*. He certainly didn't remember ever meeting his real mother. He had believed his father when he said she was dead. Ian was now more certain than ever that he was dreaming, but he had to ask. "Are you my full-blooded brother?"

"Yes." His answer was brief, but Ian again had the sense that Áedan was hiding something.

"Okay, I'll play, Áedan." Ian arched a black-winged eyebrow. "So we are supposedly immortal," Ian stated, giving Áedan a look clearly filled with skepticism, "but I almost died."

"Actually, we are half. We have many of the same strengths, but not all. And even immortals can be killed in the outer world. It was close with you, Ian."

Ian's temple began to throb as the events leading to his arrival resurfaced freshly in his mind. "I was poisoned, and you and Mrs. MacShane saved me. But who poisoned me?" His head was reeling as he tried to reassemble the events of that last night.

Áedan shrugged almost angrily. "Miranda. But we will speak of this later, Ian. There are some things I would like to tell you now to prepare you for your time here."

Miranda? No! He didn't want it to be true! He had wanted to believe her. He had wanted to trust her, but a part of him had known. A deep sadness tore at his heart before he harshly chained it down. He realized he had let himself hope for some semblance of a family, and it was all a lie. Ian allowed the cold fist of self-preservation to slam down on his emotions. He ruthlessly thrust the hardened inner shell that had fostered him through his early years firmly back in place.

"Wait, Áedan," Ian frowned, "how did we get here? I remember being at dinner, and suddenly, I felt really sick. Then ... you and Mrs. MacShane were helping me. We were running, and then I was ... *drowning! You threw me in the loch!*" Ian accused indignantly, abruptly pushing himself up in an attempt to rise from the bed.

"No, Ian, I did not throw you in the loch." Áedan sighed and moved forward, placing his hands on Ian's shoulders. He gently guided the glowering young man back down, forcing Ian to look directly into his eyes. He lowered his powerful body onto the edge of the bed, sitting just far enough away that Ian could not easily reach him with a fist should that become his intention. Ian's emotions were unstable at best, and he really couldn't blame him.

"In order to save you, it was necessary to bring you to Niamh. It is not easy to gain entry into this world, and I had to open the way quickly. There was an amulet hidden in the frame of the photograph you have always kept with you. I used it to call to Niamh but still needed to get you across the loch to the Castle Island. She met us there at the gateway."

The Castle Island? Ian remembered nothing of that. "So ... we swam?" Ian asked in confusion. His head was beginning to ache.

"No. I had a rowboat moored under the old pier. It couldn't be seen from the shore, but we had to swim beneath the pier to reach it. I'm sorry, Ian, if you believed I would harm you. I was afraid we would be discovered at any minute and needed to get you away quickly."

Ian listened in numbed silence as Áedan continued, "I know you are tired, Ian, but before you rest, let me tell you a little about our people."

"Our people?"

"Yes, Ian. Our people." Áedan stretched out his long legs and shifted into a more comfortable position. His tone was mild, but the underlying importance of the information he was imparting was clear.

"Have you ever read any of the myths of the early inhabitants of Scotland and Ireland?" he asked, a kind of quizzical expression on his face.

"Not really," Ian answered, his brain now pounding out a brutal, hammering beat in rhythm with his heart. "Obviously, growing up, I had a fascination with the history of Scotland, seeing as how I was born here ... uh ... there," he said, correcting himself hesitantly, trying to focus on Áedan instead of the bruising tattoo in his head. "But," he shrugged, his words slowing and becoming slightly slurred, "after a while, it seemed less important. I may have read something in ... um ... passing or in a literature class, but ... honestly, for some reason, reading about Scottish ... uh ... history always gave me ... a ... uhm ... headache." he finished vaguely.

"That is probably because it triggered memories that were bound and your brain was attempting to retrieve them," Áedan said, watching him more closely. "It is truly a shame that you were deprived so thoroughly of your heritage," he added sadly. "It seems you may be in need of a brief history lesson, though I am not certain you are up to it just now."

"You want to give me a history lesson?" Ian asked, incredulity etched into his young features. He rubbed his eyes and then pressed the fingers of both hands against his temples, stark exhaustion leaching all color from his skin. "I think I'm done for now, Áedan," he said blearily. His head was really throbbing now. As much as he wanted to ask more questions of Áedan, he could no longer brace himself against the *headache from hell*. He shut his eyes against the light that was now sending spikes of lightning into his brain and shuddered as his entire body tensed against the stabbing, rhythmic assault.

A swish of fabric told him that Caitria had returned. He looked at her through half-closed eyes as he struggled to force air into his lungs between the rapid searing bouts of bone-deep, pulsing pain.

Caitria took one glance at Ian and immediately rushed to his side. She allowed her displeasure to show on her angelic face as she turned to Áedan.

"You spoke of things that should have waited." Her tone was polite, but Ian registered the underlying reprimand.

Áedan cocked an arched eyebrow. "He must be told something, Caitria." His tone was polite as well, however, contained no hint of apology.

"Not until he is further recovered," she insisted. Caitria placed warm, gentle hands on Ian's forehead, and immediately, he felt the throbbing headache lessen.

"Rest well, Ian," Áedan said gently. "I am sorry you have had to learn of our world in this manner. I will return when you are stronger."

"Áedan should not have spoken to you of your history." Caitria's voice was as soothing and gentle as tinkling bells on a cool, light breeze. "If you attempt to force your memories, you will experience pain. Your knowledge of our world must be unbound in the proper manner."

"I asked him questions, and he answered some of them. I don't think he intended to hurt me." Ian felt the strong urge to defend Áedan. He'd just found out he had a brother, and though he had denied it to Áedan, he was beginning to believe all that he had told him. That knowledge was worth any pain he might have suffered in the revealing of the truth.

"Shhh, now. Let me help you. You will break your fast, and then you must rest." Caitria was suddenly the stern healer.

As soon as he swallowed a bit of the warm, salty broth, Ian fell into a deep, exhausted sleep. Blond angels—no, goddesses; no, *angels*—kept him company in his dreams. They sang lulling, healing chants with their silvery, clarion voices and promised him all would be well.

He awoke once more, feeling infinitely better than the first time. His gaze swept the now-shadowed room, noting he was still in this strange and beautiful *otherworld*. He felt far more alert but astonishingly calm. He was still here, so his dreams had been real. Probably.

Niamh, as though aware he had just awakened, entered with a goblet filled with the cool, refreshing minted drink that had revived him earlier. Her smile filled the shadows with sunshine as she seated herself on the bed beside him.

"You are much recovered," she said softly as she offered him the goblet. "Drink slowly, and then we will see if you are able to rise."

Her neon-blue eyes watched him thoughtfully as she helped him hold the chalice while he sipped its contents. Immediately, its rejuvenating properties hit his system. His head cleared, and his body felt as though he had never been ill.

"The effects will not hold," she warned. "You will feel stronger for a short time, but this new vigor will level out quickly. You will feel better, but not entirely healed. It will take a little more time for you to completely regain your strength."

Are you still in my head? he asked silently.

Yes. I apologize for this intrusion, but it is necessary that I monitor you during your illness. It is the only way I can be certain you are receiving what you require to become well.

Why are you helping me?

You are a child of the Tuatha.

Ian nodded, acknowledging the irony of the situation. No longer was he questioning his sanity. Or theirs. It seemed he believed Áedan's tall tale, and he was cautiously accepting his presence here.

"Am I a prisoner here?" he asked, testing his boundaries. "I'd like to get out of this bed now, if it's all right with you."

"Ian," she said gently, "you are free to go anywhere you would like as soon as you are able, though there are some things you must understand about this world. Why would you believe yourself to be imprisoned?"

"I can't imagine, *Niamh*. Are you going to knock me out again?"

She tilted her head, regarding him with those inhuman, neon eyes. "Ahhh, I understand. You were upset when I helped you rest. I merely calmed you so you might heal."

"You took away my free will."

"You were distraught," she said serenely. "I but calmed you. It is my nature. You cannot heal properly without rest." She said this so simply, as though explaining it to an unreasonable child.

Had he been acting unreasonably? Maybe. He was normally far more easygoing with people, strategic in his approach to adversity, preferring to assess situations before becoming confrontational. He hadn't been acting like himself lately. This whole situation since his arrival in Scotland, and *beyond*, had definitely pushed him to the limits of his control. Almost everything he had encountered recently had been like a trip down the rabbit hole, and he simply didn't trust it. And Niamh was so ... how did he even begin to put her into any kind of equation?

Her manner was so warm and compassionate, benevolent and caring, that he felt truly awful about challenging her. But it was that same feeling of safety that she instilled, of wanting to agree with her and do whatever it took to please her, that he didn't trust. He already knew she could control him if she wanted to.

"What *things* do I need to understand, Niamh?" he asked. "You said that once before but then refused to answer me."

She sighed. "You were not strong enough. You do not realize how ill you have been, and I did not want to tax you further."

"I'm fine now."

"Yes, for the moment, though you will tire quickly." She sighed once more as he made to protest. "It is not my intent to distress you, Ian. I will tell you what I can."

He arched an eyebrow as she placed her hand on his forehead and then stroked back his tousled dark hair. She traced her fingers lightly over his cheek and jawline and then returned to smoothing back his hair. The touch was strangely intimate, yet she seemed not to notice.

Maybe because like Caitria, she was a healer and touching just came naturally. Though as he thought about it, Caitria's touch was rare and always highly impersonal.

He really didn't know what to think about Niamh. She was a complete enigma, like nothing he had ever imagined existed anywhere in the world. Maybe, as he had imagined before, she was some kind of angel. She had strange and truly awesome abilities, and he somehow recognized that those he had experienced were just the tip of the iceberg. She was beautiful, mysterious, intimidating, and yet at the same time, compassionate and caring.

She was a puzzle, a paradox, formal yet warm, reserved yet completely comfortable invading his space. It was that contradiction that kept him off-balance with her, that underlying power and that aura of being completely untouchable. Ian couldn't imagine anyone being foolish enough to even accidentally brush against her without her permission.

A thought began to form in the back of his head, but he had to be wrong. *Hadn't Áedan said something about ... He'd had so many other things on his mind he hadn't pushed, but—no, it was impossible. She was far too young, close to the same age as Áedan, and it certainly wasn't the kind of thing one asked a complete stranger.*

Niamh had tilted her head for a moment, that mysterious Mona Lisa smile playing about her mouth. Was she listening to his scrambled thoughts again? If she was, she gave no indication as she finally began to address some of his questions.

"As you move about in this realm, Ian, the things you see and some of those individuals you meet here will trigger memories. When that happens, you may find yourself once more in pain. Your memories are bound. If you try too hard to push through the block, you may be uncomfortable, as you discovered earlier when Áedan spoke with you. You may go wherever you wish among our people, but until your memories are reopened, one of our healers will be nearby at all times, should you have need of them."

Hmm, babysitters? Or jailers? Ian wondered before he could stop himself. He was becoming paranoid again that she was reading his every thought, and it was ridiculous. He couldn't stop thinking, so he just needed to go with whatever was happening here. For now.

"Bound? Reopened?" he asked aloud. "What does that mean exactly?"

"You were sent into the mortal realm as a baby," Niamh said in that pure, musical voice of hers that drew him in and lowered his defenses like nothing else he had ever experienced. "As a child of the Tuatha, you wield great Power and your intellect is vast. Even though Magic no longer exists in the mortal realm, you would have retained ties to your heritage and memories of your past. Too much knowledge at a very young age is not always ideal, especially if others do not exhibit the same tendencies. Your differences would have set you apart from others until you were old enough to understand they must be guarded. Your memories of the Tuatha and certain others"—she hedged, though she looked him fully in the eye, and he could tell she was not going to elaborate about whatever *certain others* meant—"were bound before you entered that other realm, both for your protection and ours."

"Bound?" he repeated.

"Buried so deeply within your mind that you would not remember without help," she answered. "This allowed you to grow up among the mortals of that world free of responsibility for a time, as much a human child as possible. Had circumstances been different, you would have been aware of our world, of your true origins no later than the age of eight. We would have begun to open your memories at that time. They would have been fully unchained by sixteen."

He let out a long, slow breath. *All right, then.* He had asked for that, but this was a lot to take in.

"What kind of memories could I have had that were so important to *bind* if I was only a baby when I left? And why was I sent there?"

"Things will become clear to you soon," she said in that cryptic way of hers.

"When will you *unbind* my memories?"

"Soon."

"Why do you do that?" he asked, cocking his head to one side as he puzzled her out. "Refuse to answer me?"

"It is for—"

"For my own good?" he interrupted in exasperation.

"Yes." She smiled warmly.

"All right, Niamh." He ruefully returned her smile, shaking his head in defeat. It was like bashing himself against a rock to get anything out of her. Áedan had been far more forthcoming. He'd have far better luck there, he decided, and it would be much less frustrating. She was certainly like no woman he had ever before encountered, but he had to admire and like her despite her aggravating tendency to dismiss his questions. "It's fine," he returned with resigned amusement, "for now."

"Perhaps you would like to bathe. It will be a good test of your strength. I will help you rise, and we will see if you are strong enough to walk to the bathing chamber. Áedan will assist you, if you so desire."

Ian didn't exactly feel dirty. Someone must have cleaned him up at some point while he was unconscious, which he didn't even want to think about, but it would feel good to wash off the poison he could feel eking out of his pores and the lethargy that still permeated his bones and hazed his mind.

"A bath sounds great, thanks. I don't need Áedan to help me, though."

"The warm bathing pools will be much too far for you to walk to this first time, I think. Your bathing chamber is only a few steps away, though it sits under the spray that falls from the high mountain peaks. Without Magic, the water is cold—freezing, actually—so at the very least, he can warm it and then wait for you outside."

She seemed at least to understand his need for privacy while he washed. Ian didn't even want to think about how awkward that situation would have been if she insisted that someone stand over him in the bathroom.

Áedan walked behind him across a narrow-columned bridge leading from his room. It was open to the elements except for the roof but made completely private by draping vines and trees. As Niamh had said, it wasn't far, perhaps only twenty feet away, but the incline was fairly steep, and he was out of breath before they reached their destination.

The bathing chamber wasn't quite what he had expected. Like the open-air chamber where he had slept, this was simply a smaller version of the sparse, temple-like structure.

The room was round, supported by stone columns with a domed ceiling but surrounded by a sheer wall of flowing water on three sides. He could actually hear the thunder of the falls as it struck the roof, and yet the sound was strangely muted. A fine spray misted the air, though like his bed chamber, the room seemed somehow sealed against the outer environment. A comfortable, ambient temperature pervaded the space.

To the far side, three steps led down to a small open platform situated directly beneath the falls, enclosed at the outer edges by waist-high balustrades. A continuous deluge of water, sparkling like a shimmering veil of iridescent silver, struck the platform before flowing out between the fretwork of the railing.

A wide bench with folded linen sheets sat against one column to his right, while a low round urn roughly the height of the bench resided near a column to his left. A *toilet?* Ingenious, really, though he couldn't remember needing to use the bathroom since he'd been here. Water flowed from the sidewall through a slender horizontal channel, falling into it like a fountain that receded as he neared. He caught his breath. *Magic? Of course.* Everything here was a seamless blend of Magic and ingenuity. Brilliant. Beautiful.

Áedan watched as he took everything in. "Niamh thought you might be more comfortable with that." He angled his head at the stone urn. "Though our bodies do not seem to require such things here. Perhaps because this world is filled with so much healing Magic, wastes, and toxins are constantly dispersed from our cells and blood." He shrugged. "We do not have the same bodily functions as you would in the mortal world. You should not need it. Nevertheless, it is there." His eyes twinkled with that same mischief he had noted earlier.

Huh. He was right. That was convenient. What else was different about this place? He had no doubt it was going to be just full of surprises.

Ian sank down on the bench and discarded his clothes, allowing them to fall haphazardly where they might. Niamh had spoken the truth. The rejuvenating effects of the minted drink were short-lived, and his strength was quickly waning. He needed to get this done before his weakness became a liability and forced him back to bed. This really sucked. Other than the occasional pounding yet fleeting headaches, he had never been sick a day in his life.

He staggered to the three stairs, leaning heavily against the tall twining stone columns, and then braced his hands on the balustrade rail as he entered the deluge. The waterfall was so powerful that it nearly knocked him to his knees.

Holy hell! Ian was scrubbed clean in an instant and backed out of the downpour as quickly as he was able. That was certainly an experience. At least the temperature of the water had been comfortable. He couldn't imagine stepping into that torrent if it had been ice-cold. The warm blast had been more than enough of a shock to his system.

Once more safely ensconced in his bed, Ian watched Áedan as he settled his tall muscular body into a high-backed chair that had replaced the uncomfortable stool during the time they had been gone. Leaning his elbows on his knees, he regarded Ian with that same unfathomable expression that made every nerve prickle with the awareness of the barely contained force of Áedan's Power. He had heated the waterfall with a flick of his wrist and had lifted Ian as though he weighed nothing.

To his chagrin, Niamh had been right about him needing Áedan's help. Ian would not have made it back to this room if his tall muscular *brother* had not been there. He had never felt so weak in his life.

"How long have I been here, Áedan? Niamh isn't exactly cooperative when I ask for information." Ian broke the silence.

"She doesn't want to cause you pain." Áedan exhaled and then made himself more comfortable in the chair. He leaned back, stretching his long legs out in front of him. "Three risings of our sun, though I cannot say exactly how long in the mortal world. Niamh is aware that you must return as closely as possible to your own timeline, so she will be holding back the turn of our tides as much as she is able."

"Time is that different here?"

Áedan inclined his head. "Yes."

"And she is that powerful?"

"Yes."

"So you do mean to send me back, then." It was both a question and a statement.

"Yes, Ian. You must return. Miranda cannot be allowed to inherit our lands. They must not pass from our family. I am unsure of her exact agenda, but I can say with certainty that it is nothing good."

"Why aren't you there? Why doesn't anyone seem to know anything about you?"

"It is complicated."

"You've already said that. How complicated?"

"You will understand everything soon. I do not want to cause you pain either, Ian."

"That's becoming a pretty convenient answer for everyone," Ian stated.

"Nevertheless, it is true."

They regarded one another evenly in a kind of stalemate.

"You have seen me, Ian," Áedan finally relented, "when you were still a small child, though you were far too young to understand in what capacity. The politics of our family must be maneuvered carefully. The stakes are quite high, and we cannot risk discovery. You can imagine the implications and fear that would arise if the existence of our kind became known."

"You mean the Tuatha?"

"Yes." Áedan gave him an assessing look. "Does that information hurt your head?"

"No," Ian lied.

"Look, Ian, this is not the time to speak of this. I promise we will return to this topic soon, but I wanted you to know that you will be here only a short time and that your questions will be answered before you go."

At Ian's blatant look of disgust, he reiterated, "I promise."

Ian huffed out a disgruntled breath. "Your accent is different from Niamh and Caitria's," Ian observed. "Sort of British. And you seem more familiar with modern speech. They don't use contractions. You do. But I suppose you can't comment on that either."

Áedan raised a black-winged eyebrow and gave Ian that amused, slightly exasperated look he was becoming so familiar with. Ian still couldn't help the jolt of recognition he experienced each time he looked into the face so like his own.

"You ask a lot of questions, Ian."

"I have a lot of questions, Áedan."

Áedan laughed outright. "Yes, Ian, I can imagine. All right, yes, I have spent much time in the outer world," he said noncommittally.

"And … ?"

"That is all I am prepared to say about that for now."

"Okaaay, sooo …" Ian searched for something he might tell him. "Why don't I have Magic?"

"You do. It is bound with your memories, but it will still try to flow to you here. You should not attempt to wield it. It would be dangerous until you understand what you are doing."

"When will Niamh open my memories?"

"Soon. I cannot say how quickly. She has many other concerns demanding her attention just now, and it cannot be rushed." Again that inscrutable sidestep, that infuriating avoidance of his question.

Ian huffed in frustration.

"Look, Ian, Caitria would flail me if I left you in the same state as earlier. It was not my intention to injure you in any way."

"You should let me be the judge of that, Áedan. Right now, I think the pain is worth the answers."

Áedan regarded him in that penetrating, indecipherable way of his.

"You seem suddenly very accepting of our world, Ian. What has changed?"

"I've decided to stop fighting it. Either I really am here or I am going to wake up soon in my own bed. Either way, I'm going to take full advantage of this experience. And you were right. I have dreamed all my life about … I don't know … maybe not this world exactly, but ancient times, strange events, people and places that should only exist in books and movies. So why not embrace it?"

"As you say, Ian," Áedan shot him a grin. "So well … right, then." Áedan's tone was still slightly reluctant. "Perhaps we might begin with a history lesson of sorts. Are you strong enough for that?"

Áedan's eyes, mouth, chin, even the dimples that appeared when he smiled were identical to Ian's own. Again, Ian was taken off guard by the face that was his mirror image.

"Sure. Bring it on."

"You must tell me, though, if your head begins to hurt. I insist, Ian. You will find your answers soon enough without this discomfort."

"I'll be fine, Aédan." Ian reassured him, as though Aédan was the younger of the two and he was suddenly in charge.

Aédan once more cocked that winged black-as-midnight brow at Ian, silently telling him he hadn't missed his not-so-subtle attempt to shift their roles.

"All right, then, let me tell you a story, a fairy tale, if you will, that I doubt you will have heard." Aédan made himself even more comfortable in the chair. Hooking one leg over its arm, he shifted slightly sideways in a kind of lazy sprawl that stabbed at Ian's memories.

Ian blocked the odd pain that pierced both his head and his heart. He felt strangely like a child all tucked in for a bedtime story. Though part of him protested that he was too old for this, ironically, the thought was not unpleasant. He could not remember ever being told a bedtime story, although surely, he must have at some point when his father was still alive.

Aédan's voice was deep and resonant, with the same compelling purity of Niamh and Caitria's, though completely masculine. It drew him in in much the same way. Ian laid his head back against the soft cushions and allowed himself to relax. The deep, rich drone washed over him with a soothing sense of déjà vu.

"The Tuatha are an ancient, noble race who have been called by many names, but the last was by the ancient Celts. They were known as the *Tuatha dé Danann*, the *people of the goddess Danu*. The Tuatha are proud, peaceful, and benevolent and, as you have seen, not so different in appearance from humankind, though taller than average and, without exception, strikingly beautiful."

"Yes," Ian mused. "I have noticed. Are they all blond?"

"Yes. All have that unique, very straight silver-blond hair and blue eyes. They are similar to humans in many ways, except for a kind of inner glow and the brilliance of their eyes. The incandescence easily gives them away. Their eyes especially shine with a kind of luminosity that no human exhibits."

Ian shifted as he adjusted his pillow, pushing himself up a little higher in his bed. He didn't want to nod off just when he was finally getting some answers.

"Comfortable?" Áedan asked, raising that brow once more in that slightly mocking way of his.

"Yes. You may continue," Ian returned haughtily, mimicking his brother's arrogance.

Áedan's eyes twinkled. Ian recognized that same luminous glow that he had noted in the two women now that Áedan had drawn his attention to it, but his brother's was not nearly so noticeable. His eyes had a burning intensity about them that was striking but not so glaringly different as to brand him as a being of a different race.

"This ancient race," Áedan forged ahead, "the Tuatha dé Danann, arrived at the dawn of man from far beyond the stars on enormous ships carried on the mists to our world, putting ashore on what is now the west coast of Ireland. Eventually, they spread throughout the Isles."

Ian arched a brow. *Fairy tale, indeed.*

"Shortly after making land, the Tuatha were attacked by an enemy who had followed them here from some distant realm. They were a violent Magic-wielding race known as *Formorians*, bent on the conquest and subjugation of other worlds. They were intent on seizing the superior Tuathan ships in hopes that they could be used to navigate back across the vast expanse of stars to find the home-world of the Tuatha."

Ian gave him his best *"you have got to be kidding me"* look as Áedan continued, undaunted.

"Our warriors fought fiercely and were able to defend our people against this scourge, but barely. In the midst of battle, the Tuatha burned their own ships rather than allow their capture by the Formorians, refusing to see this plague let loose on other worlds."

Ian settled in without further comment. *Why fight it?* He had asked for this, no matter how far-fetched.

"And so deeply saddened, the Tuatha settled into their new world, knowing they could never again return home. It had been a necessary sacrifice, made for the greater good, and they were determined to forge a useful and productive life for themselves and their children. The enemy finally retreated, leaving us in peace, and our people thought, *hoped*, they would not return. After a time, we began to let down our guard, believing that the Formorians had turned their eyes to other conquests, to other worlds, content with stranding our people here."

"We?" Ian questioned.

"What?"

"You said *we* let down our guard."

"*Our people.* I was not yet born when this occurred."

"So it is hearsay."

"Yes, Ian, like the history of Britain or America, though no mortals still remain alive from those early days. Some of our Ancients still live among our people."

Ian's eyebrows disappeared into his hairline at that statement. "Sorry, Áedan, don't mind me. I won't interrupt again."

Áedan pinned him with a mildly exasperated look but continued.

"Unfortunately, the Tuatha later learned that the Formorians had not left as they had thought. During the battle, their own ships had also been severely damaged, thus stranding them as well. Instead, the Formorian raiders had begun to infiltrate the northeastern Isles, and some of the early ancestors of the Vikings began to worship them as gods of chaos and wild nature. The Formorians are enormous horned beasts similar to the legendary Greek Minotaur, though far more human in appearance. Their features are much like ours, though coarser and more pronounced. The points of their horns arc upward and are shaped like a crescent. This is the true origin of the Viking helmet. The Norsemen wanted to emulate their barbaric gods."

Ian fought a sharp pulse of pain in his head, though he hid it from Áedan. He didn't want him to stop talking. How could something like *horned beasts* be triggering his memories in such a way as to make his head hurt so badly? It made no sense, but he wasn't about to ask.

"This isn't in any history book," Ian stated. Despite his promise, he couldn't help his questions.

"No. This was long before written history, centuries before the Roman Empire invaded the Isles. The people there at that time lived in small groups or villages, barely scrounging to survive. There were also many nomadic tribes scattered throughout the Isles, moving from the north to the south with the seasons."

Ian dug his fingers into the corners of his eyes, rubbing at the scratchy burn, trying to concentrate on what he was being told.

"The Tuatha were compassionate and generous with those they came in contact with," Áedan continued, "and tried to help better the lives of all those they found here. They taught those early people the secrets of nature and herb lore and helped them use Magic to speak to the plants and the wildlife. They helped with the growth cycles of crops and controlled the elements so that no one would go hungry. They were even able to teach certain mortals with special gifts to wield small amounts of Magic for healing and for summoning fire, wind, and rain—of course not in the way that the Tuatha were capable of. Many of those same mortals were the forebears of Druid priests. The earth was abundant in wild Magic at that time.

"But some mortals became jealous of the formidable powers of the Tuatha and greedily sought more. They plotted to imprison our people and force them to share the secrets of their all-encompassing Power. They were not content to ply only the small amounts of elemental Magic the Tuatha had taught them to wield."

"So humans use Magic? I've never heard of anything like that. Surely, the whole *mortal* world would know if that was possible," Ian commented.

"This was long ago, Ian," Áedan reminded him. "Magic no longer exists in the mortal world. And even when it did, and even had they wanted to, the Tuatha could not share something that was not theirs to give. They are of an entirely different race and could no more bestow their vast Power on another than they could teach mortal men to become immortal. Our people grew disheartened with the cruelty of humans and the constant wars and began to seek a place of sanctuary away from the barbarity of mankind."

"Couldn't they just pretend to be mortal?" Ian asked.

"As I mentioned, it is difficult for Tuatha to walk unnoticed among mortals," Áedan answered patiently. "All are unusually tall, with pale blond hair and vivid, almost incandescent blue eyes. They are extraordinarily beautiful and graceful, far more so than any human. They emanate a kind of aura or inner light."

"Like Niamh," Ian commented.

"Yes, although Niamh is exceptional, even among such powerful immortals. Her light is by far the brightest. The others do not illuminate the darkness as she does. Their glow is subtler. It is more as though the strength and purity of their souls shine from within."

"According to you, we are half-Tuatha, but our hair is dark," Ian pointed out.

"Yes. We look like our father, although our eyes are more like our mother's."

"We don't glow."

"We exude a kind of veiled energy. People are drawn to us in the mortal world, Ian. Have you never noticed how often people stare at you?"

"No," Ian denied uncomfortably, but deep down he acknowledged Áedan's statement.

"We are different, Ian. You know this is true."

"I guess I never thought about it," he defended. "I am taller than most people. People can't help but notice me."

"Exactly my point. It is all but impossible for you to go unnoticed, and it isn't just your height. It is even harder for a full-blooded Tuatha."

Ian stared intently at Áedan as if examining him under a microscope. *There was ... something different about him*, he admitted. *Something very compelling and charismatic, although it could just be his personality, couldn't it? Well, maybe genetics had a little to do with it, but ...*

Áedan cocked an eyebrow and cleared his throat under Ian's scrutiny. "Anyway," he continued with an amused smile hovering at the corners of his mouth, "eventually, the Tuatha were attacked by an enormous army of mortal warriors called the Firbolg. Their weapons were crude, and this new enemy was easily defeated. However, it was not the end. Others came with the same intent. These attacks, especially after all the gifts and kindnesses bestowed upon the earth's people, made the Tuatha even more determined to withdraw from the realm of mortal man."

"Were all the mortals intent on harming the Tuatha?" Ian asked

"No, of course not. As in all of mankind's history, it takes only a few greedy and ruthless individuals to wreak havoc upon the many gentle souls who would live in peace. As I said in the beginning, the Tuatha were peaceful and benevolent and sought only to help those they encountered. Most mortals were appreciative and even worshipped the Tuatha as gods, although that was not what our people wanted.

"Eventually, for their own safety and peace of mind, the Tuatha combined their formidable Magic and created this world. In the beginning, it was an isle perpetually veiled in mist, secreted away in the midst of an archipelago far to the north of what is now known as Scotland, but still part of the mortal realm."

"An archipelago? A volcanic chain like the Hawaiian Islands?"

"Yes. Scotland is part of a massive archipelago consisting of over seven hundred islands. In those ancient times, there were more than a thousand, and though they were hidden, sailors could still reach our shores by following the brightest star in the constellation of Skatharia, the Warrior Maiden of the North. And many tried, though the journey was fraught with danger and the magical mists were designed to throw ships off course, confusing and disorienting those who sailed them. Still, some managed to find us. Mostly, those seamen were simply bent on adventure, but enemies like the Formorians also constantly sought to breach our shores."

"Skatharia?" Ian repeated the name of the nonexistent star cluster. "I've never heard of that constellation."

"No one in recent history has. It disappeared from the night sky at the same instant as more than three hundred islands were plucked from the sea and carried through a rift in the very fabric of the world."

"What?" Ian nearly choked in blatant disbelief.

"How do I explain this? We are not exactly in a completely separate realm, even though we refer to our world as that, but in a kind of … *in-between realm*, if you will. It took incomprehensible and near-catastrophic Magic to hurl us through the rift. Its creation was an act of sheer desperation in a time of war."

"But we—I mean, you are still connected to the mortal world through … *portals?* So in essence, you can come and go as you please and mortals could come here."

"It is not nearly as simple as it may sound to make the crossing, but yes, it is possible to enter our world from the mortal realm and for us to enter theirs. As I said, we are separate, but not entirely. The mists surrounding us can sometimes even be seen on satellite imagery, but this isle, this archipelago of over three hundred islands, can no longer be accessed by the human world without strong Magic, nor is it corporeal there in any real sense in that world."

"So satellite imagery can see these islands, but you don't exist, or only *sort of exist*, in the mortal world?" Ian had to watch his tone so as not to antagonize Áedan. This was all too unbelievable, but he didn't want him to clam up.

"Satellite imagery can only *see* the mist. It cannot see *through* it. And when the mists do appear in the human world, the constellation of Skatharia also reappears as a blurred image within the northern lights. It is as if we are in a constant state of flux with the mortal realm, similar to the ocean tides or the earth's position with the sun, coming closer and then drifting away. If we want to make a crossing, it can only be done when we are at our nearest point."

"When the mists appear?"

"Yes."

"So no one noticed three hundred islands disappearing off the northern coast of Scotland?"

"The remote north," Áedan corrected, "and as I said, this occurred in antiquity. And yes, though I am certain some did notice, these Isles were already so shrouded in myth and mist and had long been spoken of as a place where ships did not dare to sail that after a decade or so, the memory blended into obscurity."

"I need an aspirin."

"Should I stop?"

"No. I want to hear all of it, Áedan, as impossible as this all sounds."

Ian pushed his fingers through his hair, making it stick up in all directions. Some part of him was actually buying this story. Áedan was actually making this all seem *plausible*. It must be the headache. It was erasing all good judgment.

"Just try to keep an open mind, Ian." Áedan had honed in on his thoughts. "On some level, you know the truth of what I am telling you."

"I have to admit, Áedan, this is the perfect fairy tale. All it needs is a princess and a dragon."

They assessed one another for a moment like two birds of prey that had wandered into the other's hunting territory, neither backing down.

After a moment, Áedan's eyes lit with laughter. His expression reminded Ian of the photograph of his father. The mischief in his eyes and that hint of a smile that brought out those deep dimples on either side of his mouth were the exact image of Daniel Thorne's amused *"I've got a secret"* look. He was so similar in appearance to their father, just a lot younger. There was absolutely no way Ian could deny their relationship. And if it was true this man was his brother, then what did it say about the rest?

"O ye of little faith." Áedan flashed gleaming white teeth in a challenging smile. "Of course there is a princess in this story, and also dragons, of sorts. Also, many magical creatures chose to align with the Tuatha and joined us in securing and defending this realm."

"What kinds of magical creatures?" Áedan was right. This definitely had all the elements of a fairy tale.

"All kinds, Ian. You'll see. You will meet some while you are here."

Once again, that mischievous light lit those dark features. "Shall we continue, or are we finished here?"

Ian couldn't help but grin back. Truth or no, he enjoyed Áedan's company, and this tale was fascinating, no matter what he pretended. He didn't want to believe it, but he was having some difficulty forcing himself *not* to. Anyway, what else did he have to do?

"In that case, please go on." Ian airily granted his magnanimous permission.

"I think they failed to beat you at your boarding school. What is the world coming to?" Áedan retorted in a bored, long-suffering tone.

"All right. I must backtrack a bit in my tale in order to tell you about the princess. We must return to an earlier time, when our Court was still a part of the human realm, long before the fabric of the world was torn asunder."

Ian rolled his eyes at Áedan's storyteller's drama.

Áedan lazily settled into his chair, continuing in his normal deep tenor, while Ian did much the same, getting as comfortable as he was able. Áedan's voice was rich and deep and soothing in a way that Ian could not explain. It floated over him, comforting and lulling in its richness and purity, and soon, he forgot his exhaustion and the pounding jackhammer in his brain that never quite seemed to go away.

"Over the course of many millennia," Áedan began anew, "the Tuatha came and went between their mist-shrouded archipelago and the mortal world. They acted as guardians of the Isles, continuing to help where they could, healing the sick, harnessing the elements, and training those who were adept in Magic. But the world was changing.

"After the rise of Christianity, their presence began to endanger those they would have sought to help. As the Romans invaded the south, some of our people joined with mortals to hold them back, but it became more and more apparent that our presence among those humans was making them weak. They had become dependent upon us to fight their wars, ensure their crops yielded, provide for them in far too many ways, instead of taking responsibility for themselves.

"As the Roman Empire crumbled and their soldiers, who had spread out over the world like locusts, imposing their harsh rule, finally withdrew, the Tuatha realized the time had also come for them to withdraw completely from the mortal world.

"Their presence was a constant source of debate between the pagans and the Christians, and their mortal followers were being persecuted, burned, or imprisoned. Their time in that world was at an end. Our people had done enough. They no longer belonged.

"As the Tuatha were in their final stages of departure," Áedan sighed, "the Formorians once more attacked.

"It seems they had only been biding their time, drawing followers to them and building their own armies while the Romans had weakened and decimated the hemisphere. Their timing for conquest could not have been more perfect. The Tuatha were all but gone, the tribes of Caledonia were weak, and the Isles were an ideal place to stage their conquest.

"The irony is that had they simply waited until the Tuatha had removed entirely, they might have prevailed.

"The Formorians were cruel and vicious, and the Tuatha understood that the people of the earth would face a great apocalypse with the brutal horned beasts as their masters. Our people realized it would take the combined forces of both mortals and immortals alike to banish this ancient magical enemy. The Formorians were a powerful, ruthless race, but not indestructible, and their impulsive instincts to dominate often left them shortsighted.

"The Formorians were prone to mistakes, often lashing out in anger where a cooler head would have prevailed, reacting to the immediate situation instead of strategizing. They frequently challenged one another and even their leaders, which caused chaos and dissention within their ranks.

"Like jackals, theirs more closely approached that of a pack mentality instead of one of strategy. The stronger gang up on the weaker. Only the most brutal were able to survive, but not always the smartest. This tendency to fight and challenge one another made them far less effective than their fearsome Magic and superior strength should have allowed them to be.

"And there is also a very real difference in intellect between their Ruling Elite and their foot soldiers. The members of the ruling class are few. Coups abound, and the jackal mentality prevails, even at the highest levels. However, their king is a merciless survivor. He has shown himself to be utterly ruthless, cold-blooded, and indestructible. He surrounds himself with others like himself and keeps them in check through fear and intimidation. He is actually quite brilliant in many ways, though I believe that it is only his unwillingness to delegate any real power to anyone other than himself that has kept the Formorian armies in check for so long. No one makes a move without his express consent. Autonomy is not permitted, and retribution is swift."

Ian roused himself. "You said *is*. Are they still alive, then?"

"Yes, Ian," Áedan said grimly. "Very much so."

"That's actually quite … terrifying. Why aren't they still attacking us?"

"I'm getting to that part. Patience is a virtue, Ian. Haven't you learned that yet?"

"Hmmm. I guess not. Sorry," he mumbled.

Ian made no further comment as he settled back. Anyway, it was easier to listen than talk. Talking reminded him how much his head hurt.

"The Formorians' first mistake when they launched their assault on the Isles, other than not waiting for the retreat of the Tuatha," Áedan went on, "was that they did not secure all fronts or shore up escape routes prior to their initial attack. There were holes and gaps in the chain of command due to the strife within their ranks. This left them vulnerable and hesitant to move beyond their initially assigned positions or to do anything but kill and plunder within their designated borders. They arrogantly believed their superior strength and formidable Magic would overcome any obstacles in their path.

"But perhaps their biggest mistake was when they kidnapped a Tuatha princess, one much loved by our people. She was a very powerful Ancient, the sister of the Tuatha king. The king of the Formorians wanted her as his consort and was willing to wage war to get her. Had this not occurred, it is possible the Tuatha would not have been so quick to confront the Formorians or even realized in time what was occurring."

"So at last we reach the part about the princess." Ian tried to smile. His head now throbbed severely, but no way in hell was he going to let on.

"Yes, Ian. I promised you there was a princess in this tale." Áedan glanced at the dark shadows beneath Ian's eyes. His gaze was troubled as he asked, "Should we save this for another time?"

"No." Ian's voice was weary, with none of the earlier sass, but he wanted Áedan to continue. "Don't stop. I really do want to hear this."

Áedan looked to be considering whether or not he should. For all of Ian's earlier bravado, it was obvious he was exhausted.

"Please, Áedan," he pushed. "Don't leave without telling me the rest."

Áedan sighed and shifted in his chair, bringing both feet to the floor. He rested an elbow on a knee, propped his chin on his fist, and regarded Ian thoughtfully for a long moment.

When Ian was certain he would refuse, Áedan finally leaned back once more and continued.

Ian flashed a weak smile of gratitude. He knew that Áedan was aware of how much he wanted to understand this world he had suddenly been thrust into, regardless of his many skeptical questions.

"The Tuatha reemerged with a vengeance and fought a brutal war against the Formorians for nearly two hundred years," Áedan said. "Unfortunately, it was a battle on many fronts, as the warring mortal tribes attacked on all sides as well, not always clear who was their true enemy."

"Did they get the princess back?" Ian asked.

"Yes, eventually, but not without many casualties on both sides."

Ian grinned despite his acute fatigue. "I thought you were going to tell me she was rescued by a handsome prince." He tried for a teasing tone, but his voice was slightly slurred.

"Well, I suppose in truth, she was." Áedan flashed his dimpled smile. "But that is a very long and involved story best left for another day. You are growing tired, so let me hit the high points so you can rest."

Ian nodded groggily. "Thanks, Áedan, for telling me these things, no matter how far-fetched."

"You wound me, Ian." Áedan placed a hand over his heart in feigned distress.

Ian grinned. This stranger, his *brother*, would have done well upon the stage. The high-backed chair creaked under his weight as he settled back once more, stretching those long black-clad legs. Ian again noted how powerful he appeared. This man definitely looked capable and dangerous enough to have fought in those early battles he spoke about.

"The Formorians soon found ways to make incursions into our Isles." The storyteller's voice returned with its rich, lulling tenor, and Ian drifted as he listened, trying to stay focused. He did want to hear this tale, *all* of it, or at least as much as this dark warrior was willing to tell.

"Though our shores were veiled, their scouting ships were relentless, and it was only a matter of time before they stumbled into our world. We set stronger, more powerful safeguards against our borders, but their ability to wield Magic allowed them to move freely through the mists. The Formorians also became more and more aggressive, more and more lethal in their dealings with others. They became true predators of the Northern Isles, fearing no one, using their dark Magic for every vile and evil act they could conceive. Their warriors were unconscionable dealers of death bent only on inflicting pain and chaos. Those who were not killed outright were enslaved until they were no longer of use for breeding or sport. The Formorians became an immense danger to all within the Northern Isles, mortal and immortal alike.

"The Tuatha, as the only other Magic wielders strong enough to confront them, became their staunchest enemy and the only hope for peace within the Isles, yet our people were vastly outnumbered. Our children are few and precious. The Formorians breed with their captives, creating armies of half bloods. All were aware that once conquered, there would be nothing to stop the bloody incursion from expanding to other continents.

"The Formorians preferred to strike from the sea, having built a vast fleet of shallow-draw ships, but we could not hope to confront them on the vast oceans. They were far more ruthless than the Vikings, who later emulated their tactics. Their Magic made them unstoppable. There were even some among them with the Power to allow their ships to sail upon the clouds.

"Anger and outrage against these attacks escalated until mortals and immortals alike agreed that the Formorian reign of terror could not continue. The Tuatha decided upon a course of action that would have been unthinkable and unconscionable even a few years prior, but they no longer believed there was a choice.

"Because the Formorians possessed tremendous physical strength and a formidable ability to control Magic, the Tuatha saw only one course to save the earth's people. They chose to bind the earth's Magic."

"I don't understand what you mean by that, Áedan. How can you *bind* Magic?"

"Magic is in everything, Ian, the soil, the rain, the wind, and the trees. It flows in the lakes and rivers and oceans and in all living things. When the Tuatha bound the Magic of the earth, it meant that all Magic was trapped, or chained. It could no longer be summoned. No matter how powerful the wielder, it became impossible to call or command Magic."

"I still don't understand," Ian commented.

"To wield Magic, one must draw all the many threads and currents of magical energy from the elements and nature. He then must channel it into his body and then weave it into a force mighty enough to create the desired effect for good or evil."

"But how?"

"I know you don't fully get what I am saying, Ian," Áedan interrupted, "but you will once your memories are opened."

"Again with the memories," Ian complained.

Áedan gave him a dry look and shrugged. "There is only so much I can do, Ian. I'm already pushing the boundaries by telling you anything at all."

Ian tried not to glare. "Okay, Áedan. Just … keep going."

Áedan's blue eyes twinkled at the impatient tone, but he complied. "Without the earth's Magic to wield, the Formorians, although physically stronger, were as vulnerable as those they tried to conquer and were far easier to defeat. Without Magic in the mortal realm, however, it meant that immortals, both Tuatha and Formorians, who had been virtually impervious to death, could now be easily killed."

Ian's eyes widened as he grasped the ramifications of this.

"This leveled the field significantly for all, and the Tuatha hoped this would end the conflict. They were wrong.

"Even after the loss of their ability to wield Magic, the Formorians did not give up their bloody campaign. They stayed and fought. The Formorian king sent wave upon wave of expendable foot soldiers at the combined mortal and Tuatha forces, believing their superior physical strength could still prevail. He escalated his use of mortals as hostages, killing and enslaving them, using them as pawns in his demands of surrender.

"As the fighting intensified, the Formorian king became even more determined to recapture the Tuatha princess. She had become a fanatical fixation. He would broker no treaty of peace without the guarantee that the princess would become his consort. He was certain that she was the true source of the bound Magic, and he was correct in that assumption."

"*Wait!* This Tuatha princess was able to bind the Magic of the *entire planet?*"

"Yes. She was that powerful, and that is the reason the Formorian king wanted her to rule at his side."

Ian gazed in wide-eyed shock at the raven-haired man who looked and dressed as though he could have been a warrior in that ancient world.

"Of course, this was unacceptable to the Tuatha." Áedan's clipped British accent held a note of anger that sounded as though he was discussing a recent battle instead of telling a tale of something that happened in antiquity.

Ian noted the muscle that ticked in Áedan's jaw. However long ago, the events of that war seemed to infuriate his grim-looking brother. He watched the fury play across Áedan's face as he spoke about an ancient clash that still had the power to inflict tremendous ire.

"The loss of so many Tuatha warriors, who had also been some of the most powerful of our Ancients, had nearly decimated our people." Áedan unconsciously rubbed his temple as though his head, too, was beginning to ache. "All understood that without their princess, they would quickly fall. Her Power was unequal to that of any other, even the Formorian king. They realized he sought to use her to ensure his victory, and every one of them, to the last man, woman, and child, would have given their own lives to ensure her safety. The alternative was unthinkable."

"Why haven't I ever heard about a battle against these Formorians in any of our history books?" Ian asked. "I can't imagine something like that being overlooked. Surely, the entire world would still be buzzing about some epic battle fought in Scotland against some supernatural horned beasts that wanted to enslave the world. I've never even heard the name Formorian before."

"Scotland, Ireland, and the Northern Isles," Áedan corrected. "This history is so old, Ian, that it is considered myth rather than fact, but you will come across it from time to time in ancient Celtic literature. So many lives were lost, and few, if any, used any form of written language. It was passed down verbally in story form from generation to generation until it became nothing but an obscure legend. There is often more truth to mythical stories than most would like to believe."

"I suppose I should have been studying myths and legends instead of world history in school, then," Ian muttered. "So what happened?"

"The Tuatha knew they could not continue in this way. The death toll was insurmountable. Our people could not sustain the losses, and they had no hope of defeating the Formorians on land when they still had infinite fleets of warriors scattered throughout the seas. It had been a mistake to attempt to win a war amid the vast Isles, where the Formorians had so much room to maneuver.

"Our people realized they would have to draw the enemy, every last one of them, into a trap where they could be defeated, or the world would never be safe. And so they devised a desperate plan to force the Formorians from the mortal realm once and for all.

"The foundations had already been laid to permanently seal off our Isles from the outside. We decided to bring the Formorians with us and then contain them within the outer one-third of the atoll. They would have numerous islands on which to settle, but no more victims to enslave or wage war upon."

"That sounds pretty risky," Ian observed.

"Yes, the plan had its risks, but since the Formorians no longer had the ability to wield Magic, Tuatha leaders believed they could assure the safety of our people. The idea was to combine our ancient knowledge with Magic to force the Formorians … how do I explain this … *through dimensions* into a realm far beyond the mortal world and far beyond our own borders. We planned to seal them into a plane where they could never again breach the mortal realm without crossing through the kingdom of the Tuatha."

"I'm not sure I understand. How can you do that? How can you move through dimensions?"

"It is not easy to explain. Remember, Ian, our Ancients possessed elemental knowledge unequal to anything understood by mortals even to this day. They also had the benefit of near-infinite Magic, because literally, *all* the world's Magic was flowing to our shores."

Ian nodded, though he truly couldn't fathom such an advanced civilization with such futuristic knowledge living so simply and looking as though its inhabitants had stepped from the pages of a Shakespearian play.

Áedan must have been monitoring his thoughts like Niamh did, because he reminded him, "Remember, Ian, though medieval in appearance, the Tuatha possess nearly godlike power."

Ian's stoic expression compelled Áedan to explain further.

"How should I put this? You've studied science in your American school, right?"

"Yes, Áedan," Ian responded dryly. "America is not nearly as backward as you might imagine."

Áedan quirked a raven brow that said louder than words just how much his brother was pushing his luck.

"So look around you. Everything you see appears solid, though in reality, it is not. All matter is made up of smaller elements—atoms and energy, for lack of better words—that are actually in constant motion. All these individual elements spin or travel within a specific *frequency*.

"If we change this frequency, speed it up, slow it down, move it to a higher or lower echelon, almost like you would tune a radio to a different channel, you can literally *phase* into a separate dimension. Like the radio, the other channels are still there, but you can no longer hear or see the signal because the frequency is specific to the new radio station you have chosen."

Ian nodded again. Like everything else, it made sense, in a kind of bizarre science-fiction-fantasy sort of way. *Just go with it*. He had already experienced things here that defied any rational explanation.

"So ... are you good with that, Ian?"

"Sure, Áedan. Why the hell not?"

"Where'd you learn to be such a smart-ass, Ian?"

"Dude! Boarding school. You should try it sometime."

"Okay, then." Áedan shook his head in helpless resignation.

"So our people implemented the first stage of their plan to imprison the Formorians into a separate ... *dimension*"—he looked pointedly at Ian, defying him to comment—"by letting it be known that the entirety of all the Magic that had disappeared from the world, and all the new elemental Magic that was being born from the void, was flowing to the Mountain Court of the Tuatha. Rumors were spread throughout the Isles that the entire northern archipelago was adrift in Magic and only there could it be reclaimed. All one had to do was find a way into the mist and navigate northward, following the constellation of Skatharia.

"It was the most dangerous secret we could have divulged, but nothing short of that would have brought the entire Formorian armada into these Isles."

"Was that the truth? About the Magic, I mean. That it was all flowing to the northern archipelago and the Mountain Court?"

"Yes. The three hundred islands within our misty atoll were the only places in the world where Magic still existed. This had been accomplished with arcane knowledge held only by the most ancient of our people and had served as a source of protection since the Tuatha first removed centuries earlier from the Southern Isles."

"Southern Isles?"

"Geographically *southern* from us. Scotland and Ireland."

Ian's brows lowered as he tried to picture the geography of Great Britain and Ireland.

"So the mists were like a physical barrier?"

"Not exactly, Ian. The mists shrouding the northern archipelago protected these Isles and were infused with Magic that disoriented and confused anyone sailing within their boundaries.

"Our protection has always depended to a high degree on the mist's ability to instill a pervading sense of fear and disorientation as one approaches our Court, growing stronger and stronger until panic and a sense of madness ensues. It is impossible to shield against that suffocating, all-encompassing sense of terror invoked by the mist. It was our security system in the mortal world during ancient times, and it still serves us now in much the same way against the Formorians.

"During that final war within the mortal realm, ships could not pass easily through the mists without the express permission of the Tuatha, and so in essence, they gave it."

"So you just let the Formorian ships sail in?" Ian was incredulous.

"Yes. It was a huge risk but deemed the only way to contain them. The Tuatha princess used not only the Magic but also herself as a pawn.

"The Formorian king came after her as she knew he would, expecting to harness the great Power of our realm as soon as he crossed through the atoll. And he brought his entire army with him, as our warriors had hoped.

"Our people cleared the path between the mortal world, seeding the Isles with small bits of Magic, enough to make it believable, enough to entice them, to make them hungry for more, but not nearly enough to give them the strength to wield as a weapon.

"And so they came, lured by the promise of renewed Magic and near invincibility, a vast invasion force encircling the outer ring of our Isles. Hundreds of Formorian ships rode the waves that day, and in their galleys came thousands upon thousands of our most reviled enemy, passing through the magical atoll.

"Immediately the entire atoll was sealed, and the Magic withdrawn.

"With so little Magic, the journey through the mist had weakened them greatly. Before they reached our Court and before they could call enough Magic to defend themselves, the mist closed around them, stranding them within its disorienting borders.

"As you can imagine, this infuriated the enemy forces, and they sailed on with a vengeance, determined to conquer us all. They had realized too late that this maneuver, in reality, meant life or death for them, freedom to rule themselves, to terrorize the Isles, or imprisonment in a world not of their choosing.

"The war had now escalated into a personal vendetta for their king, and he was even more bent on capturing our princess, regardless of the losses sustained to his fleet. I think this was the moment when we realized we had underestimated his ruthlessness. He was willing to allow the virtual genocide of his own people, thousands upon thousands of his own warriors, to be slaughtered in the pursuit of his own goals."

Ian's eyes were as round as saucers.

"As our people amassed the Magic to send the Formorians into that separate dimension, they broke through our defenses. We were unable to hold them back.

"They fought viciously. A cornered animal with nothing to lose is always the most dangerous, and they were indeed cornered. They pierced the protecting mist and sailed into the inner circle of our atoll.

"Once through that inner ring, being creatures of Magic like the Tuatha, they were able to reclaim their Power and summon the Magic they needed to resist being banished into that other plane."

"Wait, Áedan. So the plan to force the Formorians into another dimension ... backfired?"

"In essence, yes."

If Ian thought this young warrior had looked grim before, he was mistaken. Áedan's dark features held such primitive wrath that had Ian not been fairly certain his brother meant him no harm, he would have been scrambling to get far away. The anger and Power rolling off him filled the small room like a thunderhead. Ian warily assessed the glowering man as he continued to speak.

"Yes," Áedan said again, barely controlled rage edging the beauty of that melodic voice. "It was the catastrophe we had hoped never to face. Suddenly, the Magic of our realm became theirs to harness. Our people had been so certain of their superiority, but they had not counted on the unimaginable strength and ruthlessness of the Formorian king or his ability to command and manipulate the Magic of his Ruling Elite. It was like nothing we could have fathomed. The Magic was no longer solely ours. Our Magic became *theirs*. Their Magic became *his*. And like our own princess, his abilities had already been vastly superior to any of his followers. It was an unmitigated disaster."

Áedan took a slow, deep breath and slicked his long black hair away from his face. Those nearly inhuman eyes burned like blue fire.

"The Tuatha, though enormously outnumbered, fought a brutal and ugly war, eventually forcing the Formorians back through the mists, but were unable to imprison or expel them from our world. We could not reclaim the Magic they had appropriated. They were far too strong.

"At the height of the battle, when all began to fear we might fail, the Tuatha princess called forth arcane Magic so primal that even our Ancients feared its use. Summoning *Origin Power*, the slumbering wellspring of our sleeping ancestors, the nascent source of *All* that came before, she awakened fearsome Magic never before wielded by the Tuatha.

"This Power was so formidable she nearly lost control. Realizing her terrible need and our great peril, she supplicated herself, beseeching the Might and Grace of ancient gods … and she was answered.

"The wellspring burst to overflowing, our princess was pulled into pure, spiraling light, and she was … unmade. Her body became a spinning vortex of energy unrecognizable in form. All believed she was lost to us forever, devoured in that blazing maelstrom. Our people cried out, their grief inconsolable. All understood this was the end for us all.

"When all hope seemed spent, our princess suddenly reformed, emerging out of that pure, intensely hot light.

"She was once more restored to us, and she came with a vengeance.

"The princess harnessed Magic so vast that only our goddess Danu should have been able to wield it. She should not have survived, but she did. It changed her, though. It was like experiencing a nuclear explosion, mushroom cloud and all.

"Afterward, her Power became so infinite that she could barely contain it.

"Instead of banishing the Formorians, she pulled the entire archipelago into this *in-between* realm where we now exist. She hurled the Formorian fleet away from our Isle to the outer rim, but they became trapped here with us.

"I believe wielding that vast Power frightened her to such a degree that she did not seek to create a second rift into another dimension, even if it meant expelling the Formorians once and for all from this realm.

"It was enough to have saved two worlds and won the battle.

"She then shielded our Isle in a nearly impenetrable mist. Our world, our safety zone, became much smaller that day, but we prevailed.

"The enemy resides in the outer two-thirds instead of the one-third we had planned, but we have managed to hold them there."

"So we … this island is in the inner circle?"

"Yes. This is a rough analogy, but if you picture an archery target with a bull's-eye in the center and three concentric outer rings, you can imagine our basic geography, although we are somewhat more elliptical in shape.

"The Power it took to achieve this is indescribable. Many lives were lost, both mortal and immortal. Defeat, however, would have meant, if not total annihilation, then at the very least the enslavement of both the human and the Tuathan worlds.

"But as I said, it was not without cost. Afterward, her Power became so infinite that she could barely contain it. It became a constant struggle to keep it chained and exacted a tremendous toll on her energy and abilities.

"All the Magic that had flowed from the world now flowed directly to our princess, and it became necessary to find ways to release it safely, to spread it out and expend it without creating another cataclysmic event.

"It was a great risk, and still is. The Formorians reside within our realm and continuously search for ways to invade but cannot breach our shores without us knowing. Even though the mists surrounding our borders confuses our enemies and puts them off course, there have been instances when they have been able to stumble through our barriers. I believe they have learned that the fear and disorientation they experience signals they are close to our shores, and if they can ignore that overwhelming sense of dread long enough, they can break through our defenses.

"Our princess must remain constantly vigilant, and our people must always be prepared for war."

"Sic vis pacem para bellum," Ian murmured under his breath as the Latin phrase suddenly pushed its way to the forefront of his brain. *"If you wish peace, prepare for war."*

"Yes. That has been our family motto for centuries, as well as that of the Tuatha."

"So the Formorians do have Magic now?"

"Yes, they have Magic. During that final battle, they broke the bonds that kept it chained to our Court. Magic flows freely within the entire atoll.

"And our princess is a conduit for far more Magic than she can control. She must disperse it, and this realm is hungry for it, but no matter how much she saturates these Isles, she cannot release as much as she needs. The Formorians have more Magic than they can use, as do we."

"So in a way, you lost the battle?"

"No. We sustained great losses that day, but the Formorians were sealed into a plane where they could never again breach the mortal realm without crossing through the kingdom of the Tuatha. However, as I have said, it comes at great cost.

"Much of what is witnessed as the aurora borealis is the Formorians waging war against us, spending their Magic against our shields. No massed army can penetrate our barriers, our princess is too strong, and the mist is sentient in a way difficult to describe.

"But small groups with rowboats, or even a single shallow draw ship using no Magic, can slip through the mists. They sail in one by one then gather their forces in the inner atoll. The disorientation of the mists should make this impossible, but for centuries, they have still managed to find their way across. Although so far, never in great enough numbers that we cannot defeat them.

"The Formorians have the outer two-thirds of this entire atoll and Magic to wield aplenty, but their thirst for conquest never dies. They could have peaceful lives, but they choose to attack us even to this day."

"Couldn't you give some of the Magic back to the mortal realm?"

"It has always been a topic of consideration, Ian. In those past ages, there were many far-reaching repercussions once the earth's Magic was bound. The absence of Magic also meant that the knowledge of plant and animal speech, the Magic for healing and growing crops, and control of the elements were also withdrawn.

"During those ancient years, the Tuatha had given the earth's people great gifts that had become commonplace in their lives, and without these, humans began to suffer and became angry. There were droughts and floods, food was not as plentiful, and many who were sick and injured could not be healed. Many, especially the Druids and other pagan priests, demanded the Magic be unbound.

"The Tuatha refused. The decision was heartbreaking, but the alternative was unthinkable. The Tuatha worried that if the Formorians found a way to return, and should they find the earth's Magic restored, in their anger they would not hesitate to decimate the planet. The Formorians were cruel and vicious, and the Tuatha knew that the people of the earth would face a great apocalypse with the Formorians as their masters.

"Some Tuatha stayed for a time to help the earth's people learn to plant and grow, build and heal, without the use of Magic, but most removed to this realm."

"Some Tuatha still live in the human world?"

"No longer. Those that had stayed to help again grew weary and disheartened with the cruelty of humans and the earth's petty battles. When a new foe arrived, the Milesians, from the northwest of the Iberian Peninsula, the Tuatha chose to withdraw for good. The Milesians were mortal and, although powerful, were not an apocalyptic threat. Humans were left to fight their own wars and control their own destinies. The Tuatha retreated through the mist and permanently sealed all the gateways between the worlds, except two that have remained well hidden.

"And you can imagine what would happen in this present age if Magic was to suddenly be restored. The earth is fraught with violence. With the invention of satellites, airplanes, and space ships, global war prevails. You live in a world constantly under threat of erratic world leaders, terrorists, and the true possibility of nuclear and chemical genocide."

The retrieval of these memories sent Ian's brain into a kind of shrieking overload that pierced his skull like long jagged shards of glass. He breathed through the pain and hid the trembling of his hands beneath the blanket, hoping Áedan didn't notice.

"So this princess," Ian finally asked, hoping Áedan didn't detect the slight tremor in his voice that he could no longer mask, "she is still alive?"

"Yes."

"*Niamh* is the Tuatha princess, isn't she?"

"Yes," Áedan answered after a brief pause. "You can feel her Power?"

"Oh yeah," Ian confirmed. "Being close to her is kind of like standing in the eye of a hurricane. It's all calm and peaceful where you are, but you can feel that the swirling winds and lightning are all around you, and if you move one way or another, you'll be blasted to *hell*."

"Well, that's an apt analogy, though I'm not sure I would have put it quite like that." Áedan's eyes twinkled with humor.

"She doesn't look very old," Ian remarked.

"We're immortal."

"So we don't ever grow old?"

"Not as long as we remain within this realm."

"We age in the human world?"

"You and I. Not full-blooded Tuatha."

"Oh." Ian had to think about that for a moment. "We're not as strong as full-blooded Tuatha?"

"We are as strong or stronger than most. Our physiology is just slightly different. I am not sure why. You and I seem to require the intense saturation of Magic that we are exposed to here to remain youthful, though I believe if Magic still existed on the mortal plane, we would not age after reaching our prime. Full-blooded Tuatha don't seem to need that same exposure to Magic. They"—he searched for a way to describe what he was trying to explain—"*are Magic*, though no one is as powerful as Niamh."

"Huh!" That was a lot to think about. It opened the way for so many more questions, but already, Ian's head was spinning. "So I guess Niamh could squash me like a bug with just a thought," he commented.

Áedan nodded in amused agreement. "Yes. If she wanted to."

"So I probably shouldn't challenge her anymore."

Áedan shrugged and grinned. "Probably not, Ian," he said with a wink. "If you know what's good for you."

"She does seem quite patient, though."

"Yes. Always. She is our greatest treasure, although she is somewhat fragile due to the immense Power she wields. It takes a tremendous toll on her."

Way to make him feel really rotten about pushing her to answer his questions.

"I still don't understand how we are involved, though," Ian said seriously. "You know, the Thorne family."

"That is another epic tale, Ian, best left for another time."

"Why?"

"You and your questions!" Áedan protested in complete exasperation. "I'm beginning to feel like you are a machine gun and I'm the target. Enough!" His wry grin and laughing eyes softened his protest. "Once we open your memories, you will understand everything."

"But—"

"How is your head?" Áedan demanded, changing the subject.

"Perfect," Ian lied.

Áedan studied Ian closely. His skin was nearly the color of parchment. He looked wan. "I don't believe you."

"Just tell me the rest, Áedan."

Áedan expelled another exasperated breath. He rose and put his hand to Ian's head. "Goddess, Ian! Why didn't you say something!"

Ian immediately felt a soothing warmth flow between himself and Áedan as the pain lessened. Áedan staggered slightly and then shook his head at Ian as if in disbelief.

"I am not a healer. I cannot take your pain away like our healers can, but I can help a bit." Áedan rubbed his temples as though they suddenly ached.

"Did you just take my headache into your body?"

"A little. I am sorry I am unable to do more."

"Don't do that, Áedan." Ian was speechless. "I don't want you to be hurt because of me. I mean it. I am fine."

"It will disperse from my body in a few moments. I am sorry I did not stop speaking sooner. I should have realized. I will call Caitria."

"No, Áedan! Please," Ian implored with something akin to panic. He grabbed Áedan's wrist as he moved to turn away. He *needed* to know. *Needed* to understand, and if he allowed Áedan to walk out of his room now, who knew when his questions would be answered? "At least explain why our family is involved."

Áedan sighed and stared Ian full in the face, noting the dark hollows beneath his eyes, the ashen pallor of his skin, and the slight tremor of his hand. What stood out the most, though, was the determined fire in his eyes and the uncompromising demand for the truth. Áedan put himself in Ian's shoes and caved.

Ian's hand fell away the moment he knew he had won. Áedan cuffed him gently under the chin and returned to stand behind his chair, propping his hands against the high back.

"To this day, the Tuatha place themselves in great jeopardy in the defense of the mortal realm," Áedan reluctantly said. His misgivings were apparent, but he answered with the respect he felt Ian deserved. "If the Tuatha should fall, the Formorians will once again become a threat to all mortals."

Áedan crossed his arms and leaned his elbows on the chair's back, regarding Ian as though searching for words to explain the question his brother had asked.

"There are two gateways from this plane into the mortal realm. These two portals are both concealed and secured within properties long held by our family.

"If the Tuatha were to become overrun, it would then become the duty of a Thorne descendant to destroy the gates. Our family provides the last and final defense against the Formorian threat. This has been our responsibility as guardians of that realm for many centuries. Miranda's little scheme has endangered the entire mortal world."

"How would we do that? Destroy the portals, I mean."

"Enough magical objects have been hidden within our lands for us to permanently seal the gate. That would be a last resort, used only to prevent the direst of catastrophes."

Ian's raven-winged brows soared as Áedan continued.

"The Formorians have had eons to hone their skills and plan their strategies. They have little else to do, it seems, but test our defenses and plan our demise. They are becoming an almost-constant threat. Our mists disorientate their armies, but still, they occasionally find their way through. Should their armies overrun our shores and we be forced to permanently seal the gateway between our worlds, this would cut off the only retreat for the Tuatha as well."

"Couldn't Niamh just create another rift?"

"She is too afraid of destroying everything in existence, and rightly so, Ian. No, this would become a battle once more against our people and theirs, fought here in this realm to the last man, woman, and child.

"It is highly possible that if we ever reach that point, we would face the annihilation of our race, as we would be forced to fight the Formorians to the death. We are uncertain that we could prevail against their vast numbers. Our people were nearly decimated in the wars. Our children are few, and we do not procreate quickly. Many mated Tuatha were sundered in those years of conflict."

Ian listened to the wild tale Áedan had spun. Everything in his intellect told him this story was a fairy tale, pure fabrication, but all he had to do was look around at his domed stone room and the vast, lush landscape with its breathtaking waterfalls cascading from the sheer verdant mountains surrounding him. The people here were truly different. Real, palpable Power emanated from the three he had met, and he couldn't deny his connection to Áedan. In appearance, he and Áedan were literally identical, but there was definitely more to it. He felt it. Deep down, a part of him felt the truth of what Áedan was saying. Somewhere inside of him, memories stirred but were just out of reach. This place was *familiar* to him. These people seemed familiar. It could be an elaborate hoax, but *why*?

"So my dad, *our* dad, was a guardian? And when he died, it would have fallen to me to take his place, but I was too young?"

"Something like that, yes." Áedan's shuttered expression told Ian that wasn't all there was to this.

"And why couldn't you take over?"

"No one is aware of my existence, though I have done as much as I am able. I cannot suddenly appear from nowhere to claim my place as an heir. I would undergo far too much scrutiny from the courts, and it would draw too much attention to our family."

"And DNA testing is out of the question." Ian's brows drew together in a deep frown as he looked in alarm at Áedan.

"Yes. I am aware they took your blood. This was an unforeseen crisis we had not prepared for. We are attempting to do damage control. You can understand that our blood is entirely unique and would raise far too many questions."

"Has anyone actually studied the difference? Scientifically, I mean."

"A little. Our DNA strands have a triple helix instead of a double, like mortals. It is simply far too risky to do more, should any samples of our blood fall into the wrong hands."

Ian couldn't have felt guiltier.

"We really don't seem so different from everyone, though," Ian commented. "Earthlings, I mean."

Áedan's mouth quirked into a broad smile. "Earthlings?"

"You know what I mean." Ian returned a sheepish grin. This conversation taken out of context sounded absurd.

"Yes, Ian, we are like humans in many ways. By remaining in the mortal realm, we forfeit our ability to wield Magic. While we do not age at precisely the same rate as humans and are resistant to most diseases, we are still susceptible to injury, and we can be killed."

"I thought you said we are immortal."

"I believe I explained that earlier. I should have said *almost* immortal. So far as I know, we are endowed with near-eternal life so long as we do not sustain certain fatal injuries. You are tiring, Ian," Áedan said, standing. "We can discuss this at a later time. I think this is more than enough for you to think about for now."

This time, his tone brooked no argument.

"Many of those here will not speak English well or not deign to speak it at all. It has been long since any have heard that language, and it would have been in a far more archaic form. Still, most will try. If you search your mind, you will find our tongue comes easily to you. If not, it will once your memories return."

Ian dazedly laid his head back against the soft cushions of his bed. His temples throbbed.

"You are tired," Áedan once more observed, "and Caitria returns with food. If you are able, I will see you again tonight in the Great Hall."

Ian forced himself once more into a sitting position. He couldn't let Áedan leave yet. He still had too many questions. "Wait, Áedan. I still don't understand why you stayed away. Why didn't you let me know I had a brother?"

"You have seen me, Ian" was all he would say, and he turned to leave.

"Wait, Áedan! Is … my mother still alive?"

"Yes."

"Who is our mother, Áedan?"

"Áedan!" Caitria hissed.

"It's not a secret, Caitria." Áedan's chin lifted in that arrogant way of his as he challenged the incensed healer.

"Who is our mother?" Ian repeated.

The answer came unbidden. "*Niamh!* She's Niamh, isn't she?"

"Yes, Ian, she is Niamh," he answered.

"But … how?"

"That is her story to tell."

"Áedan! You will cease this at once!" Caitria took one look at Ian and immediately rushed to him. She glared at Áedan, her beautiful silk dress wafting like the wings of a wrathful angel.

Ian could actually feel the rise of her Magic as she confronted the powerful, dark warrior nearly twice her size.

"I warned you, Áedan. Can you not see how ill he is? Must I ban you from his side?"

Áedan ran his intense blue gaze over Ian's drawn face. "Ian?" he asked. "Have I hurt you?"

"I'm fine."

"It would seem you are not," Áedan censored as his winged brows creased into a frown.

"It was worth it. Thank you for telling me the things you did. Do you really have to go?"

"We will talk again."

"Not until he is further recovered," Caitria insisted, silk still billowing about her slim figure, dulcet voice like steel.

"Rest well, Ian. Caitria will see to your *physical* health. Mentally, however ... it seems you will have to wait for any more of your questions to be addressed." Áedan sketched a courtly bow to Caitria and winked conspiratorially at Ian as he exited.

As she had done earlier, Caitria placed her hands on Ian's forehead. Immediately, the pain lessened.

"He knows better," Caitria hissed under her breath. "A banquet is to be held in your honor this night, and you must regain your strength so you may attend."

Ian groaned as he recalled the last banquet in his honor, comprising abject humiliation, haggis, and poison, leading to his near-death experience. Maybe he should feign a relapse and remain in bed.

Caitria smiled indulgently and made it clear that she could indeed read his mind. "You will enjoy the festivities, Ian. No one would attempt to harm you here."

CHAPTER VIII

As the evening shadows fell, Caitria guided Ian along a gentle downward-sloping path toward the Great Hall. Glowing torchlights had been lit throughout the landscape, guiding their way. Ian realized that this sanctuary of temples and terraces had been constructed within the protection of sheer green walls of jagged mountains, their towering summits shrouded in heavy mists. Great waterfalls, white and frothy like wedding veils, dropped from dizzying heights, and smaller rivulets snaked through ridges and spurs. Small rocky pools and ponds were everywhere Ian looked.

Just as Áedan had conveyed, all those they encountered along the way were extremely attractive and fair-haired. Ian was met with gracious bows and acknowledgments of welcome.

The sounds of music and laughter spilled from the interior of the enormous Great Hall as they entered through the massive arched doorway, and Ian was struck by the kaleidoscope of color and activity within. Richly dressed individuals in colorful silks and satins danced and twirled. The room was a cacophony of opulent hues. While all those in attendance were dressed regally, some even being armed with sheathed swords and dirks, Ian thought they looked like a bunch of blond teenagers dressed up for a theater production of a *Midsummer Night's Dream*. Everyone looked so young! *These people are immortals,* Ian reminded himself.

All around him, voices sang and laughed and conversed in a soft, lilting language foreign to his ears. The effect was heady and dizzying. There was no doubt he was far from anything remotely recognizable in his own world.

Caitria guided Ian through the high-spirited throng to a raised dais at the far end of the room. She then led him up three stairs and seated him at a long table in a place of honor to the right of a golden, high-backed throne. The music ended, and all those seated throughout the room stood, as did Ian. The entire assembly stilled as *Niamh the Radiant* entered.

Ian caught his breath as he noted the shimmer of glittering white light that sheathed her entire body. She appeared as though billions of diamonds covered her skin, her hair, her long trailing dress, enveloping every inch of her, flowing around and away from her like trails of luminous stardust or the final delicate remnants of fireworks on a breeze. The air surrounding her sparkled and churned with those seemingly infinite white filaments of fiery light.

She fluidly raised her arms as though throwing off water after a swim, and suddenly, almost reluctantly, the shimmering, sentient brilliance lifted away, dispersing into a shower of floating sparks that drifted throughout the hall and high up into the rafters, adding a soft flickering illumination to the shadowy recesses like thousands of miniscule stars.

"They are *Lumen Faeries*," Caitria whispered to Ian. "They seek out Niamh wherever she goes, but especially in the gloaming, as darkness settles upon our Court. They can be pesky little creatures, but she is patient and kind with them. It is as though they have appointed themselves her diminutive guardians, lighting her path at night and defending her most fiercely if they perceive any sort of threat."

Ian nodded sagely as though he actually understood, though his wide-eyed gaze surely gave him away.

Niamh majestically made her way to the dais, greeting those who amassed around her as she glided forward and then up the stairs.

She held her arms out, as though embracing all who stood before her as her golden light grew in strength, briefly touching each and every person within the hall until she illuminated the room like a fiery star. She then bade them to continue with their entertainment. She moved to lightly embrace Ian and then gestured for him to sit.

As her intense golden light faded once more to a gentle glow, the lilting music and dancing resumed.

Ian stared at Niamh in unconcealed awe, barely daring to believe what his eyes assured him was true. Could this *goddess*, this dauntingly powerful entity from the archaic pages of ancient myth, truly be his mother? The idea was ludicrous. It was impossible to reconcile any part of his early existence with the reality before him. She hadn't seemed quite so *otherworldly* or nearly as intimidating when she had visited him in his little room. Of course, at that point, he hadn't truly believed any of this was real.

"You are much recovered," Niamh observed warmly. "Áedan tells me you spoke at length on certain topics, while others have yet to be addressed." She inclined her head slightly, showering her incandescent blue gaze over Ian. "There is yet time for answers, Ian. Feast, enjoy this night's entertainment. Tomorrow will be soon enough to speak of the questions still unanswered."

As before, the purity of her voice pulled him in, washing away his resistance, leaving him with the desire to do whatever she asked of him. He gave himself a strong mental shake. Just that quickly, she ensnared him. He no longer felt as suspicious or threatened by her power over him, but it was still alarming that he should so easily want to hand over free will.

Áedan approached the dais, bowing first to Niamh, and then greeted Ian. Caitria, who had been hovering nearby, shot Áedan a warning glare before stepping down to dance. As Áedan conversed with Niamh, Ian took stock of his surroundings.

The Great Hall was a magnificent palatial room with soaring ceilings. Towering ivory columns carved like massive gnarled oaks twined with ivy soared skyward, splitting into intricate lacy stone boughs, branches and leaves that provided an elaborate and sophisticated structural support to the crescent curve of the ceiling. Tall unglazed gothic arched windows allowed the balmy night breezes to travel freely between the crowded room and the deepening twilight shadows. Dripping white candles glittered in the high ivory branches, casting flickering silhouettes over the dancers. The spacious hall was an enchanting fairy land and needed no other adornment to enhance its beauty.

Ian's gaze was suddenly drawn toward the grand arched entry, his focus rapt. A stunning young woman with long white-blond hair braided at her temples and dressed in a similar manner to Áedan, wearing a long-sleeved, high-necked black tunic, leggings, high boots, and a belt cinched at her waist, stepped into the throng.

Immediately, the dancers spread out and away from her as she glided like a beautiful wraith into their midst. He noticed the sheathed sword at her back and the jeweled dirk at her side, as well as the other numerous knives and blades glittering from various gem-encrusted armbands and custom scabbards.

It was as though he had felt her presence before she even entered the hall. She was the only woman Ian had seen who did not wear a gown.

A tall menacing Amazon of a man dressed nearly the same, minus the jeweled armbands, entered at her back. His narrowed ice-blue eyes swept the room, as though daring anyone to approach. Like the woman, his white-blond hair was braided at his temples and fell long and unbound to his waist.

Still at her back, they crossed in unison through dancers, who parted before them like the biblical *Red Sea*.

Ian couldn't take his eyes off the mysterious female. She moved through the room with the grace of a lioness, a great predator exuding strength and confidence. Blazing blue eyes met his, and for a moment, time simply stopped. He was drawn into those smoldering blue depths.

He realized he was holding his breath and forced air into his lungs. Her scent engulfed him, filling his senses with something primal and intoxicating. Of all the people whirling and dancing in the hall, hers was the singular scent that dominated them all, not heavy, not cloying like perfume, but pure, exhilarating *Power*. She smelled like lightning and rain before a storm.

Her chin lifted, and her eyebrows creased in a frown as she shot Ian a dark look of utter loathing.

Ian's heart stuttered. Stepping onto the dais, she glared down at him, princess to peasant, as she passed. He could feel the Power emanating from her as she brushed by him, not gentle or peaceful like Niamh's, but volatile and intense. She carried an aura of danger about her nearly as potent as the Amazon guarding her back.

Ian was stupefied. Without exception, everyone he had met had been gracious and welcoming. Had he unknowingly done something to earn her hostility? He felt an almost violent tug of recognition. Something about her riveted him. He couldn't take his eyes off her.

Then suddenly, he knew. *This was the woman from his dreams!* His heart wrenched inexplicably, and her unexpected animosity struck a dissonant chord deep within. Confusion reigned for a moment as he fought to appear unaffected, struggling to bring his warring emotions under control.

Áedan, noting the expression on Ian's face, scanned the direction of his gaze.

"Who is she?" Ian breathed, attempting to slow a heartbeat that was racing like he had just run a marathon.

Áedan paused before answering. Ian didn't miss the cloaked look Áedan exchanged with Niamh over the top of his head. "She is a commander of the Elite Guard." His tone was cautious.

"I feel as though I should know her," Ian ventured, trying to keep his own tone light.

"Put her out of your mind for now. You're meant to enjoy the night."

"But who is she, exactly?" Ian insisted.

"I told you. She is a warrior. She is second commander over the Elite Warriors of the Tuatha."

"She's dressed like you."

"Yes. Only warriors of the Elite Guard bear the right to these colors. We are few." Ian waited, but Áedan seemed disinclined to say more.

"So she's your boss?"

"Not exactly." Áedan evaded. "I maintain autonomy unless we are under threat."

Okay. That was about as clear as the murky loch Ian had nearly drowned in.

"She seems to dislike me." It felt easier to make it a statement than to ask why.

"Don't worry about her right now, Ian. And stay away from her," he added as an afterthought. "She's as likely to stick a sword in you as look at you. You need to keep your distance."

"Great," he muttered under his breath. "Welcome to the twilight zone." He took one more look at the glowering beauty.

"A sword, huh?" Ian faced Áedan with a rebellious smile. "It could be worth it." This reckless fascination was so unlike him. Females rarely turned his head, but his attraction to this one was off the charts. And she was sooo out of his league, but still …

"Ian …," Áedan warned.

"Who's the guy?" Ian asked darkly.

"He is high commander of the Elite Guard. Do not challenge him."

"Why would I?"

"I don't know, Ian. How strong of a death wish do you have?"

"So they're together?"

"It doesn't matter. You need to turn your attention elsewhere."

The supercilious beauty shot them a look of cool disdain, as if she had heard their conversation. After bowing to Niamh, she glided regally to the opposite end of the dais, the blond gladiator no more than a step behind. *Much too close!*

Ian fought the urge to get between them. Áedan was right. He really needed to get a grip. He had never reacted this way over a female, and he didn't even know her. He didn't recognize himself. He was feeling stark, ugly *jealousy*.

The fact that she was a stranger and he had no right to be feeling such strong emotions toward her seemed to make no difference. Nor did the fact that the looming warrior guarding her back could take him out before he could blink. *Probably.* He sized him up as he would any opponent. Three inches taller, thirty pounds heavier, hard, solid muscle rippled beneath that fitted black tunic, and he was armed with knives and a sword. *Yeah, he'd be a challenge.*

Niamh's warm golden glow surrounded Ian, infusing him with that deep sense of comfort that was becoming all too familiar.

"Why do you keep doing that to me?" Ian asked irritably.

"It is for your own good, Ian," she replied serenely.

She was right. Ian had no idea what had gotten into him. He was really feeling combative toward the hulking blond Adonis. So much for the calm, cool image his friends had of him.

Áedan lowered his tall muscular frame into the seat next to Ian, directing his attention to the many beautiful women swirling about the floor in their colorful, flowing gowns. He made certain to draw Ian's eye to several that he assured him were without *mates,* which Ian quickly discerned meant they were available.

Ian began to feel that inevitable restless disinterest as when Braxton pointed out all the pretty coeds to him in the school gym. Some things were the same the world over, he decided. No one had ever captivated him like the dangerous female warrior, whose irresistible scent of lightning and rain was still sending shock waves through his brain. Even from far down the dais, her elusive fragrance enveloped him in a way that made him utterly and completely aware of her.

He had always been quick to tell himself that those females his friends tried to interest him in just weren't his type. He guessed he'd just discovered what his *type* was. He seemed to have a thing for the deadly, *get-anywhere-near-me-and-die* kind of girl. Who knew? Talk about playing with fire!

Maybe he did have some hidden death wish he'd known nothing about until now.

Ian tried to feign interest but couldn't keep his gaze from returning to that cold beauty at the far end of the table who pointedly ignored him.

As the dancers began to take their places at the laden tables, a sweet, spiced amber wine was poured for everyone. Ian had never tasted anything so delicious and drained his cup. The sweet amber liquid stole languorously through his body, leaving behind trails of euphoric warmth. Immediately, more was poured for him. Áedan raised his eyebrows and laughingly removed the goblet from his hands, signaling a server for water. "Go easy on that, Ian. It's not like anything you're used to. You may heal quickly here, but tomorrow, you'll wish you'd never set eyes on the stuff if you drink too much of it."

The meal was the most incredible thing Ian had ever experienced. He dined on and sampled so many sumptuous dishes that he lost track. There were rich, savory pies and glazed roots and vegetables prepared with nuts and herbs. There were buttered wild mushrooms so tender they melted in his mouth. There were creamy, airy concoctions with ingredients that Ian could never even guess at but were amazing. He thought he had never tasted anything so wonderful until he was served the many varieties of fragrant honeyed fruits, spiced and honeyed nuts, delicate sugared flowers, and sweet, decadent cakes.

Ian watched the blond immortals with complete fascination, and slowly, the realization dawned on him that he was actually a part of this astonishing, enchanting, magical world. He listened to the laughter and music and the smatterings of conversations all around him in that strange, lilting tongue that was somehow so familiar though he couldn't quite understand the meaning. Hearing the Tuathan language was like searching for a word that you knew ... that was on the tip of your tongue, but your brain just wouldn't quite cooperate.

A feeling of unreserved happiness began to spread through his being. He didn't yet feel a true connection or true sense of belonging to these people or this world, but the loneliness and isolation that had engulfed him throughout his life were beginning to recede. Somehow, even though his brain still refused to give up the memories, he was aware that certain unexplained bits of his life were beginning to fall into place, almost like the pieces of a puzzle that had once been whole and were once again being reassembled.

Niamh introduced Ian to a steady procession of majestic Tuatha, while Áedan asked Ian questions about his life and the years since leaving Scotland. He also shared hilarious stories about various people in the hall, and his quick wit and merciless humor reminded Ian of Braxton. Ian imagined that Áedan was as incorrigible with these immortals as Brax was with everyone he came in contact with. He was aware that the conversation was kept light and inane and away from anything contentious, but he didn't feel so much as though they were intentionally keeping things from him as trying to see to his enjoyment of the evening.

A couple of times Ian asked Áedan a question that had either Caitria or Niamh sending threatening looks his way. Áedan simply shrugged and grinned and moved on to a different topic, silently telling Ian he would have to wait.

Ian had to admit, the throbbing, intermittent headache he had felt since awakening in this world was barely a dull memory, and the reprieve was such a relief that he was on board with keeping it from returning.

The connection with Áedan was immediate and comfortable, as though he had known him all his life, and they readily fell into easy dialogue and banter. Ian began to enjoy himself immensely. If only he could have kept his eyes from constantly straying to the blond beauty on the far side of Niamh, he would have said this was the best evening he had ever spent.

His eyes persistently sought her throughout the meal, although he attempted to disguise his interest, not wanting her to notice his attention and further incur her wrath. Ian was intensely drawn to her. He found her completely mesmerizing. Each time his eyes lit upon her face, he had to force himself to look away. He felt like a planet swept into the irresistible orbit of the sun. Or more realistically, like an out-of-control meteor crashing into the fiery surface of the sun, being consumed as it hit the blazing atmosphere but unable to stop its descent.

As many times as he looked her way, only once during the evening did the arresting warrior woman focus her full, scorching attention on him.

It occurred when an animated Tuathan girl bringing Ian an icy goblet of water had sloshed a bit onto his sleeve as she placed it next to his hand. As the pretty girl leaned in close to brush the moisture away, her flirty, vivacious smile broke into tinkling, mirthful laughter. Her shining blue eyes netted him, snared him somehow, dancing invitingly into his own bemused gaze.

As Ian smiled back at the enchantress, an unmistakable rush of prickling, bristling energy surged over him, turning the attention of everyone at the table toward its source.

The stunning blond warrior leveled her fierce glare on Ian. As their eyes met, that same shock of recognition rocked him. Her vivid blue eyes blazed bright and angry, turbulent storm clouds swirling beneath her aloof mask.

The subdued Tuatha girl quickly pulled away from Ian and hurried on. The aloof beauty icily assessed him for a long tense moment and then haughtily turned to speak to the formidably handsome high commander at her side.

Ian studied the forbidding warrior who had entered the banquet with her. He was similar in looks to the other Tuathan men, though he exuded raw, visceral power. He was ageless, with perfect golden skin, long straight blond hair, and a face that looked as though it was flawlessly carved from a block of living marble, more striking than any classic Greek statue.

Ian felt that same immediate animosity toward her companion as when he had first seen him. The tilt of his chin was far too arrogant, and there was a wild and dangerous quality about him. The blond Amazon was sitting much too close to that captivatingly beautiful woman, he decided, and the sudden enmity that rose in him took him by complete surprise. He recognized the instantaneous return of that same vicious stab of jealousy he had experienced when he had first set eyes on the lethal couple.

Couple. He didn't like that term either. The fact that they were obviously together cut into him like a sharp knife, shooting adrenaline through his veins and making him want to fight something. Or *someone.* Never in his life had he reacted this way to any situation, and especially to any female, nor had he ever felt so completely out of control.

He jerked himself into the real world. Hard. This was just getting beyond ridiculous. Ian had no idea who the haughty beauty was, but she obviously despised him for some reason. And she was an immortal, probably many years older than she appeared. She was so far out of his league in every way. She'd never look twice at someone like him, would she? Nevertheless, he stared darkly at the pair before finally tearing his gaze away.

He really needed to pull himself together. His fixation on this stunning female was far beyond anything he'd ever experienced and was beginning to border on obsession. *Get a grip, Ian,* he reminded himself for who knew how many times that night. It had been so frequent that he'd lost count. Still, something in him insisted he should know this disquieting warrior, and everything in him protested her proximity to the other male.

He looked up to find Niamh thoughtfully watching him. Her soft, radiant glow brushed against Ian, and a sense of warmth and contentment stole through him. This time, he actually appreciated her interference. He was tired, confused, and filled with an unnatural anger that was beginning to alarm him.

"Nice trick." He gave her a self-conscious smile.

"Be at ease, Ian," she said gently. "Things are not quite as they appear." She didn't elaborate, and Ian didn't ask, feeling embarrassed to know she'd read his thoughts.

CHAPTER IX

Ian galloped through a burned village. The acrid smell of smoke mixed with the stench of blood and salty brine of the sea stung his eyes and seared his lungs. The evidence of the brutal and senseless massacre saddened and enraged him.

At his side rode Áedan. Icy northern winds whipped long raven hair away from their faces as the two identical brothers grimly searched for survivors. Bodies of men who had tried to defend their homes lay where they had fallen, crimson stains spreading out beneath them upon the cold, packed earth.

His powerful black warhorse thrashed its armor-clad head nervously, and nostrils flared as they waded through the dead. A collapsing roof sent showers of hot embers high into the air, and his mount reared to strike out with hoof and teeth, ready to meet their assailant head-on. After so many years, they were no longer horse and rider but a cohesive team honed in combat, protecting one another on and off the battlefield. Ian reined him away from the spiraling sparks. "Easy, Demon," he soothed, forcing the high-strung beast under control.

"There are no women or children here. This is like the other villages," Ian uttered harshly.

"The Formorians have taken more slaves," Áedan grimly acknowledged. The fearsome warrior reined in his own massive black stallion, turning in a circle as he studied the surrounding terrain. Feral light flamed in seething blue eyes as he took in the senseless slaughter.

Ian scrutinized the spirited midnight-black mounts that he and his brother so easily restrained. His gaze moved to the unrelieved black leather garb they both wore, and he somehow knew that this identical guise had become a tactic used by them to confuse and intimidate their enemies. Black metal armor resembling dragon scale and heavy gauntlets protected their upper bodies, while thick leather leggings and thigh-high boots completed the menacing and ominous image of otherworldly apparitions. Sheathed swords were strapped to well-muscled shoulders, and round bronze shields and an assortment of other lethal weaponry were secured close at hand to metal-studded saddles. Similar black armor protected the heads, chests, and bodies of their immense warhorses.

He and Áedan were called Demon Warriors by their enemies, and they had worked hard to propagate the fear and mystique of the growing myth. Time and again in battle, they seemingly materialized from the shadows, converging on superstitious enemies, raining down retribution like terrifying wraiths from the fires of hell.

Ian tensed as a mounted column of men crested the ridge behind them at a heavy gallop. A lone rider broke away, spurring hard to reach the pair. He immediately recognized the indomitable face of a warrior with the same features as his and his brother's. As the fiery black stallion and black-clad rider thundered toward them, the man's name was suddenly in Ian's head. Ian hastened his mount forward to meet the third so-named Demon Warrior, Gabráin, father to both he and Áedan.

Fear of their skill and might had done much to strengthen their otherworldly allure. Legends had grown until it was rumored there was a legion of unearthly Demon Warriors leading armies of invincible gods in a crusade to cleanse the world of the evil that had overrun it.

It was true that many immortals numbered among their ranks, though the majority of this army of dark legend was mortal. All were committed to ridding the world of the evil monsters bent on enslaving its people.

"Two more villages have fallen," Gabráin reported grimly as soon as he came abreast. "I have just received word that Danii holds a Formorian army at the sea gate to the north, but her numbers are small. Her intent is to free the newly taken slaves. You know as well as I that she will not withdraw until she succeeds or is slain."

Ian swore, signaling their combined troops to follow, as he urged his horse into a dead run. Fear and anger beat at him. Danii! What in the name of all the devils in the underworld was she doing here? He had to reach her.

"Stay alive, Danii, you just stay alive," Ian raged in his head over and over as he mercilessly pushed his great warhorse through trees and scrub and over precipitous rocky terrain. Man and beast covered distance at a dangerous pace, flying like the "demons" they were both named.

As he topped the rise overlooking an angry gray sea, Ian could see that Danii fought hard to hold the line of horned beasts and conscripted mortals that made up this faction of a Formorian raiding party. The beasts were immense and powerful, with the bodies of men and the heads of something from a nightmare. Their two lethal-looking horns rising above them like a crescent made the Formorians appear almost bull-like; however, the cunning, sentient awareness in their half-man, half-beast faces was chilling.

Perhaps a hundred women and children cowered in fear as the Formorians used them as shields against the resolute blond Tuathan force. In the shallow waters of the inlet at the marauder's backs, single-mast longboats stood ready to sail, oars out, should the wind desert them.

"Damn these Formorians and their Norse ships to hell!" Ian swore again as they began loading women and children into the boats. He was aware that once on the water, the light, shallow-draw vessels would be impossible to catch.

Ian knew without looking behind him that Áedan and Gabráin had split their forces. After years of battle, the three commanders were highly skilled and cohesive, and he was aware that even now, they were maneuvering around from opposite sides in an attempt to flank and contain the invaders. The Tuatha numbered only two score or so and were vastly outnumbered but fought valiantly.

Ian ordered his own men into the fray as he converged on the fierce blond Tuathan fighter wielding her sword against an enormous horned creature. Its powerful muscles rippled as it swung an axe with all its might at the courageous young woman. Ian urged his mount even faster, but before he could reach her, she easily ducked the intended deathblow and pivoted, shoving it back with a booted foot to its powerful chest. It grabbed her leg as she made contact, and she rode up on the monster, using its own momentum. With one spectacular and graceful arc, her shining sword swept cleanly through the thick, muscular neck of the enormous beast. The head landed with a sickening thud, and she kicked it out of the way as another attacker took its place.

For a moment, Ian couldn't breathe. She was glorious in her fearless assault and deadly skilled proficiency. He knew she was an unparalleled fighter, and yet he was furious that she put herself at such extreme risk. She wasn't using her Magic. Somehow he understood that she couldn't summon it, and without its protection, she was completely vulnerable. Without her Magic, this immortal woman could actually die!

His fear and fury at seeing her in such peril escalated until he could barely think rationally. Bearing down on her, long black cloak billowing behind like great fiendish wings, looking for all the world like the spawn of hell he was purported to be, Ian savagely beheaded her foe then swung her up onto his saddle.

"Danii! What are you doing here?" he demanded roughly. "You could be killed!" He wanted to shake her. What part of the fact that she was no longer impervious to death didn't she get? He stupidly repeated his question, as if it would do anything to alter her stubborn determination to rescue these mortals. He understood the source of her intense hatred toward the vile brutes, but nothing, absolutely nothing, was worth her immortal life!

"Don't you understand your life could be forfeit in this world?"

"As could yours, Idan. Let me down!" She shoved against him, but his grip was like iron. "There are innocent children down there!"

Ian deflected a blow that would have blindsided Danii, maneuvering his mount away from the fray.

"Release me!" she demanded. She shoved harder against his chest, her voice nearly frantic. "Put me down! Every moment we delay, more are taken."

Ian suppressed the dread that pierced his heart and grudgingly let go. She leapt into the skirmish once more, and he watched as she took on another monstrous beast. He barely dodged a war hammer, realizing his error nearly too late. He had allowed himself to become distracted, which never happened to him. His focus in battle was always absolute. This woman made him crazy!

He attacked with resolve, bringing his sword down again and again against his foe, determined to guard Danii's back and end this incursion quickly.

Áedan and Gabráin had entered the battle and now engaged the enemy to either side as Ian and his men drove at them head-on. The Formorians began to retreat, hastily shoving as many of their captives as possible into the waiting boats. Ian knew that these people would be brutally used as slaves and also as hostages to ensure that their conscripted mortal armies did not betray them upon pain of the deaths of their wives and children.

The biting wind caught the sails and quickly carried the laden longboats out to sea, far beyond their reach. Danii dropped to her knees in defeat. "So many lost today," she cried as Ian knelt at her side, wrapping her tightly in his arms. Crushing the courageous blond warrior to his chest as he scanned the bloody battlefield, Ian fervently sent thanks to every god he could think of that she was unharmed. He was acutely aware that Danii could so easily lie among the dead and dying. That thought terrified him as no monster on the face of the earth had the power to do.

"Never again, Danii, do you hear me? Never again!"

Ian came awake to the knowledge that he was losing his mind. The ferocity of the battle was still upon him, his adrenaline pumping. He could still hear the screams of the dying, the clash of swords and weapons, and could smell the horses, the horned barbarians, and the blood. He could feel the icy, blustery ocean gale on his face. But his arms were empty. The woman he had held only moments before was gone.

He forced himself to stand, staggering to the arched entrance of his small templelike room. He leaned heavily against the cool, carved stone, staring out over the vine-draped terraces and misty waterfalls that shone like glistening ribbons of silver in the moonlight.

Danii! Her name was Danii. And she had called him … *Idan?* Ian was beyond confused. Like the others, this dream had seemed so real, and yet how could it be?

He had definitely been the man in his dream, but older and in a different time. Áedan had been older as well, although *Danii*, he breathed her name into his soul, appeared no older than she had earlier in the Great Hall.

His sweat-slicked body trembled, and his head pounded. He needed to get out into the fresh air. He needed to clear his mind so that he could think rationally about what was happening to him. Nothing here made sense. The more answers he received, the more questions he had. There were just too many gaps in the story he had been told, and he had no idea how to reconcile any of it with the reality of this immortal world and the dreams that kept him on the razor's edge of insanity.

He wanted a shower, but the icy deluge in his bathing chamber held absolutely no appeal. Funny how he turned to water when he needed to clear his head. Not a day had passed while growing up in Hawaii that he hadn't either swum in the ocean or in one of the pools that dotted their campus.

Ian grabbed a linen sheet from his bathroom and then made his way down a sloping, overgrown path to one of the bathing pools Caitria had shown him.

Stripping off his clothing, he waded into the steaming water of a pond fed by a thermal spring. Velvet moss covered the shallow, rocky ledge surrounding the small pond, and a miniature frothy waterfall dropped from a rock formation above through ferns and tangled vines. Wild mint and rosemary draped into the water, infusing it with their pungent, fresh scents.

Ian leaned his head back against the mossy bank as the warm water gently lapped over his battered body, and wondered again if he could be dreaming—except he had never had a dream within a dream. It could happen, he supposed. Or maybe he was simply going insane. Crazy people didn't really know they were crazy, did they?

His dreams, though, were just too real, too detailed. In them, especially the ones lately, he had always been older and in another time. Could he be remembering another life? He supposed it was possible. It was certainly not much stranger than the idea of being dropped into an immortal realm where people had supernatural abilities and never grew old or died. He struggled with memories that were just out of reach. His mind held the answers. He knew it did. He desperately wanted to uncover the truth and, more than ever, needed information that was deliberately being withheld from him.

He floated in the soothing water as fireflies flitted and sparkled throughout the lush landscape. Or were those the *Lumen Faeries* that followed Niamh? They were really quite beautiful, no matter what they were. Overhead, stars blanketed the sky like millions of glittering diamonds, and he tried to make out the different constellations. Were they the same as those that could be seen in his world? The night was cool and peaceful. Ian closed his eyes, breathing in the earthy-scented air, and allowed his mind to drift.

His thoughts turned to Danii, and he felt an unexpected pain in the region of his heart. He could see her face as clearly as though she was standing in front of him, and he was suddenly overwhelmed with sadness. Rising from the water, he quickly dried off, donned his clothes, and returned to his room.

Ian lay awake for a long time, his thoughts in turmoil. Finally, as the muted orange blush of early dawn gently crept upon the world, he drifted into a restless, fitful sleep.

I am in the Mountain Court of the Tuatha, and I have a mother and a brother! Ian thought incredulously upon waking. His gaze swept the carved ivory stone of the tall domed chamber in which he slept and the sweeping green expanse of tree limbs and lush, draping vines that cocooned the small dwelling.

Part of him still could not accept that any of this was real. Again, he wondered if he could be dreaming this place, these people. If so, this was a really long and detailed dream. And what of the blond warrior woman? *Danii?* The name felt right. He knew without a doubt it was hers. How could he know that without being told? His reaction to her was too intense. And his dreams of her were, well, the word *intense* was a definite understatement.

The clatter and echo of horses' hooves from below drew Ian from his bed. Animated voices carried up to him from somewhere near the Great Hall, Ian guessed; however, the gracefully swaying willows and flowering foliage obscured his view.

He quickly pulled on his tunic and boots and then fastened his belt as he hurried through the sloping maze of vegetation.

As he neared the lower terrace, Ian was completely unprepared for the sight before him. It wasn't horses Ian had heard but *creatures from myth*! Áedan had told him all kinds of magical and mythical beings lived in this world, but some part of Ian had believed it was said in jest. He couldn't have been more wrong. *At least twenty centaurs milled about the courtyard!*

The powerful, dark-haired men with the sleek bodies of horses congregated around Niamh as she serenely greeted them. Their faces were strong, with broadly chiseled patrician features, framed with long wild manes of hair and ears like that of horses poking through. Their upper human arms, chests, and torsos rippled with muscles, and their powerful horses' bodies blazed with untold strength.

Niamh was speaking to them in that soft, lyrical voice as Ian came into view. The centaurs as a unit turned toward Ian, placed their right fists over their hearts, and inclined their heads in a quick show of respect.

Ian was thunderstruck. He fisted his right hand over his chest, returning the same greeting, and approached the creatures.

The largest of the centaurs came forward and spoke to Ian in a guttural, sibilant language that he couldn't understand, though it tapped at his memory in the same way as the lilting tongue the Tuatha used. He looked helplessly at Niamh.

"We have not yet reopened his memories, T'airneach. Thus, he yet comes to our world as would a stranger," Niamh told the centaur in her softly accented English.

"Ahh. I understand." The enormous creature regally inclined his head once more as he addressed Ian in slightly halting English. "I am T'airneach, the leader of our tribe." His voice was rich and strongly accented. "It has been long and long since we last set eyes upon one another, Idan."

Again, that name, Idan?

Ian inclined his head, as had the centaur leader. How was he supposed to respond in this situation?

"It is an honor to … meet you once more," Ian returned, trying for the same formality in tone. It was the best he could do.

"Your return was heralded throughout the Veil. It is a shame we are forced to renew our acquaintance under such dire circumstances."

Ian raised an ebony brow. Was he talking about Ian being poisoned or some other dire circumstance? Once more he looked to Niamh. This time, he had absolutely no idea what his response should be, and Niamh stepped to his side to assist him.

"My son is unaware of the circumstances facing us at this moment in time. Until his memories are restored to him, he cannot possibly understand the significance of what has occurred."

"When will you do this thing?" the centaur inquired gravely.

"Soon. Today. It is imperative he return immediately, as the danger is too great should we be forced to wait until Samhain."

What the heck?

"Then my brethren and I would be honored to assist."

"My thanks to you," Niamh solemnly replied. "Your added reinforcement would be a welcome safeguard."

What. The. Hell?

"Ian came to us grievously injured," she continued. "We have not yet had time to assess the danger we now face from the outer world. We will meet shortly in the Great Hall so that we may understand fully our risk and our options in his world as well as the threat to our borders. You will join with us, T'airneach?"

The immense dark-haired creature nobly bowed his head in assent.

"Our warriors even now assemble," Niamh again spoke. "Please join them. You will find refreshment there, and we will provide the same for those who remain here in the courtyard. We will convene as soon as all arrive."

Ian felt as though he had been punched in the gut. "You're sending me back today?" he asked in disbelief. He had only just discovered he had a family, *an immortal family*! He had just begun to allow himself to believe he was a part of this astonishing world, and *now they wanted to send him away*?

Her golden glow expanded, and he hurriedly stepped back. "Please stop doing that, Niamh! Stop trying to control my feelings."

"I only wish you peace, Ian," she said sadly. "Our time together is short, and I would have you well and whole before we are forced to part. I feel your confusion and anger, and though I cannot prevent our farewell, I can help you find solace before you leave us."

He searched Niamh's serenely beautiful face and was suddenly enveloped in such bone-deep, mind-numbing sorrow. She was a shining golden jewel in the sunlight, exquisite and mysterious beyond anything he could imagine. *And she was his mother*. Now, he was never going to get to know her or understand how he fit into this world.

Actually, that had been the problem his entire life. He didn't fit in anywhere. He was far too brilliant by any *mortal* standards, and he constantly had to hide his knowledge. Finally, he was beginning to understand why information came too easily. It was as though he *absorbed* it. He never had to study. He just … *knew*. Sometimes it was as if he actually picked thoughts and facts out of other's heads.

One of his teachers, who had known him since his first days at his school, had always called him an old soul, and it had rankled, because that was how he truly felt.

He was the responsible one, the serious one, always looking after the others, always working behind the scenes to keep his friends out of trouble. He was extremely protective, always seeing to their care and happiness.

Sometimes he felt *ancient* and tired beyond measure. He felt as though he had to hide who he really was, that he was an impostor. Ian had worked hard to fit in, but he had never really belonged. It wasn't so much that the others knew it, but he knew it. And now, when he finally had a chance to understand what was wrong with him, she was going to send him back.

There is nothing wrong with you, Ian. Of course she heard his thoughts, and she had answered in his head.

Niamh faced Ian, knowing without being told of the distress he felt.

"Ian, you are my son, always and forever in my heart. How I wish you could remain here within the Veil, safely at my side. You are of my blood and also of the blood of my most beloved husband. You and Áedan are all that is left of him, and I cherish you both more than you can possibly know."

She paused as her voice became husky. Tears glistened like diamonds in her jewellike eyes, and Ian felt the waves of intense sadness she suppressed beneath the serenity of her smile.

"You have both made great sacrifices to ensure the safety of our realm and the outer world from whence you came, and I could not be more proud to name you my children. I have often wanted to call you home and let the mortal world deal with its own problems, but long ago, we chose a path that cannot be easily altered or abandoned." She paused. "Walk with me, Ian. You must attend this meeting as well, for it affects all who dwell on both sides of the gateway."

As they turned up the path toward the Great Hall, Ian wondered what had happened between his parents and why his father had been married to someone else before he died, but he didn't want to distress Niamh by asking her that question. Perhaps he should ask Áedan. As soon as he thought it, he realized his error. He might as well have said it aloud, and he felt truly guilty about his errant reflections.

She sighed. Of course she was aware of what Ian was thinking.

"Immortals do not love as mortals do, Ian," she said softly. "Throughout the eons of our existence, it is likely that there will be only one to whom we completely give our hearts and whom we call *soul mate*, or as in your world, husband or wife, though that human bond is nowhere near as strong. Our souls recognize each other, and it is forever done. We are bound to that person for all eternity. Your father, although mortal, was such to me, and I to him." Her radiant golden light dimmed slightly. "Daniel Thorne was not the person you believe him to be."

"Obviously, if the two of you were … *soul mates*." He used the word she had. "I don't understand why you weren't together, though."

"Daniel Thorne was not my mate," she said gently.

"I don't understand. Are you saying … Daniel Thorne wasn't my father?"

"In many ways, he was, Ian, but he was not who you thought he was."

"We look exactly alike, Niamh. Even Áedan looks like him."

"Forgive me, Ian. I should have said nothing. I could speak to you now of many things, but you would find much confusing and even difficult to believe," Niamh said softly. "Soon, we will open your memories, and then you will understand why I hesitate. Had you remained in Scotland, I would have gradually unsealed your memories and imparted the knowledge of our world. You would have known me in the early years of your childhood. By the age of sixteen, your memories would have been fully restored to you. You are a powerful being, Ian, and it was necessary to allow you to grow up in the outer world as wholly mortal as possible, without the great burden of the knowledge that you will shortly regain."

"Áedan already told me this."

"Ahh, yes." She tilted her head in that way of hers that told him she was rifling through his memories. It no longer unnerved him as it had in the beginning. "It seems he did."

Ian felt his frustration grow. He didn't want to wait. Why wouldn't someone just answer his questions? Why all the mystery? Why wouldn't Áedan or Niamh just tell him what was really going on?

He felt the soothing touch of Niamh's golden light and her gentle voice in his head. *Be patient a little longer, my son.*

She turned her neon-blue gaze upon him, and he felt its impact in every cell in his body. Her eyes were clear and unshuttered, and for a second, it was as if he could see the vast infinity of the universe in those boundless, fathomless depths. It was a deep and endless place where all knowledge, all truth, all that ever was, and all that ever would be resided.

Her Power was like the blast of an atomic bomb in the initial phase as the atom splits. She was the quiet before the roar of winds ruptured the sky, the surreal, breathless peace before the destruction of the world. She was the beginning and the end of all things. Ian could see and breathe and feel the godlike power in her. She was like nothing imaginable or explainable, and he was suddenly awed and humbled by her presence.

He realized he needed to stop pushing her and trust that she knew best. Everyone in this place revered her and adhered to her decisions. He was fortunate she hadn't already blasted him into oblivion.

Her lips quirked into that serene Mona Lisa smile of hers. "I would never blast you into oblivion, my son, though I must admit that at times, you do try my patience."

"You know it's just wrong that you know absolutely every thought in my head," he groused. The deep dimples on the sides of his mouth appeared as he broke into a wry smile.

"That is my right as your mother. Do not human mothers do the same?"

"I'm sure they would if they could read minds as well as you can." He laughed. There was absolutely no way of getting around her. Áedan must have had a heck of a time growing up in this place. She was certainly like no mother he had ever known or expected to have.

Ian would have liked to ask Niamh why she had sent him instead of Áedan into the mortal world, but he knew it was time to put his questions on hold. As she had said, all would be answered soon enough.

Probably by the end of the day, he mused gloomily, and then he would once again be sent back to his own world.

The thought was a bitter pill on his tongue. He would have liked more time to explore and learn about this magical realm of the Tuatha. He would have liked to come to terms with this part of his heritage. And he wasn't at all certain he was ready to return to his old life, especially with his murderous witch of a stepmother out for his blood.

As they arrived in the Great Hall, a golden Tuatha girl in the flowing, colorful medieval garb that he was becoming accustomed to brought Ian a goblet of the minted, honeyed beverage that had helped him heal so quickly. Thirteen others, including two centaurs, were already at one of the long tables on one side of the room, and Niamh and Ian joined them.

Ian recognized four men and two women from the previous night's banquet, as well as Caitria, Áedan, T'airneach, and the cold, beautiful warrior who had glared at him last night.

Danii. She took his breath away. She stood near the large table surrounded by the others, and for a moment, the room seemed to shift under his feet. He locked onto the stunning immortal and couldn't look away. Nothing and no one else existed. His world narrowed to the fiery blond warrior from his dreams. She was magnificent! Her eyes blazed, and Ian could tell she was spitting mad. The air actually crackled around her, and small sparks of brilliant light arced from her body. Ian couldn't seem to tear his gaze away from her face. He was so focused on her that he nearly stumbled into Niamh. The sudden jolt brought him back to reality.

As they reached the table, Áedan was saying something in the Tuathan language that Ian couldn't understand, but his tone was unmistakably sarcastic. His comment was met with an audible gasp by the others in attendance. All eyes at the table turned to Danii as she furiously spat out a response. Ian noticed she fingered the hilt of the long jeweled knife sheathed at her side.

Several pairs of eyes veered to Ian and then back again to Danii as he waited to see if she would actually turn the weapon on his brother. Why had everyone glanced his way for that brief moment before looking quickly away?

Áedan simply raised his winged eyebrows and regarded her with a mocking grin. The tension at the table was palpable as Niamh and Ian seated themselves.

Niamh's golden glow brightened, enveloping all those present. Ian felt a wave of tranquil serenity invade his body and realized that Niamh had just effectively settled whatever argument the others were having.

"We will use the English tongue in this forum so that Ian may understand the proceedings and participate," she regally informed those assembled around her. Her tone, as always, was as soft and pure as delicate strains of music on a summer breeze, but there was an underlying command and warning that whatever challenge had been issued was at an end.

As Niamh introduced each person, Ian held his breath. He already knew the blond spitfire's name from his dream. He was certain he was right. Ian's pulse leapt as Niamh spoke her name aloud. *Danii.* What was this intense reaction he had to her every time he was in her presence? She literally rocked his world with the earth-shaking ferocity of an erupting volcano. It was all he could do to focus and remain outwardly calm when she was anywhere near him.

The blond male warrior from the previous night was introduced as Hakan, high commander of the Elite and Court Guard. Danii was named commander of the Elite Guard, and another powerful male, Einarr, commander of the Court Guard. Two other warriors, Gilbrandr and Vidarr, received the titles of captains of the Elite Guard, while Áedan was formally introduced as commander of Niamh's personal guard.

Hakan. Ian now had a name for the too-handsome man who had put his teeth on edge by his proprietary presence at Danii's side the night before. He narrowed his eyes slightly as he assessed the Tuatha warriors. Power clung to each of them like a second skin. Even though their perfect, classically chiseled faces seemed youthful, there was something dangerous about all of them, even Danii.

Their eyes held too much knowledge, as though they had seen the creation of the cosmos, the beginning and end of the universe, and every other unfathomable mystery indecipherable to mortal man. Perhaps they had.

They were all very tall and powerfully built, with muscles rippling beneath their clothing each time they moved. Even Danii, although highly feminine and curved and perfect in all the right places, exuded palpable, flagrant strength and possessed toned, athletic muscle. The formfitting, belted tunic and leggings only emphasized her narrow waist, long legs, and other feminine features that he tried not to stare at.

God, Ian! He harshly reined in his thoughts. *Stop staring at her! Stop staring at her body!* He was acting completely out of character.

Danii's eyes met his and glared. Ian knew she'd read his mind. He glanced away immediately, embarrassed that he couldn't seem to control his attraction to her. The situation was intolerable. Maybe he did need to go home, where no one was aware of his unguarded observations.

Caitria and two other women, Aileas and Eithne, were introduced as healers. Their colorful clothing wafted around them as they moved, and all three seemed to flow like water, their bodies ethereal and almost insubstantial. Their energy was soft and gentle, light and soothing, like the elusive gossamer brush of a butterfly wing.

And the last, Alastriona and Arthfael, a sister and brother, were introduced as the *Keepers of the Past.* The two *immortal librarians* were polite and solemn and very similar in appearance. Arthfael intently perused an ancient-looking piece of parchment, while his sister nudged him slightly to get his attention as Niamh made the introductions.

T'airneach stepped forward, presenting the other centaur as L'aoch, his second in command. L'aoch, like T'airneach, was immense and powerful. The centaurs were beings of enormous strength and dignity, yet Ian could feel their wildness, almost taste it on his tongue. It filled the air, feral and untamed, like crashing whips of lightning in a thunderstorm, and he knew they were even more dangerous than the Tuatha warriors.

"Now, we must all be made aware of the details of what has transpired at Thorne Manor," Niamh stated. "Áedan, you will tell us what you have learned, and then Ian will give us any other information he believes can be helpful to us."

"The witch is now in control," Danii interrupted in a deadly voice. "Áedan has failed in his duty to safeguard the bridge between our worlds, and for the first time in centuries, we face threat from the mortal realm."

"Be calm, daughter." Niamh's voice was tranquil, and her light glowed even more brightly. "All here have sacrificed much in defense of the portal. Emotions must be set aside while we debate how to best contain the damage."

"You are correct, Danii. The fault is mine." Áedan spoke quietly. "There is nothing I can do to change the past, though I would forfeit my life if it could be undone." Pain etched his handsome face, and his voice conveyed his misery. "We have begun to suspect that Miranda may have guessed that Ian is ... different. She has tested his blood, and possibly mine as well, and by now knows that there is something highly unusual about it. If this is the case, she is much more dangerous than we at first believed."

"How could she get Ian's blood?" Danii demanded. "And *flaming gods*, Áedan, how could she get yours?" Her tone was scathing.

"I'm sorry," Ian uttered, looking around him at the stunned immortals. "I didn't know there was anything unusual about me at that time. I allowed her to take it." Part of him was truly distressed that he might have endangered these people, but another outraged part of him defensively insisted that if he was supposed to keep secrets, someone at some point in the past seventeen years should have bloody well stepped up to let him know.

Amid the gasps and cries of disbelief, Niamh's tranquil voice again filled the room. "What is done cannot be undone. We must understand the extent of the damage so that we may prepare our defense." Her soothing warmth once more washed over those in her presence, easing the tension.

"My blood was on an old rugby shirt," Áedan said quietly. "At the time I chose to keep it, the technology did not exist for DNA to be studied."

Ian's eyes turned to Áedan in confusion.

"The rugby shirt that belonged to my dad?"

"Yes, Ian," Áedan answered grimly.

For a moment, Ian couldn't think. He studied Áedan's dark, handsome features, trying to put the puzzle pieces together. He was missing something, something really important, but he couldn't get his brain to function. A memory in the back of his mind tried to push through, but it wouldn't surface. His head felt like it had been split open with a knife, and Niamh immediately placed her hand to his temple, drawing out the torturous, shooting pain.

"No one ages here, am I right?" He looked around at all the immortals who appeared to be just out of their teens even though he knew them to be hundreds or even thousands of years old. "Does that mean when you spend time here, your body rejuvenates at a cellular level? Does that mean even if you're old, your body becomes younger if you return here from the outside world?" His head split again with another thrust of knifelike pain.

Again, Niamh touched his temple, dulling the impact.

"Do not try to force the memories, Ian. They must be opened in the proper way, or you will suffer greatly." Niamh's tone was gentle.

"Yes, Ian, you are correct," Áedan answered him.

Niamh rested her neon gaze on Áedan in mild but clear censure.

"You're my dad!" Ian gasped in shock. Suddenly, it was all coming together.

"Not exactly." Áedan's tone was noncommittal.

"You're Daniel Thorne!" Ian accused.

Áedan assessed Ian for a long moment before answering. The others in the room remained quiet. The hushed, strained silence was nearly deafening. "Yes, Ian, I *was* Daniel Thorne."

"But how? Why?"

Áedan closed his eyes for a moment and breathed deeply before facing Ian fully.

"Why didn't you come back?" Ian's voice barely concealed his hurt.

"I couldn't." He looked to Niamh, who nodded for him to continue.

"I will shield Ian from the pain. He deserves to know." She laid her hand gently across his temple once more while Áedan spoke.

"I was severely injured that day in the boat, Ian. A scuba diver in the water shot me with a speargun and then dragged me overboard. The spear sliced through my chest and nicked my heart. I fought him off you as he tried to pull you under, and I eventually drowned him, but I was in really bad shape. I thought we were both finished."

Ian stared at him, aghast.

"Niamh knew somehow. She always seems to know when we are in mortal danger, and she brought me here after getting you to shore. But it took too much time for me to heal. Because of the abundance of Magic in our world, no one ages and there is no natural or inevitable death. Anyone entering from the outside regenerates quickly. Our bodies heal at a rapid rate. As our cells regenerate, so do our bodies. The ravages of aging fall away until we are youthful and perfect, always in the prime of our lives."

Ian continued to stare speechlessly at him as Áedan tried to explain.

"It took many days to heal completely. I already appeared twenty years younger by the time I was able to return. It would have been impossible for me to try to take back the identity of Daniel Thorne, especially with Miranda in the picture."

Ian was stunned. He allowed it to sink in. Of course. It all made sense now. Or did it really?

"Why were you pretending to be Daniel Thorne?"

"It is as I told you when you first awoke, Ian. Our family has always guarded the gateway to our world." He hesitated. "It was my turn."

"So are you really my brother?"

"Yes."

"Who is our father?"

"His name was Gabráin."

Ian already knew. This was the formidable raven-haired man from his dream with features so similar to his and Áedan's.

"Where is he?"

"He died long ago."

"And he was mortal?" Both Áedan and Niamh had already told him so, but Ian felt the need to ask again.

"Yes. He was a great warrior, Ian. He was a very great man."

Confusion reigned in Ian's head. As before, the more answers he received, the more questions arose. None of this added up to any explainable timeline.

Danii firmly intervened. "This is unimportant at this time. We must cease this talk of Gabráin." She glanced at Niamh, who now clutched the edge of the table so tightly her fingers were white. Her golden skin was nearly as bleached as her gown, and her eyes held a tragic, faraway glaze. The three healers rose in unison.

"You know this upsets her," Danii hissed to Áedan. She then faced Ian with near-blinding focus, her inhuman blue eyes blazing with disapproval. As always, the force of her gaze hit him with the impact of a tidal wave. "You will understand everything when your memories are opened, Ian," she stated stiffly. A hint of something like bitterness tinged her voice.

How many times had he heard that exact statement in the past two days?

"You will cease to demand answers." Danii's voice had now gone soft and low, not with the purity of Niamh's, but deadly serious, with a threatening quality that made the hair on the back of his neck stand up. "Or I will be the one to return your memories to you, and I vow you will not be happy with the way it is done. Niamh cannot sustain this constant barrage."

Ian was completely taken aback. *Had she just reacted to his thoughts about being told over and over again he must wait for answers? Had she just read his mind?* Of course she had. It seemed he was unable to keep a secret or a stray thought from anyone in this place. She had definitely just threatened him, and there was no doubt about her animosity toward him. He just didn't understand why.

Áedan moved to get between them, but Hakan got there first, his arm briefly circling Danii's waist as he positioned her to his far side.

Everything in Ian railed at that casual display of possessive intimacy.

"For now, we will concentrate on what we must do to repair this situation." Hakan's voice was a deep, pure rumble filled with absolute, unyielding authority. His stern, uncompromising visage promised swift retribution to anyone foolish enough to cross him.

The room turned suddenly icy, and Ian pivoted to see that Niamh's golden light had become a cold, wintry shade of gray.

A frosty sheet of crystal began to form on the walls and floor and every surface of the room. Enormous icicles emerged and glistened from the stone branches overhead. A glaze of thick, solid ice quickly spread to enclose the gothic arched windows.

The centaurs lifted their heads, nostrils flaring, their hooves scraping the stone floor as they shifted uneasily. The warriors tensed, energy flaring around them as though preparing some magical defense. Crackling flares of energy built up around their bodies, and blue balls of fire shimmered in the palms of their hands.

Hakan linked hands with Danii as they cast a shimmering blue shield around all those present, while within the bubble, Áedan cast another similar shield over Ian as a double reinforcement. It insulated him from the cold and dulled the sound of creaking wood and stone as ice flowed over every surface like a rapidly moving glacier, pressing up and outward against the carved interior, stressing the building in which they stood nearly to the breaking point.

Arthfael quickly seized his parchment from the rapidly icing table, stashing it into his tunic for protection, while his sister, wide-eyed and panicked, did the same with two scrolls, tucking them safely into the folds of her dress.

Caitria and the other two healers immediately surrounded Niamh, while a soft golden light gradually began to force its way through the silvery arctic ice. The three women began to glow more and more brightly as shades of amethyst, violet, and then deep purple swirled and mingled with the dilute golden light. A warm breeze swept through the room, chasing away the frigid air, gently wafting the colorful silks of their long flowing dresses. They resembled vibrant butterflies lifting and dipping their wings in flight.

The ice receded slowly at first and then completely, leaving the Great Hall surprisingly undamaged. The air smelled fresh and damp, like the aftermath of a storm. The three healers stepped away from the wielder of so much fearsome and destructive Power. The golden light of Niamh the Radiant was not nearly as radiant as before.

"I will be fine," she assured the three healers. Her beautiful face was once again a mask of serenity and composure, although everyone present could feel her distress. She faced the others. "My apologies," she said with great dignity. "It is imperative that we continue."

"I am truly sorry, Niamh." Ian was horrified and chastened that he had been the cause of this.

"No harm was done. You are not at fault, my son." Her placid, neon gaze touched each person in the hall. "Please, let us resume. Our time grows short."

An uncomfortable silence ensued as Áedan and Hakan turned their attention to Niamh. It was obvious that the three engaged in some kind of mental conversation that the others were excluded from.

Finally, Áedan grudgingly nodded and cleared his throat.

"As has been so eloquently pointed out"—Áedan glanced acerbically at Danii—"Miranda is in control for now. British law has granted her that right until Ian's eighteenth birthday, though MacTarran's exhaustive efforts have made it nearly impossible for her to gain any permanent autonomy over Ian."

The others restlessly settled back into place at the table as he began to speak.

"As you know, though dangerous, it was necessary for Ian to remain in the mortal realm after my *untimely demise* so that control of the portals would not pass from our family. He could not simply disappear from sight and then reappear years later without serious legal ramifications. It has always been our precedent to maintain a smooth, unbroken, and unchallenged line of inheritance. Also, his extended disappearance would have thrown the running of our estates into chaos, and I am certain Miranda would have immediately stepped in to claim and possibly dispose of our properties with no one to naysay her.

"Ian was removed from the United Kingdom three days after his fifth birthday and placed in a highly secure American boarding school. We have had guards around him since his arrival there."

Ian looked at him in utter shock, while the others nodded in agreement, as if this was old news. He guessed it was to everyone but himself.

"By law, as Daniel Thorne's wife and a presumed heir, Miranda is entitled to reside within the walls of Thorne Manor. Between Niamh's ghostly appearances and the MacShanes' efforts at various subtle forms of sabotage, as well as their assistance with additional and diverse hauntings, we have thus far been able to dissuade her from staying on the property. However, it seems she is ready to change that."

"The screaming banshee Mrs. MacShane told me about was Niamh?" Ian asked, slightly flummoxed, looking at his *mother* with renewed interest.

"Miranda was the screaming banshee. Niamh was the avenging specter from the gates of hell who chased her all over the manor and then threw her out into the rain." Áedan grinned and winked at Niamh. "No one could have done it better." The levity lightened the mood as Niamh returned his amused smirk with her own innocent, Mona Lisa smile.

Ian couldn't help but grin as well, imagining Miranda fleeing in terror from this paradigm of regally composed serenity. It seemed the others were also picturing the event. Even Hakan's stern, unsmiling mouth twitched, and the corners of his eyes crinkled slightly as he regarded Niamh.

"She had injured both my children," Niamh stated simply. "It was time for her to leave."

"Agreed," Áedan continued, amusement still coloring his voice. "As I was saying, the will was to be read on the twenty-first of June, the twelfth anniversary of my … ah, Daniel's death. It names Ian as sole heir to the Thorne Estate and all its holdings. However, it also provides a substantial financial settlement for Miranda and allows her use and access to any and all the Thorne properties for as long as she lives.

"The MacShanes are also named and granted their cottage and access to Thorne Manor and its lands for the duration of their lives. There is no further provision, as it was assumed that Daniel Thorne would live a long and healthy life and Ian would not inherit until he was well into his adult years. Other than the provision for Miranda, this has been the standard means of inheritance by our family for centuries."

"So there is no provision in the event of Ian's untimely death?" Arthfael inquired.

"No," Áedan replied curtly. "I must assume that Miranda believes if Ian is killed, she will inherit everything. Certainly, without any other living heirs, this would normally be the case. However, the purpose of the sealed codicil attached to every Thorne *last will and testament* for the past several centuries is to ensure that our properties do not pass from our line. It is the safeguard against just such an event as we have now. Though Thorne wives have been few throughout our dynasty, procedures have always been implemented to assure our properties remain within our control.

"The codicil is notarized and witnessed, but blank and unsigned by me. As soon as it is released to MacTarran, I will see to it that Miranda is stripped of all rights. It will probably be necessary to provide some financial benefit to her. Otherwise, it would draw undue suspicion, but the settlement will be small."

"Her life should be forfeit for her treachery," T'airneach growled aggressively. L'aoch supported his leader's decree, looking feral and deadly. The two centaurs shifted restlessly, their manes whipping and their nostrils flaring, as though readying themselves to charge through the portal and dispatch this reviled enemy of the Tuatha.

Niamh predictably sent out her golden light, though it was slightly less robust than usual. The tension lessened to a small degree, though the mood remained edgy.

"I could not agree with you more," Áedan said tightly. "There was no shortage of volunteers among our clan, I can assure you. Miranda was left alone because we assumed the courts would make her their problem. It has always been our goal to avoid scandal. The questions and media attention surrounding my death had brought our family too much into the spotlight already.

"Miranda's disappearance or premature death in the wake of my own would have created an outcry for an in-depth investigation into every aspect of our family dealings. This was something we could not afford. The fallout would have been too extensive, potentially exposing certain eccentricities concerning lines of succession as well as other more obvious observations about the lack of Thorne wives within our lineage.

"Also, too many good people have covered for us in small ways throughout our many lifetimes. We could not afford to expose them or put them at risk.

"It seems, however, that they failed in their investigation to uncover enough evidence against Miranda. I am thinking now that perhaps we should have planted some. This new attack on Ian has me thinking we should have allowed our allies to remove her."

Ian listened in stunned silence. These revelations were like something out of a suspense novel. "We have allies who know about us?" he asked, trying to grasp the extent of the network of safeguards and deception surrounding his family.

"Yes, Ian. They are few, but they are loyal. Certain of our clan have guarded our secrets for many generations now. Some carry our bloodline, though it is highly diluted."

Interesting.

"Unfortunately, because of the mysterious circumstances surrounding Daniel Thorne's death, the authorities insisted the will be placed in a sealed vault until I—*he* could be declared legally dead. This is why twelve years have passed between my disappearance and a lawful succession. Even Alan MacTarran was not allowed access to the document once it was placed into the bank's keeping."

"So as it stands, Áedan, the sealed codicil is blank and you cannot amend it until your return, and only if MacTarran can obtain it for you before the will is made public. *Your wife*, Miranda, is set to inherit not only an enormous sum of money but also *has* and will *retain* unrestricted access to the Thorne estate. And she has just made another attempt on Ian's life because he was left unprotected upon his return to Scotland. Correct me if I am wrong." Danii's statement was low and dangerous and dripped with condemnation.

"No, Danii, you're correct about everything except that Ian was unprotected. Our people surrounded him, and still he was attacked. No one foresaw the poison or that Miranda would strike so blatantly." His jaw clenched in a telltale sign of anger before being quickly disguised with one of his sarcastic smiles.

"However"—Áedan shot Danii a wolfish grin—"Ian is not dead, the estate is at present in complete turmoil, with Miranda once again the center of an investigation, and"—Áedan winked at Ian—"the armored car transporting the Thorne will has been hijacked on its way from the Royal Bank of Scotland. Nothing will happen for a few days while the authorities investigate these latest events. By now, the will is in MacTarran's possession. We still have time to change it."

"Does this not seem somewhat risky?" Alastriona spoke up, her words halting, her accent pronounced. "Will not the document, this *will*, be suspect when it reappears?"

"The truck will be found intact once we return. Hopefully, in the interim, its disappearance will throw even more suspicion on Miranda. This was the best we could accomplish on such short notice."

"Armored car ... truck?" Arthfael inquired. "This is something like a chariot?"

"More like an enclosed wagon without the horses," Áedan told him.

At his frown of confusion, Áedan locked eyes with him. He must have somehow sent a picture of it into his mind.

"Ahhh." Arthfael's scholarly face lit with understanding. "Quite ingenious for mortals."

"In truth, Áedan," Niamh remarked, "I am surprised that Miranda would have attempted to take Ian's life, especially in the way it occurred. It was extremely foolish, and I do not see what she hoped to gain. She must have realized that Ian's death or disappearance would only place her once more under suspicion. You know her better than any of us. Surely, she could not be that reckless."

Áedan's face darkened, and a muscle worked in his jaw. "I thought I knew her. Obviously, I know nothing of what is in her mind," he forced out through gritted teeth.

"You are certain this is her doing?"

"Who else? No one but Miranda has anything to gain from our deaths."

Áedan rubbed his temples, looking drained. "Our greatest dilemma is how to safeguard Ian once he returns. It is of paramount importance that he return quickly. However, we are positive he will be in great jeopardy as soon as Miranda knows he is still alive. He is still considered a minor and thus subject to Miranda's guardianship for one more year. Until we can make the codicil public or arrange to have her arrested, he must be safeguarded."

"So you will need to return with him and contact Alan MacTarran before anyone can become aware of Ian's presence," Hakan stated. "How swiftly can you make changes to the codicil and arrange for the armored car to be recovered without suspicion?"

"That depends upon how fast I can reach MacTarran. He will be expecting us but will, of course, have no idea how quickly we will be able to return."

"Do you have anything to add that might be of benefit to us, Ian?" Niamh asked.

"I'm not sure." Ian hesitantly looked at Áedan as he thought back. "Mrs. MacShane probably filled you in on everything that she knew about. I saw you with her in the kitchen the night Miranda arrived." His brows creased in a frown. "Miranda brought in Dr. Maynard for a reason, though. I overheard them talking about me not having a birth certificate. Maybe that has something to do with why they took my blood, and my dad's ... uh ... *your* jersey. They might have been wanting to prove I'm not really your son."

"We are virtually identical in looks. That was a foolish track to take, although it seems they did indeed find something." Áedan looked furious. "Miranda's crimes are multiplying by the hour."

"Do I have a birth certificate?" Ian asked doubtfully.

"Yes, Ian. Though it is a forged one, it will pass muster."

"I can't think of anything else right now. What did you mean about eccentricities concerning lines of succession and Thorne wives?"

"That is a question best saved for later."

Ian clenched his jaw, resisting the urge to glare at Áedan.

"I can't possibly understand a fraction of what is going on here unless you at least bring me up to speed on a few things, Áedan," Ian said in frustration. "Because you won't talk to me, I have no idea what might be helpful, just as I was clueless about the blood ... and everything else," he added darkly, refusing to give ground.

Áedan exhaled a deep breath of air, looking to Niamh for guidance.

"You asked for my input," Ian pressed, "but how can I give it without some common point of reference? You continuously refer to things I know nothing about as though they're common knowledge. Honestly, Áedan, I'm as tired of asking questions as you are of hearing them. Obviously, everyone here knows things that make sense of all this, but I really don't have a freaking clue what's going on. So why don't you just wave your magic wand now and do whatever mojo you need to do to bring my memories back so we can quit with all the this cloak-and-dagger crap?"

Ian hadn't raised his voice—in fact, he'd tried hard to keep it level and unemotional for Niamh's sake—but he was really done with this.

"It's not that simple, Ian, or we would have, but you are correct." Áedan looked to Niamh once more.

Niamh sighed. "I should have opened your memories prior to this meeting, but there has been no time since your arrival," she said to Ian. "I have no doubt this will simply raise more questions for you. However, Áedan may answer if he is so inclined."

"All right, Ian," Áedan said, "I will try to explain this as simply as possible. Our lines of succession are not always straightforward. There has always been a direct chain of inheritance from father to son. However, Thorne wives have been a rarity, and this has, at times, presented a problem so far as the legitimacy of heirs.

"Throughout the many centuries we have stood as guardians"—Áedan now spoke slowly, as though he was choosing each word carefully—"we have married for political alliances and only when absolutely necessary. We tend to find ways of introducing our offspring into the world without the complication of mortal women who must be brought into our confidence. In this day and age, it is fairly straightforward. Unmarried women within our clan who have either lost a child at birth or themselves died in childbirth have provided us with the means to introduce new heirs. It is far less important in this age that we marry. However, in times past, this was not so. Many of our wives have had full knowledge of our world and *pretended* to carry our heirs."

Ian looked at Áedan as though he'd lost his mind.

"I warned you, Ian. You now have a hundred more questions than you have answers to."

A dangerous chill filled the room, and Ian looked to Niamh, but it was not her this time. Danii radiated a cold, palpable fury that made Niamh's brief sojourn into the arctic winter feel like a mild spring day.

The blast of arctic air was immediately contained. Danii stood, chin up, shoulders back, eyes blazing, as did the other three warriors in a show of respect and solidarity. Only Hakan remained in his seat. As always, his harshly beautiful features were an unreadable, dangerous-looking mask. His narrowed eyes were his only tell that something untoward had occurred as he and Danii exchanged a succinct nod.

"I am finished here, Áedan." Danii's voice was as clipped and icy as the gust that had come and gone so quickly. "I must return to my duties. Gilbrandr"—she addressed the striking warrior next to her—

"you will remain here and apprise me of the proceedings at the conclusion of this forum."

"Yes, Commander," he answered formally. He crossed his right arm over his chest, fist over heart, and gave a sharp nod of assent.

Danii returned the gesture of respect to him and to the other two warriors still standing at attention. She then acknowledged the centaurs in the same way, warrior to warrior. It was a surreal scene of majestic decorum, highly charged yet fraught with a boding sense of peril.

T'airneach and L'aoch gravely inclined their heads, returning the warrior's salute.

Ian had no idea what had just occurred. He stared dumbfounded as Danii pivoted with formal dignity before stepping away from the table.

"We cannot wait to open his memories." Distress rolled off Niamh in waves, and Ian hoped she would not have a relapse. "This disjointed disclosure of information is difficult for all of us and cannot continue."

Niamh suddenly stilled, as though listening to something the others could not hear. Danii immediately halted, while the others surged to their feet.

Immediately, Niamh raised her arms, and a cool, dense mist engulfed all those in the room. *We are under attack. There is no time to wait for the rest of our warriors.*

Ian heard her words in his head. His feet left the ground, and he experienced a sense of swift, flowing movement and disorientation. The mist swirled and eddied around his body, twining itself around him like ghostly, silken vines. He felt strangely lightheaded yet pleasantly cool and buoyant at the same time. He didn't drift so much as stream through the open windows, across the courtyard, out past streams and forests, and then high over peaked mountains and cliffs.

Ian stumbled slightly as his feet regained a solid surface. He found himself standing on a rocky shore and watched in awe as what appeared to be hundreds of Viking ships filled the skies and crested the waves through the churning waters of an endless turquoise ocean.

Áedan, Danii, and the three other warriors spread out in front of the small group, drawing their swords. Danii's blade glowed with a fiery blue light that arced like lightning. The others' burned with a cool white flame. T'airneach and L'aoch quickly brandished their own blazing swords and separated, flanking the group and taking up positions on the outer perimeter. They rapidly pivoted, eyeing the forest and the high ridges rising from the dense green trees behind them.

Niamh moved forward into the midst of her warriors, raising her arms skyward. Dark storm clouds instantly descended over the ocean. Swirling winds and rain assaulted the small group on the beach so that it was difficult to stand.

While the others struggled to maintain their balance, Niamh seemed to gather the chaotic force, pulling it toward her in a display of unimaginable Power. She then unleashed the full brunt of the storm's fury on the advancing ships. Clouds boiled, and lightning arced from her fingers through the sky, striking at ships and forcing them back. Her long blond hair flowed behind her like a cape, and her white dress billowed over her body like a ghostly shroud. She was fearsome in her domination of the elements, and Ian caught his breath at the sheer magnitude of her ability.

Just as suddenly as it had begun, the seas began to calm, and although the angry clouds still whirled around the encroaching armada, it appeared almost as if a glass dome had been positioned over the ships.

Ian shifted uneasily and glanced at his companions. Each wore a look of utter fearlessness and determination. The small band of immortals stood confident and undaunted against the thousands of invaders sailing menacingly into the harbor.

Niamh withdrew the force of her winds, and an eerie stillness enveloped the ocean. Ian felt disoriented for a moment, as if time had simply stopped. It was a surreal sensation akin to floating through a dream without will or form.

A dark figure appeared in the sky and slowly moved toward the beach. As it drew near, Ian gasped, realizing the form coming toward them was a man. He advanced on them as though walking on an invisible surface, his arms held out, away from his sides. His long black hair whipped in an illusory wind, and he was dressed in a similar manner to Áedan and Danii, although his clothing appeared shiny, as if it were made of metal.

"Ahh, Niamh! Is this any way to greet an old friend?" His voice was rich and deep, and he honored her with a low bow, as though they were meeting in a medieval ballroom instead of in the midst of a battle.

They were speaking an ancient language that Ian suddenly realized he understood. Somehow, he was drawing the information to him through his connection to Niamh. He didn't question why; he simply accepted it.

"Tyr. You breach our borders. You bring your warships to our shores. How should I greet you?" Niamh's voice was soft and melodic. She remained unruffled and spoke politely, as if merely inquiring about the weather.

"My dear, surely the time for animosity between us is long past. We have come to offer a truce. We would welcome an alliance between our two great races."

Ian recognized that the man's smile did not reach his cold eyes. His voice was beautiful and beguiling, as was the man himself, but he was too perfect, too beautiful. Something about him wasn't right.

Look with your mind, Ian, not your eyes. He heard Niamh's voice in his head. *He only appears beautiful. He uses glamour to fool us. He is a monster.*

"You request a truce when even now you prepare your attack. It has indeed been long, Tyr, if you have forgotten that I know your thoughts as soon as you think them."

"My lovely Niamh." He shook his head as though in mock disbelief, as his dark eyes avariciously roved over her body. "You ever misjudge my motives." His voice took on a coaxing quality, its tenor as pure and beautiful as that of any Tuatha. "Let us speak together like the old friends we are. Have you forgotten that we once fought on the same side, that we wanted the same things, that we were once allies?"

"Tyr," Niamh said sadly, "we have never wanted the same things. Treachery and lies have no place among allies, and you deal wholly in both. Leave our shores now before I am forced to destroy you."

He stiffened, his demeanor changing abruptly. "I see that you have your weak *human* children at your side." The word *human* was a snarl. "Who guards the bridge from the mortal world?" he asked silkily. "No one? What a pity. Perhaps I will visit your humans."

"You will not win this battle, Tyr, and you cannot enter there without crossing through our world."

"You were always too fond of those pathetically feeble mortals whom you have protected for untold millennia," he spat in anger. "They are not worth the dirt you scrape from your shoes. They know nothing but greed and war and destruction, and yet they break so easily. They care nothing for their own kind. You do humans a disservice by allowing them free reign and free will to destroy their planet. You are a *god*, Niamh. It is right that the earth's people should revere and serve you. Think how much better off they would be to be ruled and guided by you."

Tyr's beautiful face turned crafty, and for a moment, the true beast that he was flickered there. Ian saw a great horned creature with an enormous and powerful body. His skin had a bronze tint to it, and his large mouth had a twisted, cruel quality about it that made Ian shudder.

"We could reign over the humans together, Niamh." His face and voice were once again beautiful and pure. "Think of what you could give them. Release the Magic you have bound to this place and allow it to flow freely over the earth once again. No more war, no more famine, only peace and prosperity. Humans have shown time and again that they cannot provide for themselves, that they cannot refrain from heinous violations against one another. They cry out for a benevolent liege."

"Tyr, you would rule more brutally than the worst human in the history of their race. This I cannot allow. You are the very reason we were forced to bind the earth's Magic. When our people were sent out by our goddess Danu across the vast black ocean of stars and eternal night, it was not with the intention of conquering or enslaving those we found. We were charged with their protection and that of their home-worlds. We burned our ships so your people could not journey back through the stars, could not subjugate and enslave other races. It was our solemn oath to our goddess that we would safeguard those we encountered, and it is our resolve to keep our promise to Danu. You would destroy the bountiful earth that gives all of us life and sustenance as casually as you would squash an ant."

"Your fate is sealed, then, Niamh." Tyr's voice was a velvet purr. "You will perish with the rest of the frail mortals you would protect. It is only a matter of time."

Niamh suddenly tensed and raised her arms in a sweeping movement as the other Tuatha brandished their swords high. The centaurs closed the circle, and Niamh slammed a barrier around the group as a hail of fire and spears of lightning were hurled at them. But she was not quick enough. Ian's breath exploded from his lungs as a blistering fireball struck his shoulder, slamming him to his back.

"Protect him, Áedan!" Danii cried out over the chaos of flaming projectiles and the sizzling arc of arcane blades as centaurs and Tuatha blocked and dispersed the evil Magic. "He cannot shield himself, and Niamh must focus all her strength on the Formorians." She swung her sword, deflecting lightning bolts and fire away from Ian.

The searing pain in Ian's shoulder quickly intensified to an unbearable inferno of scorching torment. Razor-like tendrils burned and snaked their way up his neck and face and down into his chest toward his heart. He rolled to his knees with a cry of agony, unable to bear the torturous pain.

Caitria and Eithne were suddenly at his side, pushing him back down. A shock of icy energy pounded into his chest, and biting, wintry crystals pulsed against the rapidly spreading fire consuming his body. Ian's heart stuttered, missed a beat, and then another, as a fiery fist began to crush his lungs. The fist wrapped around his heart and squeezed. Blood flowed from his nose and mouth, and Caitria screamed, "Niamh, he's dying!"

A tremendous sense of calm suddenly washed over Ian. He could feel Niamh's presence within him. She was everywhere, filling him and surrounding him with her soothing essence. Somehow she was simultaneously shielding those on the beach, forcing back the enemy ships, and healing Ian from within. He could feel her pushing out the fiery venom, extinguishing it cell by cell. Her soothing chant filled him with peace even as his connection with her made him aware of the enormous effort she was exerting to hold back the enemy ships.

He heard the sounds of many people running and shouting as they were joined by hundreds of immortals. Centaurs and other winged creatures charged from the forests, taking up positions of defense.

Linked as he was to Niamh, Ian was aware of her connection to the thousands of sentient minds as well as her immense Power and utter control over the infinite forces of nature. The entirety of the earth and its beasts awakened to do her bidding. Even the elements arose at her command. Such abilities as she possessed were simply beyond the realm of imagining. As Tyr had said, Niamh was truly a god, for only a god could have such all-encompassing knowledge and wield such formidable Power.

Caitria and Eithne took up the chant, and Ian once again experienced a sensation of being surrounded and filled with healing warmth as the essence of both healers flowed into him.

The link was very different than his with Niamh. Both women exuded a comforting, healing energy, but their inner touch was light, far less potent. There was no universal connection to the minds and thoughts of others and no sense of being one with nature and the elements. Niamh's Power was unparalleled, and Ian realized with a certainty that his mother was extraordinary, even among other immortals.

As his pain subsided and Niamh withdrew, Ian once more questioned how it was possible that he could belong to any part of this world. These immortals were the mystical beings of myth, the great gods and goddesses of legend. How could any of this truly exist?

Laboriously shifting his focus back toward the battle, Ian noted that both Danii and Áedan still guarded him, defiantly standing between him and the invaders in a position of readiness and defense. He frowned as he noticed bright-red blood smeared across Danii's face. Had she been injured too? If she had, she showed no other sign of weakness as she fearlessly faced the Formorians.

Niamh stood on the rocky shore like an avenging angel, her white dress and long platinum hair whipping in the deadly storm winds she commanded.

Some of the defenders shielded and deflected the Formorian's fiery onslaught, while others hurled bolts of lightning against the intruding ships. Other immortals stood behind Niamh, and it seemed to Ian that they were focused on adding their strength to hers.

As the storm increased to lethal intensity, Niamh rose high into the air, gathering the black roiling gale into a deadly sphere. As its winds and lightning escalated to a terrifying level, she hurled the complete force of the fearsome tempest against the Formorians ships. They were blasted back as if struck by a nuclear bomb. The sea began to churn and swirl, and an enormous maelstrom opened beneath the Formorian armada.

Before the defeated fleet could be pulled beneath the hungry waves, Tyr appeared once more in the sky. Spreading his arms wide as he had done before, he gazed at Niamh with a mix of fury and utter yearning.

"Spare my people, Niamh. We will withdraw. You have my word."

"Your word, Tyr?" Her white gown billowed, and her hair streamed around her as she faced him in all her golden glory. She was like a sun breaking through the darkness, a brilliant, fiery star shining over a sea of endless night. "For how long this time? How long before you attack us again?"

"One day, Niamh, you will understand that we are not enemies, but brothers and sisters. One day you will understand that your pacifistic nature does more harm than good by allowing those less worthy to sully and destroy a planet of immense abundance and beauty."

Tyr moved in closer, slowly gliding forward upon the air, arms still wide, as if in supplication, but there was no contrition in his face.

"I ask you, Niamh"—his voice was low and beguiling—"how long before the mortals destroy their planet entirely? The earth is dying. You have stripped it of its Magic, and its nature deities now seek refuge elsewhere. The water, sky, and soil are contaminated, and without the healing and regenerating properties inherent in the Magic you suppress, the earth will soon perish. The greed of the mortals already destroys all that is good and pure. How long before their wars and bombs decimate all that is left? Think, Niamh. Is the earth better off now than when we reigned? Are its people better off being controlled by the corrupt regimes who sell themselves to others for power and gold than they were when they worshipped us and we gave them laws to live by?"

"Tyr, we were charged by our goddess to help and defend, not to conquer. You talk of greed and corruption, yet you and races like yours seek to subjugate the earth and take its riches for yourself. You would enslave or eradicate the population, and this we cannot allow. If it means we must suppress the Magic, then so be it. Until you understand that it is better to live in peace with others, whether as powerful as yourselves or not, you can never be allowed to dwell there. We have inhabited the earth for millennia, and it is our home. We are part of its history and culture. We are part of its myths and legends. While it is true that we were once worshipped and honored as deities in its early history, we used our Power and status to teach and heal. Our presence there was peaceful. Again, I say to you, Tyr, we do not seek to conquer but to coexist peacefully. We withdrew because of *you*. We bound the earth's Magic to keep *you* from using it to conquer and destroy. The most dangerous enemy the earth has is *you*."

Tyr made no discernible movement, but somehow, he appeared more threatening as Niamh spoke. His expression remained calm and even, but a slow darkness emanated from the air around him. Ian hoped Niamh knew what she was doing, because he didn't trust Tyr not to attack her at his first opportunity.

"How foolish you are in your beliefs, Niamh. The earth needs the Formorians to survive. And we will have it! You simply delay the inevitable. It would be a shame if the Tuatha must perish in order for us to accomplish this. You have never learned to share."

"Be gone from our shores, Tyr. It is only our inherent respect for all life, which you so despise, that has kept you alive for so long. Do not test our benevolence, or you will lose."

Tyr sketched an elegant bow to Niamh, accompanied with a mocking smile.

"This is not the end, my queen. You are destined to rule at my side. Perhaps it is *that knowledge* and not your benevolence that stays your hand." He placed his fingers to his lips, his eyes promising things that made Ian's skin crawl as he and his force faded into the dark, roiling clouds that swept them out to sea.

Áedan knelt at Ian's side, his blue eyes blazing. "How do you feel, Ian?" His tone was angrier than Ian had ever heard it.

"He wants our mother? *Eew!* That's just ... sooo wrong on so many levels," Ian slurred. His head fell back as he rode another wave of fire in his shoulder. It burned like the devil but wasn't nearly as intense as before. The healers had done something to him to make him more comfortable. But as the pain began to subside, he found himself as loopy as the time he and his roommates had downed a contraband bottle of whiskey.

Ian saw the corners of Áedan's mouth twitch into a humorless smile before his world went black.

CHAPTER X

Ian made his way down the verdant, sloping path toward the Great Hall. Willow boughs swayed and rustled in the faint, fragrant breeze, and birds called out to one another high above him in the lacy branches.

He moved stiffly. The wound on his shoulder burned and tugged if he twisted or turned too quickly, and he couldn't yet take a deep breath. But all things considered, he was doing pretty well for having survived the second attempt on his life in under a week. In fact, other than panting for breath and feeling as though someone had shoved a fist through his heart, he was peachy. Maybe he could try for one more near-death experience before the week's end, just to round out his summer vacation.

Actually, Ian knew he had been very lucky. Niamh and the healers had gotten to him quickly this time, so his recovery had been amazingly fast.

One more night here, he mused as he gazed in awe at his surroundings. One more night in this astounding, beautiful, *hazardous* paradise, and then he would be home.

But what was he returning to? He didn't even want to think about what waited for him on the other side of the portal. He'd worry about that later when he got a chance to talk to Áedan, as immediately after the battle, those still standing had closeted themselves to talk strategy.

The clash with the Formorians had taken its toll on everyone, and between his time with the healers and Niamh's own need to recover after such a formidable expenditure of Power, Ian had been given a brief reprieve before this ceremony, this *opening of his memories*, could take place.

A blond, black-clad woman approached from below, eyes downcast as if in thought. The fading rays of sunlight shone like glowing amber off her pale hair and elicited sparkles of iridescent color from the jewel-encrusted hilt of the dirk she wore at her side. Her movements were graceful and sure, the smooth gliding rhythm reminiscent of a lioness's, her warrior's training evident in every step she took. Her face carried a vulnerability he had not seen before. Her expression revealed an inner sadness that surprised and distressed him. His heart reached for her, and he felt an ache that had nothing to do with his injuries.

As she glanced up, their eyes met and locked. A tangible current of awareness flowed between them, and his entire being reacted with an intensity that shook him. For an instant, her compelling blue gaze flooded him with a warmth that took his breath away. His still-healing heart stuttered, and his stomach flip-flopped. It was as if his soul called out to hers. He was encouraged by the unexpected spark of acceptance in her eyes. She had protected him fiercely during the battle. Was the disconcerting animosity she had displayed toward him behind them now?

The corners of his mouth lifted in a cautious smile, and for a moment, he thought she would return it.

There was a sudden unguarded flicker of alarm, as though she had just become aware of her surroundings. A look akin to panic or confusion, like a wild thing caught in a net, instantly replaced the unguarded show of emotion before she shut him out. Once again, she donned the cold, haughty facade she seemed to wear whenever he was near her. She sidestepped him, looking away. It was apparent she was not going to acknowledge his presence as she passed, but he needed to know why.

"Danii?"

She halted, unsmiling, face averted, that self-possessed mask now firmly in place.

"Yes, Ian?" she asked tautly.

What could he say to break through the ice? He desperately wanted to end the hostility she seemed to feel for him. "I wanted to thank you for today. You saved my life."

"Niamh saved you," she said curtly, "not I."

"You protected me. You didn't have to."

"It was my duty, nothing more."

"You seem to dislike me, and I would like to know if I have done something to offend you."

"I barely know you, Ian." Her statement was clipped, but something in her demeanor told him it wasn't quite the truth.

She moved to step around him.

"Wait, Danii, please." Ian felt the urge to place his hands on her shoulders, to turn her so that he could look fully into her face. He wanted—no, *needed* her to look him in the eye. He resisted reaching for her with difficulty, aware that such an overture would not be welcome. "I know this sounds crazy, but I've had dreams about you my entire life. I feel like I know you."

She hesitated once more. She was so beautiful, with the sun caressing her perfect golden skin and the breeze pushing gentle fingers through that long pale hair. She continued to gaze past him at some distant point of interest, shoulders back, chin high, but she didn't move away.

"My dreams about you always seem so real." Ian hesitated. Should he really be saying these things to her? Maybe not, but he couldn't stop himself. "I don't always understand them." He cautiously watched her expression as he spoke. He didn't want to frighten her away or to make himself seem even crazier than he already sounded, but he needed to speak to her of these things. He needed to see her reaction to his words.

"Sometimes it seems as though I'm a different person and we're in a different time, but whenever I look at you, it's as if we are linked in some way. When I'm near you, it's almost as though I can't breathe. Please, Danii, just … talk to me for a minute. Don't run away."

She released a long, slow breath and faced him fully. "Ian, we were … friends once, a long time ago. You will appreciate why that is no longer so when Niamh opens your memories."

That was the last thing he expected from her.

"When, Danii? When were we friends? How? Every time I ask a question, I'm told I will understand when Niamh opens my memories. Why all the mystery? There aren't any holes in my life. I'm seventeen. The years up until the time I was five are a little hazy, but how much can there be in my past?"

He reached for her wrist, and she gave him a dangerous look that dared him to touch her. He stopped himself, but only just. Their relationship in his dreams was so familiar. At times it was difficult to remember that they truly did not know one another. Or did they? What had she just told him? *We were friends once?*

"Danii, *please*. Tell me what's going on here. Tell me the reason why you hate me so much."

"*Hate* is not precisely the word I would use, Ian." Her voice was as icy as her demeanor. "You will recognize soon enough why our friendship is impossible." She strode away from him without looking back.

Ian watched her go, an elegant and regal warrior princess from a fairy tale. He was so drawn to her. He couldn't get her out of his mind. Nothing he could do or tell himself could make him stop thinking about her. His dreams of her were all too intimate, all too intense. It was as if she had stepped into his body and taken out a piece of his soul.

Although teenage girls, and even older women, had often flirted and tried to get his attention, sometimes to the point of stalking, he had never been interested in any of them. He'd almost begun to wonder if there was something wrong with him. His friends had teased him about being too shy to ask a girl on a date, but Ian knew it was something else.

Danii's face was the one that had haunted his dreams. She was the one he thought about and compared all the others to. He just hadn't known she was real. He didn't understand why or how, but he knew he had already given her his heart. That was why he could never imagine himself with anyone else. But Danii, the woman from his dreams, his beautiful, immortal warrior princess, was so far out of his reach his heart hurt.

An informal evening meal, nothing like the lavish banquet from the night before, had been laid out in the Great Hall when Ian arrived. Tables were laden with tureens of an incredible creamy wild mushroom soup, platters of buttery flatbread, similar in texture to pancakes, though slightly thinner, finger-size yellow squash, rolled grape leaves stuffed with a mixture of spicy grains and vegetables, and fragrant bowls of vibrant, fresh fruits and candied nuts. Several ice-cold pitchers of water and the same sweet wine that Áedan had warned him off of were also placed within easy reach along each of the six stone tables.

Minstrels played lilting melodies as Tuatha strolled in and out, eating, drinking, and visiting with one another. The tables still resided along the edges of the hall, freeing the central space for those who wished to dance.

It was a dazzling scene straight from the annals of a medieval age yet quite welcoming and pleasant.

The ability to understand the language of the Tuatha that he had been granted during the morning's battle had apparently disappeared with Niamh. Ian found it frustrating that something he had so clearly understood one minute could be completely wiped from his mind the next.

As Ian hesitated near the entrance, Caitria joined him, guiding him to a sparsely filled middle table, where he could face the room and enjoy the gaiety. Four other males, already enjoying their supper, courteously greeted Ian in an old, formal style of English, and they exchanged pleasantries for a moment.

Almost immediately, colorfully gowned women began to gravitate to their corner of the hall, greeting first Caitria and then Ian. Soon his table was filled with a bevy of lovely, high-spirited Tuatha females. As more and more arrived, the four males were crowded closer together until they were finally pushed out entirely. They gave Ian polite but rueful smiles as they abandoned him to the undivided attention of the fairer sex. All the vivacious women spoke to him in the same Old World English as well, although some more haltingly than others.

He was relieved when a while later, Áedan joined him, and the throng of females laughingly made room. Áedan seemed immensely comfortable amid this all-female company, joking and teasing and conversing easily.

Ian noticed, as the night progressed, their grasp of modern English became better and better. It seemed the Tuatha possessed the capacity to learn at a rapid rate. The two dark-haired males among a colorful, high-spirited sea of pale blond women ate and drank and laughed as the long shadows turned to night and the moon climbed high, casting its silvery light over the world.

Caitria excused herself early, and Ian noted that Niamh did not make an appearance.

Ian knew the moment Danii entered the room. He felt her presence like the earth awakens with the sun. His pulse quickened, and all his senses burst to life. Among all the other aromas and fragrances in the hall, her light, intoxicating scent of lightning and rain immersed him, like mist settling over the mountain peaks. No one else seemed to notice. So why was *he* so affected by her?

She joined a table of warriors, putting her back to him. He forced himself not to acknowledge the pang of hurt he felt that she wouldn't even look at him. Ian knew he really needed to get over whatever this was between them. He was surrounded by a dozen beautiful women, each one vying for his attention, and still, his focus seemed to be on the only woman in the entire Court who couldn't stand the sight of him. He resolutely turned his eyes away from her table, determined to enjoy the pleasant and flattering company at his own.

Hakan strode into the hall shortly afterward, and Ian noticed that the Tuatha, males and females alike, scattered before him as he crossed to join the others. It was like watching a lion move through a herd of gazelles. Most Tuatha possessed a certain polite but aloof composure. They were regal and elegant, but almost eerily serene, much like Niamh.

This phenomenon, reminiscent of the previous night, as Hakan and Danii had crossed through the dancers, made Ian take pause. It was almost as though his own people were afraid of the tall supercilious warrior. There was a darkness about him, a barely concealed rage. Hakan was a dangerous predator in their midst, and they recognized it.

Whereas Danii had seated herself with her back to the room, *probably so she could ignore Ian,* Hakan placed his back to the wall. Again, the menacing hunter scoping the terrain.

The warriors put their heads together in conversation. Ian recognized Gilbrandr and Einarr from earlier, as well as a few others who had joined the battle. The men were all young looking, and though masculine in appearance, they were beautiful and graceful in the way of all Tuatha. Their long pale hair and flawless, youthful skin gave the illusion of innocence. But there was also something hard and lethal about them that the others did not exhibit.

A hush fell suddenly over the hall, and Ian glanced up, surprised to see Danii approach their table.

"I seek a word with you, Áedan, before your departure on the morrow," she said formally.

Áedan rose, inclining his head cordially, and the two moved a few paces away to converse. Ian's hearing was far better than average, but the pair immediately resorted to the Tuathan tongue. Ian, to his credit, learned nearly as quickly as the Tuatha and was finally beginning to comprehend bits and pieces of their language. It was as if a veil was slowly lifting from his mind, but not yet enough to understand Danii and Áedan's conversation, though he was certain it concerned him.

Their discussion quickly escalated into some sort of argument, and Danii haughtily swept from the great hall, Hakan and Gilbrandr in her wake.

There was a buzz of furtive dialogue and then the gradual return of normal conversation. Ian noticed the covert glances his way.

Later, as he and Áedan left the hall, Ian asked, "Why don't you two get along?"

"Because I remind her of times far in the past, of things we would both like to put behind us."

"Why do you antagonize her, Áedan? Why do you two dislike each other so much?"

"I don't dislike her, Ian. There was a time when we were very close." He hesitated. "I remind her of someone whose loss almost destroyed her, and our little game of verbal war keeps us both sane."

Ian felt strong emotion take him. He suddenly felt jealous and territorial. "How close?" he asked edgily.

"We were friends, Ian. Nothing more." Áedan's blue eyes were shuttered, and he gazed at Ian with something he couldn't quite fathom.

Friends? That was the second time today that word had been bandied about.

Ian tossed for a long time before he finally slept. Tomorrow, he would return to the mortal realm, apparently with all the mysterious answers he had been seeking since his arrival. Too bad he couldn't have retrieved those memories beforehand. He would have enjoyed this world more knowing the language and understanding his own history. And it was evident that many he had encountered here knew him, or were at least familiar with him in some way, which made him highly uncomfortable and put him at a disadvantage.

His shoulder still hurt from the fire blast. Caitria had said because it was *dark Magic* and had sent its poison throughout his system so rapidly, it would heal slowly. He had to be careful not to move too quickly or twist, or the wound still broke open and seeped.

Finally, his eyes closed and the soft roar of waterfalls lulled him into a dreamworld he was all too familiar with, only this time, it was different. He was different.

He was young, no more than ten or eleven years old. It was dusk, and long shadows were enveloping the Mountain Court in its journey into night. Flickering torches began to dot the terraced paths, casting their dancing play of light over the landscape and across the intricately carved structures of the kingdom of the Tuatha.

He breathed in the crisp, clean scent of mountain pines and mist as the last yellow rays dropped behind the tall spire-like ridges high above. The air cooled noticeably as the sun abandoned their Court, and he automatically summoned a trickle of Magic to warm himself.

A furtive rustle in the shadows and stealthy movement caught his attention. He knew his kingdom was under siege. Guards were everywhere, and yet someone sought to elude them. Someone small. Someone dressed in colorful purple silk, with long pale hair that shone like a moonbeam in the dying light. She was swatting away some curious Lumen Faeries, the same glittering entities that were always attracted to his mother.

"Go away," she hissed to the Faeries. "You must leave me alone!"

Ian often found himself drawn to this particular girl. He was enchanted by her selfless nature and inner strength. She was of the Healing Caste, and, though younger than him by a season, already rumored to possess formidable abilities. But why was she sneaking about unprotected when enemies were known to have breached their shores?

He moved in quietly and caught her wrist before she could disappear into the night.

"Danii? What are you doing?"

She jumped guiltily. "Hush, Idan! You will give me away." Her tone was indignant, as though he was the one slinking around in the shadows. She tugged to release his hold, but he held firm, refusing to budge from her path until she answered.

"Just return to the hall, Idan," she commanded, her voice a low, nearly desperate whisper. "Pretend you did not see me."

A satchel was slung over her shoulder, and she carried blankets and a long coil of rope. Her bundle was almost too big for her delicate frame, but her expression was resolute.

Ian's eyes widened as he took in every aspect of her bizarre appearance.

"I am not certain this is the eve to be running away from home, and you are hardly dressed for climbing trees," *he quipped, flashing her a disarming smile.* "Perhaps you should reconsider your adventure until there is less danger about."

"Go! I mean it. Leave me now before someone sees us!" *she insisted in that same urgent whisper.*

"I think not, Danii," *he answered in an amused tone, though he lowered his voice to a similarly hushed octave.* "You appear to be up to something that could get you into trouble, are you not?" *He eyed the rope and blankets, winged eyebrows arched.* "Do you not know our shores are besieged by Formorians? You see the guards. What are you thinking?"

"Nothing you should concern yourself with." *She refused to meet his eyes.*

He placed his hands on her shoulders, turning her so she was forced to meet his inquisitive gaze. He was a full head taller, but she stood her ground. Lifting her chin in stubborn defiance, she squirmed to get away, but his hold was too strong.

"Tell me, Danii, or I will not allow you to leave."

"Allow?" *She glared indignantly.* "You have no right to interfere with anything I choose to do."

"You think not? It is unsafe to wander about just now. What is so important that you must creep about, hiding your presence from everyone? Why would you willingly place yourself in danger?"

"You are going to attract the guards," *she hissed in frustration.*

"Then tell me, or I will take it from your mind."

She gasped. "That is disrespectful! I cannot believe you would even think of invading my mind without my permission. This is not one of your and Aedan's games, Idan. I made a promise. I cannot tell you."

"Then I will see to it that you do not leave the Court."

Her jaw dropped in utter disbelief at his audacity, blazing blue eyes shooting daggers at him.

"Yes, I know you have some scheme in mind that involves leaving the protection of the Court. And no, I did not take that information from you. You should learn to shield your thoughts better."

She stamped her tiny foot, and that stubborn chin lifted a notch higher.

"I have all night, Danii. Do you?"

"All right, Idan. You force me to break a vow," she said with so much anguish in her voice that for a moment, he felt guilty, but not enough to allow her to leave. Not tonight. Not with enemies all around them. She was so young, so fragile. He could not allow her to wander about by herself unprotected

"I would force you to do more than that to keep you safe," he told her truthfully.

"I have a friend. She is injured."

"Why do you go to her alone and in secret?"

"She is not accepted by our people."

"Our people shun no one but the Formorians."

"She is Selkie."

Idan's eyebrows shot to his hairline, and he choked. "You cannot be serious."

Danii stamped her tiny, silk-clad foot once more. "This is why I told no one," she spoke angrily through clenched teeth.

"You cannot go to her on this night."

"I must. She is my friend. She called to me. None of her kind are close enough to reach her in time."

"Why cannot another healer do this or at least accompany you?"

"You know our people are afraid of them. If she sings to them, they will be ensnared."

Ian eyed her warily.

"So how did you befriend her? How do you know of her injury?"

"We speak to one another sometimes. We can reach across great distances. I felt her pain and heard her cries. She was attacked. She barely escaped and is dying. I must go to her now. She is running out of time."

Ian looked incredulously at the determined young girl. There was something about her that drew him. She affected him in a way that no one else ever had. It was an unsettling connection that he felt to the core of his being and seemed to erase every bit of common sense he possessed. That confusing connection just now made him want to support her in her crazy scheme, overcome any obstacle to make her happy, but above all, demanded he keep her safe. He knew if he told anyone, she would be prevented from leaving.

The internal struggle to see to her happiness and at the same time see to her safety set up a dilemma he wasn't certain he knew how to overcome. He could not find it in him to deny her, and he would not betray her trust. But he needed to make her see reason.

"You cannot go alone, Danii," Ian insisted once more. "I know my mother would aid you, even in this."

"I made a vow to keep her presence a secret from our people!" Again, Danii jutted that stubborn chin in a way that assured Ian she was determined to do this no matter what he said. "She is injured. She needs my help, and I will not refuse her." She grasped his hand, blue eyes pleading, beseeching, and he melted. Every bit of common sense he had flew away like wisps of dandelion fluff in the wind. "You cannot tell anyone or—" She broke abruptly off as a guard wandered too close for comfort, tugging Ian into a crouch beside her.

This was completely absurd, Ian thought as he watched the guard stroll past. And it was even worse that he was buying into her plan. Despite her insistence and his unexpected reaction to her, he knew he had to try once more to appeal to her rationally, logically.

"You know my mother would not allow this friend of yours to suffer, Selkie or no."

"She trusts no one but me! By detaining me, you are wasting precious time that she does not have."

"Then I go with you. You cannot do this alone. It is too dangerous. You need me, and I would never allow you to go off like this by yourself."

"I made a vow to keep her secret, Idan! I cannot take you to her, and I will not allow you to risk yourself against our enemies. As you have said, our shores are besieged by the Formorians. It is my choice to aid her on this night, but I will not endanger you."

"You cannot go alone, Danii." There was no compromise in his voice. "Decide." His voice was hard and impassive, and no matter her protests, he was not going to back down. "I will assist you in this if you are so determined to risk yourself for this friend. I will not allow you to go to her without someone to guard you."

She assessed him dubiously. "You are nearly the same age as I."

"Yes, but my father has already begun to train me, and my Magic is strong. I will protect you."

"You are not afraid that her voice will ensnare you?"

"I will have to take my chances. How is it that you are immune?"

"She is female, as am I. I am far more resistant. And she is my friend. She would never harm me, though I can guarantee she will not welcome your presence."

"You are not going alone, Danii." *He was unflinchingly resolute.* "We are finished with this discussion, unless you wish me to inform Niamh."

"You are not my keeper, Idan."

"No, Danii, but I can easily summon someone who is. If you wish to save your Selkie, let us go now while we are still unobserved."

Danii huffed, and her eyes flashed blue fire. "You wish to become her slave?"

"If she is truly your friend, she will not seek to harm me. Besides, her allure is only short-term with our kind, I have heard," *he added, hoping that myth was true.*

"Nevertheless, her voice is beguiling."

"I will manage."

"I have warned you, Idan."

Her tone carried annoyance, but something in her eyes told him she was grateful for his presence. The graceful mantle of Power and self-assurance she carried belied her extreme youth. Though her features were ethereal, her stature delicate, she exuded a barely contained, visceral force. She was a contradiction of childlike innocence and goddess-like Power, and already, despite her age, she carried herself like a queen. But Ian knew that underneath the facade, she wasn't nearly as confident as she maintained.

"I will think of something when we arrive," *he stated briefly, unwilling to argue further.*

"Then hurry, Idan. She is in great pain. If you are coming, we go now!"

Ian shouldered her rope and satchel then rolled and secured the blankets to her pack as they skirted the guards, staying to the shadows until they had left the Court far behind. He easily shielded their thoughts and intent from their people, having had much practice in screening his mind from his mother, one of the strongest and most powerful goddesses ever to live. He was highly adept at shielding his brother as well, as Áedan had a certain penchant for getting into trouble. He now found it easy enough to extend his talent to include Danii. As strong as she was, her defensive powers were weak. Perhaps because her true skills lie in healing, and in that endeavor, she must open herself to others, not close herself off, as Ian was prone to doing.

When they had gone far enough away that they were no longer in fear of discovery, Danii broke the silence. "You can never tell anyone about this," she adamantly whispered to Ian.

"You are acting under the assumption that we are going to survive this night." He hoped he was joking.

"Stay or come," she answered in exasperation, "but you must swear to never tell."

"I will keep your secret, Danii."

At her tense look, he held up both hands in surrender. "I swear."

"How far do we travel this night?" he inquired mildly. It was a question he should have asked earlier, but caution and silence had dictated otherwise as they made their imprudent escape from the safety of the Mountain Court.

"She is to the north. She sought shelter on the windward side of our Isle in hopes that the Formorian ships would seek the calmer waters to the south or in the Western Bay."

"Formorians?" Ian articulated incredulously.

"Yes," she answered tensely. "It was they who hurt her."

"How is that possible if she could simply sing to them?"

"I do not yet know. She called to me over great distance, and she was already too weak to do more than seek my help and impart to me her location."

"Are you certain she is still alive?"

"Yes. I can still feel her essence, but she is failing."

"Why the rope?"

"She is in a cave at the bottom of the cliffs. We will have to climb down to reach her. Or swim in from the ocean."

Ian faced her in utter disbelief as he came to an abrupt halt. "Are you insane?"

"Possibly." She tugged him onward, not slowing her ground-eating stride upward through thick vegetation and sharp, rocky crags along a nearly invisible animal trail. And though their night vision was exceptional, possibly on par with many of the night-dwelling creatures they heard scurrying through the low brush, only the fact that the silvery moon was nearly full and the sky clear and cloudless made it possible for them to traverse the rough terrain.

"You are not dressed for this, Danii. Your clothes are already in shreds, your shoes are completely inadequate, and if we must swim, the water will weigh you down in that mass of billowing silk. What are you thinking?"

"I possess no clothing other than billowing silk gowns, Idan. It may have escaped your notice, but females do not dress in practical male attire. For some absurd reason, it is frowned upon by our people. Probably some archaic rule enforced by the males of our race to keep all of us powerless females in our place." Her voice, though defensive, dripped sarcasm. "As I said, help me or not, but get out of my way."

"No, Danii. You must know how treacherous it will be to climb down to a cave at the base of a cliff in complete darkness. This would be dangerous even in daylight. Have you ever even been to the Northern Cliffs?"

"No, but we have a rope. If for some reason it is inadequate, you will turn your back and I will strip down to my undergarments, and I will swim. Enough, Idan! I am not some delicate flower that you must protect. You and Áedan would never hesitate to embrace such a challenge. Do not allow yourself to believe that because I am a female, I am any less determined or capable of reaching that cave."

"I will give you the determined part, Danii." He didn't know whether to admire her bravery and audacity or shake his head at her sheer recklessness. He had always thought healers to be peaceful and gentle. There was nothing soothing or tranquil about Danii. She was all fire and aggression. If they lived through this, he was going to insist that his mother set guards on her day and night.

Twice they came upon Tuatha sentinels, and they were forced to backtrack, staying low through the underbrush until Ian could find alternate routes for them while he mentally shielded their presence. He hoped if they came across a Formorian patrol, he would be able to do the same.

Danii's dress snagged on everything, leaving a trail that a blind man could have followed, until finally, Ian drew his knife and cut away the ridiculous train and much of the excess fabric.

"This is Eidersilk, is it not?" he asked in exasperation. "I thought it was supposed to be nearly indestructible. How is it your gown is so fragile?"

"It is the weave," Danii told him wearily. "Gossamer fine so it floats and billows," she added with some asperity. "Your clothes are made differently, so they wear like iron. Our rope is a similar weave to your clothing. Virtually indestructible."

"Ah. How do you know so much about this?" he asked, more for something to pass the time, although he was mildly curious.

"While you and Aedan are training with the guard, Idan, I am learning important things, like weaving Eidersilk," she told him sarcastically.

Oh yes. This girl was pure fire.

As they topped the rise, the buffeting northern winds suddenly bit into their skin, cold and sharp as splintered shards of ice. Ian was loath to leave the relative sanctuary of the jagged rock formations that had sheltered them thus far from the ferocious ocean gale. They staggered, bracing their backs against the ragged ledge, and blinked to clear the tears that suddenly marred their vision, brought about by the stinging wind as it whipped across their faces.

The enormous expanse of heaving black ocean spread out before them, lit eerily by the moon. Frenzied white-tipped breakers tumbled relentlessly across the plunging, shifting surface as far as the eye could see.

Far below, pounding waves crashed against the rocks before exploding upward in sprays of ghostly white, striking high upon the cliff face.

The ocean was dangerous tonight, menacing and angry. The hazardously sheer precipice beneath them was wet and slick, promising untold peril. And there would be no swimming in these treacherous waters.

Dark shapes silhouetted against the waves, rising and disappearing in the rough swells, alerted Ian that their hope of avoiding the Formorian ships was an empty dream.

There was no beach to make land, but Ian could not discount the possibility of patrols on the ground or within the higher mountain peaks. From their vantage, they could see practically the entire northern coast, and he was certain an enemy as cunning as these inhuman invaders would not neglect such an advantage.

Ian put his mouth to Danii's ear so he could be heard over the thundering surf. He pointed, his face grim. "Those are Formorian ships out at sea, Danii. I am certain there are foot soldiers throughout these mountains and sentinels high up on the summits. We are fortunate we have not already run across them. We must take care not to be seen. The cover of darkness is in our favor for now, but we must not be caught out on this mountain in daylight."

Ian assessed the cliffs below, taking in the many darkened depressions that looked to be caves or deep hollows in the rock face. "Do you know where she is, Danii?" This task was becoming more unfeasible by the moment. "We cannot possibly search all these caves."

"Yes. I can feel her. If we can make our way to the left of that tree"—she drew his attention to a scraggly bush jutting out over the cliff's edge—"we can drop straight down. The tide is coming in, but her cave is still quite high above the waterline. It will be tricky, but I think the rope is long enough to reach."

Ian looked over the ledge to determine the exact spot Danii was pointing to. Tricky was an understatement. They would need to find something secure to anchor the rope to, and he wasn't certain anything was available. He did not want to trust their lives to the stunted bush barely rooted in the crumbling stone. He would need to scout for something better.

He moved Danii back within the relative shelter of the rocky ledge they so precariously clung to, enough out of the wind so they didn't have to shout, though he was aware they needed to establish some better form of communication. *Danii? He pushed gently into her mind.*

She gasped. He knew it was an intrusion. Usually, only family members used this intimate form of communication with their young. Adults had different rules, but children were strictly protected from the bombardment of unsolicited mental interaction. However, Danii had already said she was in communication with the Selkie. She had obviously established a mental pathway and seemed comfortable enough using it. Ian's mental link shouldn't be too different, he hoped. He had only ever used it with his own brother and mother.

Yes, Idan? Her answer was clear and strong. There was nothing tentative about her Power.

Wait for me here while I find someplace to secure the rope. He untied one of the blankets and pushed it into her hands. *Try to get warm until I return.*

She thrust it right back at him. "I am going with you. She cannot last much longer. Do not coddle me, Idan. We must hurry." She spoke to him aloud over the din of the ocean, her tone sharp.

Ian released an exasperated breath. "I was not—oh, for goddess sake, Danii. Your feet are bloody, and you are shivering. I was only trying to give you a moment to rest while I find something that will work for us." He turned away, tired, frustrated, and incensed. He was nearly at the end of his patience. He had had enough of this spikey, maddening female.

Danii reached for his arm, staying his retreat.

"I am sorry, Idan."

He resisted, but her grip was firm. There was far more strength in those small graceful hands than he would have believed.

"Idan! Please wait!"

He halted, jaw set, but allowed her to retain her hold.

"I am sorry if I have seemed ungrateful. I am not certain I could have done this without you." There was a small catch in her voice that tugged at him despite his ire. "I did not want to slow us down or appear weak. I feared you might force me to turn back. You have been wonderful, so wonderful to bring me this far."

Ian could see that Danii now fought back tears. He was at a loss. She had been so strong, pushing them both incessantly for hours without any thought of rest or complaint. Suddenly, he saw beneath the outward show of invincibility to the exhaustion and vulnerability of the ten-year-old child.

Ian narrowed his eyes as he fully took in Danii's appearance. Her normally golden complexion was as pale as the white bluff on which they stood. Her face and arms were cut and abraded. Thin lines of congealing crimson crisscrossed and marred her delicate skin, where thorns and bushes had caught and sliced as she passed. And she shivered in the icy wind. She was a healer. Surely, she should have closed the cuts on her skin and healed her feet as they traveled. And she was freezing?

"Why are you so cold, Danii? Do you not know how to warm yourself with Magic?" Ian demanded to know.

"Yes, Idan. I know how to use Magic. It may require everything I have to save my friend. I cannot afford to waste any of it on myself."

Ian's mouth fell open. "You refuse even to heal the injuries you have sustained to reach this place?"

"Her name is Shanara, Idan, and I am so afraid for her. She is my only friend, and she is dying. I cannot ... I will not lose her."

Ian took a long, slow breath of chilled, briny air into his lungs. Danii's steadfast devotion and loyalty to this friend of hers astonished him. He had thought her selfless before they set out, but he was seeing sides of her that he never imagined.

"We are nearly there, Danii." He released his anger and looked around with renewed resolve. They had come this far. Somehow he would get her safely to the bottom of the cliff.

The shrubby little tree jutted from a depression about fifteen arm spans to their left, and they needed to get just beyond that point. Directly above the cave Danii had indicated was another rough ledge, though small and dangerously sloped. If they could reach that spot, it was possible they could rappel straight down. They simply had to reach that exact location, somehow, across impossibly steep and unstable terrain.

Ian led Danii away from the raging ocean's edge and back across a series of irregular fissures and wind-beaten rocks. They made their way through a narrow crevice and then were forced to climb an abrupt ragged spire before finding another low, tight opening through the mountain. He didn't want to take them too far, lest they overshoot their objective, but he needed to be certain they had gone far enough before turning back toward the cliff.

As they worked their way around another rock formation, jumped a thin seemingly bottomless fracture, and then scaled another high crag, Ian mentally asked a question that had bothered him since he and Danii had spoken on the ledge.

What do you mean the Selkie is your only friend, Danii? Ian had been stunned by her admission.

There was a long pause, and for a moment, Ian thought she would not answer. He was about to apologize for using the mental pathway without her permission, even though he believed it unwise given their circumstance to continue yelling at one another over the wind and risk being heard by their enemy, when she responded.

Exactly what I said, Idan. Our children are so few, and there are no others my age besides you and Áedan. The others are all so much younger.

What about the healers? Are you not close with any of them?

They are kind to me, yet I feel …
Her hesitation lasted too long.
What, Danii?
They are adults, yet I feel as though they are afraid of me sometimes. Or … I do not know … intimidated. They say my Power is more vast than any have seen for millennia, perhaps approaching that of Niamh. Even my mother's pales next to mine, but it is still raw and unpredictable. It frightens me. I cannot always control it.

Ian had no idea. Danii always seemed so sure of herself, so confident. Ian had never been alone. He'd always had his brother. There had never been a question of Aedan's presence in his life. Ian had always just known he and his brother would be there for each other. And his mother, Niamh, was so formidable neither sibling had ever worried about their own emerging Power. She was always able to intervene before either he or Aedan could even come close to causing some dire catastrophe with their unruly, fledgling Magic.

Shanara knows how it feels to be different, shunned, alone among many. We do not judge one another. I cannot imagine a world without her in it. Please, Idan. We need to get to her as fast as we can.

We are nearly there, Danii. Can you still feel her?

Yes.

I did not know, Danii. I did not understand that you were so isolated.

There was another long pause, and Ian did not want to intrude any further into her thoughts if she was finished speaking to him.

I should not have told you those things.

I am glad you did. We all need friends. And now you have two.

A sudden intense joy flooded him, filling him up to overflowing, and he realized he was feeling Danii's reaction to his declaration of friendship. His heart did a strange flip-flop that nearly had him missing a foothold.

He really needed to concentrate instead of thinking about the tiny, mercurial, bundle of trouble following so closely behind him.

They scrambled over one last boulder as they reached the spot they had sighted from the area far to their right. Ian warned Danii away from the edge, afraid of the loose scree that might send them toppling over the cliff. The icy wind battered them, and it was hard enough to brace themselves between the eroded rock formations without the added danger of sliding gravel. He edged forward on hands and knees and then lay on his belly, brushing as much of the loose debris as he was able over the edge. The rock was solid underneath, and he was heartened as he continued to clear a stable place to stand.

Like Danii, Ian was reluctant to summon his Magic, but for an entirely different reason. If, as he suspected, the Formorians had taken up positions all around them, he didn't want them to detect their presence by an expenditure of unnecessary Power. All Magic users felt the surge of energy when Magic was summoned. The impression was usually proportionate to the amount and proximity, unless the wielder was very skilled at shielding.

Ian assessed the area around them, unsure what should be used to anchor their rope. At this elevation, the entire northern coast was nearly barren of foliage. The combination of violent ocean gales and dense, nearly solid rock gave trees and other vegetation little opportunity to thrive.

He considered the large boulder at his back. If he formed a slipknot, the loop could be dropped completely over its rounded surface and then pulled taut at its narrower base. They would have to hope the rock was solid enough to keep the line from pulling under its foundation or dislodging the boulder entirely. Neither he nor Danii weighed much, but Ian wasn't certain he was willing to trust their lives to the unstable underlayment beneath the stone. Or he could tie off farther back, around a tall jagged spire of granite. This alternative appeared infinitely safer, but he wasn't certain the rope was long enough to reach the cave if he did.

The last thing they needed was to step off the cliff with insufficient length to attain the small opening while being buffeted by the strong, erratic winds. This descent was going to be difficult enough without releasing the line before their feet were on solid ground. If they slipped, they would find themselves in the rough ocean, amongst the crushing waves, either dragged out to sea by the undertow or battered cruelly against the rocks. Had he been with his brother, Ian admitted to himself that the two of them might have been crazy enough to try it, but no way would he risk that with Danii.

The spire was safer, he decided. It would cost them time if it didn't work, but Ian could tie it off quickly. He had done this sort of thing dozens of times, though granted, not under these conditions.

Finally, flinging the rope over the edge, and then leaning out to observe its position, it was as he had suspected. It was too short, but not by much. He could feel Danii's escalating anxiety, and it added urgency to his movements, but he was not going to risk making foolhardy errors after they had come so far.

Ian was going to attempt this descent with a girl who had probably never even climbed a tree. And he was going to keep her safe, somehow, no matter what else occurred.

He secured the line at the base of the much-closer boulder and tugged. He motioned Danii to help as they pushed the bulk of their weight against the rock. It did not budge or shift even a fraction. It would have to do.

I am going to go first, Danii. I need to be beneath you if you lose your grip—

I will not lose my grip.

And, he continued, *it will be easier for you to climb down in this wind if I can stabilize the rope at the bottom. Tell your Selkie that I am helping you so she does not decide I am an enemy.*

She is barely conscious, Idan, but she knows. Just go!

Danii was shifting from one foot to another in her anxiety to get them moving.

Do not take the line until I am on the ground, Danii, Ian warned. *Wait until I tell you.*

She nodded impatiently. He felt her strong urge to push him out of her way and leap over the edge, but she yielded to his unbending command.

As long as the wind didn't bash them against the cliff face too severely, or the rising tide didn't wash them into the sea, they should both be able to do this, he assured himself.

Ian had accused Danii of being insane, but participating and enabling her in this was sheer lunacy.

A sudden prickling of Power crooned a warning that a Formorian patrol was somewhere nearby. It was the merest brush, sly tendrils of seeking Magic, questing out into the night.

Pushing Danii to the ground, Ian landed nearly on top of her small form. The indignant squeak of surprise and abruptly choked exhale conveyed that the landing hadn't exactly been soft.

Sorry.

She mumbled something unintelligible as Ian moved off her. Beneath them, the dark rope slithered like a long snake against the white cliff face. He was going to have to use a trickle of Magic to hide it.

Just do it, Idan! Hurry! Danii was in his head, reading his thoughts. The forbidden intimacy of it, the prohibited intrusion, should have disturbed him, at least a little, but the urgency of their situation and the danger made it necessary. And it felt almost natural to have her there, sharing his mind. Her mental touch was so different from his mother's or brother's. It was like Danii herself, ethereal yet powerful, determined yet principled and selfless.

He shrugged it off. This forced intimacy was a necessary consequence of their predicament. It was definitely easier with her knowing what they faced.

Can you locate their position? *she asked.*

Ian stealthily sent out his senses and felt Danii tentatively do the same.

Stop, Danii! *he said urgently into her head.* You have not learned to shield your Magic. Your touch is light, but they still may detect you. Let me do this.

Mentally connected as they were, Ian perceived her dismay, but she withdrew immediately.

After a few moments, he responded. I believe we have time to make the climb. They are still some distance behind us. We can only hope their sentries do not turn their attention to this portion of the cliff face while we are dangling out over the sea.

We will have to chance it, *Danii insisted.*

Even if they do not see us, it is still possible they may stumble across the rope. I can cloak it for a time, but if they get close enough, they will sense the Magic.

Do it now, Idan, *Danii demanded, the surrounding air thrumming with urgency.* Can you conceal us as well?

Yes, but it will require stronger Magic, though I believe I can shield most of it if we go quickly.

Then climb fast, Idan. *Danii was already hauling him to his feet.* I will do the same.

Ian cast his cloaking Magic and lowered himself over the side, climbing swiftly hand over hand, pushing against jagged outcroppings of rock with his feet as he fell lower and lower beneath the rim. Strong winds battered him against the cliff face, and the rope swayed wildly. Sea spray splashed against the sheer, pale rise, making it slick and treacherous, reaching higher and higher as if to drag him down.

Ian was strong and experienced enough to withstand the ravenous barrage of icy wind and clawing sea, but he wondered how Danii was going to manage. Perhaps he should have rigged a harness and lowered her, but he doubted she would have agreed. The additional time required would have been unacceptable.

Reaching the darkened hollow, shiver spirits ran up Ian's spine as he swung cautiously into the yawning cave mouth. No moonlight penetrated its unnerving maw, and though his people possessed formidable night vision, his eyes would take a few moments to adjust—long interminable moments in which he would be vulnerable to the mysterious creature now inhabiting the cave. He sent up a silent prayer to the goddess that the Selkie would not attack or, worse, sing to him.

Still retaining the rope, Ian dropped guardedly onto a wet, gritty floor. He winced as a mixture of sand, scree, and solid rock crunched under his feet. So much for his plan of a stealthy entrance. A rustle of movement toward the back alerted him to the Selkie's presence. At least he hoped it was Danii's injured friend, and once more, he winged a prayer to his goddess that if this unknown being decided to bespell him, she could at least wait until he got Danii safely on the ground.

"I am here to help you," Ian whispered into the darkness, hoping the creature understood, before turning his attention to the bluff above.

Come now, Danii.

She didn't hesitate. Ian's first time stepping over a sheer descent with nothing in his hands but a rope between him and excruciating injury, if not outright death, had sent his adrenaline into overdrive. He had needed a moment to prepare. But Danii launched herself off the cliff without even a moment's thought to her safety.

Her bravery both humbled and scared the ever-living hell out of him.

Ian stabilized the rope as Danii made her descent. He watched, heart beating a staccato rhythm, as the punishing gale thrashed her ethereal form again and again against the hard, unforgiving rock. Her dress billowed and tangled as long pale hair flowed wild and free. Her spectral form hovered high above, silver and ghostly surreal in the moonlight. She glided and drifted like some exotic wind creature, an elemental spirit from times of olde, brave, beautiful, and fierce, as the buffeting winds streamed over and around, whipping her from side to side.

At last, Danii dropped into his arms, her feet barely touching the ground before she rushed to the Selkie's side.

Ian's heart found a more natural rhythm, and he gulped air into starved lungs that had forgotten to function during the courageous young apparition's harrowing descent. He moved in warily behind her, his eyes adjusting quickly to the stygian darkness.

A white seal, slashed and bleeding and bound with a sinisterly glowing barbed cord, lay near the back wall of the damp cave. Her large dark eyes watched soulfully as he approached. She shuddered, making a sound between a sigh and a groan, and her eyes slowly closed as bright, frothy blood oozed from her mouth.

Ian feared they had arrived only to watch her take her final breath. Dark, nearly black blood pooled beneath her, leaching into the sandy floor, and Ian could see the bloody smear where she had dragged herself from the ocean to her present location. How could any creature still be alive with these types of injuries?

Danii placed her palms over the dying seal, and Ian watched in awe as her hands began to glow with a soft purple light he had seen other healers wield. As it grew in brightness, Ian realized he would need to shield the cave's entrance so no hint of her Power leaked out into the night. The luminous purple light would draw the attention of the enemy more surely than any errant Magic they might have used in reaching this place.

He cast his cloaking Magic over the entrance and strengthened the shields surrounding the three of them. Danii's healing energy was surging, bathing the cave walls in shimmering violet light. The flames grew brighter yet like a bonfire, consuming both her and the little seal until they were engulfed in the raging, unearthly conflagration.

The shallow lesions began to close before his eyes, and then the deeper ones slowly knit until only long red scars remained.

As Danii lifted her hands, allowing the warm, healing light to fade, the wounds reopened. Ian looked on in horror as one by one they reappeared. It was like watching an unseen hand inflict the damage anew.

The Selkie cried out in such agonizing pain that Ian was certain it would end her.

Danii murmured softly, soothingly. Her voice was gentle and reassuring, speaking comforting words that Ian couldn't quite hear. Even as bedraggled and dirty as the trek across the mountain had made her, and as small and waiflike as she now appeared, kneeling so carefully on the cave floor beside the injured seal, she still exuded an aura of utter grace and composure.

I need your knife, Idan. *Danii's voice in his mind was urgent yet calm. He was witnessing the true healer in action. She reached back without taking her eyes from the dying Selkie, knowing he would comply. Her focus on the injured animal was absolute.*

As Ian placed the hilt into her outstretched hand, the weapon began to glow with a quiet infusion of Magic. A translucent flame flickered along its length, cool and lambent as blue ice, softly lighting the darkened cave. The dancing blue light cocooned the space, giving the illusion of being underwater.

Danii touched the blade to the Selkie's bindings. A sizzling crack then a small explosion erupted from the contact, sending sparks in all directions. The Selkie chuffed out a heart-wrenching sound, trembling and groaning in unimaginable anguish.

Danii's hand shook as she lowered the blade.

Idan, *she met his shocked gaze with troubled eyes as she spoke quietly into his mind,* the rope is imbued with vile fell Magic. I have never attempted to diffuse anything like this before. Have you ever seen this?

No.

I saw our healers neutralize this type of Magic once, but it took many of them, working together in tangent. Do you think you can assist me?

I have no idea what I am doing, Danii. I might injure her further.

Your Magic is strong. I can feel it. I will guide you.

I will try. *Ian could think of no other recourse. He would have to go along with her plan.* Tell me what to do.

Danii hesitated for a moment, as if undecided about something. Can you continue to hold the safeguards against the cave opening while sharing your Power?

I believe I can. I do not feel unduly strained with the amount I am expending thus far.

I also feel you cloaking our Magic. Are you certain you are able to take on the additional drain of your energy without jeopardizing the defenses you have wrought for us?

I will make certain I do. We have no other choice. His tone was grimly resolved, though he was less than optimistic about what he was getting himself into.

You will have to touch me, and I will draw the energy from you. The first time, it can be … uncomfortable, frightening even, and it is very demanding. I promise I will not take more than you can safely give, but you will have to trust me not to harm you.

After witnessing her loyalty to this injured creature, he wouldn't hesitate to trust her with his life.

Take what you need, Danii.

He placed his hand on her shoulder and lowered his mental shields. The bond was immediate. If he had thought the mind connection was intimate, this was complete and utter exposure, the opening of his soul, the baring of all that he was, the sharing of all his secrets. All his barriers were swept away, and he literally melded with Danii. They were no longer two separate individuals. Breaths and hearts sought the same rhythm, the blood in their veins surged and sang in synchronous harmony, cells and atoms exchanged information to the most infinitesimal detail, fusing minds and bodies into one single perfect entity suspended in time.

Their joined energy exploded like a beacon, and Ian had to pull back slightly to reinforce his defensive shields against such an intense onslaught of raw Power the two of them seemed to be generating. He had been utterly unprepared for this and hoped no hint of their magical essence had escaped for the Formorians to lock onto.

Danii gasped.

Is something wrong? He knew he should not have attempted this. He was not a healer. He had no idea what he was doing.

No. I have never felt this strong a connection to anyone before. Our combined Magic is … really powerful.

Oh! Well, that is a good thing, right? He hadn't caused irreparable harm, then. He was definitely out of his comfort zone. *I can feel what you are doing. It is as you said, a little … uh … terrifying, actually, but … amazing.*

Ian tuned himself to Danii's own very different essence. He could see through her eyes, feel through her body, know what she was thinking as she began to trace the threads of fell Magic woven so maliciously into the bindings.

He experienced the initial invasive tug as she began to draw on his energy, tentative at first, but then more insistent. His first instinct was to resist, snatch himself back from their shared bond, as one who had placed his hand into a flame would jerk away, but the direness of her need kept him there. He quickly understood that for every small amount she took from him, she was giving a hundredfold. She was being far too cautious, safeguarding him at her own expense to a far greater extent than necessary. And she was rapidly approaching burnout. He drew a deep, calming breath and gave to her freely.

As he once more melded fully with her mind, Ian felt the malevolent resistance of the bonds, the dark, tainted poison woven into the fabric, pushing against the purity of Danii's Power. The bindings hummed with a discordant resonance, like the strings of an untuned harp strummed raucously by a diabolical hand.

Vile Magic emanated from each and every strand, its fused sum undulating with biting, unadulterated evil.

Danii passed her hands over the barbed rope, tracing the intricately intertwined strands. Slowly, much too slowly, the evil bonds began to respond. One warped thread at a time changed color, untangled, unraveled, became smooth. The pitch and tenor transmuted to a nearly harmonious congruence.

Ian recognized the enormous toll this metamorphoses was demanding from Danii. Her own Power was nearly depleted. She was rapidly approaching crisis. She had stopped herself from taking too much from Ian and was risking herself rather than request anything beyond what he could comfortably give.

Well, to the insidious gods of the underworld with his COMFORT! Ian cursed inwardly. He didn't care if she caught that thought or not. Ian focused fixedly through their shared link and then flooded her with his own powerful essence.

The bindings instantly glowed bright white, resonating clear and pure, harmoniously synchronized to the clarion rhythm of their combined energy. The twisted fell Magic lost its hold, tangled strands fully unraveling, dispersing back into the ether.

Danii once more lifted the knife to the imprisoning but now magically benign bindings. Ian's blade, as before, glowed blue, an icy, flaming torch against the pressing darkness, dealing easily with any residual evil.

As the bonds fell away, Danii breathed a sigh of relief.

"I really need to get one of these," she commented, reverently sliding her fingers along the glittering blade like another might caress a beautiful piece of jewelry.

"It is yours if you promise never to do anything like this again."

Danii reluctantly laid it aside, giving Ian a wistful look that plainly said she would not, could not, promise anything of the kind.

He sighed. Knowing Danii as he was beginning to, Ian reflected despairingly that she would probably become embroiled in something even more hazardous before a full turning of the moon was upon her. It was not in her nature to sit idly by while others were in need.

"They cut out her tongue, Idan, so she could not sing to them." She spoke aloud, her voice hushed and sorrowful.

Though they were no longer merged, she was still easily reading his thoughts. And while her words were by no means an apology, they were a defense of her need to act, her need to make right a heinous wrong.

The thing was, Ian understood and agreed with her, dangerous as their situation was. She shouldn't feel the need to defend or apologize for what she had done and would do again, he knew without any doubt, under similar circumstances. He was utterly awed by her selflessness and courage.

Once more, she placed her hands over the little seal now freed from the befouled prison. As Danii's violet light unfurled over the thrashing creature, it shed its pelt like a person removing a cape.

In its place, a woman—a white-haired, pale-skinned, very naked woman—lay amid the blood and discarded rope. Oozing crimson slashes and angry, mottled bruises marred alabaster skin where, only moments ago, white bloodied fur had been. A strangely beautiful necklace made of pearls and iridescent seashells encircled her neck. Its weave was lacy but substantial, reaching in an arc from her throat to her chest. Otherwise, she was as bare as the day she was born, if she was born. Knowing nothing about their kind, she could have sprung fully formed from the sea for all the knowledge Ian possessed of this mysterious race.

Ian gazed in wonder as healing Magic bloomed full and strong from Danii's outstretched palms. It was as though even the elements of the earth and spirits of the air and ether had recognized her need and heeded her call. Or was the Selkie, now freed of the malignant bonds, contributing to her own healing?

Somehow, as exhausted as Ian knew her to be, Danii had managed to tap a hidden well of enormous Power. Her light engulfed the Selkie, bright and fiery as a comet, blazing over her body like dazzling whips of lightning. Then as quickly as it had flared, it was extinguished, leaving the cave once more in utter darkness.

Ian quickly turned his back, not certain what he should do. His people were known to be quite conservative in their manner of dress and the amount of skin revealed in public. Never in his life had he seen a woman unclothed. He gathered the blankets and glanced over his shoulder.

Danii was slumped against Shanara, long hair spread wildly down her back and onto the cave floor like skeins of tangled platinum silk. Her face was paler than that of the Selkie's white, nearly translucent complexion.

Ian rushed to her side, lifting the tiny crumpled form gently into his arms. For all her formidable Power and attitude, Danii was as slight and insubstantial as a sylph.

I am well, Ian. Just so incredibly tired. She pushed to a kneeling position.

Ian wordlessly handed Danii the blankets and watched in amazement as once more, the shallow slashes and then the deeper lacerations crisscrossing the Selkie's battered body began to close. This time, they remained so. The fell Magic of the Formorians held no sway against such formidable Power as he had witnessed.

"Idan," Danii spoke quietly. Her voice sounded lifeless, frail. He could feel her exhaustion and also was aware that far more would be needed from her. From both of them. This bit of healing was only the first round. She was far too young to have attempted what only an army of their most talented healers should have undertaken. And yet she had already accomplished the impossible. But at what cost?

"There is honeyed mead in my pack. It is infused with a healing restorative. Can you bring it to me?"

Digging through the pack he had carried across the mountain, Ian discovered the bottled beverage. As he uncorked the flask, the sweet warmth *of distilled honey and the fresh, reviving scent of mint hit his nostrils. He passed it over to her as he inventoried what else she had brought.*

Two honey cakes wrapped in fig leaves and a small package of dried fruit made up the bulk of the contents. At least she had thought to bring something for herself, though she had partaken of nothing during their long trek.

Her exhaustion beat at him. They were both tired, but the long night was far from over.

"You must eat something, Danii," he said, removing one of the cakes. *It was little enough, but it would help.*

"We both must, Idan. There is still much we must do."

He turned his back once more as Danii wrapped Shanara in one of the blankets and placed a second under her neck and head as a support. Already, her breathing was better.

Knowing what she required of him without being asked, he helped to support the Selkie while Danii dripped a little of the mead into her mouth. She choked, and Danii turned her head to the side as she coughed crimson bile onto the floor.

Her tongue has begun to heal, but she needs to expel the blood. The knowledge stole softly into his mind. Danii's link was becoming like a comfortable shadow, a part of himself that he was barely aware of until suddenly she surprised him with her presence.

Once more she dripped the mead into her friend's mouth, and once more, the Selkie choked. Danii patiently tended her until she could swallow a small amount.

Shanara's deep black eyes watched the young Tuatha girl as she worked over her. Ian could tell they were communicating. Occasionally, her soulful gaze tracked to him, but he felt no animosity from the injured woman, only an acknowledgment of his presence.

Danii passed the bottle to Ian. "You should drink some of this. We must undertake a second healing, and it will help maintain your strength. I fear I will once again require your help."

"You first, Danii. And you will eat now," he insisted. "You cannot hope to continue for much longer unless you do."

She placed her hand over Shanara's forehead and then sat back, accepting the food. Breaking it in half, trembling fingers pushed a divided portion back into Ian's hands. He had no idea how Danii was still functioning. She was barely hanging onto consciousness.

Danii haltingly consumed the cake, drank a small amount of the mead, and then leaned back against the cave wall, eyes closed, face as bleached as the chalky cliffs above and below. Only the faint, shadowed bruises under her eyes added any color to her otherwise-blanched complexion.

Ian finished his own less-than-satisfying portion and then turned to the cave entrance. The three sips of minted mead he had allowed himself had done much to revive his flagging strength. He knew that every drop was precious and that Danii had intended all of it for her patient. But the reality of their situation made its consumption necessary. Neither of them could afford to succumb to the sickness the excessive expenditure of Magic could produce. He feared they were both rapidly approaching its onset. Especially Danii.

The moon now soared high above this hidden sanctuary, casting its indifferent light over the menacing shapes of dozens of ships still out at sea. More had joined the floating nemesis since their climb down the cliff. What were they waiting for? Were they gathering for a massed attack against his people? These treacherous waters to the north of their Isle would undoubtedly be the last place their Tuatha warriors would expect the Formorian fleet to gather, though the looming threat of attack would surely guarantee his people had eyes everywhere.

Should he reach out to warn his mother? Only if it appeared the ships were moving to the west or if too many more amassed, he decided. He needed to give Danii a little more time, and there was the not-so-small problem of the vow he had given her. He sighed. Better to be known as an oath breaker than to allow this evil to descend unaware on his people.

Ian reinforced his safeguards and then joined Danii against the wall. The Selkie watched his movements, and he advanced slowly, trying to appear nonthreatening. Goddess knew she had reason enough to fear any but her own kind.

After a brief rest, Danii took another sip of mead and crawled back to the Selkie's side. The creature stirred as she neared but did not open her eyes. Her breathing was shallow and labored. She was still barely a heartbeat from the Dark God's ever-beckoning embrace.

Danii placed graceful hands over the huddled form, and lavender light softly lit the darkness, flowing like a transparent stream over and around them both.

Idan. *He heard the soft plea in his head and was immediately at her side.* I am sorry to have to ask …

He did not give her time to finish before touching her shoulder, joining his essence with hers. The connection was as before, and immediately, the soft light became a living blaze, taking on the deep, vibrant purple of intense healing.

Shanara's breathing became easier. As Danii gently pushed back the blanket, Ian could see that the angry red scars had turned pink, as though they were days old instead of hours.

"It is raining," she remarked, looking toward the cave mouth. She ripped a length of cloth from her dress and passed it to Ian. "Do you think you could wet this so that I can clean away some of the blood?"

He took it as she gently brushed back the wild tumble of stark-white hair matted against the Selkie's feverish skin.

Danii washed away as much of the sticky crimson carnage as she could under their inadequate circumstances. Ian could now see that this injured woman, this fabled creature from myth, was beautiful in a slightly unnerving way and strangely alluring. There was a certain unsettling magnetism about her. Her presence was becoming more compelling as she grew stronger. He feared the rumors might be true. If she decided to speak, would he be enslaved, lost forever in her thrall?

Danii urged the Selkie to drink. This time, she was able to swallow more easily. Ian was alarmed to note that the depleted little healer's movements were becoming sluggish. Drooping eyes were rimmed with pale purple bruises, and her lips were tinged an anemic shade of blue.

Ian rescued the bottle from near-lifeless hands as she collapsed next to the daunting creature and did not move. Even, shallow breathing told him Danii had fallen into an exhausted sleep. She lay quiet and motionless for a very long time, so long in fact that once more, Ian began to wonder if he should break his vow and attempt to reach out across the enemy-subverted mountain they had trekked to contact his mother.

When he had promised to keep Danii's secret, Ian had in no way envisioned the scope of this endeavor. Danii's adventure had seemed more the romantic quest of a sheltered young maiden, not the dangerous reality *of the brutalized creature she had come so far to rescue or the dank, gritty cave providing dubious shelter from a vicious and lethal enemy.*

He would certainly never again underestimate the steadfast loyalty or the terrifying courage and determination that drove her. Nor would he underestimate the total disregard for her own safety or the single-minded capacity to land herself in trouble up to her stunning blue eyeballs.

He was aware his mother already knew of his absence and was attempting to locate him. The insistent brush of her mind was becoming increasingly demanding, but thus far, he had been able to block her. If he opened himself to her even the smallest bit, she would find them. They were both going to be in so much trouble when they returned.

Ian sighed. He was not going to think about that right now. He knew Danii would not leave the Selkie until she was well enough to defend herself. Much could happen between now and that time. He was under no illusion that they were in danger. And he had no doubt they had many obstacles to face before they reached home, if they reached home.

He should not have given his vow to Danii. Had he not, however, he was entirely certain that she would have found a way to ditch him and struck out alone. He would worry about the consequences of their actions later.

Danii shivered in her sleep, a forlorn bundle of shredded purple rags with a dirty face adrift in the shadowy play of light. How could such a tiny being possess such an indomitable spirit and wield so much Power? And yet she lay freezing amid the scree and broken shells, like a piece of flotsam or driftwood, scattered like so much debris upon the icy floor.

Ian sent a trickle of heat, enfolding her in warmth. Her abrasions and injured feet had healed during that first rampant blast of healing when they had combined their Magic, or she would still be suffering from her own injuries. She had given everything she had, to the very dregs of her soul, to the healing and held back nothing for herself.

Ian listened to the steady fall of rain from the upper lip of the cavern and stared out at the ever-lightening sky. Vertical streaks of lightning slashed the heavens, followed quickly by the deafening boom of rolling thunder. The incessant roar of the ocean and savage waves crashing against the rocks provided a portentous backdrop against the surrealistic cocoon of the dim shelter. He breathed in the close, damp smell of rain and storm clouds mixed with the pungent scent of brine and fish and seaweed.

The night was waning, and with it their cover of darkness. They could not get far in this storm, nor could they afford to be caught out in daylight with virtually no concealment from the eyes of their enemy. And if Ian was under any illusion that the Formorians were brutal, barbaric beasts, Shanara's condition reinforced their deadly intent.

They would have to wait out the day and try to leave after nightfall. Oh yeah. They were going to be in sooo much trouble.

Repelling another strong mental push from the direction of the Mountain Court, Ian began to wonder if it would be preferable to face a horrific death at the hands of the Formorians rather than confront the wrath of his mother.

For a long while, he watched the ominous black ships out at sea. Somehow, even in this gale, they were managing to hold their positions, neither succumbing to the massive swells nor being swept too close in to the treacherous rocks along the coast. Soon, he would have to make a decision.

Returning to the darkened interior, Ian knelt beside the two huddled forms. He knew from their bond that Danii was only sleeping, but she had been out for so long he monitored her for a time to be certain. Finally, she began to stir and then awakened abruptly with a start.

"Oh! I am so sorry! I have slept overlong." Shadows still rimmed lackluster blue eyes, and fatigue lay heavy over stooped shoulders and drawn features. She moved slowly, carefully, like an invalid recovering from an illness.

Ian helped her sit without comment.

"You needed it. Are you stronger?" What else could he say? She looked as though the smallest breeze might crumble her to dust.

"Yes." She immediately checked her patient.

Shanara's spiky white eyelashes flickered up, revealing those depthless black eyes—ancient, vigilant eyes that weighed the world at a glance and saw everything.

"The dawn is not far off." Danii's voice was resigned. There was no need in stating the obvious fact that they would now be trapped until nightfall. "We must attempt at least one more healing," she said softly to the Selkie. "I am hopeful that this will give you enough strength to return to the sea or to seek a safer shelter."

"Danii," Ian said hesitantly, "I am unsure if you are able to do this again. As a healer, you are as aware as I what will happen if you burn your

Magic. You will be weakened to a state where I will be unable to help you, and I will be forced to call our people to save you."

"I am aware of what you think, and I will not push myself to that point! You gave me your vow, Idan! You will not contact our people."

"You have already taken yourself to the very edge twice."

"Shanara is nearly healed but still too weak to return to the ocean. I will not leave her in a state where she cannot defend herself."

"I know. I understand your sense of duty."

"It is not duty, Idan. It is love."

Ian sat back on his heels. There was no arguing with her, and since it appeared they would indeed have to remain here for another day, she would have time to recover before they were ready to return. If she didn't kill herself first. He hated to think what might have happened if he hadn't insisted on accompanying her, if he hadn't been here to lend her his Magic.

He eyed the Selkie with renewed interest. How had this wounded creature engendered such loyalty from such an unlikely ally? His eyes narrowed as he wondered suspiciously. Was it enthrallment?

"No, Idan," Danii retorted indignantly, "it is not."

Still in my mind? he asked mentally.

She ignored him completely.

Ian opened the pack and divided the second honey cake. "Will she eat some of this?"

"No. Her diet is mainly sea lettuce and fish. But the mead will make her stronger."

"It is still dark enough. Should I"—he shrugged—"climb down and try to harvest some from the rocks?"

Danii was quiet for a moment as she communed with the Selkie. "No. There is no need at this time."

"What is she saying to you?" Ian asked curiously.

"Shanara reminds me that it will be dawn soon. She insists that we do not endanger ourselves further by remaining with her, but I will not leave until I am certain she is well enough to take care of herself."

Ian eyed the Selkie suspiciously. "If she did not wish to endanger you, then why did she ask you to come?"

"She did not ask me to come. She reached out to me to say good-bye." Danii's eyes filled with tears, and she swiped them angrily away.

Ian was taken aback as he stared into those fathomless black eyes. There was truly an undeniable bond of deep trust and friendship between the two. At some point in time, he would like to discover how such a thing had been forged, but now was not the time for asking.

"Danii," Ian hated to remind her, "there is still the issue of the rope. It is glamoured for now. The Formorians may not notice it in the dark, thinking it some sort of vine, but if we must leave it until sunrise, they will find us."

"Then what should we do?"

"If I release it, we will not be able to climb back up the cliff, especially with your strength so depleted. I am not certain you could have made it anyway."

Danii glared.

"Look, Danii. We must be realistic about our situation. It is possible that we could leave here at low tide and make our way across the tidal pools and boulders until we can reach a ledge or something, but I am very certain of one thing. We cannot swim. It would be suicide."

"Can we not discuss this later?"

"No. We must think about this and devise a plan. If I use more than a trickle of Magic out in the open, either to help you climb or somehow keep us afloat in the waves, it will be like a beacon, pointing whoever is out there our way."

"I realize this." *The weariness in her voice went straight to his heart.*

The Selkie stirred, placing a slender, strangely elegant hand upon Danii's wrist. The two locked eyes.

"Shanara says she has a plan for us."

Ian eyed the Selkie warily. "Do I even want to ask?"

"Do not be disrespectful."

He stood slowly, regarding the pair, narrowed blue eyes flashing a warning that Danii was on the verge of pushing him too far. "My apologies, my ladies," *Ian said in a voice rife with sarcasm. He sketched a courtly half-bow as elegant as would merit any social event in the Great Hall.* "Forgive my ill manners, but I was under the mistaken impression that we are surrounded by an armada of Formorian invaders. Perhaps you are aware of something I am not."

Ian passed her a portion of honey cake, although he was sorely tempted to throw it at her.

"No." She huffed out a breath. "Yes. I am sorry, Idan." Danii's hands trembled as badly as before she had rested as she accepted the food. She was in much worse condition than she was letting on. He pushed the mead into her hands and insisted she swallow a good amount.

This situation was untenable, but losing his temper would help no one. They were both exhausted, hungry, and anxious about their precarious predicament, but Danii was far worse off than him.

The Selkie's liquid black eyes met his gaze, sending an involuntary shiver up his spine. They were cunning eyes, depthless and soulful, filled with secret ancient knowledge. Could they really trust her?

"So what is her plan?" he asked in a resigned voice.

"She has some friends. You know, the playful sea creatures we often watch from the shore. They will help us."

"How?"

"She says they can swim with us so we will not drown."

"There are Formorian ships at sea. How will we avoid them?"

"She says we must trust her."

That was really the crux of it. Despite what Danii thought, could they really trust their lives to this feral creature of the sea? Danii obviously believed in her enough to have risked her own life to save her.

Ian walked to the cave's entrance, angling his face up, allowing the rain to fill his mouth with fresh, cold water. He swallowed greedily. He was terribly thirsty but would take no more of the mead. The two females needed it far more than he.

Sending the merest trickle of Magic along the snaking vine, he released the rope. As its length slithered from the top of the cliff and then free-fell into his hands, he hoped he was not making a mistake.

It was possible he could rescale the bluff, but to do so in the dark, under the same conditions he had experienced the night before, and without any sort of safety line would be the height of madness.

Ian knelt beside Danii as she prepared herself for what he hoped would be the final healing. Goddess. He had no idea how she was going to find the strength. She swayed, and he wrapped an arm around her shoulders. She leaned into him until he was physically supporting her.

"I do not believe this is a good idea, Danii."

"I must, Idan. Both you and Shanara are fighting me now, and I do not have the energy to argue anymore. Please, just help me one last time."

His eyes met that of the Selkie, and something in that black gaze reassured him that she would not allow Danii to come to harm.

Danii began as before, only this time her light was barely tinged with the faintest blush of color. Ian sent his essence, his Power, his energy straight into her body, using the ever-growing potency of their connection to force his strength through their bond. The light grew until suddenly it burst open, intensely bright and true, turning the rich, deep healing purple he had come to recognize.

Even with the infusion of his Magic, Danii was depleting herself to a dangerous level. He knew she was once more taking only the minimum of what she needed from him. He pushed back through their bond, insisting she accept more, flooding her with Power.

The healing light blazed to a fiery inferno, light fully engulfing the Selkie, until only the barest outline of her form could be seen through deep-purple flames.

Finally, it was enough. It had to be enough, as Danii collapsed, unconscious in his arms.

The Selkie stirred then pushed to a sitting position. Danii's eyes immediately fluttered open as the cool, pale hand touched her forehead.

Shanara held the residual mead to Danii's mouth, forcing her to consume the last of the drink. She inclined her head toward Ian, a slight, enigmatic smile playing about her lips. Black eyes shone with primordial awareness, wholly terrifying in their intensity.

An icy chill crawled up Ian's spine. Was this the moment where she obliterated his mind?

The creature threw off her blanket and rose, an intimidating being of awesome and fickle Power. Dangerous? Absolutely. Ian had no doubt. Would they, or at least he, now become the recipient of her outraged wrath?

Her body still retained violet-pink scars from her torture, and Ian wondered if the marks would ever completely heal. Dark Magic was an evil that once implanted, rooted and twined quickly with its insidious poison. He had heard it spoken of in whispers. It was a vile curse, difficult to entirely banish. Once infected, its corrupted taint never fully vanished.

Ian averted his eyes, trying to keep them on her face. This daunting creature seemed completely unembarrassed with her nudity, and though long white hair covered her pale slender body, mostly, Ian was certain his cheeks were flaming.

Protector of the goddess child, Daénaeria Solais dé Lorelle ad Ruadh dé Danu, who shall be so named in your time, Righter of Injustice, Defender of All, Bringer of Light, Dispellor of Darkness ...

The clarion voice was a silken lullaby in his head, soothing, pacifying, frightening in its ability to reach so easily into his very soul.

Stark-white hair streamed over bare ivory skin, falling nearly to the ground, long and tangled, lifting and wafting softly in an unseen breeze as powerful Magic flowed to her. Ian could sense it in the air, smell its elemental tang of sea and salt and wind, feel its feral swirling essence, its need to heed her siren call.

Gathering what energy he still had, Ian threw a barrier between them, hastily seeking some way to force the sentient, alien presence from his mind while his thoughts were still his own.

The pale, unearthly creature tilted her head as though listening to something Ian could not hear, as though seeking some hidden secret he could not fathom. Black eyes looked deeply into his, that mysterious, knowing smile reaching into the depths of his being.

You, Son of Danu, have no need to fear me.

Ian pushed against the mental intrusion, but it was no use. The silken descant continued to insinuate itself, softly weaving through his being, spreading out like drops of dye upon the surface of water.

Tendrils of melody took root, twining themselves into his very being, a subtle song, a mellifluous wash of color, snaking through his mind and body until he was saturated with the longing to lose himself in its promise, in the harmony and safety and color of her voice.

And then suddenly, he was released from her spell. He was left with the knowledge that her touch had been meant to soothe, not frighten.

I, Shanara, Daughter of the Sea, one born in times immemorial of the shifting winds and raging tides, bestow upon you, Son of Danu, a life debt. I proclaim that this debt shall be honored.

From this moment on, through the vast turning of tides, the ever-ending journey of the blazing God of Light and his consort, the Luminous Silver Goddess who follows in his wake across the night sky, through the eternal passing of seasons, throughout the ages and unto the end of days, my life shall remain forfeit for yours until my debt is honored.

The glorious, fearsome creature then turned to Danii.

This debt and more, unending and eternal, I bestow upon you, Daénaeria Solais, my truest friend, my staunchest ally. For without you, child goddess of the Tuatha, Bringer of Light, Defender and Dispeller of Darkness, she who shall lead and protect her people in the coming war, my soul would have journeyed to the Dark God still bound in filthy chains of vile and evil Magic, had not you given back my life.

She had included Ian in their communion so that he would know the strength of her gratitude and understand the binding oath that had been bestowed upon them both.

Was this the truth, then? Were they safe from the Selkie's enthrallment and wrath? But oh Goddess! She was in possession of Danii's true name! And she had bequeathed a coming Legend that only their goddess Danu should know, a destiny that upon hearing it had given Ian chills, yet one Ian was certain Danii would fulfill.

How had this fear-provoking entity come by this knowledge? Had Danii been foolish enough to share her true name with this ominous creature?

What she spoke of revealed the deepest knowing of a person's soul, the deepest access to thought and mind. How could she know a future yet to happen, lives yet to be written?

What was this pale, alluring creature exactly? Selkie? Yes. He had seen her change forms. The bloody pelt still lay against the cave wall where she had discarded it. But there was so much more. Siren? A mythical entity even more dangerous to their people than the Selkie, with its enslaving song, a terrifying being of utter chaos and absolute dominion able to ensnare the minds and souls of men, able to send legions to their deaths.

Yes, Idan dé Niamh dé Danu, ad Gabráin mac Domangairt, Descendant of the Hereditary Line of the Goddess, Descendant of the Hereditary Sword of Nuada, soon to be called Living Sword of Nuada, wise beyond your years, who shall also be named Sage Leader, Staunch Protector, Ruler and King, he who rises from chaos, he who shall unite the world. It is the gift of our people to know such things.

Adrenaline raced through his bloodstream. How could she know any of this? She had just spoken his true name and also named his ancestors, something very few had any knowledge of. What was she?

Our people are known by many names—Selkie, Siren, Instrument of the Dark God ... This knowledge of a person's soul, of his every fantasy, his every dream and his very destiny is the secret that grants our kind sway over all creatures.

Yet I have already sworn that you have nothing to fear. I have bequeathed you a life debt. There is no higher gift one may bestow to another than a life for a life. My life shall be ever forfeit, yours to claim for as long as I draw breath, until payment may be rendered. We are forever linked. We are now and forever family.

Ian was dumfounded. He had done none of this for reward of any kind, much less a sacred life debt bestowed by a creature of such fearsome Power. Her promise of safe passage was more than enough.

"I am honored," Ian said humbly, forcing himself to meet those fathomless eyes. "I will accept the bond of family with gratitude, my lady, but there is no debt." *Perhaps he should not have dismissed her goodwill so hastily, but in good conscious, he could not allow it to stand. He had come because of Danii, but he would have done no different for any creature once he discovered the horrendous torture she had sustained at the hands of the Formorian beasts.*

She gave him that mysterious, enigmatic smile and raised her elegant hand to touch the center of his forehead. His third eye. A pale filament of blue light flowed between their hearts, connecting them irrevocably.

It is done. The debt shall stand.

Ian could actually feel that thread of light take hold. It was definitely done. He hoped his mother never found out what had occurred this day.

Daénaeria Solais dé Lorelle and Idan dé Niamh, I would say to you one thing more. You have bound your destinies together this night in a way you do not fully understand.

Danii and Idan looked at one another in confusion.

You will know the significance of this in time. Now heed me, you must leave soon. Your people have secured the waters and shoreline that are kissed each day by the last light. Even now they guard the blue harbor. It would be safer for you to return there instead of crossing back across the mountain.

"How can you know that?" Ian asked.

I know many things, *she answered cryptically.* I also know that your goddess queen searches for you even now.

Ian was already uncomfortably aware of that fact. Niamh's push against his mind had grown frantic. At this point, he was honestly weighing the option of never returning.

"It would be great if we could return by water, but we are not like you," Ian reminded her. "Danii is exhausted, and we cannot possibly swim that far in this rough sea. And Formorian ships even now watch this part of the coastline. If the surf does not crush us against the rocks before we clear the shore, the undertow will surely carry us far out into the ocean. We would either drown or be captured."

I have said my friends will see you safely to your people. It is not so far to the crescent harbor, where the God of Light seeks sleep each night, if Kiar and Neira swim with you.

"You are speaking of the Western Bay?" Ian asked uncertainly.

Yes. The sheltered inlet where your people swim and play. Once past the northern reefs, the waters are calm. If you can hold your breath for short intervals, Kiar and Neira will dive with you beneath the waves, where the current is untroubled by surface storms. Let them know when you need to ascend for breath.

Oh Goddess! Was she really serious? Ian could probably do this, would have actually found this to be a fabulous adventure, but Danii? No way! They would need to think of something else.

Danii touched his arm. "This is our best chance, Idan. I trust Shanara. We will be safe."

She did look better. Whatever Shanara had done when she touched Danii's forehead had helped her immensely. He eyed the Selkie with cautious respect.

"If you believe you can do this, Danii, then I agree this is our best hope of returning safely to our Court," Ian reluctantly assented.

Shanara removed her pearl-and-shell necklace and placed the treasure around Ian's neck. For all its delicate appearance, its weight was surprising. The mystical object felt unnaturally warm where it touched his skin and seemed to hum with some unseen Power. A tingle of awareness shot through his veins. This was a potent amulet, an extension of Shanara's own life essence.

She smiled, those enormous black eyes capturing his gaze. *This will shield you against what is to come.*

Her smile was stunning, if unnerving. Perfectly straight, sharp white teeth gleamed like the rarest pearls. Her appearance was transformed into a vision of such exquisite beauty that Ian lost his breath. This was the visage of the Siren, the mesmerizing, enthralling face of an enchantress.

Ian swayed for a moment, blinded by the sheer brilliance of her guise.

With a knowing gleam, the Siren steadied him, placing a hand on his shoulder that cleared his head. Pale fingers then trailed across his chest, caressing the confection of pearls and shells affectionately as one might a lover.

Kiar will return this to me when you reach your people.

Filtered through the defensive armor of the necklace, Shanara's mind touch was wild—as untamed as the sea, as tempestuous as the storms battering the coast, as capricious and volatile as the northern winds sweeping across the high mountain peaks, leveling everything in its wake.

Ian was immediately and immensely grateful for the talisman he now wore, for he now had a vague sense of the workings of her mind. He knew she had plans for the armada still gathering out at sea. He was going to need this object, this shield infused with such formidable Magic, against the madness and pandemonium that was to come, against the hell she was about to unleash on her enemies.

I owe you a life debt. My life forfeit for yours, *she reminded.* May the gods see you safely through the sea, may your journey be swift.

As they stood toe to toe, Ian was shocked to realize that this unnerving creature, this intimidating force of nature, who easily rivaled the fiercest of Tuathan warriors in her ability to instill fear, stood barely taller than him. At eleven summers, he still had far to grow. Like Danii, she held such formidable Power within such a small form.

Ian found his voice. "Truly, there is no debt, my lady." Placing his right fist over his heart, Ian bowed his head, his courtly protocol instinctually coming to the fore. "We are grateful for your assistance," he said formally.

They exchanged another knowing glance before she released him with that enigmatic smile. He tried not to shiver. Those sharp white teeth were truly daunting.

Shanara, hand splayed, palm facing down, swept her arm from left to right in a horizontal arc, and the raging waves below the cave calmed.

Ian was amazed to see two gray snouts emerge from a narrow trough of flat ocean. Black liquid eyes, much like Shanara's, assessed them, though the creatures were far different from the seal-like animal from which she had transformed. The pair poked their sleek heads through the foaming green water and chattered a greeting. With their jaws open wide, even though their pink mouths were filled with long rows of little sharp teeth, they looked to be grinning. Ian couldn't help but grin back. They exuded such playful energy that he could do no less than feel an immediate, delighted bond.

His people had no specific name for these playful fish, but something from the recesses of his mind filled in the blank. These were dolphins! And they weren't fish at all, but highly intelligent mammals.

This is Kiar. *The larger male chattered once more, acknowledging them.* And this is Neira. *The smaller female sent a splash of water their way as though warning them they needed to hurry.*

The brooding pewter sky spit cold splats of rain and freezing sleet, and Ian shivered as they stepped from the sharp rocks into the frigid waves. Storm clouds hovered low and bloated, erasing the demarcation of sea and sky. Far to the east, the barest wash of pale orange peeked feebly through the gloom, warning that dawn was not far off.

"Can you warm yourself, Danii?"

"I am fine, Idan. I need hold nothing back now that Shanara has regained her strength."

Kiar and Neira met them at the water's edge. Already wet to their waists, their second step submerged them completely, and Idan sputtered as the icy water flowed over his head. They treaded water as the pair swam up underneath.

Ian suddenly knew what to do as the sentient creature somehow aligned their minds. He understood immediately that this being was highly intelligent, unconcerned with the beasts of the land, but unhappy about those within the floating vessels hunting the inhabitants of the sea.

Kiar's mental touch was far different from Shanara's. It was almost as though Ian was receiving pictures, mental images of how to grasp the strong dorsal fin and align his body over the back of the immensely powerful sea creature. Kiar's hide was soft and slick yet also surprisingly tough. Beneath the rubbery gray skin, a layer of insulating fat stretched over sleek muscle.

Kiar and Ian skimmed the surface as they accustomed themselves to the feel and rhythm of one another's bodies, and then Ian was counseled to hold his breath as they dove beneath the waves.

The cold, salty sea washed over his head, immersing his senses with underwater sights and sounds as they cut swiftly and easily through the viscous green realm.

The dim green light filtering from above provided a peaceful haven as they wove their way between submerged rocks and shoals and dense forests of tall golden kelp before heading out into open ocean.

This was the best thing he had ever done! If he hadn't been worried about how Danii was managing, and of course the small matter of the enemy ships so close now he could nearly smell their Magic along with their cloying musky stench, Ian would have counted this one of the best experiences of his life.

Neira came alongside, and they surfaced for a quick breath. Danii threw back her head and laughed with the same exuberant joy that had Ian grinning from ear to ear. What an adrenaline rush to swim with these noble creatures!

Ian looked back toward the cave as they cleared the rocks.

Shanara, now lit like a glowing beacon of light, long white hair whipping wildly in the storm, stepped out onto the cave ledge and raised her arms high to the elements. It was something he had seen his mother do when she summoned immense and powerful Magic.

A voice filled his senses, Her voice, that same beautiful siren song she had gifted to him earlier, but magnified to an unimaginable degree. It floated on the storm, descended from the heavens, reached to every quadrant of the cloud-swathed northern sea. The song filled his soul to overflowing, breathed longing and new life into his weary senses. He hungered—hungered—for its promise, for its source. Every silken chord affected him, drew him, but not as before and not as it was doing to the Formorian invaders.

The siren song engulfed every miserable, malevolent soul aboard the enemy ships, wrapped them in loving arms, enslaved them with its intoxicating spell.

The enchantress summoned them to her side, where they would be sheltered by her beauty, slaked by her body, consumed by her magnificence, granted every wish, every fantasy, every unfulfilled dream.

The necklace shielded Ian, but he was highly aware of the incredible pull, the urgent longing to turn back, the captivating call of the Siren. He yearned to lose himself in Her voice, to return to the cave, to succumb to Her spell.

The sound of shouts and the wooden thwap of oars brought Ian's attention to the dark ships silhouetted against the gray sky. Hastily raised sails billowed madly before catching the wind. The dark fleet turned directly toward land, heedless of the hazardous shoals and jagged coastline.

Ian understood. Her song was irresistible. How could any being deny Her call?

Ships sailed directly at the cliff where the enchantress stood, singing to her victims, compelling them forth with her haunting voice. Boats floundered against the treacherous shoals, crashed against the cliffs, broke apart against jagged rocks, but still they did not drop their sails. The horned beasts frenziedly fought one another amidst the wreckage as their ship's hulls splintered, trying to get closer to the wielder of their fate, the instrument of their doom.

Shanara threw back her head and laughed, white teeth gleaming as the enemy who had wrought such pain descended to the depths of the ocean.

No wonder his people were terrified of these feral creatures of the sea. Their unbound Power was fearsome to behold.

Kiar chattered and clicked, sending unpleasant images into Ian's mind. Neira splashed water into his face, and Danii grabbed his hair and yanked, forcing him to look fully into her furious blue eyes. "I warned you, Ian! Now, snap out of it!" she demanded ferociously.

The diversion was enough; the spell was broken. They floated above the waves long enough to watch the carnage unfold and the wreckage begin to wash ashore before heading northwest.

Kiar and Neira easily towed them through the churning seas along the sheer cliffed coast. It was like nothing Ian had ever done. To swim and bond with this noble creature, to glide like a fish, slipping so easily and quickly through the water, to become one with the other creatures of the sea! Nothing could ever be better than that!

Ian could feel the difference in temperature as they rounded the farthermost point of their Isle, and the four crown-like spires that sheltered the Western Bay came into view. Even the water was a different color here, not the forbidding, murky green and slate gray of the storm-ridden north, but a brighter hue of vivid aqua and even turquoise in the shallower depths.

He heaved a great sigh of relief until he spotted the Tuatha warriors on the beach and the incensed goddess in their midst dressed in flowing white. Another powerful female dressed in bright scarlet stood at her side. Flaming gods! Danii's mother was there too!

Kiar and Neira brought them close to shore, where their feet could touch bottom.

Tuathan warriors stared in astonishment as the pair emerged from the surf like two half-drowned sea creatures, Ian mostly unscathed, but Danii in her ragged, streaming silk, flashing far more skin than was acceptable amongst their puritanical people.

Kiar accepted Shanara's necklace, clamping it firmly between strong jaws, and Ian gently stroked his rubbery gray hide in farewell. It was time to face the music, and he knew it was not going to be pleasant.

Lorelle rushed to her daughter, and though Niamh kept pace, she appeared merely to glide, serene and unhurried, toward the errant children. Ian knew better. He was still blocking her, but the angry push against his mind told him more than he wanted to know.

"I would expect this kind of behavior from Aédan, not you, Idan. Would you care to explain what has occurred?" Niamh tilted her head as if listening to something. Her golden voice washed over him, its soothing cadence belying the censure of her words.

Ian and Danii exchanged looks.

You promised, Idan. Danii's words were in his head on that forbidden mental path they had forged under such desperate circumstances.

Ian hesitated.

"Danii, tell me where you have been!" Lorelle demanded.

Heads down, the pair exchanged another silent look.

"Idan is shielding both their minds!" Lorelle exclaimed angrily. "You have no right to intrude on my daughter's thoughts, Idan!" Lorelle lifted Danii's stubborn chin, forcing her to look directly into her mother's stormy eyes. "You will tell me where you have been, Danii." She stamped a silk-clad foot in precisely the way Danii was prone to. "Now!"

"It is not Danii's fault," Ian said, jumping in to defend her. She was exhausted, about to collapse. He had indeed made her a promise, and she had already been through enough.

No, Idan. You cannot take the blame for this. My mother is furious. She will see you punished.

Danii opened her mouth to deny that it was Idan's fault.

Say nothing, Danii! *Ian commanded.* They cannot take the knowledge from your mind as long as I shield you.

I cannot prevent it once we are separated. She is so angry she will have it anyway.

Merge with me like you did in the cave. I will show you how to block her from your thoughts.

They inched closer, surreptitiously clasping hands, but kept their union hidden within the sodden folds of Danii's once-beautiful gown, which now hung like strands of seaweed.

She took the information easily from Ian's mind. The bond they had forged was strong and true, their mental path entirely different from the ones shared with their parents.

"I talked Danii into going with me," *Ian spoke before Danii could. He squeezed her hand, warning her not to disagree.* "We went to the cliffs to see if we could spot the Formorian ships. We got caught out between the Court and their patrols and had to wait out the night."

My mother is so angry with you. I cannot allow her to blame you for this. *Danii insisted once more.*

Do not say a word, Danii. I gave you my vow, and I will keep it. *Me* wanting to see the Formorian ships is something they will believe. It is completely unlike *you*, however. If you deny my words, they will only ask more questions. Whatever my punishment, it will pass soon enough and was worth the price. *He thought of the Selkie now wholly healed and free from the vile chains.* Yes, whatever happened to him, it was worth it.

"What cliffs?" *Lorelle demanded.* "Where were you? Our warriors searched and searched. They would have found you had you been on the rise above the bay."

"The cliffs overlooking the North Sea," *Ian mumbled.*

Idan! *Danii's alarm rang in his mind.*

We need to keep it simple, Danii. I promised I would not tell about Shanara, and I won't. But the rest of the truth is what it is.

"You what!" *Lorelle nearly screeched.*

For a healer who habitually spoke in soothing, dulcet tones, this was an enormous indicator that she was on the verge of some dire act. Although as an envoy of the Healing Caste, she had sworn never to harm or do violence to another. It was possible this was the only reason she had not already blasted Ian back into the bay.

"And you dragged my daughter into this?" Lorelle asked in disbelief. "You took Danii all the way to the North Sea, skirting goddess only knows how many Formorian patrols? What were you thinking to place yourselves in such danger? How could you be so foolish?"

Niamh pensively placed her hand over Ian's heart, the exact spot where Shanara's thread of light had connected when she bestowed her life debt. Once more, she tilted her head as though hearing something the others could not.

"You must calm yourself, Lorelle," Niamh said softly, her radiant light flowing out, enveloping the furious healer, soothing all who stood in her midst.

"You are keeping something from us, Idan," Niamh said to her son. "You have kept me from your mind, refused to answer my summons, even to assure me of your safety. You will tell me why."

"It is as I have told you. I wanted to see the Formorian ships, and I persuaded Danii to go with me, but there were patrols. I did not want to use my Magic in case the Formorians should trace it back to us. I blocked you to keep us safe. Danii was not at fault." The lie rolled easily enough off his tongue. So many years of keeping his brother out of trouble had given him the ability to think fast, but still, Ian felt enormously guilty for this untruth he was forced to tell his mother.

"This behavior cannot pass unpunished, Niamh. Idan must be held accountable for his dangerous actions."

"And so he shall," Niamh said serenely. She continued to assess Ian and Danii in that composed, nearly detached manner of hers. "However, it is more imperative at this time that we know what they observed. Idan, you said you saw Formorian patrols."

"Yes, and there were ships out on the North Sea."

"How many ships did you see? Our warriors are watching the coast. We must be certain they are aware of the threat."

"Uhmm"—Ian looked at Danii before he answered—"dozens. But I'm pretty sure that's not going to be a problem anymore."

"What do you mean?" Niamh was quiet for a moment as she mentally communed with their warriors. "Our warriors have been watching the coast through the night. There is debris in the water, the wreckage of ships washing ashore up and down the coast. They report that at some point during the early hours, enemy vessels began sailing into the rocks. What do you know of these events?"

Say nothing, Danii.

"Nothing," Ian answered as guilelessly as he was able.

"Danii?"

She shook her head, wide-eyed. "We do not know anything."

Niamh assessed her disgraced son and the exhausted girl at his side. "There is more to this than they are telling."

The bedraggled pair shifted uncomfortably under her scrutiny as they mutely stood, hair dripping, seawater streaming off ruined clothing into an ever-growing puddle at their feet.

"Take it from his mind," Lorelle insisted heatedly.

"I cannot forcefully read his memories without doing damage," Niamh said calmly. Ian was highly aware, however, that his mother's serene demeanor was not as perfect as it appeared.

"Danii, you will tell me!" Lorelle insisted.

Danii gazed once more at Ian.

"He is influencing her. They are communicating mentally! You know that is forbidden!"

My mother will take it from my mind, *Danii said wearily on their mental path,* or Niamh will see it in yours. What are we going to do?

I can continue to shield your thoughts, Danii. I know I can, because I protect Áedan all the time to keep him out of trouble. I promise I will protect you. Our Magic is stronger together, haven't you noticed? What has passed will remain secret so long as we maintain our link.

Ian's dream suddenly morphed, as only dreams can, and he found himself with Danii, clean and dry and dressed in the customary attire of their Court. She gasped as he placed the priceless dagger she had so admired into her hand.

"This is made of literium, from our home world," she said in wonder, watching the translucent blue flame flit along the blade as it merged with

her Magic. "Like Nuada's Sword of Light," she breathed, as she touched the sentient weapon with reverence.

"The metal is torterium. It contains but a single shard of literium. It is an amalgam, forged with elements found in the mortal realm."

"It belonged to Nuada. I cannot accept this, Idan. It is too precious and too rare."

Rare like Danii, he thought, watching the sun shimmer off her golden skin and long blond hair.

"I would be pleased if you would keep it for me. Wear it, use it. Perhaps the memory of our adventure will keep you out of trouble."

"I cannot vow to stay out of trouble. You said in the cave it would be mine only if I did." She flicked a strand of long dark hair out of Ian's eyes with a sassy grin. "Truly, Idan, I cannot," she said, reluctantly attempting to return it.

"I am going into the mortal realm. I will take a mortal blade."

"You are taking this punishment in my stead."

"It will not be so bad. We go to our father's people to learn the ways of humans. It could have been much worse."

Once more, Ian's dream changed. He was in the courtyard near the Great Hall with Áedan. They were both grown, older than Ian was now.

"Have you seen Danii yet?"

"No. Why?"

"She is dressed for war. Besides the dagger you gave her as children, she is carrying a wicked-looking sword. Most males give their sweethearts jewelry, Idan, not weapons. That was your first mistake with her, brother."

Ian's jaw clenched in frustration as he looked skyward. She was going to be the death of him. "She is her own person, Áedan. She has her own reasons for the path she has chosen. What makes you think I can control her?"

"All are aware she is your destined mate. Everyone seems to acknowledge it but the two of you."

Yeah, he knew. He just didn't want to push Danii. And with all the warring factions in the mortal realm, there was no place for attachment.

"She should remain safely within the Mountain Court," Áedan stressed. "The battlefield is no place for one of our women. Why is she so determined to ride with us against the Formorians?"

Ian understood her reasons, though he didn't have to like them. "She wields powerful Magic and is an able warrior," he answered wearily. "Gabráin will not deny her. We need all the help we can get." Though Ian wished his father would refuse. He had already fought with both of them long and hard over this subject. He did not want to see her in danger.

"You will allow her to go?"

"I allow nothing. Gabráin thinks to use her as a healer on the battlefield." Use her! He hated that word. "Little does he understand the tremendous toll those abilities demand. She cannot heal and fight at the same time."

"Then stop her."

He cast a tight-lipped glare at his brother.

"You try stopping her," Ian responded bitterly. "You are as aware as I that the death of her mother at the hands of the Formorians, as well as our experiences with those evil beasts as children, has rallied her to this cause. With our father enabling her, she is riding with us straight into the mouth of hell!"

"Goddess help you, brother. She is going to be a handful."

"What does that mean?"

"You have not looked at a girl except Danii since you were eleven. Can you truly keep your attention away from her if she is in danger on the battlefield?"

No. It would be impossible. "She will be only one woman for me to worry about, unlike you," he said, turning it back on his brother. He really didn't want to discuss this anymore.

"Me?" Áedan asked in mock innocence, widening his eyes and placing his hand over his heart as though his brother's words had severely wounded. "I am quite certain I have no idea what you are talking about."

Ian was aware he was attempting to lighten the mood. He allowed himself to be pulled into the diverting banter.

"Oh yes," he snorted, rolling his eyes skyward. "I am sure you don't." He elbowed his brother good-naturedly. "You do enough looking and flirting for both of us, and then I get dragged into it because they can't tell us apart. One female will be far easier to keep track of than the legion of women you have chasing you, on the battlefield and off, and then me by default," he added. "They say the Formorians are gods of chaos. They have nothing on you and your endless horde of females."

"*Hell yes. I love women!*" Áedan slapped him on the back with a huge grin.

Goddess, Idan groaned. *This was going to be a long campaign.*

Ian woke with a splitting headache that nearly dropped him to his knees. *"WHAT THE FREAKING HELL?"*

Memory? Or *dream?* The pounding tempo of his skull said his money was on the memory. But how? It was as if he was dreaming someone else's life. At the age of eleven, he had been imprisoned safely within the high walls of the International Academy of the Pacific, in *Hawaii*, surrounded night and day by teachers and bodyguards.

And Danii had continuously called him by that name again. The name everyone seemed to know but him. *Idan.*

Another flash of memories, or whatever the hell they were, surfaced, along with an even stronger headache.

He and Áedan were in some ragged medieval garb, fishing and mending nets. Another flashed of them plowing fields with archaic tools, harvesting a field of wheat with a scythe. One more emerged of the two in a muddy courtyard, aggressively practicing with swords as chickens clucked indignantly and scattered out of their way. But they were both so young, the same age as in his dream with Danii.

Ian was now certain he was losing his mind. These things were *IMPOSSIBLE!*

More images and jumbled scenes swamped him. It was like the floodgates of a dam had been pried open as he was swallowed up in frenzied, disjointed scenes from lives he couldn't have lived. It was as if that dream, that mind-blowing dream of Danii and him as children, had unlocked something, some secret past that couldn't possibly be his.

Once again, his sleep was ruined by chaotic thoughts and questions so ridiculous, so *crazy*, that he couldn't begin to sort them. He tossed until the first orange rays of dawn chased the God of Night from the magical realm of the Tuatha.

CHAPTER XI

Niamh led the intimidatingly large procession of immortals into the lush green forest to a circle of gnarled ancient trees. As they passed beneath the densely tangled canopy, Ian experienced a sense of deep inner peace. Here within the shelter of the great, proud oaks, the Magic of this world felt even stronger, the connection to all of nature more profound. It was as if these trees had been a part of this forest since the beginning of time, quiet keepers of the wisdom of the ages. These colossal guardians of the woodlands seemed to bend toward them, a subtle shifting of trunk and leafy branches, as though aware of their presence. Ian gazed in awe at these silent sentient observers to the ritual about to take place.

He had attempted to speak to Danii before everyone assembled for this mystifying ritual but had been unable to get her alone. Ian was driven to ask her about that dream no matter her protests. His mind was in such turmoil; he *needed* to clear this up before the ceremony.

She stood now among her warriors. They were an intimidating group to behold, bigger than most, well-muscled and savagely armed for war, but he was not going to let that stop him.

The one called Gilbrandr glared as he approached, but Ian was undaunted. He would have his answers, even if he had to challenge that pretty-faced captain of Danii's to get them.

He nodded a cautious greeting to the dangerous-looking group of men and then addressed the sole woman in their midst.

"Danii." Ian took her arm amid glares from her warriors and gasps from various others. "I need to speak with you." She stiffened but did not pull away. "Please," he added, although it was clearly a demand, not a request.

Gilbrandr put his hand over Ian's, a hard lock meant to painfully extricate it from Danii's wrist.

Ian refused to relinquish his hold as he stepped closer, placing his mouth against her ear. "Daénaeria Solais," his voice was formal, a whisper only she could hear, yet a command nonetheless, "will you talk to me?"

Her eyes glittered. A heartbeat passed, and then another. Gilbrandr's gripped tightened. More eyes turned their way. Finally, her voice broke the hostile silence.

"It is all right, Gilbrandr. I will speak with him."

The outraged warrior inclined his head to Danii then scowled warningly at Ian before releasing him. Still bristling, he stepped back, allowing Ian to pull his commander a little away for privacy.

"I had another dream about us last night."

She gazed at him stonily, giving him nothing.

"We were kids in a cave, and there was a Selkie. Formorian ships were crashing into the cliffs, breaking apart upon the rocks. Was that real, or is this some kind of …" Ian raked his hands through his hair. "God, I don't even know. Was that … a memory, Danii? Reincarnation? A dream of another lifetime? *My* lifetime, with *you?*"

She hesitated, assessing him fully as though taking his measure. For the first time since he had arrived here, her eyes held something other than loathing.

"The memory is real," she said softly. "You helped me and then took a punishment that should have been mine. You never told."

A fragment of knowledge pushed into his head, followed by a sharp pain. Funny how he was almost getting used to that piercing ice pick shredding him from the inside out; it was happening so frequently here. "But you told someone."

"Yes. I confessed to my mother. I could not allow her to believe that you had behaved dishonorably or that you had endangered me, when it was I who endangered you."

All eyes were now turned their way. Her voice had been so low only Ian heard her answer, but now she spoke tensely into the hushed silence. "They are waiting for you, Ian. You will have all the answers you seek soon enough."

"The memory is real?" Ian had known, but still he was stunned by her admission.

His eyes bored holes into Danii as Niamh gracefully beckoned him to the center of the clearing.

"Go," she insisted, extricating herself from his grip. "They are waiting."

THE THORNE LEGACY BOOK II

BITTER LEGACY

Ian Thorne must return to the mortal realm, for the portal to the *otherworld* has been left unguarded, and there is a dire risk that Miranda may attempt to usurp their lands or may even have discovered the secrets his family has guarded for millennia.

As the Formorians step up their incursions, amass their war ships, and prepare to invade the Veiled Isle, Ian is torn between aiding in the defense of his newfound people and the need to return to the world of humans. He has only just discovered the truth about who he really is, *Idan MacGabráin*, a powerful immortal warrior born centuries in the past. And he is tired, so very tired, of the endless masquerade he has been forced to endure, of the lies he has been forced to tell, while living among others so different from himself. And worst of all, of the binding of his memories and his Magic.

Danii must once again ally herself with Idan to defeat the great horned beasts bent on the destruction of the Tuatha, as their combined Magic has always been more formidable than any other but Niamh's own godlike Power. They are strongest together, but can Danii forgive Idan's betrayal from centuries past long enough to fight once again at his side? Can she overcome the fury and heartache and the decisions made by the mate she once would have died for before she kills him herself?

As Niamh struggles to restrain an all-consuming Power never meant to be wielded by any but the ancient gods, her precarious Magic is becoming more dangerous and unstable than anyone knows. She must set into motion a series of events that will change the lives of those around her for all time while she still has the strength, for she has seen glimpses of a future where she dwells in darkness. What those visions mean, she cannot say, but she must hold herself together long enough to safeguard her people from the Formorians and from herself before all is lost.

BITTER LEGACY is the second installment of *THE THORNE LEGACY*. Secrets will be unveiled, lives will be forever changed, and even greater sacrifices will be demanded as two worlds collide and Idan comes to terms with choices made in antiquity and the *bitter legacy* of his life.

GLOSSARY

Ancient – *refers to those born at the creation of the world, or those immortals who have lived eons longer than others of their kind*

The "before times" – *before the sundering*

binding of Magic - *to chain Magic so that it cannot be summoned, to usurp Magic so that it flows only to one person or geographical location*

binding of memories – *to chain or bury memories so deeply that they cannot be recalled*

Centaur – *a creature with the head, arms and torso of a man, and the body of a horse*

Elementals – *Elemental spirits of nature and Magic, earth, air, fire and water, born at the creation of the world*

The "mist" – *sentient mist created by the Tuatha that rings and protects the Veiled Isle*

Magic – *('Magic,' as opposed to 'magic') transformative force of creation, born of nature, inherent in all magical entities*

Power - *innate strength and ability to wield Magic, innate ability to command the forces of nature*

Selkie – *a creature which assumes human form on land, and that of a seal in water*

Siren - *a feared creature whose beguiling voice can enslave the minds of others*

The "sundering" – *occurred during the Great War between the Tuatha and the Formorians, when the mist-shrouded archipelago of nearly three-hundred isles, including the Veiled Isle, was pulled into a separate closed realm, inaccessible from the human realm except by two portals or gateways*

Talis of Tara - *ancient talisman imbued with potent Magic, originally created by Niamh for Gabráin as a means of summoning her and opening the portal between realms*

Veiled Isle – *also known as the "Veil" and "Isle of Mist" – island home of the Tuatha dé Dannan*

Tuatha dé Dannan – Otherworldly Immortal Children of the Goddess Danu

Niamh the Radiant - *Goddess-Queen of the Tuatha (also known as the Golden Goddess)*

Danii – *(Daénaeria Solais) –Commander of the Elite Guard, warrior, formerly of the Healing Caste, mate to Idan, (Elemental entities refer to her as 'the golden one,' in the before times, and the 'Goddess of War,' after the sundering.)*

Ian Thorne/Idan MacGabráin – *second born son of Niamh and Gabráin, warrior and king in ancient times, twin brother to Áedan*

Áedan MacGabráin – *Commander of the Queen's Guard, warrior, first-born son of Niamh and Gabráin, twin brother to Idan*

Gabráin – *warrior, king, mortal mate of Niamh the Radiant*

Hakan – *High Commander of the Elite Guard and Court Guard, fierce warrior and general from the time of king Nuada.*

Gilbrandr – *Captain of the Elite Guard, second-in-command to Danii*

Lorelle – *Healing Caste, Danii's mother*

Caitria – *Healing Caste*

Einarr - *Commander of the Court Guard, ancient warrior and general from the time of king Nuada*

Nuada – *Tuatha king and brother to Niamh (killed in battle long before the sundering)*

Arthfael – *Keeper of the Memories (immortal librarian)*

Other inhabits of the Veiled Isle
T'airneach – *centaur king*
L'aoch – *centaur general*
Shanara – *Selkie/Siren, primordial being of formidable but capricious Power, born at the dawn of creation*

Formorians – Immortal horned Gods of Chaos
Tyr – *Formorian king*

Rune *– Formorian general and powerful mage who has the ability to harness lightning and storms, and to sail Formorian ships amidst the clouds*

Thorne Manor *– ancient palace built in the 1500's, official Scottish "seat" of clan Thorne*
Miranda Thorne *– wife to Daniel Thorne, step-mother to Ian Thorne*
Maigrid MacShane *– cook and housekeeper at Thorne Manor for over fifty years.*
Hamish MacShane *– groundskeeper, husband to Maigrid*
Moira *– village girl helping Maigrid MacShane*
Lord MacTarran *– barrister, executor of the Thorne estate*
Sir Lawrence *– friend of Miranda*
Dr. Maynard *– friend of Miranda*

IAP (International Academy of the Pacific) *– Elite, highly secure boarding school in Hawaii*
Braxton Marcus *– Ian's best friend since the age of five*
Devon Marcus *– Braxton's father*

ABOUT THE AUTHOR

As the second-to-last child of parents who grew up during the Great Depression, Winter Adaire was taught from a young age to be thrifty, to make do and be grateful for what she had. As a result, she discovered early on that books filled with the most wonderful adventures could be borrowed from the library and that dreams and imagination were free.

As an adult, Ms. Adaire has amassed a ridiculously immense library of her own, which she no longer has to share, but still often finds that her favorite stories are the ones that spring from her own imagination.

She has a background in dance and martial arts and has also accumulated various academic degrees throughout her life. She travels the world whenever the opportunity presents itself, thrilled to explore all those exotic lands she read about as a child. She is an avid admirer of ancient architecture and insatiably picks up the language, legends, and fables of different cultures.

Ms. Adaire has a supportive husband who also travels constantly and a beautiful daughter now in her third year of college.

She resides in the mountainous lake country of Southern California, where she kayaks, hikes, and shares her back deck with a bunch of bossy blue jays and a family of very persistent raccoons in summer. In the winter months, she and her most faithful writing companion, a blue-eyed cat named Valhalla, enjoy the snow from afar. Valhalla has become an indispensable part of the creative process and is brilliant at knocking pens, notes, and research papers to the floor just when a plotline gets a little tricky, or lying across the computer keyboard when she is certain the story is going in the wrong direction or it is time to break for a cup of tea.

Ms. Adaire concedes that "one must choose one's battles" and also "give credit where credit is due."

CPSIA information can be obtained
at www.ICGtesting.com
Printed in the USA
LVOW03s0717301017
554271LV00002B/286/P